$\cancel{8}$/14

P9-BZJ-155

A MAD, WICKED FOLLY

A MAD, WICKED FOLLY

Sharon Biggs Waller

Viking
An Imprint of Penguin Group (USA)

VIKING
Published by the Penguin Group
Penguin Group (USA) LLC
375 Hudson Street
New York, New York 10014

USA ◆ Canada ◆ UK ◆ Ireland ◆ Australia
New Zealand ◆ India ◆ South Africa ◆ China

penguin.com
A Penguin Random House Company

First published in the United States of America by Viking,
an imprint of Penguin Group (USA) LLC, 2014

LIBRARY OF CONGRESS CATALOGING-IN-PUBLICATION DATA
Biggs, Sharon, date–
A mad, wicked folly / Sharon Biggs Waller.
pages cm
Summary: In 1909 London, as the world of debutante balls and high society obligations
closes in around her, seventeen-year-old Victoria must figure out just how much
is she willing to sacrifice to pursue her dream of becoming an artist.
Includes bibliographical references.
ISBN 978-0-670-01468-2 (hardback)
[1. Artists—Fiction. 2. Sex role—Fiction. 3. Love—Fiction. 4. London (England)—History—
20th century—Fiction. 5. Great Britain—History—Edward VII, 1901–1910—Fiction.] I. Title.
PZ7.B4837Mad 2014 [Fic]—dc23 2013029858

Printed in U.S.A.

1 3 5 7 9 10 8 6 4 2

Designed by Kate Renner

For my aunt,
Shirley Atchison Steinert.
Thank you for believing in me
and for being my very first editor,
all those years ago.

A MAD, WICKED FOLLY

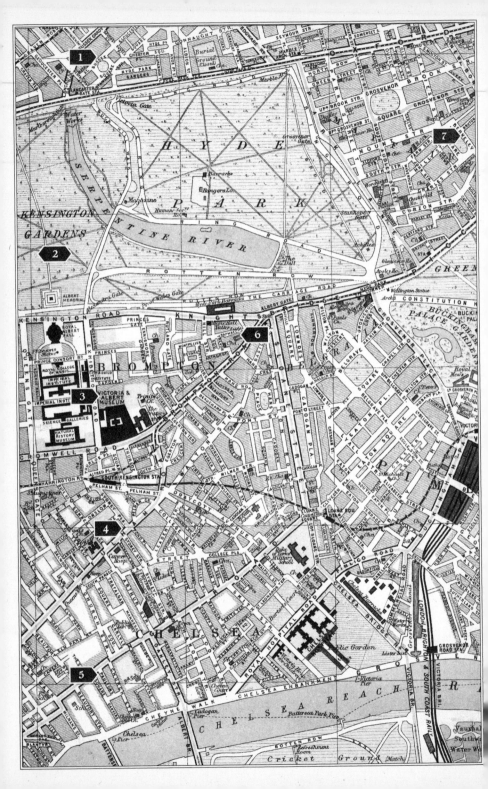

LONDON
circa 1909

1   Will's flat
2   Kensington Gardens
3   Royal College of Art
4   Sylvia Pankhurst's
    studio
5   Vicky and Edmund's
    new house
6   Women's Exhibition at
    the Prince's Skating Rink
7   The Darling residence
8   Freddy's house
9   Royal Academy of Arts
10 Piccadilly Circus
11 Trafalgar Square
12 Horse Guards
13 Houses of Parliament
14 WSPU headquarters

I am most anxious to enlist everyone who can speak or write to join in checking this mad, wicked folly of "Women's Rights" with all its attendant horrors, on which her poor feeble sex is bent, forgetting every sense of womanly feelings and propriety.

—QUEEN VICTORIA, 1870

I NEVER SET OUT to pose nude. I didn't, honestly. But when the opportunity arose, I took it. I sat with the other artists that morning in Monsieur Tondreau's tiny atelier in the French village of Trouville waiting for Bernadette, our usual model, to arrive. Some tinkered with their charcoals and pencils; others adjusted their easels. A few of the artists stared at the stage as if the model would magically appear if they looked hard enough. Monsieur bustled around in his canvas smock, moving the model's chair into the light, plumping the bolsters. The studio smelled of turpentine, linseed oil, and charcoal, and there was no sweeter perfume in the world to me than that.

Étienne, one of the other artists, yawned, leaned back in his chair, and closed his eyes.

"Hungover, old fellow?" his friend Bertram whispered. "Is fair Bernadette in the same state?"

Étienne grunted a warning but did not open his eyes.

"Poor Étienne," I whispered. "He looks unwell, Bertram. Let him be."

Bertram reached for his pencil, sharpened it with his knife, and began to sketch a cartoon of Étienne. "It's hard to feel sorry for a chap who has inflicted illness upon himself and caused the malaise of our model, once again." He added devil's horns to the line drawing and then nudged Étienne's boot with his own. Étienne cracked open one bloodshot eye and then closed it. "He lacks the artist's discipline but possesses all of his foibles."

"We all have our faults, Bertie." I knew I shouldn't side with Étienne; he was a rapscallion. But I also knew him to be a talented artist, and this, in my eyes, meant he'd earned the right to roguish behavior every now and then.

"If he had half your discipline, my dear Vicky, he would be lucky," Bertram said.

I smiled and began my own sketch of Étienne, this one with angel's wings. Bertram saw what I was doing, grinned, and shook his head.

I had made Bertram's and Étienne's acquaintance last autumn when I was drawing my dearest friend, Lily, in the village square. They plonked themselves down at our table as though we knew them and watched me as I worked. I was about to tell them to keep to themselves when Bertram blurted out, "You're very good." But then he spoilt it by adding, "For a girl."

After I found out they were students of a local artist, Marcel Tondreau, and studied with him at his atelier, I wouldn't let them leave until they told me about him. I was self-taught, apart from a few watercolor classes at finishing school, and I had always longed to attend an atelier like that, but my parents did not approve of such a thing. I begged Bertram and Étienne to introduce me to the artist. To my delight, I found that Monsieur was a rare person in the world of art. He didn't care if the artist was male or female; he let the work speak.

All of the other artists at the atelier were male, and none of them gave me a thought apart from the occasional curious glance. I did not blame them. Most females drew things that did not matter.

But the other artists were wrong about me. I didn't fill my head with airy nothings or paint watercolors of kittens and flowers meant only for decoration; I wanted so much more.

When I was ten years old, I laid eyes for the first time on a painting called *A Mermaid*, which hung in the Royal Academy in London. The mermaid's eyes seemed to call to me, telling me that creating someone like her was within my grasp. And like her maker, J. W. Waterhouse, I wanted to be considered among the best artists in the world. I wanted critics to laud my work. But most of all, I wanted to express myself through my art as I fancied, and not be told what or whom I could draw or paint. For all of these dreams I needed knowledge and connections with other artists who could introduce me to the mysterious society that made up the art world.

No one at my boarding school, Madame Édith's Finishing School for Girls, knew I attended the atelier— not the headmistress nor any of my fellow students, apart from Lily, who helped me sneak away. If they knew, it would be hell's delight, because Monsieur Tondreau's atelier was not the kind females should frequent. At Monsieur Tondreau's we drew from the undraped figure—the nude. No woman of good breeding would ever do such a thing, which was another reason why female artists were not taken seriously. Sometimes women could draw from nude statues without fear of scandal. The Victoria and Albert Museum in London held drawing classes for women, but the instructors covered the male statues' bits with tin fig leaves. Apparently, gazing at a statue's male anatomy was equivalent to staring into the sun.

Monsieur Tondreau glanced at his pocket watch and sighed. "*Alors.* I think that Mademoiselle Bernadette will not be with us today." He leveled a look at Étienne, who was cradling his head in his hands. "So. We say good-bye for the day, or we have a student pose." Monsieur's gaze flitted over the artists briefly and then lit on Bertram.

"I'm not doing it again." Bertram raised his voice over the artists' calls of encouragement. "Once was enough."

"Who wants to draw your scrawny carcass again anyway," came a voice from the back of the room.

"I nominate Étienne," Bertram went on. "He's the cause of all this grief." He stood up, grinning, and dragged Étienne to his feet by the shoulder of his jacket. Several students shouted out in agreement. Étienne took this all in humor for about ten seconds before slapping his hand over his mouth, turning a very sickly shade of yellow, and running for the back door that led to the outdoor privy. Sounds of retching echoed through the room.

"Can you not find a model who resists Étienne's charms, Monsieur?" one of the artists asked. "This is the second time Bernadette has failed to show after a night out with him."

"I'm sick to the back teeth of drawing the blokes,"

Bertram added. "Hell's bells, I can draw my own phallus at home. We need to draw women, Monsieur."

"I will try, but it is difficult to find women who are willing. Or one whose father will let her." He looked over the group again, but his eyes did not fall on me. "If no one will volunteer, then I shall bid you all farewell. À demain."

"Why does she not pose?" demanded Pierre, a burly artist from Paris, who had pointedly ignored me from the day I walked into the studio. "Everyone here has had a turn. Why not her?"

I twisted in my seat and scowled at him. "My name is Vicky!"

Pierre shrugged. "I only learn names of people who matter, *Vicky*."

"Don't be an ass, Pierre," Bertram said. "She's just a girl."

There it was again: I was just a girl.

"*Pardonnez-moi!*" Pierre replied. "I thought she was an artist. She pretends to be."

I turned back in my seat and stared at my easel. I felt the gaze of several of the artists fall upon me. Everyone in the room *had* posed before. Everyone but me. And that awful voice inside me started up. That little voice that always carped at me when I didn't feel confident about my work: *No wonder none of the artists give you a thought. Why should they? You aren't really one of them.*

It was true, wasn't it? I wasn't willing to do what the other students did for art. Who was I to call myself an artist? If I didn't take my turn, then I would always be *just a girl*. Certainly never an artist in the other students' eyes. And then the words burbled out: "I'll do it! I'll pose."

Monsieur Tondreau's whiskered face registered surprise.

Pierre looked taken aback for a moment, but then I thought I saw a little flicker of respect in his eyes. "Well, then, mademoiselle. I was wrong. Maybe you aren't pretending, after all." He bowed slightly, sat back down in his chair, and began to set up his easel.

"I didn't mean *you*, Vicky," Bertram said.

I stood. "The other artists here have taken their turn. Pierre is quite right. I should do my bit."

"A moment, gents." Bertram took me by the elbow and led me off to the corner. He leaned in close. "Vicky, you know female models have more to lose than male ones. No one cares if a bloke gets his kit off."

"If I'm going to be a student here, treated on equal terms, then I have to be willing to do everything that they do," I said. "There can't be two sets of expectations, one for them and one for me, the only girl in the class. How will I earn their esteem if I don't pose?" I threw a glance over my shoulder at the students watching us. Pierre sat with his arms folded; the look of respect was now replaced with a sneer.

"Are you going to try to tell me that you care what Pierre thinks? That great buffoon? The only one you should care about is Monsieur Tondreau, and he thinks the sun shines out your arse. Take my advice: let your fabulous work speak for you, and forget about what everyone else says or thinks. Pose if you want to, by all means, but don't do it because you feel you have to. A model should never be forced; you know that, Vicky."

"I'm not forced." I jerked my arm out of Bertram's grasp and marched to the front of the room. I wouldn't say that I

SHARON BIGGS WALLER

wasn't afraid, because I would be lying. My legs were trembling so much I was surprised my knees didn't clack together.

Mercifully, Monsieur came forward and helped me up onto the dais. He threw open the creaky blue shutters to let in as much light as the gloomy day would allow.

I am going to do this. I am really going to do this! I turned my back and let my breath out. I had no idea how to begin. When Bertram disrobed to model, he made it funny, pretending to be a fan dancer at the Folies Bergère, taking each item of clothing off and throwing it to us, eyes rolling comically while we whooped and shouted.

I decided to do the opposite, to act as if disrobing in front of a group of men was no great thing. I started to undo my blouse, but my hands shook and my fingers slipped off the buttons. I squeezed my hands into fists and tried again.

No one spoke a word as I undressed, but I could hear the usual bustle of artists readying their easels and drawing boards—the rustling of paper and the scrape of pencils against knives. I slid my skirt and petticoats off, put them neatly to one side, turned around and sat down on the chair. I stared at my bare toes for the longest time, unable to find the nerve to look up. It was the first occasion in my life that male eyes had seen my unclothed body. I'd never cared what men thought of me before, but now, sitting in front of their steady gaze, I wondered how they regarded my breasts, my hips, my legs. I found I wanted them to see me as beautiful. In my own experience I'd looked at the men's bodies in that way when they posed. I was human, after all, and the model wasn't a *thing*, a bowl of apples to be drawn.

Finally, I forced myself to lift my head. And I saw ten pairs of eyes looking back at me. I had no idea what Monsieur's students were thinking, because they were professional and had learned to focus their minds on their work. They knew if they gave in to any urges—leering or making bawdy comments—Monsieur would dismiss them and they'd never be allowed back.

And so the artists regarded me frankly and then bent to their work. Only one of the newer artists, a boy about my age, gaped, his eyes out on stalks, jaw dangling. I could see his throat tighten when he swallowed. I met his gaze and raised my eyebrows. Startled, he knocked over his easel, his pencils and papers scattering over the floor, earning disgusted looks from the more experienced artists. He fumbled to gather up his things, his ears red.

Bertram remained in the corner with his hands in his pockets. I tilted my head toward his easel. He hesitated for a moment, opened his mouth to say something. But then he shrugged, went back to his workplace, and began to draw.

I felt my shoulders relaxing, my nerves disappearing. I felt like Queen Boadicea taking on the Romans. I leaned forward, propped my chin in my hand, and stared out at the boys.

Now I'm one of you.

WHEN THE CLASS was over, the students—apart from Étienne, who reeled off for home—asked me to join them at a nearby café, a place they all went after class to argue about art. They had never invited me before. I had a little time to spare before I met Lily where she always waited with my school uniform, so I went along.

The only other woman at the café, apart from myself and the proprietor's wife, sat at a little table, a glass of green liquid at her elbow, staring straight in front of her, a dazed look on her face. Her booted feet were turned out carelessly to the sides, her knees wide apart. I had never seen a woman sit like that in public in my life. The art students paid her no mind, apart from Pierre, who grunted a greeting in her direction.

The artists noisily pulled several tables and chairs into the middle of the room, creating a table that would accommodate all of us. No one glowered at them or told them to hush up or to put the tables back. Instead the proprietor came over and shook everyone's hands, then surreptitiously slid a large basket of crusty bread onto the table, despite the disapproving glare of his wife. Several of the students fell on it, grabbing the bread with their bare hands. I knew it was probably the only meal they would have that day. Bertram had told me that many of them spent their extra money on paint—and wine—instead of food.

The proprietor returned with a carafe of red wine. I could not return to school with wine on my breath, so I asked for coffee.

Pierre poured a glass of wine and stood up, holding the glass in my direction. "À la vôtre! To Mademoiselle Vicky! For . . . how do you say in English . . . saving the day!"

The other artists held up their glasses; some banged the table; a few clapped.

I pretended it was nothing, but I knew I would hold

their acceptance close forever, like a treat I could take out and savor anytime I wanted.

The conversation turned into an argument. This one was about whether painting subjects like a mother and child was maudlin pap. Bertram said it wasn't; Pierre said it was.

"What do you say, Mademoiselle Vicky?" Pierre asked, squinting at me through a plume of cigarette smoke.

"*Ça dépend*," I said, carefully, knowing that Pierre fully expected me to launch into a statement about how lovely a mother and child were to look upon. "It depends upon what you're trying to say, what emotion you want to conjure within the viewer. If you render your point of view skillfully, even the simplest subject can have meaning and purpose."

"Go on," Bertram said, leaning forward over the table. "Give us an example."

I cast about for one, and my eyes lit upon the woman in the corner. "Take a woman who has imbibed too much absinthe. If you choose her as a subject, how do you want the viewer to see her? Happy? Indifferent? Hopeless? If you want to depict her in despair, a hopeless expression on her face, her boots turned out, instead of together like a lady would sit . . . the viewer might feel her despair and have sympathy for her plight, and look on her differently from just an unladylike wretch who doesn't merit a thought.

"The same can be said of a mother and child. Perhaps they are bidding farewell to a father as he marches off to war, the family knowing not when they will see him again.

Such art can awaken feelings inside us for which there are no words. And that is hardly maudlin."

"What if the critics say that is ugly?" asked the teenage boy who had knocked over his easel.

"They are entitled to their opinion," I said. "But an artist should only worry about his or her own expression. An artist shouldn't let the critic hold the paintbrush."

"Ha!" Bertram said. "I couldn't have said it better, Pierre. I win!"

Pierre, unhappy with losing, flicked his cigarette ash in the direction of a plate. "Do you paint, mademoiselle?"

"Only watercolors," I admitted. "But I so want to learn to paint with oil. I hope Monsieur will let me progress soon."

Oils were my favorite, but they eluded me. I had no idea how to mix them to create the depth of color so sought after in the medium. My attempts in the past had been dismal. I couldn't get the feel of the paint. Worse, I constantly overloaded the brush and ended up creating an unspeakable mess on the canvas. Oil paints were terrifically difficult and most intimidating, but when one understood how to use them, the results were magical. And magic was what I craved. But Monsieur would only let students progress to painting when they had mastered drawing. Drawing was the alpha and omega of painting, he always told us.

"Oils are not a woman's medium," Pierre said. "Best to stick with watercolors, eh?"

"For God's sake, Pierre," Bertram said before I could protest. "You don't have to have *un phallus* to work with oils." He turned to me. "Don't take any notice, Vicky. He doesn't know one end of a paint tube from another. You'll get there; have patience."

I smiled at Bertram gratefully, taking care to avoid meeting Pierre's steady gaze.

All too soon, I had to make my good-byes. I reluctantly left the artists shouting over one another and smoking their cigarettes. But before I left, I quietly settled their bill with the proprietor and paid for extra bread and a hot cassoulet to be sent over.

I walked quickly through the village, needing to get back to school. But I paused when I reached the square. I saw Étienne's latest poster plastered to the side of the *boulangerie* where Lily and I always bought our chocolate croissants.

Étienne, like many French artists, made extra money illustrating advertisements. His efforts, however, tended toward the more risqué commerce. This one was for a cabaret the next village over.

FORMIDABLE

was written in bold lettering across the top. Underneath posed a woman who looked like our model Bernadette. *Quelle surprise*, I thought. Étienne had scribbled a froth of orange tulle over her lower body, but her breasts were left bare. I smiled. The poster would probably last only a day before a disapproving villager tore it down.

When I rounded the corner of the bakery, I saw that Étienne had thought of this and had managed to stick a poster high up, where no one could reach it. He must have climbed the roof and leaned over the eaves to paste it on. Already the baker was outside eyeing the poster, most likely working out a way to remove it. His wife stood at his side, clucking with irritation like a maddened hen.

Mindful of the time, I picked up my skirt and broke into a run. When I arrived at our meeting place, Lily stepped out onto the path from behind the tree.

"Lily, I have so much to tell you! You wouldn't believe..." But my voice trailed off when I reached her. Her face was white as milk, and she held my uniform bundled against her chest.

"Oh, Vicky. Tell me it isn't true!"

"True? What are you talking about?"

Lily chewed her lip and shifted from one foot to the other. Her complexion began to change from pale to bright pink. Her curly blonde hair had escaped its combs and formed a wild halo over her head.

"Give over, Lily, you're frightening me."

She clutched the clothing tighter. "Did you really take your clothes off in front of men?" she blurted out.

"Pardon?" I was dumbfounded.

"It's all over school," Lily went on, breathless. "Mildred Halfpenny said she saw you undressed, sitting in front of a crowd of men. She must have heard us talking about the art studio and followed you. You know what an eavesdropper she is."

Mildred Halfpenny. My nemesis. Mildred had been jealous of me the moment she laid eyes on me. She hated that I was Lily's dearest friend; the idiot thought she had more claim on her because their families had summered together in Germany once. And she thought she was better than me because my father had a plumbing fittings-and-fixtures holding while *her* father owned a lingerie company. As if knickers and petticoats put her higher in the social standing than toilets and wash-hand basins. I called her the Royal Princess of Petticoats once, and her face turned so purple with rage that I thought she was going to choke.

How could Mildred have seen me? The window by the model's dais looked over the river. She must have tiptoed round where no one ought to go and peered in the window. Who knew that clumsy oaf could be so nimble?

"Is it true?" Lily stepped forward, her face pleading.

"Our model didn't show, so I . . . volunteered." I tried to sound like I didn't care, but I wasn't doing a very good job of it. In a daze, I took my uniform from Lily and went behind the tree to change.

"You volunteered?" Lily's voice was climbing higher. "Volunteered?"

"It was my turn." My mind whirled, trying to work out what to do. I would just have to brazen my way out of it as best I could. I dressed quickly and stepped back on the path. "It's Mildred's word against mine. I'll say she mistook me for someone else. I wasn't there. Madame Froufrou won't bother to check. You know what she thinks about the artists in the village. She won't get within a mile of the place." I certainly hoped this was true. It was my only chance. And a slim one at that.

Lily looked down at the ground and bit her lip. "It's too late," she whispered. "I'm so sorry, Vicky. You know I'm not very good at hiding things. Madame Édith called me into her study and started asking me all these questions about the art studio and if you went there. I tried to lie, but my face went all red and I started stammering. . . . You know what Madame is like, the looks she gives. She got it all out of me. I had to sneak out just to meet you here. I had to warn you." Lily paused for a moment and then went on, her face grave. "Madame has already sent a telegram to your father."

"My . . . father?" I whispered. The shock of it made my cheeks tingle and my limbs go weak. Panic rose hot and fast inside me. I might have felt like Queen Boadicea before, but I had forgotten one important fact about the Iceni warrioress: in the end, the Romans had crushed her.

My father. That was it, then. My time in France with the artists was over.

Two

Cherbourg, France, Cunard Steamship Line,
Wednesday, third of March

I STOOD ON THE deck of the steamship and looked out at the seaside town of Cherbourg. Gray clouds scudded overhead, and a brisk wind whisked the sea into foamy waves. The damp air seeped into my bones. I shivered and wrapped my arms about myself. The weather had chased the rest of the passengers below long ago, but Cherbourg was my final glimpse of France, and I was loath to look away. My chaperone, one of the school's maids, stood just behind me at a respectful distance, but I could hear her little noises of dismay as the waves lapping the sides of the ship grew heavier.

The steamship's vast engines rumbled to life, the sailors cast off the lines, and the boat began to make its way across the Channel toward England. Toward home.

I was leaving France under a veil of scandal and humiliation. The scandal was bearable. The girls at the school loved any chance to gossip, and I didn't care about their chatter, but the humiliation bit through me to the bone. I had just proven myself to the artists, and now I was being sent back home to my parents like a naughty little girl who had misbehaved at a party. *What do the artists think of me now?*

The immediate punishment for posing nude was acceptable to me. I was expelled from Madame Édith's Finishing School for Girls—good riddance to bad rubbish. No more marching about with books on my head to perfect my posture. No more elocution lessons hammering home the proper diction of words as though one's fate in life depended upon it. No more listening to inane conversations about how the hockey pitch was flooded or what sort of pudding would be served at Sunday lunch—usually the same old jam roly-poly, so I don't know why the girls yammered on about it.

My expulsion would have been welcome if it hadn't meant saying good-bye to Monsieur's art studio forever. I had not had a chance to say farewell, not even by letter. When I went to ask Lily to take a note to the studio, she looked at me with red-rimmed, tear-filled eyes, and I put the note back in my pocket. Lily was in trouble enough for helping me; I did not want to add to her burden.

Yes, the immediate punishment was bearable; the unknown punishment was the one I feared.

A sailor carrying a coil of hemp rope over one shoulder paused on his way across the deck. "Best you go down below, miss," he said. "There be weather kickin' up, make no mistake. Wouldn't want to fish you out of the water."

"Thank you," I said. "I'll go down in a moment."

"I'll leave you to it, then." He tugged at the brim of his hat and then continued on to his task.

"Go ahead to your cabin, Anne-Marie," I told the maid.

She bit her lip, looking unsure. "*D'accord,*" she finally said, and turned for the stairs that led to the cabins.

I sighed and returned my attention to the shoreline, watching until Cherbourg grew smaller and smaller until it was just a tiny dot in the distance, and then it vanished into the horizon. The first drops of rain began to fall, as the sailor had predicted, and the wind gusted, sending the ship's flags snapping.

I made my way below, weaving around my fellow passengers, the deck rising and falling under our feet. I found my cabin, turned the key in the lock, and swung the door open.

"Hell's teeth," I muttered.

My cabin was a mean little cupboard with only enough room for a cot and a small washstand with a pitcher and basin atop. The bed was dressed with an old woolen blanket that looked like it might be crawling with noisome creatures. The meanness of the accommodation spoke volumes. My father always paid for me to travel in a first-class cabin with a sitting room. I dreaded small spaces, and my father knew it.

All right, Papa, you've made your point, I thought, struggling to wash my face over the little bowl as the ship pitched to and fro.

The crossing grew even more fitful, and I spent a good part of the night with my head hanging over the basin. When the seas calmed and my nausea abated, I fell into bed, exhausted. But sleep was far away.

There was enough light from the bedside candle lamp to see by, so I took my drawing book out of my art satchel and opened it. Sketches of my friends from France flipped past: Lily, sitting on a stone wall by the sea, gazing at me with a mix of admiration and exasperation, her eyes so wise and merry; Étienne, smoking a cigarette and squinting, his hair tousled as if he had just woken up. And then I paused on my sketch of a nude Bertram, posing contrapposto, weight on one foot, hips and shoulders twisted to the side, a look of embarrassment and amusement on his face, as if he couldn't quite believe what he had let himself in for but he found it funny all the same.

Sadness and longing filled me. Tears threatened and I pushed them back. The aching sense of loss I could do nothing about. Crying about what might have been would take me nowhere.

I put my pencil to the page and began to sketch the features of the sailor from memory. I was halfway through the picture when the boat tipped so steeply that I tumbled off the bed. I struck my elbow on the frame of the cot and landed on the floor in a heap.

The cries of the other passengers drifted through the cabin walls, accompanied by the sounds of china crashing to the floor and trunks slamming into walls. A moment later the sea settled and the ship righted itself. I hauled myself up and rubbed the life back into my tingling elbow. My sketchbook had come to a rest upside down against the doorframe. Several pieces of paper had fallen out and lay scattered over the floor. I was always collecting bits of things and shoving them into my sketchbook—posters, leaves, newspaper cuttings. I was a magpie that way. I gathered them all up to shove them back into the book when one of them caught my eye.

ROYAL COLLEGE OF ART,
ANNUAL SUMMER SHOW, 1908

It was last year's program for the show of students' work. Bertram had it in a wodge of bumf he was discarding. I wanted some sketches he was throwing out, so I'd fished it all out of the rubbish, and that's when I found the leaflet. The Royal College of Art was one of the most prestigious schools in England; many of the country's finest artists had studied there. Bertram had attended the RCA. Although he left after a year, he said he'd learned a great deal about fundamentals. Monsieur Tondreau often said that without fundamentals, an artist would always struggle.

I sat down on the edge of the cot, holding the leaflet. I could never return to Monsieur's studio, but I didn't have to give up on instruction. I could apply to the RCA. My drawing book held proof that I understood the technical challenges of art, especially anatomy. I had a treasure trove of those forbidden drawings. I would need a letter of reference, but I could get one from Bertram or from Monsieur Tondreau. I knew Bertram's address. He worked and lived in a tiny studio off the village square. I would send letters to both of them as soon as we docked.

Then I reminded myself that I was in disgrace and my parents might not be so disposed to let me go to art college. Besides, I already knew what my father thought about women going to college: there was no reason to educate a girl as a boy, he believed. The only value to a woman of good breeding was as a wife and mother.

Forget it, I thought. I slid my feet under the blanket and laid my head on the lumpy pillow, trying to ignore the spring that poked me in the backside. *If I were a boy, this wouldn't be an issue. If I were my brother Freddy . . .*

I sat straight up then. Freddy! Perhaps I could enlist my brother's aid. A year ago, he'd defied Papa and left the family business. He embarked upon a career in publishing instead of taking the reins of the family business. Papa did not speak to him for nearly six months, and refused to change the name of the business, hoping the "son" in Darling & Son Sanitary Company would see the error of his ways. There was a rapprochement at Christmas, and now my father behaved as if Freddy's career decision had been his idea. If I could get Freddy on my side, he could speak to my parents for me.

I imagined myself at the RCA show, standing next to my work of art, wineglass in hand, listening as the president of the Selection and Hanging Committee told the gathered crowd why my painting had been chosen and how I was considered among the best of my generation.

Maybe bidding France farewell wouldn't be so unbearable after all.

Three

I N THE MORNING, we disembarked at Southampton and I put my letters to Bertram and Monsieur Tondreau in the pillar-box. A sailor helped load my trunks into a hansom cab and tipped his cap when I handed him a coin. When Anne-Marie and I arrived at the train station, a porter hurried out, collar turned up, shoulders hunched against the rain, and settled me into a first-class carriage, which heartened me. Even better was the sight of my brother, Freddy, on the train platform at Victoria Station in London, leaning on a walking stick, his homburg hat tilted at a jaunty angle.

I alighted from the carriage, and Freddy hurried to greet me, a look of affection tinged with concern on his face. "There you are!" He kissed my cheek and then took hold of my valise. "Welcome home. Mother was going to send the footman, but I wanted you to see a friendly face before heading into battle."

"What's the news of home?" I asked as we moved through the station.

"Oh, the usual. Mother is dragging Dad into the twentieth century, or at least attempting to. She's had a telephone installed."

"That *is* news. What brought that on?"

"Mrs. Plimpton had a sudden rush of blood to the head and had one fitted, so now all the ladies in her social circle have to have one, too."

My mother was ever the trend follower. Years ago she had taken after Queen Alexandra's style, which boasted high collars and tiered pearl chokers, all of which were really only meant to hide a scar on the queen's neck. If the queen's deformities meant a high neckline, then who was my mother to argue? At least she didn't parrot Queen Alexandra's limp by shortening one shoe heel as many of her friends had. When I was home at Christmas, Mamma had changed our Mayfair townhouse from a dark, old-fashioned abode to one with a more light and airy sensibility, as was now in vogue. Chintz and pastel fabrics, potted palms and aspidistras abounded. My father was the opposite and clung to the old ways like grim death.

"Papa has agreed?" I asked. "I thought he said a telephone in the home was an intrusion."

"She talked him round, and the thing was installed last week."

"Heavens."

I watched while Freddy saw Anne-Marie onto the next train and arranged for a cab for us, so capable and self-assured. He had not always been so. Our father used to remark on Freddy's every movement, correcting him constantly. My brother was much older than I, ten years, but I remembered him spending most of his teenage years, while not at school, avoiding our father.

We settled in the cab and the horse set off, harness jangling. The first signs of spring were about. Daffodils and narcissi poked their noses through the grass in Green Park. A weak ray of sunshine broke through the gloom, and several people sat on park benches, faces turned toward the warmth. Motorcars chugged past our cab, trailing smoke, tires hissing on the damp tarmacadam. The smell of wet wool, coal fires, and the tang of horse sweat got under my nose, but it was a welcome scent. London never failed to make me happy, so I tried not to dwell on my sadness at leaving France.

"Well, how grim is it?" I asked.

He frowned. "Fairly grim, Petal. I'm not going to lie to you."

"Is Papa very angry, then?"

Freddy regarded me in silence for a moment. "Angry? Vicky, you took your clothes off in front of a group of men."

"You make it sound so sordid, Fred. It was an art class. It's what we do."

But Freddy was shaking his head. "That makes no difference to our father. He doesn't care a whit that it was in the name of art or what have you. Word has gotten round. Apparently some of the girls at Madame Édith's wasted no time writing to their parents, and now Mother's social circle knows."

"I care not what her social circle thinks."

"You should care. Your behavior did much damage, Petal. You know Dad has lost Sir Hugo Northbrook's regard? That is a lot for him to swallow."

"What does Sir Hugo's regard have to do with any-thing? Lily Northbrook is my dearest friend."

"Sir Hugo had been paving the way for Dad to gain a royal warrant. The royal residences are updating the plumbing, and he was going to introduce Dad to the pro-curer. If Dad supplies the fixtures, he'll be on his way, but now, because of your actions, he may have lost his chance."

What Freddy said filled me with guilt. Royal warrants were marks of recognition for those who provided goods to King Edward. The *By Appointment* stamp was a highly coveted item; even more was the beautiful royal crest that decorated the receiver's place of business. My father had made it his life's work to gain one. Thomas Crapper & Company had installed thirty lavatories in the king's country seat, Sandringham House, as well as fixtures in other royal houses years ago. Crapper was Papa's bête noire, and the mere mention of the name sent him into a fury. To lose another royal contract to that company would be a terrible blow.

Freddy looked at me in sympathy. "Not to worry. I'm sure Dad will find someone else who can help. He's already working the chaps he knows at the Reform Club."

"Papa probably wants to roast me over an open fire now," I said.

"I think that would be the least of your punishments. He's very angry. Roasting would be a merciful death, I should think."

"Do you have a whiff of anything?"

Freddy shrugged. "No. I do know that another finishing school is out. No one would have you."

"It would be nice if someone asked me what I'd like to do. I'm not a child."

"Go on," he prodded. "I know you've a scheme or two hatching in that mind of yours."

"I should like to go to college."

"You're wasting your time," he said. "Dad will never give his permission, even on a good day when all is right in his world. You know what he thinks about higher education for females."

"Yes, well, that's where you come in. You're going to help me convince him. Louisa Dowd goes to medical university. Times are changing." Our neighbor's daughter attended a medical school that admitted women.

"You want to be a physician like Miss Dowd, is that what you're saying?"

"No! I would not want to have snotty children sneezing all over me and people complaining of piles and digestive difficulties. And Lord knows the places on a person she'll have to look to make her diagnoses." Freddy screwed his mouth up, trying not to smile. I could always make him laugh. "But I should like to go to art college."

"Why? You already know how to draw and such. Why do you need to go to college?"

"I want to learn more, and I want to paint, and if I'm going to be able to exhibit my work, I need contacts in the art world who will help me along that path."

"Exhibit?" Freddy looked dubious.

"Just leave it, Freddy. I want to go, and my reasons for going are my reasons. I'm not going to explain myself." I was growing frustrated. What if Freddy refused to help me?

"Fine, then—you'll also need Dad's coin. University is expensive."

"I'll earn a scholarship."

"And if you don't?"

"I don't know. I suppose I can earn money ... somehow."

"Oh, give over, Vicky; how?"

"Can you pay me to illustrate your novelettes?"

"Oh, no. Not a chance. Penny dreadfuls aren't the place for women's pictures of bowls of fruit and bunches of flowers. We print drawings of highwaymen and demon barbers of Fleet Street. Not appropriate subjects for a girl."

I pinched him on the arm. "I don't draw bowls of fruit! Nor do I draw bunches of flowers!"

"Ow!" He rubbed his arm. "All right, then. You don't draw fruit. You needn't resort to violence to make your point."

"Just let me have a chance. Please, Fred."

"No. It's utterly absurd."

"Why is it so absurd? I can illustrate as well as any man. These are modern times, and women are still treated as nothing but pretty dolls or lapdogs!"

"Nevertheless, Dad would never forgive me if I allowed such a thing. I've just returned to his good graces, and what with Rose in her confinement, I simply can't risk another row."

"What does Rose's lying-in have to do with it? Papa cares not a fig about babies. I doubt he'll even make the journey across town to see it when it's born. Much too taxing for him, I'd say. And then when it starts yelling and squalling, as babies are wont to do, he'll be first out the door."

"It?" Freddy tilted his head toward me.

"Very well. Her! Charlotte would love a little sister."

"Him, I'd prefer."

I opened my mouth in retort.

He held up his finger. "A sister needs a brother's guidance to rub along in life."

I shot him a filthy look. He laughed.

"I feel very sorry for your future husband, my dear. I can picture him now, living his life so innocently, unknowing of the mischief his future wife will create for him."

"Ha-ha. Very amusing, Freddy."

"But the point is, Vick, that Dad will be happy to cut my allowance again if I should stray. No. Sorry, I cannot risk it."

"But you make your own money!"

"A publisher of a start-up tuppenny novelette company makes very little. Certainly not enough to feed a family and keep home and hearth together." Freddy grew quiet. His face was pinched with strain. Suddenly I understood what it had cost him to break from our father's expectations. I took his hand. "It maddens me to admit it," he said. "But I need the old man's money, too. I suppose I'm just as much of a lapdog as you, Petal, when it comes right down to it." He squeezed my hand. "I'll tell you what, I'll mention this art-college idea of yours to Mother, but that's it. The rest is up to you."

"Thank you, Freddy!" I kissed his cheek. "I'll never ask anything of you again."

"I highly doubt that, Petal," Freddy said.

Big Ben rang out three o'clock as the cab reached

Parliament. I was surprised to see a crowd of women in front of the gates near the House of Commons. London was a city of men, and women did not loiter. They traveled through on their way home or to the shops. Women who stood about were considered of ill reputation. But these women didn't seem to be concerned with their reputation, ill or otherwise.

The cab stopped for traffic, and I leaned toward the window. What was most unusual was that the women were of various classes, from upper-class to working-class. I could tell by the way they were dressed. A woman handing out leaflets wore an expensive-looking fox stole around her neck; her wide-brimmed hat was trimmed in feathers. A woman in less fashionable dress, probably middle-class, stood talking to her. She was tiny and as thin as a rake. She wore a plain navy suit, called a tailor-made, with a gray bow tie. There were several working-class women too, who looked as though they had just left the factory floor, feet in clogs and shawls around their shoulders. I had never seen a collection of mismatched women so united. My mother, and every woman in her social circle, would have fainted dead away if forced to mingle with such a mixed group.

The men on the street seemed as curious, gawking at the assembly as they walked by. I noticed several posters hanging on the iron railings, bracketing the women. On one was a stylized drawing of Joan of Arc. She held a trailing green banner with the word

JUSTICE

blazoned on it. Étienne could not have drawn a better poster.

Just as I was thinking this, a police constable ripped it down and tore it in half. A younger constable stepped forward to deal with the second poster, but he didn't rip it. Instead, he removed it carefully from the railings, rolled it up, and handed it to the tiny woman.

Who were they?

"Votes for women!" the woman with the fur muff called out, solving the mystery for me. She turned to thrust a leaflet at a passing man, and I saw that she wore a sash across her jacket with the letters WSPU.

I knew that WSPU stood for Women's Social and Political Union. It was headed by Emmeline Pankhurst and her daughter Christabel, who was so famous she had her own waxwork at Madame Tussaud's and her face on playing cards. All the girls at my finishing school were agog over Christabel's beauty and her sense of style. Certainly not over her political views. Not at Madame Édith's Finishing School for Girls.

"Suffragettes!" I said. "In the flesh!"

Freddy leaned across me and snapped the window shade down.

I flung the shade back up just in time to see the man snatch the leaflet from the woman's hand, pitch it to the ground, and stamp it under his heel. Undaunted, she shoved another at the next passerby. "Votes for women!"

The traffic snarl cleared and the cab moved forward. I turned to Freddy. "What are they doing in front of Parliament?"

"Never you mind."

"Oh, come off it, Freddy!"

Freddy sighed. "They picket Parliament every day demanding the vote, leafleting, fixing their ruddy propaganda to the railings, and mucking things up. Christabel Pankhurst and her cursed mother have led their merry band of suffragettes into all sorts of shenanigans, as of late." He grimaced. "They do it for attention, to grab newspaper headlines. But not for much longer. You see the chaos they cause—traffic and all sorts. The prime minister is going to put a stop to that nonsense soon enough."

I pressed my cheek against the window of the cab, eyes straining to keep the spectacle in sight for as long as I could. The cab turned a corner, and the suffragettes vanished from view. I sat back. "They meet there every day?"

Freddy looked alarmed, sensing looming disaster. "Don't tell me you're going to join them."

My fingers began to itch as they always did when I saw something that I wanted to draw. "I have no plans to join them. But I'd love to draw them."

My brother muttered something under his breath. I couldn't hear what he said exactly, but it was something along the lines of *here we go again*.

FREDDY ESCORTED ME home, and I begged him to come inside so as to dilute some of Mamma's anger toward me.

Freddy stayed for tea. Our mother was too civilized to chastise me in front of him, but she eyed me above her teacup, pinky crooked somewhat accusingly in my direction.

Finally, Freddy made his good-byes. I sat nervously while Mother saw him to the door. Freddy leaned in to kiss her cheek and then paused. I couldn't hear what he was saying, but from the look upon her face she didn't like it. She closed the door behind Freddy and walked back into the sitting room.

"Do you want to explain yourself?" she asked in an even tone that I recognized as controlled anger.

"I—"

"I know not what to do with you, Victoria! Undressing in front of men?"

"It was for art, Mamma," I said, trying to keep the defiance out of my voice. That would only lead me into more trouble.

My mother had an artistic bent herself, but she turned her talents to the decorative, drawing her own patterns for needlework, painting the odd watercolor landscape for the hallway. She could never understand what it took to become a real artist.

She played with the pearls at her throat. "Such reckless behavior will lead you down the path to ruin. And now, your brother has just told me that you wish to go to art college. I'll tell you that your father will not allow you to attend."

I said nothing. What could I say? My opinions, thoughts, and desires meant little in my own home and always had. Freddy was right. I should have known better.

"You've disappointed us, Victoria." She crossed to the credenza to look through a pile of fabric swatches that lay there. She picked up her embroidery hoop and sank into the chair.

"I'm sorry, Mamma. I really am. But . . . please don't punish me so harshly. I really want to go to art school. How about this? At least let me apply. If I get in, then—"

"Denying you art school is not a punishment, Victoria! It's for your own good. What kind of mother would set her child up for failure?"

"I didn't do anything wrong!" I could hold back no longer.

My mother smacked her hoop down on the seat so hard the bamboo cane snapped. "What you did, Victoria, was beyond the pale. You're very lucky that you didn't do this after you came out. The scandal would have been irreparable, and your father and I would have been unable to save you. You would have been lost."

Her blast of anger caught me so unawares that I shrank back. My mother had never raised her voice to me in that way. Never.

"You'll not walk out of the door until your father and I have decided what to do with you. I have nothing more to say. Go upstairs." She picked up her hoop and tutted at the damage. "See what you've gone and made me do."

As if I had the power to make my mother do anything. If I did, I certainly would do more than make her break a bamboo embroidery hoop.

THAT FIRST NIGHT my father greeted me with a cold hello when I kissed his cheek. And then one week slid into the next, and still no one said much. Dinners were silent affairs, only broken by the occasional "please pass the salt" or the clink of cutlery. I began to hope that this confinement and the cold shoulder-of-mutton treatment would be the extent of my punishment. Once it ran its course, I would bring up the idea of art school again. I could bide my time.

I had been home for a fortnight when my mother called me into her drawing room. She sat working on her needlepoint in the window seat, squinting in the morning light.

"You wished to see me, Mamma?"

Mamma stuck her needle into the muslin and put her hoop aside. "Sit down, Victoria." Her tone was the one she used when she refused to brook any nonsense, so I knew what she had to say would not lead to happy days for me.

I sat. I felt as though I were climbing the stairs to the

scaffold where the executioner waited to slice off my head. I could only hope it would be swift and not too painful.

"Now, your father and I have been discussing your prospects. Finishing school is no longer an option, so we must accept that."

I shifted. "Yes, Mamma." Well, that was a relief. I could see the executioner set down his ax.

"It's high time you lowered your skirts and put your hair up. You look a child with your hair dangling down like that. I have hired a lady's maid for you—Sophie Cumberbunch is her name. She will arrive this Saturday. Very highly recommended. Skills at the height of style, both clothing and hair. Mrs. Hollingberry employed this Cumberbunch for her daughter Joan—such a plain little thing—but Cumberbunch was able to work miracles."

"If she is so amazing, why doesn't Joan keep her?"

"Joan has married down and no longer has the means for a lady's maid." Mamma looked utterly scandalized. I'm sure she couldn't imagine a life where a woman was forced to button her own shoes, comb her own hair, draw her own bath. *Oh the horror, the shame of it!* It wasn't that difficult. I dressed myself and did my own hair. True, Mamma's dressing ritual did require assistance, but it wasn't a crime to simplify one's dress, I was sure. "Still, her loss is our gain. She will prepare your clothing for your coming-out and act as your chaperone."

"Mamma," I interrupted. "Do you think it's wise that I have a coming-out? After all that has happened, do you think I'll get one single invitation to a ball?"

My mother was outraged. "No one in my circle would

dare shun me by cutting your name from the guest list!"

"But they might! Maybe . . . maybe we could simply give the whole thing a miss. Make an excuse that I'm unwell or something?"

My mother looked as if I had asked her if I could cease breathing air. "Every young lady of quality has a debut to announce her coming-out to society. If you don't have a debut, you'll soon know what it is to be a social outcast."

I didn't mind parties—in fact, Lily would soon be home and most likely be at many of them, which would give me a chance to see her again—but this inevitable season of parties heralded the beginning of my life, as far as Mamma was concerned. There was more to a debut than balls and dresses. The reason for debuts was marriage.

Debutante balls reminded me of animals being driven to Smithfield Market for slaughter. The executioner might have set down his ax, but it was only to sharpen it.

Until a girl was brought out, she was invisible. Seen but not heard. She was only to speak in social settings when spoken to, and the response to any questions should be kept to single syllables. The best thing a girl could do before she was brought out into society was to become one with the wallpaper. I was already starting out with a blot next to my name.

"There's no guarantee now that you'll receive an invitation to be presented to the king along with all the other debutantes," my mother went on.

Even I thought this unfortunate, as I would have welcomed the chance to see inside Buckingham Palace. I'd heard there were a Rembrandt and a Vermeer hanging in the Picture Gallery. But only the crème de la crème were invited to meet the king. The fortunate debutantes each year started out with a presentation at the king's formal drawing room. The rest of the pack were considered second-rate. Mamma herself had not been a debutante; however, when she married my father, Mrs. Plimpton took Mamma under her wing and transformed her. Mrs. Plimpton had arranged for Mamma, then a newly married woman, to be presented to the king when he was the Prince of Wales. My mother was such a socking success that she and Papa climbed straight up the social ladder with barely a pause.

"I can't tell you how humiliating that will be for your father. If the palace discounts his daughter, then what hope does he have to be considered as a supplier?"

I pretended to be vastly interested in Mamma's new rug.

"I have sent a letter to the Lord Chamberlain, putting your name forward for presentation," she went on. "The summonses come out in mid-May, three weeks before the next presentation. That's not much time to unpick this mess you've made. Between now and then, you must be the picture of contrition and innocence. The first thing to do is to get you involved in a charity. I've chosen for you to join the Friends of London Churches. You'll start this Saturday afternoon at St. Martin-in-the-Fields in Trafalgar Square. The charity will be helping the ladies to organize prayer books and hymnals."

Mamma could not have chosen a more boring charity for me. "Is this the reason you called me in here, Mamma? To discuss balls and lady's maids and charities?"

Mamma looked at me in silence for a moment. "No. As I said, finishing school is out. So the next best choice is to see you settled. I think a steadying hand would do you a great deal of good, and your father has agreed. He has arranged a match for you through an acquaintance at the Reform Club. Sir Henry Carrick-Humphrey's younger son, Edmund."

And there it was. The final blow. My head was rolling down the steps. The solution to the pressing problem of Victoria and her bad behavior was marriage. My parents would also be able to wash their hands of me for good. I would now be my husband's problem.

"So soon? Why?" I asked, stunned that my mother had put such a scheme into action so quickly, especially before my debut.

"I think it's best we strike while the iron is hot. Marriage will show you are respectable. We'll announce your engagement formally the day after your presentation to the king. Before then we'll make sure word gets round that Mr. Carrick-Humphrey has shown interest, which will put the idea in people's minds that you are presentable. The sooner you're married, the sooner we can have this whole business behind us." Mamma pointed at the bellpull hanging by the mantel. "Ring for tea, Victoria."

I stood up and tugged the brocade fabric, my mind struggling to make sense of everything my mother had heaped upon me. I had met Edmund Carrick-Humphrey at our Christmas party two years ago. I could not imagine a more toneless creature. He was totally devoid of emotion, and his countenance lacked any joy or zest for life. Had he not been wearing a striped suit, his very blandness would have faded his person right into my mother's beige drapery. "But why him?"

"Edmund Carrick-Humphrey is eager to join your father at the plumbing works, as he has a very strong interest in the business," Mother replied. "His father also has connections within the king's household, which will help patch the damage you caused with Sir Hugo." She looked at me pointedly.

"So this is a business arrangement?"

Mamma flicked her fingers. "A portion of the business will be your dowry. Nevertheless, such a union would be very fortuitous for both families, particularly in light of the fact that your brother has removed himself from the business. Your sons will inherit, and your father's legacy will be assured. You should be happy you have any prospects left, my dear. A scandalous woman is not something most men would want, but Edmund Carrick-Humphrey has agreed."

"Oh, how jolly lucky for me," I said. "If my pickings are so thin on the ground, then why not leave me to find my own way? Surely I have sense enough to be able to choose my own husband, Mamma."

She clucked her tongue in disapproval. "I can quite imagine the sort of husband you would end up with. I'm sure you'd go the way of Joan Hollingberry. Her poor parents are so humiliated. A clerk! Fancy that. He doesn't even possess a tailcoat. Comes to dinner wearing a tweed jacket, as though dressed for a country shoot! No. Your father has worked very hard to rise from nothing, and he's not about to see his efforts go to waste over your passing fancies."

Papa had started out as a foreman in a pottery business in Lambeth, but he had anticipated that the flush toilet would be in high demand in the years to come. With money he'd saved, he purchased a small concern that made pressed-clay toilets. He sank every penny he had in a design he invented called the dreadnought, which prevented smells from coming back into the room. He'd forced himself to live a meager existence until the business began to pay. He didn't marry my mother until he was thirty-two. She had been the pressed-clay kiln owner's seventeen-year-old daughter. My father was immensely rich, more so than the many aristocrats who looked down on people like my parents, but Mamma liked to pretend that we weren't parvenus ourselves, still wet from a lower-class pool.

"I don't have passing fancies—"

"I beg to differ. This art-school desire of yours is a five-minute wonder, my dear. Here today and gone the next."

"It is not—"

"I'll hear no more about it. We will be entertaining Sir Henry and Lady Carrick-Humphrey, their daughter, and Edmund, who is home visiting from Oxford University, tomorrow evening."

"And if I say no?"

"If you say no, then you will make a life with my aunt in Norfolk."

"With Aunt Maude?" My voice squeaked in alarm. My widowed great-aunt lived a near hermit's existence in Norfolk. The house was dark as pitch and cold as death, and she detested art, books, and joy of any kind. Worse, she owned four smelly old Yorkshire terriers that piddled on the carpets, shed hair everywhere they walked, and bit everyone but my aunt. Every time I visited, my mother bade me read the Bible to her aloud. Aunt Maude always chose the passage about Jezebel, smiling smugly at me all the while.

"Yes, she has need of a companion—someone to read to her and fetch her things and such. Don't look like that. You're lucky we are giving you a choice, Victoria."

"It's not much of a choice!"

"I am sorry, but you must lie in your bed as you've made it. Your father is not a man to deal with when he's been thwarted, as your brother can attest. He has no stomach for nonsense. He is not prepared to support you if you don't marry. He has a horror of spinsters."

"So I either marry a man I don't know or like, or go live in deepest darkest Norfolk, shut away like a cloistered nun never to be seen again? Times are different now, Mamma. Women can marry for love. It's not like in your day."

"How would you live if you do not *fall in love*, then?"

"Other women work."

"Not women of your standing. No one would hire you. And no one in polite society will accept a woman who earns her own money. Should you like to be a charwoman and scrub outhouses? Because that's the life you will have." She looked up, and her eyes softened. "I am in agreement with you. I should not like to live a lonely existence as someone else's companion. Can you not see how I am trying to protect you from a life of penury and loneliness?"

"But if I was allowed to go to art college, I could earn my own living!"

"Who put that idea into your head? Those ridiculous bohemian artists in France? What makes you think you have the talent to earn a living as an artist? Who do you think you are? How preposterous . . ." Mamma stared down at her sewing. For a moment I thought she was going to cry. But then she picked up her scissors and angrily began to rip out the perfect stitches that outlined a bouquet of sweet peas.

Her lack of faith in me, in my talent, hurt. I couldn't bear to hear any more. "I don't care for tea, Mamma," I said faintly. "I don't feel at all well. May I be excused?" Not waiting for her answer, I stood up and left the room.

Mamma's words followed me, floating over me like a dreary cloud, as I trudged up the stairs to my room. *Who put that idea into your head? . . . What makes you think you have the talent to earn a living as an artist? Who do you think you are? How preposterous. Preposterous. Preposterous.*

When I reached my room, I threw myself on the bed and screamed into my pillow for all I was worth until my throat ached. I wanted to weep with rage and humiliation. It was as if that awful little whisper inside of me had been given a voice, and it was my own mother's. Just thinking about it set it off: *If your own mother doesn't think you have talent, then who does?*

Mamma was right. Who did I think I was? How ridiculous it was of me to think that I was not like other girls. What a jest! I was exactly like other girls. And like other girls, my life was not mine to call my own; rather it was one that would be handed over to the next responsible party as soon as possible.

I heard a creak of the floorboards. I jerked my head up and saw our maid, Emma, in the doorway, shifting her weight from foot to foot. "I'm sorry, miss. I didn't mean to bother. But you have a letter." She held a silver salver in her hand.

"That's all right, Emma." I sat up. Another story of mad behavior to report to my mother. That's what I got for failing to close the door.

Emma crossed the room and held the salver to me. I took the letter and Emma bobbed a curtsy, turned round, and scurried out, the ribbons of her white cap and apron trailing behind her.

I recognized the penmanship, the broad loops and swirls made with such confidence, the pen pressing just a bit too heavily. The letter was from Bertram. *Thank goodness!* I tore the envelope open eagerly and unfolded the page.

My Dear Vicky,

I just received your letter. I'm sorry you were punished for posing, but don't say I didn't warn you. I only hope the penalty wasn't too harsh.

I apologize for not replying to your letter swiftly, but the spring light was too good to miss and the lads and I went off into the countryside to paint. Étienne tried to find a goat so we could take a stab at replicating Hunt's The Scapegoat, *but all*

*we could find was an old donkey, and he wouldn't
keep still long enough to let us draw one whisker!*

*As far as your letter of reference goes, one
from me wouldn't do you much good, as I never
completed the course. Monsieur Condreau would
be the better choice, but he left just after you did
to visit his sister, who is ill. I don't know where
she lives. Étienne says maybe Paris but he isn't
certain. Monsieur might be back in a month or
so, but that's probably not soon enough for you.*

*In any case, I wish you well and hope we'll
meet again someday. I enclose a little gift for you.*

*With fond regards,
Bertram*

Bertram's gift was the sketch he had done of me on the day I posed.

In the drawing, I sat on a chair on the artist's dais, with one leg tucked under the other, leaning forward with my elbow on my leg, my chin in one hand, looking out at my fellow artists. The expression he had drawn on my face was one of contentment and strength. Did he really see me that way?

I dropped my head against my pillows and stared out at my room. My mother had not yet turned her redecorating attention here. It still had the same dark, fanciful furniture of my childhood; drawings and paintings I had made through the years festooned the doors of my wardrobe. Pinned onto the corner of a pastel sketch I had done of a fishmonger's cart was the RCA leaflet. I should just throw it in the rubbish. Throw it all in the rubbish. But I couldn't bring myself to.

A chance for a different life. Just a chance was all I asked. If I got into the RCA, maybe my mother would see I had talent to be an artist and talk my father round. Maybe, just as with Freddy, Papa would think my art success was his own making.

But how could I get near the RCA to apply when my mother had me on a short lead, like a dancing bear in a circus?

Then I swung my feet to the ground and sat up. Heart thudding in my ears and hope shooting through me like quicksilver, I fetched my art satchel from my wardrobe and slung it over my shoulder.

My mother might have forbidden me to walk out the front door.

But she had said nothing about the window.

MAYBE CLIMBING OUT the window wasn't such a brilliant idea.

I clung to the ancient wisteria vine and tried not to look down. A branch under my left boot snapped, and I scrambled against the wall. The trellis creaked. Of course, I had timed my climb out of the window badly and now my skirt was caught above me on my bedroom-window latch, frillies on show for all the world to see if they cared to look up.

I stifled a whimper and reached up to pat around the window ledge, trying to find the end of the skirt. I had to do something quickly, or I could possibly hang there forever with the breeze whistling round my underthings.

I yanked on the garment as hard as I could until it ripped. I hoped it wasn't too badly rent. It wouldn't do to pitch up at the RCA with my skirt in tatters.

I climbed down as far as I could and then jumped the rest of the way. The impact with the ground caused me to stumble and I sat down hard.

That was when I saw our gardener, Harold, with clippers hoisted midchop over the privet hedge, his mouth open wide in bewilderment.

"Oh!" I said from my seat on the ground.

"Afternoon, Miss Darling," he mumbled.

Blast! How long had he been there? How much had he seen? The look on his face told me he had seen everything. His ruddy, weather-beaten features were even redder than usual. His glance traced from me to my window, where a long streamer of lace hung out, billowing in the wind.

I looked at my skirt missing its wide lace edging.

I didn't care about the skirt, but I might as well have left a calling card for my mother telling her exactly how I had escaped.

With as much dignity as I could muster, I struggled to my feet, waved at Harold, and ran.

BY THE TIME I reached a busier street where I could flag a cab, I was panting like a hound, and my side ached. I found a hansom cab and directed the driver to the Royal College of Art.

The school was housed at the back of the Victoria and Albert Museum, accessed through a side entrance on Exhibition Road. In the anteroom, honored paintings from former students hung from floor to ceiling. I stopped to scan the paintings, and my eyes lit on one I hadn't seen before that looked inspired by the Pre-Raphaelite Brotherhood.

The PRB was a small group of Victorian artists famous for painting women from myth and story. Waterhouse, the painter of *A Mermaid*, was an inheritor of their legacy. I admired them so, and I longed to paint like them, but I wanted to portray men in myth and legend instead of women.

This painting before me appeared to be inspired by John Everett Millais's *Ophelia*. Millais, one of the PRB founders, had portrayed Shakespeare's character floating in her watery grave, but in this one, the painter had chosen to depict the doomed Ophelia running toward the stream. He had beautifully caught the movement of the devastated girl and the light that fell upon her hair.

I stepped closer to the work to inspect the brushstrokes. The sunlight streaming through the trees was filled with so many different colors. It was astonishing. How did he do that? This painting illustrated perfectly the reason why I had to attend the RCA. I wanted to know what this artist knew.

Footsteps came from the back of the room. I turned around to see a balding man dressed in a morning suit and spectacles walking quickly toward me. He looked annoyed, as though I had interrupted him in some important task. "We aren't open for viewing today, miss." He held his hand out toward the door. "If you'll just come back on Saturday, we're open to the public from morning to teatime."

"No, no. I . . . I've . . ." My face blushed hotly. "I've not come to view, although the paintings here are extraordinary. I've come to inquire about the application process. And the scholarship," I hastened to add, seeing the growing look of disinterest on his face. "I'm just inquiring as to when I can submit my sketchbook. I, uh, have it here if I can submit now." I fumbled for it in my art satchel, and held it out to him. To my dismay, my hand trembled. "Um . . . what do I do?" I broke off. I sounded so daft, and not at all like the sophisticated artist I wanted to appear.

His gaze flickered to my book briefly and then away. "The application window is not open."

"Oh," I said. I pulled my sketchbook back and clutched it to my side, embarrassed.

"It opens in April. All work must be submitted for consideration by the end of April, along with a letter of reference from an instructor or one from an artist alumnus of the school. If you're accepted, you'll sit the exam in July." He regarded me over his half-moon spectacles. "I should warn you, though, we only accept very serious students of the highest quality. This school turns out professional artists. If you plan to get married and have children, this may be a waste of time for you. Perhaps you should discuss things further with your parents to see what would be best for your future." He inclined his head and started to leave.

Before I knew what I was doing, my hand shot out and grabbed his arm. His eyes widened.

"I do apologize, sir," I said, finding my voice, even though it wobbled. "I plan on completing my course of study, and I very much look forward to attending the school. I'm quite serious about my work and someday I plan to see it hanging here among the works of these alumni. And not high up, sir, where no one will notice it. Right on the line of sight, in pride of place."

Goodness gracious, where did all that come from? I didn't give a fig because the look of disinterest fell from his face, and now he was listening. "Now, what is required for submission?" I let go of his arm. My voice cracked, and tears of frustration were only an inch away.

"I have some information I can give you." The gentleman went out of the room and then came back with a leaflet in his hand. "This explains it all. You must drop off what's listed by the date there. We'll review it and then contact you if you've been chosen to sit for the examination. My name is Mr. Earnshaw. If you have any problems, ask for me."

"Thank you."

"I wish you the best of luck, Miss . . . ?"

"Darling. Victoria Darling."

"Miss Darling. And I do look forward to seeing your work hanging amongst our alumni's."

"On the line." This time I did smile.

"Of course," he said, smiling back at me. "Wherever else?"

"Good day, Mr. Earnshaw."

"Miss Darling, just before you go," he said. "Present the best work you have. Very few women are given a scholarship each term. You must put your best foot forward."

"I shall," I said, and then bade him good day and left.

Outside, I took a deep breath and blew it out in relief. My knees were shaking, so I found a bench in a tiny garden nearby, and sank onto it to rest for a moment and read the leaflet:

Portfolio Requirements
for the Royal College of Art

All work submitted must have been produced within three years and dated. Only genuine sketchbooks and notebooks will be considered; loose sketches will be disregarded.

False statements made will result in disqualification.

If invited to the interview and examination, you will be requested to bring further work with you.

I stuffed the leaflet and my sketchbook into my satchel. With all that was required, what if my studio drawings weren't enough? *Put your best foot forward*, Mr. Earnshaw had said. The paintings from the alumni were so good, so well crafted and inspired. The way that artist caught the light. And then the awful voice inside me began to whisper: *You don't know how to do that. How will your work measure up?* And then my mother's voice chimed in: *What makes you think you have the talent? . . . Preposterous, preposterous, preposterous.*

I couldn't think this way. Monsieur Tondreau and Bertram believed in me. I must believe in myself.

I had, what was it? Five weeks or so before the window closed. I would just have to put my shoulder to the wheel and produce more work. Starting immediately. I wished I had subjects like the absinthe woman in France. I needed something compelling, something fiery and bold, something that would make the panel feel what my subjects felt. If I could make them feel, then they would sit up and take notice.

Suddenly I remembered the suffragettes. I stood up and started walking. If anything fit into the category of compelling, the suffragettes and the crowd that came to gawk did. I could draw the police constables, the passersby, the suffragettes themselves. A whole litany of subjects was there for the taking. Freddy said they picketed Parliament every day. I wasn't far from Parliament.

I stepped into the street and waved down a hansom cab.

Six

The Houses of Parliament

I HEARD THE NOISE even before reaching Parliament. Half of London must have been there. When I stepped out of the cab and drew closer, I saw the crowd was made up mostly of rough-looking men who didn't appear to be interested in women's suffrage. More men poured up the pavement from all directions. A few women hurried past with downcast faces, towing their children along. Some crossed the street to avoid the spectacle.

I pushed through the crowd to get a better view.

"Go home where you belong!" a sneering man shouted at me.

I stepped back, unsure.

"Shut your mouth and leave her be!" said a pinch-faced woman standing in a group of other women. She waved her hand to me: come along.

Smiling my thanks, I joined the women and found a place out of the way of the men, next to the railing. I pulled out my pad and looked through it to find a blank page.

The words of Monsieur Tondreau filled my mind. *Draw what you see*, ma chère, *not what you know.* I made some quick sweeps with my pencil, warming up, getting the measure of the crowd. I began to lose myself in the work, and my mind settled.

"Are you drawing that for the newspaper, for *Votes for Women*?" A teenage girl wearing a straw boater peered over my shoulder.

"It's just a sketch." I turned my pad away from her. I didn't like people to look at my sketches while I was working. Especially strangers.

"I wish I could draw," the girl said, and then she brightened. "I'm in the poster parades, though. We wear sandwich boards and march in a line together singing songs. It's ever such a lark. So *are* you drawing that for the paper?"

An older woman standing next to her glanced around. "Margaret, don't be so beaky."

The girl shrugged. "I'm only asking, Mum."

"Don't know how Miss Pankhurst will be heard over this din," her mother grumped.

"Miss Pankhurst?" I said. "Do you mean Christabel Pankhurst?"

"That's why so many people are about, to hear her speak. She'll be along in a moment."

I could not believe my luck. Having such a famous figure in my sketchbook would be a boon.

"Come along, Margaret. Let's get closer." Margaret's mother took her hand and set off. As I watched her tow her daughter through the crowd, I couldn't help but think how strange it would be for my mother to bring me to such an event.

The area around me began to fill, so I stepped back into an empty space next to a woman standing alone. I recognized her from the group of suffragettes I had seen the day I arrived home. She was the tiny woman who had been handing out leaflets. Up close I saw she was young, probably no more than a year or two older than me. She peeped out from under the brim of a hideous felt hat with wide eyes that made her look a little like a startled mouse. When she stepped to one side, I saw that a long iron chain trailed out from under her coat, the ends padlocked to the railings of the fence.

I was taken aback. "Is that a chain?"

She grinned widely. "It is indeed." She spoke in a flat accent peculiar to Americans.

"You're American." Most likely stating the obvious.

"Yes." Despite her small size, she had an air of fierceness about her. "And what of it?"

I turned my pencil around and around in my fingers. "I don't meet many Americans. Are you visiting?"

"I'm here for school. I was working for the vote in America, so I picked up the cause here when I arrived last year. But it makes no difference what nationality I fight for. It's the same war to me." She studied me for a moment, glancing from my face down to my sketch pad.

"Why the chain?"

"The prime minister made it unlawful to loiter last week, so the police try to move us on if we stop and give a speech. If I'm chained, and there's no key for that lock, they can't force me off very easily."

"Why doesn't Christabel chain herself, as she is the one giving the speech?"

"Because she'll get arrested. The police arrest anyone who obstructs the pavement. And Christabel can't do the work she needs to do in jail. She's too valuable. If the police come, the girls over there make sure she gets away. I'll gladly get pinched in her place."

"Why?"

"Going to jail is our way to wrong-foot the law. We're denied the rights of being citizens, so we have to be outlaws and rebels. The newspapers used to ignore us, but now they can't. Our names and the circumstances of our arrest are written in the newspapers the next day. Or course, they're as prejudiced against us as you can imagine, but all publicity is good publicity for our cause. And because of this we're willing to pay the price for our actions. You see?"

"I suppose," I replied, just to be polite. I couldn't begin to imagine why anyone would want to put herself in harm's way for any reason. To volunteer to go to prison seemed extreme.

"My name is Lucy. What's yours?" she said.

I hesitated. "Victoria," I finally said, omitting my surname, not wanting her to know too much about me.

"What? Were you named for Queen Victoria? The one who said the fight for women's rights was a 'mad, wicked folly'?"

I shrugged, not knowing how to respond.

She looked at my sketchbook again. "Are you going to join the WSPU?"

"I've only come to draw." I turned my attention back to my sketch. "I'm an artist."

"Well, this is your lucky day. We have need of artists," she said. "Cristabel's sister Sylvia is recruiting artists to assist her with a grand mural for the Women's Exhibition in May. I've been helping with it and I'm sure she'd welcome you."

"I appreciate the invitation, but I'm very busy just now." I admired the suffragettes' conviction, and certainly believed in women's suffrage, but I had little time to join such an organization. And besides, my father would have a fit of apoplexy if I became a suffragette.

Furthermore, an artist had to focus, and that left little time for anything else. It didn't matter if I joined the suffragettes anyway. One woman more or less would not make a difference.

"So you're the type of girl who lets the rest of us do the heavy lifting while you sit back and reap the rewards," Lucy said matter-of-factly.

"I beg your pardon! You don't know what you're talking about." I glanced around for another place to stand, away from her questions, but there was nowhere to go in the crush of people.

"Christabel Pankhurst always says that women who aren't willing to fight for the vote are unworthy of it."

"I agree with the WSPU, I really do," I said. "You don't have to convince me." I shifted under her frank gaze. "I told you, I'm very busy. I'm applying to the Royal College of Art and I have a great deal to do to get ready for the exam. Maybe I can donate some money or some such."

"Sylvia went to the RCA. Said the principal hated women."

My shoulders hunched up. I pressed my mouth closed and bent to my drawing.

"I do apologize," she said, not sounding sorry in the least. "I've been told I'm a bit pushy sometimes." She pulled loose a small pin from her jacket. "Maybe you'll accept this gift." She reached over and fastened it to the lapel of my coat, giving the pin an emphatic tap with the tips of her fingers. "I hope you'll wear it proudly."

I pulled my lapel up and looked at it. It was an enameled striped shield with WSPU stamped on the top and the phrase DEEDS NOT WORDS written underneath.

"If you want to make a *donation*, when you have the *time*, bring it to the headquarters." She handed me a leaflet. "Clement's Inn, just off the Strand."

Without looking at it, I shoved the pamphlet into my sketchbook, and turned away from Lucy. *What an annoying know-all!*

"Here she comes!" someone from the crowd shouted.

I stood on my tiptoes and craned my neck for a better look. The crowd near the Members' Entrance had parted to allow a dainty woman through. Several women flocked around her, protecting her. One set a wooden parlor chair down and helped her up onto it so that the crowd could see her better.

"There she is," Lucy said, rapt.

I began a quick sketch. Christabel Pankhurst was even prettier in person than in her photos. She was dressed in a coral-colored lace frock with a wide sash across one shoulder. The sash read **Women's Social and Political Union**. She had a sweet appearance, with delicate features and curly brown hair that framed her face. But her countenance was not sweet. She glowered down at the restless crowd. Several men moved up to stand in front of her, arms folded and faces grim. Another man leaned against the railing right to the side of her with a sneer upon his face. If she was afraid of them, she did not show it.

And then her stalwart expression collapsed, changing to one of dismay. I turned around and saw a square black wagon pulled by two dray horses approaching.

"Here come the coppers," Lucy said under her breath. "And they didn't even give her a chance to speak."

The women around Christabel closed ranks. Two helped her down from the chair; another threw a cloak over her head and bundled her off toward Westminster Bridge. The pinch-faced woman and the others followed. Margaret and her mother hurried away toward Old Palace Yard.

"You'd better scarper," Lucy said to me. "Quickly, unless you want to get arrested, and I doubt that you do."

But I did not heed her. I had entered the fervor that gripped me whenever I saw something I wanted to draw. It was always the same. It was as if something possessed me and forced me to capture the scene unfolding in front of me. I began a new sketch of the police van, hurrying to lay down the structure of the van and to portray the essence of the placid nature of the horses, so at odds with the ominous conveyance they pulled.

The doors at the back of the van flew open, and several constables jumped out. One of them hung back, an expression on his face as though he was embarking upon a distasteful task. He was a lot younger than the other constables, maybe only eighteen or nineteen, but he had the air of someone much more mature. He cut a very masculine figure in his uniform, with the dark-blue trousers and the long five-button tunic. He looked familiar. I had seen him before somewhere.

I began to draw his profile in the corner of the page. He had strong facial features, with a long jawline and high cheekbones. The police constable had an expression of strength, but there was a vulnerability about him that appealed to me. He would have made a wonderful model for heroic poses, like Michelangelo's *David*. I could picture him as David, standing tall, holding the slingshot over his shoulder, as if waiting quietly for the chance to unleash the rock against an enemy that was stronger than he was. (But without the stupid tin fig leaf!)

I smiled and glanced up from my sketch. The constable was staring at me, a look upon his face as if he knew me. I recognized who he was, then. He was the young constable who had rolled up the poster and handed it to Lucy.

With an exasperated *tsk*, Lucy shoved me away from her. "Go!"

I tripped forward, and the pencil skittered across my drawing, marking the sketch.

She faced the crowd. "The government levies taxes upon women as well as men, but women have no say in how that money is spent," she shouted out, her voice calm and steady. "How can we if we are unable to express our opinions by casting a vote? This is taxation without representation. America, my own country, raised arms against its sovereign for such treatment. Now women of both Britain and America are feeling their backs against the wall and we are not willing to submit tamely and without protest to political tyranny—"

"Oi, love!" a man wearing a bowler hat and a long canvas duster shouted. "You know what they say . . . hell hath no fury like a woman scorned!"

"Nay, sir, hell hath no fury like a woman denied her God-given rights!" Lucy put the heckler in his place with barely a pause. "Women of the nation have made crystal clear—"

"Clear as mud, I'd say!" the same man shouted. Others nearby laughed.

Lucy was undaunted; she leaned forward, warming to the task. "Listen with your ears then, sir, and not your eyes!"

"Wouldn't do any good, lass!" the man shouted out.

"I should think not. I feel sorry for your poor wife if you give her the same attention as you're giving me."

"He hasn't got a wife!" another man near him said.

"No woman will have him, eh?" Lucy's smile took the sting from her barb, and gales of the crowd's laughter covered the man's sheepish retort. "Now, gentlemen, if I may carry on entertaining you with my fine speech."

Lucy darted her eyes at the approaching constables, registering them for only a moment before turning her attention back to the crowd, which had increased greatly. More men had joined the fray—so many that they spilled out into the road, creating a traffic snarl, forcing omnibuses and cabs to trundle round them.

Lucy leaned casually against the railings, as though she

didn't have a worry in the world. "Working women and women in the home are in special need of the vote's protection. After all, legislation interferes with our interests just as much as, or maybe even more than, it does with men's."

A burly constable with muttonchop whiskers reached the scene first. He stepped in front of Lucy, blocking the crowd's view of her. "All right, that will be enough," he said. "So your leader's done a bunk and left you to it, eh, lass?" He took hold of the chain and rattled it against the railing, pulling at it to test its strength. His eyes traveled the length of the chain to where it ended under Lucy's coat. "Unlock this tackle now, there's a good girl."

Lucy slid away, as far the chain would allow, to the next section of railing. "As I was saying, we want the government to remove the sex disability which deprives qualified women of their just right to vote on the same terms enjoyed by men."

The constable shifted back in front of her. "Enough with that codswallop! I'll ask you one more time. Unlock the tackle."

She wagged her finger, smiling prettily at him. "Don't be rude. I haven't finished my speech."

But Lucy's humor had no effect on the constable; in fact it appeared to stoke some fury within him. He towered over her, his face filled with hatred, and I wondered for a moment if he would strike her. Lucy's calm demeanor cracked. She took another step away, but there was no slack remaining in the chain.

"If you won't give us the key, we'll just take the chain off you!" he said. "I know you've a belt buckled round you underneath your kit. Think I won't strip you starkers to get to it? Is that what you want? 'Cause that's what'll happen." He grabbed her hips and his huge fingers fumbled with the dainty feminine buttons on her skirt.

How could the police do this? I looked around wildly. Would no one come to her aid? But the men in the crowd who had been held captive by Lucy's humor turned coat once again, laughing and shouting out bawdy suggestions.

"Let go, you big gorilla!" Lucy twisted, trying hard to free herself. The constable gave up on being gentle. He jerked the placket open; the buttons pinged onto the ground like hailstones, revealing the ends of the chain latched into rings on a wide canvas belt.

The young constable I had been drawing arrived. "Excuse me," I said. And for the second time that day, I took hold of a man's arm.

He glanced at me, shook his head slightly, and gestured for me to move back.

I didn't budge. "That man is a beast!" I said. I pointed my pencil at the burly constable. "He should be struck off the force, handling a woman so. It's not to be borne!"

"Please step back, miss," he replied, firmer this time. He put his hand on the constable's shoulder. "Leave off, Catchpole. No need for that. Let's give her a chance to find the key."

Lucy looked relieved to see the young constable. I saw them exchange a small look of recognition. I was right, he was the constable I had seen that day at Parliament.

"Are you daft, Fletcher? She's got no key." Catchpole shrugged off his hand. "Our orders are to move the women along and arrest those who don't leave. And that's what I'm about."

"No need to humiliate her in the doing," Fletcher said. His voice remained calm, even friendly, but there was a tinge of warning to it.

Catchpole let go, and Lucy turned away and fumbled with the remains of her skirt. She was trembling, but her mouth was set hard.

"We have to move them along, you know that," Catchpole was saying to the other constable, who looked like he didn't care, one way or the other. "No obstructions to the pathway." His face was red and he was breathing hard. He eyed Lucy like a hungry wolf yearning to finish his freshly caught meal.

"But not this way," Police Constable Fletcher said. "Look, we'll have the hacksaws at work soon. She'll be loose in a trice."

Catchpole scowled. "Always thought you was one of them. Honorary suffragette, are you? Be wearing a skirt next if you're not careful."

The insults seemed to slide over the young constable.

"Are you all right, Lucy?" I said.

She paused in her repair of her skirt and glared at me. "This isn't tea with the queen. I'll tell you again, go home!"

And I don't know who it was, but right at that moment, someone pushed me so hard that I flung my arms out to catch my balance. My sketchbook and pencil flew out of my hands. At the same time PC Fletcher turned toward me. And I swear I did not mean to—I was only trying to stop from falling headlong—but I stumbled forward, fetched up against his chest, and wrapped my arms around his waist.

The next thing I knew, he toppled to the ground, with me on top of him. That would have been humiliating enough, but the force of the fall was so great that my forehead clonked against PC Fletcher's chin with a loud whomp. Stars dazzled in front of my eyes.

"Uhhhh." PC Fletcher let out a groan.

I tried to get off of him, but my skirts had whipped round my legs, and the more I struggled, the more I seemed to make matters worse. I had never been in such intimate contact with a man before, and if I could have sprouted wings and flown off of him, I would have done so immediately.

"Will you pack it in?" he said. "I don't wish to be rude, but you're jabbing me in a very painful area."

"Well, this is no picnic for me either!"

"I feel as though a tree has fallen on me."

"Oh, thank you very much." I scowled.

And then he smiled. And as he did so, his whole being lit up with good nature. It was as though having someone dropped on top of him was simply all in a day's work. One hand settled on my arm, as if he were walking alongside me in the park. I could feel the heat of his hand through the silk sleeve of my coat and I found I liked it. I liked it much more than was strictly proper, and I felt my body melt against him a little. His face was only inches from mine, and up close he was even more handsome. His eyes were an unusual shade: dark gold flecked with sage green, encircled by a border of evergreen. They would have been heaven to paint.

At that moment, rough hands grabbed me round the waist, jerked me off the constable, and stood me on my feet. I stepped forward to pick up my sketchbook but I could not. I was held fast by two of the other constables. Without wasting any time, they began to march me toward the van.

"Let me go!" I jammed the heels of my boots against the ground, but they didn't care one bit; they dragged me along. I craned my neck and saw PC Fletcher back on his feet. My sketchbook was on the ground near him.

"Attacking an officer of the law is bad enough, lass. I wouldn't add resisting arrest to it," one of them said.

I jerked my head around. My heart began to beat in a wild tattoo. "You're arresting me? No! Someone pushed me."

"Tell it to the judge."

"At least, please get my book. I beg you." But they would not hear me.

We drew closer to the back of the van and I could see inside. It was lined with boxes, which looked like coffins standing on their ends, with only a little barred window in the top of each one.

"Welcome to the Black Maria, lass," one of the constables said.

Seven

The Black Maria

I COULD NOT GO in there. I went dotty in confined spaces. Always had done. I could not help it.

A constable waiting inside reached out for me. When the other two lifted me up, I pulled my legs up and planted my boots on either side of the van door, not caring that my skirt flipped up nearly to my hips.

Panic swelled inside me, and I was having trouble focusing. Everything blurred in front of my eyes, skewing objects into splotches of color like one of Monet's paintings.

"Lord's sake." The constable on my right swore. "It's like trying to shove a horse though a keyhole."

"She's a live one, I'll give her that," the other replied.

The constable inside the van grabbed my ankles, yanking them off the door and scraping my right calf painfully as he pulled me in. "Makes a change from the usual thugs we get. At least she smells good," he said.

The men laughed.

The door to one of the coffins squeaked open and I was shoved inside it. The door slammed shut and a key turned in the lock. The coffin smelled of vomit and sweat, and something soft squished underneath my boot.

There was barely enough room to turn around, not enough to even to lift my arms up, so I leaned back and kicked at the door. "Let me out of here!" Great heaving sobs that started in my chest rose up into my throat, and I thought I might be sick. I kicked the door again. "Let me out . . . somebody!"

The van tilted as someone else stepped inside. I stood on tiptoes and looked through the window. Catchpole was pushing Lucy forward.

"Lucy!" I shouted. But Lucy took no notice of me. They bundled her into the last coffin and locked it. I kicked the door again and again. I would bloody well kick it down if they didn't hear me.

"You're only making things worse for yourself."

A pair of familiar eyes regarded me through the bars. It was PC Fletcher.

"Tell them I didn't attack you," I said, trying hard to keep from shrieking. "Tell them someone pushed me! You know that's the truth."

"We'll sort everything when we get to Cannon Row Police Station. I'm sure they'll release you to your father."

My father? Oh, no . . . no, no, no. "There's no reason for me to go there." My voice rose in desperation. "Please open the door. I can't bear it in here."

"Just try to calm yourself," he said gently.

"At least tell me, did you pick up my sketchbook? I know you saw it there."

Someone shouted out his name, and PC Fletcher turned to leave.

"Please get my book!" I shouted after him, with no idea

if he heard me or not. I banged the door with my fist and slumped back against the wall.

And then the van began to move, pitching me against the side of the coffin. The horses' heavy hooves clopped against the road, and the van's wheels rattled. The bells of Big Ben rang out the half hour.

"Well, Queenie"—Lucy finally spoke—"looks like you're a suffragette now."

I DIDN'T KNOW which was worst: the fear of being enclosed in the Black Maria, the dread of my parents' finding out about yet another scandal, or the loss of my precious sketchbook. If that police constable had just let me out, it would have all been fine. I could have found my book and then gone on my way. No harm done. But no, he couldn't be a gentleman. And I certainly doubted he retrieved my book like I asked him to.

"The next time someone tells you to scarper, I bet you'll listen, Queenie," Lucy called out.

"My name is not Queenie!" I snapped, outraged that she would address me with such mockery.

A light rain began to fall; I could hear the drops against the roof of the van. I pictured my sketchbook lying on the pavement, pages fluttering in the wind, drops of water plopping onto the charcoal, smearing my sketches until they were nothing but wet ashes on blotting paper. Work I'd been compiling for months, gone.

What would I submit to the RCA now? My childhood drawings? Without my sketchbook, I had no chance at a scholarship. I wouldn't even get past the application process without work to show.

No doubt about it, the loss of the sketchbook was the worst. I leaned my forehead against the door and tried to work out how my life had gone so wrong in such a short space of time.

Maybe there was a chance that my sketch pad was still there. Whether it was ruined or not, I could not let it lie there, abandoned, for some street sweeper to gather up along with the horse manure and cigarette stubs. Perhaps I could salvage something of it. As soon as the judge let me free, I would go back.

THE VAN STOPPED with a jolt, and Catchpole and the others brought us out of the coffins and into the station.

I glanced around, and dread rose inside me. PC Fletcher, the only one who could vouch for my innocence and be believed, was nowhere around. Certainly no one would listen to Lucy.

Lucy and I stood in front of the police-court judge, a hugely fat man with a doughy face that looked like it hadn't seen the sun in years.

"Not you again?" he said to Lucy. "Haven't you learned your lesson yet? Why don't you go back to America and do us all a favor, eh?" Then he lifted his chin at me. "And you. Assaulting an officer can get you three years in Holloway."

My heart began to pound alarmingly, the feeling of panic rising again at the mere thought of being held in a prison cell. "There seems to be a misunderstanding," I said.

"I wasn't even with the suffragettes. I was simply drawing them for my own pleasure. And then someone pushed me and I fell on the police constable."

The judge regarded me with a dubious expression as I protested my innocence. Then his gaze traveled down and landed on the lapel of my coat. "You weren't with them, you say?" He jabbed a finger at my lapel. "Then why are you wearing one of their badges?"

The pin! The ruddy suffrage pin that Lucy had put on me! My mouth opened, but I could not think of a word to say.

The judge leaned back in his chair. "Well?"

"I hung that on her," Lucy said. "As a prank. She's right. She's got nothing to do with us."

The judge harrumphed.

"That's a load of old pony." Catchpole stepped up. "She was in Fletcher's face as soon as he arrived, then she tackled him so he wouldn't take this un's skirt off to get to the chain."

I gasped. "You lying toad! You know full well you're the one who tried to take her skirt off." I turned to the judge. "He did. He said he'd strip her naked, too. He's a menace!"

"If you were drawing, where's your art book?" the judge asked.

"I dropped it. I'd hoped one of your constables picked it up for me."

The judge leaned forward, his chair creaking beneath his bulk. "Listen to me carefully, miss. I very much doubt that you were simply drawing. If you were, then why didn't you get out of the way when the constables arrived?"

What a stupid thing for the man to ask. "Because I wanted to draw. As I said." I caught sight of Lucy, who was shaking her head. *Shut it*, she mouthed.

"You wanted to *draw* the *police*?" the judge said, glaring at me. "That doesn't seem innocent. Care to explain?"

"Explain?" I said, a feeling of doom settling over me. I should have just said I couldn't get away, that I was trapped in the crowd. But no, once again I was my own worst enemy. "Um . . ."

Then PC Fletcher came in, shaking raindrops off his tunic. Just as I thought, there was no sketchbook in his hands.

"Hell have you been?" Catchpole said.

"Witness report. I walked back."

"She's claiming she's not with the suffragettes," the judge said. "Said she was drawing. Know anything about that?"

PC Fletcher turned around slowly and looked at me, his jaw set hard. Disgust flickered in his eyes. "Well, I don't know anything about drawing, but someone pushed her, sir. I can vouch for that."

I met his gaze with a cold look of my own. *Liar!* He'd seen me drawing. He knew he had. The words to tell him off were right there, ready to burst forth, but I caught Lucy shaking her head again, this time vehemently, so I didn't. But oh, it took everything I had to hold back.

"Wouldn't believe a word coming from him." Catchpole jabbed a thumb at PC Fletcher. "Always helpin' them out. On the take, he is."

PC Fletcher frowned at him. "Shut it, will you?"

Catchpole shrugged.

"I'd give anything to get home to my tea on time, just for once. I'll tell you that for nothing." The judge cupped his chin in his hand. "I suppose you don't want to pay the fine for obstruction," he said to Lucy.

"Not a chance."

"I'm not surprised. Looking for a news story, are you?" He sighed. "You lot will do anything for publicity."

"We're fighting for our rights, sir. Rebellion is a natural reaction to repression for any human being, male or female. If our action makes front-page news and gains sympathy for our cause, then that's the icing on the cake."

"I don't need the lecture, miss. Two weeks in Holloway." He slanted his head at Catchpole. "Take her in."

Lucy shot me one more warning look and then went off with Catchpole. She looked so tiny and vulnerable walking alongside the burly constable, but her back was straight and her stride unfaltering.

The judge turned his attention back to me. "What's your name?"

I held my breath. If I said Darling, he'd probably ask if I was related to Darling & Son Sanitary Company, and then, I was sure, one thing would lead to the next and my father would be in the know. "It's . . . Victoria. Victoria Smith."

Fletcher glanced at me and frowned. What in heaven's name was his problem?

"Well, Miss Smith," the judge said. "Most suffragettes are fighting to get into jail, not out of it. So I'm inclined to believe your story. But if I see you here again, I won't be so generous. I'm releasing you to PC Fletcher, who will escort you home. You're lucky the missus has sausage plait and plum duff on for tea, or I might not be so generous. Off you go, then. Make sure she gets home, Fletcher."

"Yes, governor." PC Fletcher took my elbow and led me out of the room.

Once we were out of the judge's sight, I yanked my arm out of his grasp.

He held his hands up. "Sorry."

I strode in front of him and out into the rain. I had no umbrella but I didn't care.

"Wait a mo'." PC Fletcher popped into the station and came out with an umbrella. "No sense catching a chill." He snapped it up, holding it over both our heads. I stepped out of the umbrella's shelter. I didn't want to stand so close to him. I was too angry.

He sighed. "I won't bite."

The rain fell harder. He stepped closer; this time I did not move away. I shivered. It was cold, and my silk coat was not lined. I could almost feel the warmth radiating from him. He smelled lovely, like wool and green grass. And despite my anger, I could not help but feel pulled toward him. I didn't understand how I could feel angry and attracted to him at the same time. Maybe it was because I yearned to draw him. When the Pre-Raphaelite artist Dante Gabriel Rossetti first laid eyes on Lizzie Siddal, he became obsessed with painting her. Maybe this was what one felt when one met a potential muse.

"Well, where do you live?"

I hesitated. Potential muse or not, I had to work out what to do with PC Fletcher at the present moment. And then I realized how I could prevent another scandal from reaching my parents' ears. "With my brother and his wife in Pimlico." The lie tripped easily from my mouth.

"Pimlico?" He sounded doubtful.

"Yes, Pimlico! What's so odd about that?"

He looked at me with that hard expression again, as if he couldn't bear to be standing next to me. "Right then, Victoria Smith from Pimlico." He said the words with a sharp beat. "Best be on our way."

"If you don't mind, I wish to go back to Parliament first."

"I do mind, actually."

"Fine then, I'll go on my own." I made to leave, but he grabbed my arm.

"Oh, no you don't. I have my orders to take you home, and home is where you're going."

I tried to twist my arm away, but his fingers were locked on.

"Who is to know?"

"I'll know!"

"P.C. Bumptious." I whispered the insult under my breath but made sure he heard it.

"Bumptious?" he said, his voice rising. "I'd rather be bumptious than a liar."

Anger swelled inside me. "Who's a liar?"

"You are."

"Me? A liar? That's rich. You're the liar. You could have told the truth right away and let me loose. But no!" The words bubbled out of me in a stream of rage. There was no holding back. "You're just like that Catchpole, aren't you? Treating women like objects . . . things to be pulled about from pillar to post." I took a shaking breath.

"For your information, I couldn't have let you go," he said. "That's for the judge to decide. And believe me, you're not worth me getting the sack."

"I don't care. I'm going back to Parliament!" I pried at his fingers, but they were like iron. "You're hurting me!"

He loosened his grip, and it was enough to jerk my arm away and run. I heard him swear. I had a little head start as he dealt with the umbrella, but then he was running behind me. I sped up. There was a crowd standing outside a pub underneath an awning just ahead. Maybe I could lose myself in the clutch of people and then cut away. He wouldn't know which way I went, and then I could return to Parliament.

But just as I reached the pub, a hand snaked out and wrapped around my waist, nearly jerking me off my feet.

"Who you runnin' from, treacle?" A tall, burly man stared down at me, a cigarette clamped between his teeth. A strong smell of unwashed body wafted from him. He looked down the pavement and saw PC Fletcher. "Ah, a copper, eh? You a pickpocket?" He looked me up and down. "Dress nicely for a thief, I'll give you that."

"Just let me go!" I pulled away, but I had lost my head start. PC Fletcher caught up and grabbed my wrist.

"Try that again and I will shackle you, right here in the street, with everyone watching, and then haul you back to the station."

My eyes fell upon the manacles hanging from his belt. I swallowed.

The burly man laughed. "Need some help, lad?"

PC Fletcher scowled at him. "You can move on!" The man leered at me once more and then returned to his friends. Fletcher returned his attention to me. "Do I have your word, Miss Smith, that you won't try to escape again?"

I wanted dearly to kick him in the shins and run, but I knew I would not get far. So I kicked a rock instead, sending it winging across the street. "Very well! You have my word."

PC Fletcher released me with an exasperated sigh. Rain poured in a stream off his helmet. "You are an impossible girl," he said.

"So I'm told." I could feel the rain dripping off my nose.

"What's at Parliament that's so important?"

"The prime minister, a bunch of MPs, quite a lot of lords."

"Oh, ha-ha. It's your sketch pad, isn't it? I saw you drawing."

"Yes, and I asked you to pick it up for me. In that police van. Did you not hear me?"

"I heard you. It's not the business of the Metropolitan Police to look after things for doers of crimes."

"I'm not a . . . a doer of crime, and you know it!"

"Besides, I'm sure it's long gone now, so you can forget about it." He seemed to take quite a lot of pleasure in saying this.

I noticed a bruise had begun to bloom on his chin where my forehead had struck him. Good. I hoped it gave him a blinding headache for days.

"Besides, what's so important about it?"

"I don't expect you to understand the value of art. It's

not a subject dullards and buffoons would be interested in," I said.

"Now see, that's where you'd be wrong. I find the illustrations on the Guinness beer adverts most inspiring."

"That's very funny," I said, not finding his sarcasm amusing in the least. "Why can't you just be a gentleman and take me to Parliament so I can find it?"

"Sorry, but no."

PC Fletcher put his umbrella up again, and we walked the rest of the way to Pimlico in silence. I dearly hoped my brother Freddy was home. He'd go along with my story. I was sure PC Bumptious would insist on delivering me right inside the door, and if Freddy's wife, Rose, received us, she'd tell him the truth about me and then some.

My hand fell against my empty satchel, slung across my chest. Freddy would take me back to Parliament to search for my sketchbook.

I couldn't help but look at PC Fletcher sideways out of the corner of my eye as we walked. He was handsome in a distracting way. Too handsome for his own good. Or mine. I caught him looking at me the same way. He grinned at me smugly and I flicked my gaze to the front.

I decided that my artistic senses had terrible taste in muses.

Eight

E TURNED DOWN Warwick and rounded the corner to Eccleston Square, where my brother lived. I had been right: the constable shadowed me right up the steps to my brother's maisonette.

PC Fletcher dropped the knocker against the door. While we waited, I removed the WSPU pin and dropped it into my satchel. I caught him watching me.

"What?" I said.

"Nothing." He let out a little laugh and then muttered something under his breath.

It took all of my will not to shove him off the porch. I imagined him landing right in the prickly bushes.

The door opened. My brother's maid of all work stood there. "Oh, Miss Darling." Her eyes widened as she took in PC Fletcher in all his law-abiding glory.

"Who is it, Becky?" a voice called out. *Blast! Rose.*

Becky stood back and let us in. "Miss Darling, madam. And she's got a police constable with her."

Rose swished into view. Rose. A painfully soppy person if there ever was one. How my fun, handsome brother got saddled with her I shall never know. But there it was. And now she was expecting their second child. My mother, who adored her, had to threaten me with dire consequences or I would never visit her of my own accord. I'd sit there leaning over my teacup listening to the grandfather clock in the hall tick down the minutes as my mother laughed and nodded in all the right places, her face a picture of contentment, ever so grateful to have at least a daughter-in-law who was so reasonable, so domestic.

Rose pursed her lips together, looking as though she had bitten down on a wasp and sucked on a lemon at the same time. "Victoria. Your mother has been ringing constantly, asking your whereabouts. For the life of me I cannot understand why you continue to get yourself into such mischief." She looked at PC Fletcher. "She's naught but a troublemaker. You have no idea."

Oddly, PC Fletcher said nothing.

"Auntie Vicky!" a little voice chimed. Charlotte, my six-year-old niece, came running down the hallway, adorable in a pink frock with a candy-striped pinafore. Charlotte had inherited Freddy's cheeky expression. It made me laugh sometimes to see some of his looks echoed in Charlotte's childish features. I knelt down and hugged her. She wrapped her little arms around my neck and pressed her nose against mine. "Auntie Vicky, will you draw me a picture?"

"Not today, dearest," I said.

She stared at PC Fletcher, her eyes enormous. "Who is that?" she whispered.

"That's a police constable," I said.

PC Fletcher bowed. "How do you do?" he said in a very formal voice.

Charlotte giggled. "Can *you* draw me a picture?" she asked him.

"The police constable's busy, darling. Come along now," Rose interrupted.

And then, thank heaven, Freddy came into the hall. "Go into the sitting room with Mummy, sweetheart," he said. Rose took Charlotte's hand, frowned at me, and then drifted into the parlor. My brother turned to me, his eyes full of reproach. "I told Mother you'd turn up soon enough." He held out his hand to PC Fletcher. "Frederick Darling."

"Darling?" PC Fletcher said. "I thought your name was Smith."

"We have different fathers," I said quickly.

My brother glanced at me sideways, but thankfully he let the comment pass by. "Well then, PC . . . ?"

"Fletcher, sir."

"Is my little *half* sister in some sort of trouble?"

"Not exactly, sir. Bit of a misunderstanding is all. She was caught up in the arrest of some suffragettes."

"Suffragettes?" Freddy's gaze cut to me.

"Yes, sir. I was tasked to bring her home."

"Oh!" Freddy laughed. "Poor sod. I don't envy you." He reached into his jacket, pulled out a little silver case, and drew out a card. He handed it to PC Fletcher. "Here's my card. If there's anything I can do to repay the favor, please do not hesitate to ask."

PC Fletcher looked at the card. "Darling and Whitehouse Publishing. You do the tuppenny novelettes, then?"

"Why, yes. You've heard of us?"

"Never miss an issue." PC Fletcher glanced down at the card again and then slid it into his pocket. "I'd best be going." He touched his hand to his hat and then looked at me; a smile lifted his lips. "Good-bye then, Miss Smith." He held out his hand. I crossed my arms, and his hand hung there in the air unshaken. He pulled it back. "Well, then. I guess that's it. Best of luck to you."

Freddy showed him out. And then he rounded on me. "What the devil, Victoria? Smith?"

"I didn't want him to know my real name."

"Of course; I should have known!" He sank down on a bench in the hall. "You're in enough trouble as it is. Now you're mixed up with the suffragettes? I knew you'd go there." He lifted his hands and let them drop into his lap. "This really takes the biscuit. I don't understand you, Petal. You have a lovely life but you do insist on creating trouble for yourself."

I loved my brother dearly, but he just did not understand what it was like to be told what to do from sunup to sundown. His life was his to call his own.

"You had a lovely life too," I said with a pointed look.

His face reddened. "It's not the same. And don't change the subject. I want you to stay away from those suffragists."

"What's so wrong with what they are doing?"

"Don't tell me they've converted you already?"

"So what if they have? Don't you think women have the same right to vote as men do?"

"It is not a question of rights; it's a question of understanding. Women know naught of politics!"

"That might be true of some, but not of every woman, surely! I'm positive there are men who know naught of politics. And if a woman wished to be informed, she'd only have to read a newspaper or two—"

"I'm not going to have this discussion with you. You show up here dripping wet and in the company of a constable and under an assumed name after haring about with suffragettes. What am I to do with you?"

"Just don't tell Father about the suffragettes . . . and the constable."

Freddy rolled his eyes. "And what am I to say? Honestly, Vicky! The things you ask of me. You deserve to take your punishment."

"If you care about me at all you won't tell."

He heaved a very exasperated sigh. "Very well."

"And make sure Rose doesn't tell either." I leaned against the wall. "You're the only one who speaks to me, Freddy. Father won't even look me in the face." I traced a finger around a lilac printed on the wallpaper.

Freddy stood up and came over to me. He put his hand on my cheek. "I know it grieves you, but in time it will ease. Just remember, no matter what, I'll always be on your side. Come along, let's dry you off and get you home."

Freddy hailed a cab, and before we made for home, I asked him to send the cab driver to Parliament so we could look for my sketchbook. We got out, and from a distance I caught sight of something that looked like my book. But then my heart sank. It was just an old box lying on its side.

My sketchbook was not there.

I searched around on the ground and saw the crushed

remains of my graphite pencil where Lucy had chained herself. The pavement was littered with rubbish; the street sweepers had not been through yet.

Someone must have taken my book.

We climbed back into the cab, and the driver clucked to his horse. I leaned my forehead against the window and watched the scenery go by. The rain fell harder, filling the streets with puddles and giving the buildings a gloomy cast. The pavement was a sea of bobbing umbrellas.

I wondered who had taken my book. I pictured one of the men in the jeering crowd ogling my work, turning the pages with his grubby hands, perhaps using the paper to light a fire to cook sausages over.

I felt a pain in the pit of my stomach. I had nothing to submit.

The book was gone; I had to accept that, so I tried to think of a way to replace half a year's work in five weeks. Still life I could probably do in the garden at home, but figure drawing was out. I needed a model for that. An undraped model, preferably. There were women's art programs in London that my mother would approve of, but they gave mostly beginner classes, focusing on watercolor for decorative paintings to hang in one's home. The thought of painting a subject suited only to matching a sofa made my artistic sensibilities cringe.

Freddy finally broke the silence. "Petal, you have to stop this headstrong behavior. Mother says you climbed out a window."

"Yes, well, maybe if I were given a bit of freedom, I wouldn't have to resort to climbing out windows."

"She said you refused to consider the marriage proposal."

I shrugged.

"I've met Edmund Carrick-Humphrey. He's a bit aimless, but most are at his age. He's a very nice chap, all in all."

"I don't give a fig if he's a nice chap. I don't want to marry him. I'm not ready for marriage yet. I have things to do first."

"You'll need money to do those *things* you say have to do. You'll have money when you get married."

"I doubt Papa will settle on me, Freddy." Although there was a tradition of bestowing an inheritance upon one's daughter after marriage, it wasn't in my father's nature to hand over a socking great wad of cash. Especially not to me.

"You haven't thought it all the way through, have you, Petal? Carrick-Humphrey comes from a wealthy family. You want to go to that college of yours so badly. Who needs Dad's coin when your husband has coins aplenty?"

Maybe it wasn't such a terrible choice. I wouldn't have to compete for a scholarship.

"And from what I know about the fellow, he's not the sort who would care what you did."

"How do you know?"

"I had a word with him at the Reform Club last week. Do you think I'd let my little sister marry a bloke without vetting him first?"

"What did you say to him?" I said, feeling somewhat heartened, yet anxious at the same time. Suddenly Mr. Carrick-Humphrey's opinion seemed immensely important.

"I told him you weren't the type of girl to sit around

a house kicking your heels, and that you wanted to go to college."

I gripped his arm. "What did he say? Tell me, Freddy!"

"He laughed and said—and I quote: 'What a corker of a girl.' So I think you have to little to worry when it comes to Mr. Carrick-Humphrey."

I sat back in the carriage's seat and thought about it. If what Freddy said was true, a marriage to Mr. Carrick-Humphrey would get me out from under my parents' thumbs and into a home of my own. And into a life of my own. Lessons at the art college began in September, so I would have to be married as soon as possible.

A little tingle sparked inside me, setting a glow of hope alight. I had a little over a month to get work together. I could do it. I was sure I could do it.

THE NEXT MORNING I awoke to the noise of snipping and of branches scraping the wall. I got out of bed and crossed to the window. My curtains billowed in the wind. The rain had gone and it was a fine day. A fine day, apparently, to cut down a wisteria vine. Harold stood on a tall ladder wielding a saw. There would be no wisteria blossoms this May.

He looked up then and saw me, a pitying expression on his face.

Only my father would have ordered such drastic action. My mother would certainly never sacrifice flowers for any reason.

I hoped that would be the end of it. I hadn't spoken to my father last evening. He had come home from work very late, missing dinner, which had become a common theme since I had returned from France—much to the dismay of my mother, who had had to turn down many invitations for lack of an escort. I knew it was I who kept him away. My father didn't want to see me or speak to me. He had always dealt with me in this fashion. But it wouldn't make any difference whether he spoke to me or not; he would never understand why I'd chosen to pose nude.

I delayed as long as I could, but finally hunger won the day. So I went to my wardrobe, dressed in the first skirt and blouse to hand, and brushed my hair, pinning the sides back with tortoiseshell combs and letting the rest fall down my back. This done, I went to breakfast, hoping that my father had been and gone.

I entered the breakfast room and saw my father sitting behind his newspaper, a cup of tea at his elbow. I hesitated for a moment, considering going back up to my room.

"Don't hang about like that, Victoria," my father said from behind his newspaper. "Come in and have your breakfast."

"Good morning, Papa." I tried to keep my voice bright and cheerful, as if nothing had happened whatsoever. I went to the sideboard and filled my plate with a boiled egg, kippers, toast, and marmalade. I sat down in a chair next to him, glanced at his newspaper, looked at it again.

TWO SUFFRAGETTES
ARRESTED
AT PARLIAMENT

Miss Lucy Hawkins and Miss Victoria Smith were arrested yesterday afternoon for obstruction of the pathway near Parliament. Additionally, Miss Smith was accused of resisting arrest and causing grievous bodily harm to Police Constable William Fletcher.

Miss Hawkins refused to pay her fine and has been jailed for a fortnight at Holloway Prison. All charges were dropped against Miss Smith.

For a moment I thought I might laugh out loud. There my father sat, calmly reading the newspaper, while another scandal involving his daughter was front-page news. I sat openmouthed, leaning in, staring at the story.

My father folded down a corner of the paper and saw me. His brow furrowed and he snapped the paper shut and placed it under his plate. My father did not like me reading newspapers. It might undo my delicate constitution.

Quickly, I turned my attention to my breakfast, slicing the top off my boiled egg. Thank goodness I had thought to give a false last name.

I'd imagined PC Fletcher's Christian name might have been something like Reginald or Rupert or Simon. Somehow the name William didn't seem to fit a policeman. It seemed more of a nobleman's name: the name of a man loyal to Henry Tudor during the Wars of the Roses, who would ride out in a suit of armor under the dragon banner of red, white, and green. Considering the kind of person PC Bumptious was, he probably would have turned coat and fled Bosworth Field directly the horns for battle were blown because his horse had thrown a shoe or some such.

"Victoria," my father said. "Your mother has asked me to speak with you."

I set the egg topper down and tried to arrange my features in some sort of bland expression that would not anger him.

"I know you have ideas for your future, but I must say that further schooling is quite out of the question. A girl's duty in life is to be a pretty and entertaining wife to her husband. She should not outshine him in knowledge, lest she show him up among his peers. Advanced study is harmful for women as it makes them discontent and unfit for lives as wives and mothers. You are quite a pretty girl, so your prospects are much more promising than Louisa Dowd's anyhow, poor thing. She is but a plain girl, and education is the only option for her."

I tried not to let an angry remark slip out, so instead I ate a spoonful of egg. "Thank you, Father." I smiled, knowing that egg yolk was all over my front teeth. So much for not angering him, but I could not help it. I hated when he came out with rot like that.

Father straightened his cravat with an angry tug and stood up. "This willful behavior of yours will stop, do you understand me? If you put one toe out of place again, you will lose your drawing privileges. I will remove your art things from your room myself."

I looked down at my plate. The smoked kipper's murky eye stared up at me balefully. My stomach churned, and I pushed the plate away.

"They should have been taken from you directly after you returned from France. But your mother convinced me otherwise."

"Mamma convinced you?" I sat back. Why would my mother have done such a thing?

He shook his head, and went on as if I hadn't spoken. "I don't understand you, my dear. What possessed you?"

I didn't say anything. What could I say that would make him understand? My father, like many people, would only ever see the tawdry side of the nude figure, which always confounded me. People flocked to the annual Summer Exhibition at the Royal Academy. There were many paintings there that depicted the undraped figure. To most people, the process was unspeakable, but the resulting work of art was not.

"You will turn your mind away from such pursuits and to marriage, where it belongs. You will be a wife and a mother, and that is all." And then he left, pulling the door shut behind him a little harder than he needed to.

I slumped in my chair. As if my life were only about being decoration for a man. Well, that decided me. I wasn't going to wait around any longer.

I quickly finished my breakfast and went upstairs to find my mother in her drawing room. "I've decided I'm going to marry Edmund Carrick-Humphrey."

My mother looked taken aback at my sudden change of heart. "I told your father you would see reason, for despite all your willfulness, you are not a stupid girl—"

"Only I have a caveat," I interrupted.

Mamma looked at me warily. "And that is?"

"Let's have it over and done with. I wish to be married by the end of August."

Mamma rose and went to look at her diary. "August twenty-ninth might do. If the Carrick-Humphreys agree, then I don't see why we can't accommodate that request. Your father and I will discuss it with them when they come to dinner this evening." Then she smiled. "I'm very happy that you've learned your lesson and have seen sense. We'll announce your engagement after the king's first court in June. You will have a wonderful life with Mr. Carrick-Humphrey. Just think of it."

But all I could think about was my college tuition paid.

Ten

Mrs. Kipling's kitchen

FTER OUR CONVERSATION, my mother invited me to take a turn round the Royal Arcade with her friends. She suggested we begin looking for things to fill my marriage trousseau, but I demurred. I didn't tell her that picking over ribbons and staring at hats was more than I could bear. After she left, I collected my charcoal and pastels from my room, took some paper from my father's study, and went out into the garden to find something to draw. At least I could practice until I had purchased a new sketchbook for the RCA admission.

Things were looking brighter. I knew my marriage would not be one of love, but I would marry the devil himself if it meant I could pursue my artistic goals. I thought of the handful of successful women artists. Most of them were wealthy and could afford to spend their days immersed in their work. I would soon be filled with the satisfaction of joining the ranks of Mary Cassatt and Evelyn De Morgan. Even Lizzie Siddal, an artist in her own right, had money of her own because of John Ruskin's patronage. Although I admired the Pre-Raphaelite Brotherhood, I did not relish the idea of having to choose between eating and purchasing art supplies, as they often had. As my artist friends in France had, too.

After an hour I began to get hungry. I hadn't had much to eat at breakfast. I could have asked for something to be brought to me, but I didn't want the footman hovering. So I decided to go into the kitchen and snaffle some of our cook's pikelets. I loved them, and Mrs. Kipling always made them up for afternoon tea. My mother didn't want me in the kitchen mixing with the servants, but it was nearly ten o'clock, and Mrs. Kipling would be taking her morning break. No one would see me.

The kitchen was in the basement, down a set of stairs that could be gotten to from the breakfast room, through a door painted white and adorned with a crystal handle on our side but covered with green baize and a gunmetal knob on the servants' side.

My mother would never drag her decorating ideas in here. The kitchen was for service only. Large wooden sinks lined one side of the room, and a monstrous oven sat on the other. A wooden clothes airer hung with stockings had been hoisted up over it to dry. The only windows in the room were at street level, and I could see shoes walking and skirts sweeping by.

I paused at the bottom of the steps. No one was about, so I tiptoed across the flagstone floor to the cake tin. I pried open the lid, took out a pikelet, and bit into it. Heaven.

As I leaned against the worktop and ate another cake, a pair of very shiny black boots paused at our window, turned, and then walked toward the steps that led to the servants' entrance. Then I heard the sound of footsteps marching down the marble stairs. I froze, the cake halfway to my mouth. Any moment now the person would knock, and if anyone came through the hallway that led from the scullery to answer the door, they would see me standing there.

The heavy iron knocker fell against the door.

I darted a look down the hallway, but no one was coming. I set the cake on the worktop and went to the door, peering through the bull's-eye glass.

The owner of those boots was a police constable. He stood in the door well, looking across the road and toward Berkeley Square.

Blast! I took a step back. Had the judge changed his mind? Had the constable come to arrest me? But how could the police trace me here without my real name or address? They would have gone to Freddy's house first. *Rose! I'll bet it was she who told them.*

I thought about running out of the kitchen, ignoring him altogether. But if I answered the door, I could send him on his way before he had a chance to speak to a servant. I lifted the latch and opened the door.

"May I help you?" I said. I tried to keep the alarm from my voice.

The constable turned around. And you could have knocked me over with a feather. It was PC Fletcher. A paper sack was tucked under one arm. His chin sported a dark-purple bruise.

"Good day," he said, bowing slightly.

I must have looked a gormless ninny, staring at him with my mouth dangling open.

"We meet again." He leaned against the doorframe as if he planned to stay awhile.

I finally found my voice. "What are you doing here?"

"I believe I have something that belongs to you. I thought you might like it back."

He handed me the bag. I opened it, and inside was my sketchbook. It was completely undamaged.

"Your address was inside the book."

"You have no idea what this means. I feel as though my life has been handed back to me." I tried very hard not to squeal with glee, like the girls at my school when they made a goal on the hockey pitch. But instead I did something equally embarrassing. Without even thinking about what I was doing, I stepped up and kissed his cheek. He smelled the same as he had the previous day, of a mixture of green grass and fresh laundry.

"Well, it's much easier to make you happy than I would have reckoned!" he said, laughing. "I thought you'd have my guts for garters."

"Did someone turn this in to the station?"

"No, I found it."

"You found it?" I glanced at the cover again. Not a raindrop on it. "But when?"

"I . . . um." He looked sheepish. He scratched the side of his face and gazed across the street for a moment. And then he turned back to me and shrugged. "Just after you were arrested," he finally said.

"When I was in the police van?" My smile faded.

He nodded.

"But at the station you said you hadn't even seen me drawing. And when we were walking home, you said you knew nothing about my book. I don't understand."

A flush began to darken PC Fletcher's face. "Let me explain. I found your sketch pad after you were arrested and hid it in the police box by Parliament. If Catchpole had found it, he would have destroyed it. Or the judge would have taken it off of you. I hate that they do that. It's not right."

I remembered the way PC Fletcher had rolled up the poster so carefully and handed it to Lucy, and how the other officer had ruthlessly torn the other poster. From the short time I'd known PC Catchpole, I felt certain he'd probably have thrown my sketchbook into the trash.

"I was going to take it to the WSPU headquarters, but then at the station you said you weren't a suffragette. You were going on about it, and you seemed angry with the other girl, so I guessed you were with the Anti-Suffrage League. I thought maybe you were drawing a cartoon, to make fun of the suffragettes—like the ones in the papers lately. I think the antis are wrongheaded, so I didn't want you to have the book."

"So that is why you were so foul to me?" I said.

He nodded. "Then I looked through the book and found you weren't an anti, just an artist like you claimed. I saw your address and your real name and I felt ashamed at what I'd done. I'd hate for someone to nick my work. Now I know why you ran off like you did. I would have done the same. Come to think of it, I'd probably have put up a hell of a fight. They're really good, your drawings. I hope you don't mind me looking?"

"No," I said. I did, a little, because an artist's sketchbook is a personal thing, but a part of me was happy that he had. "You're very kind."

"My favorite's the cartoon of the girls with the books on their heads. I had a right laugh over that one."

The cartoon he meant was a satire I did of a crushingly boring comportment class at finishing school. Madame had us swan around the room with books on our heads to teach us to stand straight. I had captioned the picture *Young Ladies' Literature Lectures.*

"Are you an artist, too?" I asked, curious about what he'd meant when he referred to his own work.

"I'm a writer," he said. "Well, I want to be a writer, that is. I write serials, like the ones in tuppenny novelettes. I want to get them published, but I haven't had any luck so far."

I remembered how he had remarked about my brother's novelettes and carefully put his card in his pocket. "Would you like me to recommend you to my brother? I'd be happy to, if it's a favor you're after."

A confused look skittered over his face. "No, not a bit of it. I was going to ask if you'd collaborate with me and illustrate my stories, like Charles Dickens and Cruikshank did. I've been told that publishers prefer illustrated stories. I've been looking for an artist, but I never found one good enough until you. I would submit them to your brother's company, yes, but I don't expect you to speak to him. I'm not looking for any favors."

Illustrating PC Fletcher's stories appealed to me greatly,

and I was just going to say yes when I realized how impossible that was. How would I leave the house to help him?

Just then I heard the clop of Mrs. Kipling's heavy steps approaching. "Is someone there?" she called. "Miss Darling? Is that your voice I hear?"

"I have to go!" I whispered, throwing a look over my shoulder.

"Wait!" he said. "What do you say?"

I shook my head. "I'm sorry. I'd best not. It's tempting, but truly I cannot."

"Oh." He looked disappointed.

The cook's footsteps grew nearer.

"I really have to go. Thank you so much for bringing the book. Best of luck!" I waved good-bye, shut the door, and dashed for the stairs, hugging my sketchbook to my chest.

Eleven

At home, a dinner party

I WAS STILL THINKING about PC Fletcher later that evening as I waited for my mother's maid, Bailey, to dress me for dinner with the Carrick-Humphreys. I so wanted to illustrate his stories, and perhaps I could have come up with some ruse to do so, but I was taking enough chances applying to art school without my parents knowing. Besides, my getting caught in the company of a working-class boy would send my father into a frenzy of anger from which he would probably never recover. Stepping down the social ladder to consort with someone below me, as I had done before with the artists in France, was out of the question. As Mamma said, *They know their place and we know ours.*

No matter. I had my sketchbook back, and my own art was what mattered, no one else's. I had so much to look forward to now. I would submit my sketchbook to the RCA acceptance panel at the end of April and sit for the exam in July.

I finally felt content. I had made a good decision to marry Edmund Carrick-Humphrey. It solved so many problems in one fell swoop. I would have my own life, my own money, and a husband who would not try to tell me what to do.

Bailey came into my room, her arms full of garments, which she placed upon the bed. She set to work putting up my hair. My hair was quite heavy and long, and it took ages for her to haul it all into place. Her deft hands combed, tugged, and pinned my hair. Finally her hands fell away from the finished coiffure and she stepped back and folded her hands, a pleased expression on her face.

I leaned closer to the mirror and turned my head to the side. She had rolled my hair into sections and pinned them along my head. The back of my hair was coiled into a bun and pinned high on my head. It was very feminine, very romantic, but it looked like it was more suited to a Greek statue.

The weight of my hair dragged at my scalp, and I put my hand up to loosen it a bit. Bailey sucked in her breath and took a step forward, her hands outstretched. Mindful of how long it had taken her to create the hairstyle, I dropped my hands into my lap.

A pin poked at my scalp, and while Bailey turned to the material on the bed, I quickly pulled the offending thing away and flicked it behind my dressing table.

But the hair ordeal was a gift compared to what unfolded next. Bailey stood waiting, holding a long-boned coutil laced corset.

I did not own such a garment. As a matter of propriety I had worn an unboned bodice since I was twelve. I should have begun wearing a boned corset at fourteen, but my first visit to my mother's corsetiere had been a disaster.

The moment the garment was tightened about my waist, a feeling of confinement washed over me. I shamed myself and started crying right then and there in the shop. My mother had been so mortified that she had had to find herself another corsetiere. She had not repeated the exercise since and left me to remain in my bodice. Until now.

"That is not mine," I said.

"Your mother wishes you to wear this." She held the corset out and waited for me to stand.

I remained sitting. "I'm not wearing that. I'm telling you now. I'm not overly fond of corsets."

"I'm sorry, miss, but your mother says. And you won't get into this dress of hers without it. You won't fit."

"How will I sit with the corset going so low down my legs? It's impossible."

"The same way your mother does. You've seen her sat down, haven't you? Now come on, Miss Darling." The look on her face belied the calmness of her voice. I knew that if her position had allowed her to, she would have screeched at me.

I sighed and stood up. What did it matter how I dressed? If this was what I had to do for marriage, then so be it. By September I could dress like an organ grinder's monkey if I wanted.

I held out my arms and Bailey slid the heavily boned corset over my combinations and around my waist and hips, latching the clasps in front, just under my bust. She began to lace the back, taking a strong tug with each new loop. The tie hissed as she pulled it through the holes. I grasped the pole of my four-poster bed to keep from being jerked off my feet as she worked her way down.

"Dash it, Bailey, it's awful tight!"

I could hear the maid breathing in my ear. She was standing too close. I could smell the carbolic soap she washed with. I took a step forward to gain some space, but she followed. The walls in the room seemed to march a little inward with every tug.

"Breathe from the top of your chest, Miss Darling," Bailey instructed. "Not from the bottom. The boning's what's worrying you. And at supper, eat only small bites and very little, otherwise you will feel sick."

I did as she said but I couldn't imagine how I would get through an entire evening in the corset. No wonder my mother took to her bed several times a day.

"I don't know how anyone can get on like this." I tugged at the coutil fabric. My hips and waist were compressed so tightly that I felt as though I were in a straitjacket in a lunatic asylum.

"You don't need to get on. That's what servants are for."

Bailey pulled a cotton camisole over my head and buttoned the front. Then she held out a pair of lace knickers for me to step into and tied the tapes at my waist. She laid a silk petticoat on the floor in a circle and held my arm as I stepped into the middle. She pulled that up and tied it.

My mother had chosen for me one of her own gowns of pale pink silk over a darker pink taffeta. It had a square neckline and a narrow skirt with a small train. I raised my arms while Bailey lifted the garment over my head and did the long line of buttons up the back with a buttonhook.

I looked in the mirror. A familiar image peered back at me.

I resembled my mother.

AT FIRST I did not recognize Edmund Carrick-Humphrey. For a fleeting moment I thought my mother was introducing me to his older brother or a cousin. I barely heard her say his name because I was looking around the room for the boy I remembered.

"Victoria, where are your manners?" my mother hissed in my ear. "Do shake hands!"

Startled, I put my hand out, and he bent over it.

My father came into the sitting room, and my mother went to join him in greeting Edmund's parents.

All I could think was that university life had done much to change Edmund Carrick-Humphrey. His looks had altered from dull, nothing boy into a strikingly handsome one. He had grown taller and filled out—no more gangly limbs. His dark hair was Macassar-oiled back from his brow. He wore his tailcoat very well, carrying himself as if he were King Edward. For a moment, I wondered if Edmund would make a good art model, but my artistic sensibilities didn't rise—still stuck on drawing PC Fletcher, apparently.

He studied me, eyeing me as if I were a racehorse he had planned to place a wager upon.

"Our parents have made a good match between us," he said. "We're a good-looking couple." He turned me so that I stood next to him, reflected in the large mirror over the fireplace. "We will be the envy of all."

His arrogance was appalling, but he was so confident in the way he spoke that I laughed. He reminded me a little bit of Étienne.

He tilted his head toward mine, watching our reflections in the mirror. "My father has dreadful taste, so I was doubtful when he said he knew the perfect girl for me. But then I remembered who you were. I don't think you remember me. I was all spots and big feet then. Certainly nothing you would look at twice."

"I remember you as being . . . very polite." I turned away from the mirror and sat down on the settee. Edmund sat next to me. The scent of his cologne wafted over. It was spicy and masculine, a mix of sandalwood and leather.

"That is very kind of you. I suppose *polite* is one way of putting it. *Terribly shy and deadly dull* is how I would put it."

The door creaked open and a girl came in. She was maybe sixteen. She was dressed in a blue lace gown with a square neckline. A large velvet ribbon held her hair at the back of her neck, but some strands had escaped and were hanging round her face. The messy hairstyle made her look charming in a slightly mad way.

She perched on a chair across from us. "So you're the wicked girl I've heard so much about."

Edmund looked at her in exasperation. "May I introduce my dear sister, India Carrick-Humphrey. Indy, say hello to Miss Darling, and keep those claws of yours sheathed."

"Taking your clothes off in front of a group of men." She studied me for a moment. "How peculiar."

"It was in an art class," I said.

"Must have been awfully drafty!" She wandered over

to the fireplace and began to inspect the bric-a-brac on the mantel.

"Indy, do shut up," Edmund said, crossing over to the side table. His hand paused over the bottles. "What would you like?"

"Gin sling, please," India piped. She picked up my mother's Staffordshire horse and trotted him along the mantelpiece.

"There doesn't appear to be any sugar here," Edmund said, scanning the contents of the table. "Gin and lemon will have to do." He handed India a glass. "Very watered down, or dear old Dad will have my head. And you?" he asked me.

"Drinks *before* dinner?"

"Not drinks. Cocktails. It's the new American thing, haven't you heard? All the smart hotels are serving them."

"Sounds beguiling, but not just now, thank you." There were too many unknowns to this dinner—corset, new gown and hairstyle, unfamiliar fiancé and his family—to add another thing to the mix, as fascinating as a cocktail seemed.

"I'm afraid you don't have a choice. You need to experience the joy that is the cocktail." He looked over the table again. "Hm, what mayhem shall we create . . . ?"

"Do her a flash-of-lightning, Edmund," India said.

"Mixers are thin on the ground here, Indy. We need gingerette and red-currant syrup for that."

"A bosom-caresser, then!" India said, collapsing in gales of laughter.

"Steady on! That requires an egg."

"I don't think our drinks tray is very well equipped," I said. "My father doesn't go in for such modern concoctions. I'm afraid he's a bit old-fashioned in many ways."

Edmund lifted a decanter and sniffed the contents. "Why muck up this quality brandy with such fripperies, anyhow." He poured two glasses and held one out to me. "Might as well start out as we mean to go on, hey?"

I hesitated for a moment and then took the glass. One drink wouldn't hurt. The woodsy, smoky scent of the liquor was strong. I took a drink like it was lemonade, which turned out to be a big mistake. The brandy seared its way down my throat, leaving a burning trail behind. I gasped. My eyes watered. "It's like drinking fire."

Edmund and India laughed.

"For God's sake, woman, don't throw it back like that," Edmund said. "You're only meant to sip it!"

"You should see the look on your face!" India chimed in with a tinkling laugh. "Hilarious!"

I tried to hand the glass to Edmund, but he pushed it back. "Don't give up. Have another. This time go easy."

I took a little sip. It was still fiery, but not as much.

Edmund studied me. "Nice, isn't it? Brandy is nectar of the gods."

At that moment, I couldn't have agreed more.

I smiled, and touched my glass to his.

Our parents never joined us in the drawing room, most likely thrashing out the details of the engagement. So while we waited for dinner to be served, Edmund regaled his sister and me with stories of university and all the high jinks the boys there got up to, pausing every so often to top up our glasses. It all seemed quite hilarious and I found myself in fits of giggles several times.

"Good lord, Edmund. She's tiddly," I heard India hiss at Edmund after some time. "Papa will blame you, you know that?"

"As if I give a toss what he thinks."

Half an hour later the gong sounded for dinner and we stood up. My mother's potted palms waved back and forth as if a tropical breeze had blown through. And the floor felt as though it had tilted to one side. I hadn't realized I had drunk so much. India was right. I was tiddly. I staggered, and Edmund caught my hand. He laughed. "Steady there, Victoria." I gripped his arm as we walked to the dining room.

I giggled and slapped his arm. "You are so funny."

"Shhhh!" India said to me. "Keep your voice down. You'll get us all in trouble."

"No, you shhhhh, China Carrick-Humphrey." I jabbed my finger at her.

"I'm India!" she said.

"Well, they're both in Asia!" Edmund pointed out helpfully.

I burst into laughter.

Mamma had placed Edmund and me together at dinner. We sat down, and Edmund grinned at me as if we shared a wicked secret.

Our footman began to serve dinner. I concentrated very hard on appearing normal, but it was most tiring. At one point I gave up altogether, set my elbow on the table, and rested my chin on my hand for a moment.

Edmund leaned over. "Try to eat something, Miss Darling. It will help sop up some of the brandy," he whispered.

As dinner wore on, my brandied haze abated a little bit. The dinner conversation was as dull as usual, with topics restricted to the weather and the latest plays in Drury Lane. My father, thrilled with having a Knight Bachelor in our own home, nodded and smiled at everything Sir Henry said, at one point even agreeing with his good opinion of the king, of whom I knew my father heartily disapproved, usually saying his lifestyle, especially the flaunting of his mistresses, was louche and not befitting his royal station. The road to a royal warrant was paved with much arse-kissing. I laughed out loud at the thought.

My father shot a look at me.

"Quite the bon vivant, quite so." Sir Henry continued his appraisal of the king, his long walrus mustache quivering.

Sir Henry may have behaved as though he were royalty himself, but he was nothing more than a parvenu. He had climbed his way up the industrial ladder, like my father had, sold his steam-powered flour mills for scads of money, double-barreled his name, and acted as though he were to the manor born. The recent knighting from King Edward for achievements in food production no more made Sir Henry a gentleman than tying a ribbon round a hen's neck made her a lady. Besides, he was just a Knight Bachelor, so the title would die with him rather than passing on to one of his sons.

"It's good we have a monarch with a zest for life," Sir Henry went on. "I never approved of Queen Victoria shutting herself away on the Isle of Wight. No, I did not."

My father had shaped his mouth into what looked like a smile. I frowned. My father was behaving like he had no spine. My father always flew at anyone who cast aspersions on our late queen.

My mother smiled wanly and played with her diamond-teardrop earring.

I felt Edmund's hand drop upon my knee under the table. I darted a look at him. He stared ahead, an innocent expression upon his face. I bit back a giggle.

"Did your Frederick attend university?" Sir Henry asked, and then went on, not bothering to wait for my father to answer. "Oxford has been the making of my youngest son here." He gestured to Edmund with his fork.

Edmund turned toward his father. A slow flush began to spread up his neck.

"Before university he was nothing but a milksop," Sir Henry continued. "Wouldn't say boo to a goose!" He paused to shovel potted shrimp into his mouth. "Tied to his mother's apron strings, he was. Nothing like his brother, Jonty."

Edmund glared, his jaw tight, but his father did not seem to notice. Edmund's fingers played with his knife, as if he would dearly love to plunge it into his father. His hand squeezed my knee hard. I tried to pull away, but he only increased his grip.

His mother, a tiny birdlike woman, chimed in. "Actually, my son was quite ill when he was a child and he—"

Sir Henry made a noise and held up his hand. "Don't interrupt."

Lady Carrick-Humphrey bit her lip and stared at her plate, her knife and fork frozen in place.

India looked from her mother to Edmund with an anxious expression.

"Had no hopes for him, no sir," Sir Henry went on. "But now, thank the Lord, he's changed into a man. Better late than never. You must make sure he learns the lesson of hard work when he joins your firm, Mr. Darling. Don't want him falling back into bad habits."

"Of course," Papa replied. "It is every father's wish for his child to find his place in the world."

Sir Henry glowered at Edmund. "He's been indulged for too long."

There was pain on Edmund's face. But quick as a flash, it was replaced by bravado. It was as if he had practiced that look a thousand times in his bureau mirror. I knew that feeling. I knew what it was like to be the misfit in the family. I reached under the table and slowly set my hand on his. He turned his hand up and gathered my fingers into his cold palm.

"Edmund's in the Oxford and Cambridge Boat Race in April," India blurted out. "Did you know that, Miss Darling?"

"I didn't." I was grateful that India had changed the subject. "How impressive, Mr. Carrick-Humphrey." The annual boat race was a famous event and had been going on a very long time, since 1829. On the day, thousands of spectators crowded the banks of the Thames from Putney to Mortlake to watch the heavyweight eights from Oxford and Cambridge race each other in their tiny, fragile boats, vying for the fastest current and often clashing their oars together in their fight for the lead. Anyone rowing in the race had his name put down in the history books.

"I'll be rowing in the stroke position," Edmund said. "You must come and watch. India will be there. I'll send a motorcar round."

India's announcement of Edmund's success seemed to have stopped Sir Henry's bashing of his son. But peace did not reign for long. Over dessert, the conversation took a turn toward the suffragettes at Parliament, especially the events of the previous day.

"I cannot believe these women. What could they be thinking?" Mother said, setting her wineglass onto the table with an indignant tap. "The *Daily Bugle* said one woman chained herself to a railing. What a disgraceful way to behave."

I stared at Mamma. If only she knew.

"I heard the police gave them a damn good thrashing," Sir Henry said. "Serves them right."

I thought about the way PC Fletcher had treated the suffragettes. Even though he was tasked to move them along, he allowed them their dignity. Sir Henry and Mamma were scornfully dismissing them out of hand. "They have a right to their opinion, surely," I said, feeling the need to defend them in absentia, as PC Fletcher had done in person.

"It's unladylike and shocking behavior," Sir Henry replied firmly. "Our government is using good judgment.

The vote should not be given to women when they turn to violence and prove themselves to be unworthy of it. This type of behavior is exactly what I predicted would happen when women joined such organizations. It quite undoes them. No sensible person would ever agree to women's suffrage. Never."

"Voting would add to our responsibilities," Lady Carrick-Humphrey put in. "That would be such a cruel thing to ask of women."

Sir Henry beamed. "Well said, my dear!"

"I don't know what they are fighting for anyway," Lady Carrick-Humphrey went on. "I don't want to be forced to vote. Politics sounds so dreary."

"You wouldn't be forced to vote, Lady Carrick-Humphrey," I said. "I think you'd be able to choose. And Sir Henry, what do you know of what it's like to be a woman?" I had the bit between my teeth and there was no stopping me. I leaned forward in my chair and tapped the table emphatically. I decided to bestow a little of Lucy's speech on them. "Doesn't the government make women pay taxes? How would you like it if you didn't have a say in how that money was spent? That's how the Revolutionary War in America began, after all."

Ha! That told him. I sat back feeling pleased with myself and glanced around. It was deathly quiet. Everyone was staring at me. India looked confused. Mamma's mouth had dropped open. Edmund, finally breaking the silence, laughed as if what I said was the funniest thing he'd ever heard.

Oh, no. The brandy might be nectar of the gods, but it must have given me a false sense of security. I had never spoken in such a way in front of my parents.

"And what do you know about this, Victoria?" There was a measured tone to my father's voice. His expression was calm, but I could see anger seeping through. I knew I had gone too far.

"I just heard some people talking," I said. My cheeks felt hot, and I hoped they weren't as red as they felt.

"People talking where?"

"I forget," I said weakly, realizing how feeble that sounded.

"Your daughter seems to have *interesting* opinions, Mr. Darling," Sir Henry said, and then smiled. But there was little humor in that smile.

"It appears so," my father said shortly.

"Do you have an occupation, Miss Darling? Are you finding yourself taxed?" Sir Henry asked, a patronizing smile on his face, as if he were addressing a naughty little girl who didn't like the flavor of her lollipop.

"No," I said. "But I—"

"Since you, like many women, don't earn money, you *shouldn't* have a say on how the taxes are spent. Perhaps you should keep quiet about things that don't concern you."

"But I would welcome a way to earn my own money."

I heard a sharp intake of breath from my mother.

"And take work away from a man? Trying to support his family?" Sir Henry demanded.

"What if I, or any other woman, had to support myself? Everyone deserves an equal chance at life, do they not?"

"Such socialistic views you have, Miss Darling." He picked up his spoon and turned his attention to his charlotte russe pudding, dismissing me.

"Just because I have an idea of my own doesn't make me a socialist, Sir Henry. Not that there is anything wrong with socialists, after all."

"Victoria!" My father was too polite to shout at the table, but I could hear the warning in his voice.

"But that's not fair," I said, looking round the table. "It isn't fair to treat women unequally. We aren't children."

Sir Henry set his spoon down. His face was pickled with anger. "I think my son will have to tie you to the table leg, young lady."

I stared at my plate. *Shut it, Vicky. Just shut it!* my saner self screamed at me. But my impulsive side, fueled by my father's rather expensive brandy, prevailed. I lifted my head and looked Edmund's father in the eye. "Let him try it."

I heard Edmund muffle a snort of laughter.

"Ladies, I think we'll go through," my mother said, bringing a halt to the exchange. So, as usual, we ladies stood up and followed her up to the drawing room, where we waited for the men to smoke their cigars and talk of subjects not meant for female ears, which, of course, meant politics. Mamma chatted with Lady Carrick-Humphrey and India, blatantly ignoring me. I stood by the fireplace and wished I could become invisible.

When the men joined us, Edmund asked me to accompany him onto the veranda. India followed us but went down the steps and wandered out into the garden. I was glad to go out, because the fresh air cleared my head a bit, and anyway I did not want to be in the same room with Papa and Sir Henry.

Edmund leaned against the railing, his hands in his pockets. "What a row, Miss Darling," he said. "The way both our fathers looked, I thought lives would be lost."

"I didn't mean to create a scene." I brushed an insect away from my sleeve.

"Blathering on about women's rights, how funny. I thought you were never going to take a breath. You are a one. I've never known the like."

I shifted under his candid gaze. "I have opinions. Is that so wrong?"

He shrugged.

"Do you agree with your father, that I should be tied to the table leg?" Perhaps Freddy was wrong. Perhaps Edmund wasn't as forward-thinking as my brother thought. Perhaps I had made a terrible mistake.

"No, of course not," he said, to my relief. "It was amusing to watch you get one over on my father. Lord knows I wish I could do the same." There was a bitter note to Edmund's words. "I'm sick of him ordering every direction of my life."

"How so? You're at school and away from him, aren't you?"

"Oh, his reach is long." He made a little noise and grinned. "Let's just say I made a bit of a mess recently. My father had to tidy it up and he was not amused."

"What happened?"

He waved his hand. "Some gambling debts. And I may have borrowed money against my inheritance that needed paying back. I'm sure they barely made a dent in his coffers, but he's demanded recompense, and so my wings are to be clipped. I get married and find an occupation or take up a commission in the navy. And life on a ship is not for me. I can't see myself sailing o'er the Spanish Main fending off all boarders. Too Robert Louis Stevenson for words."

"The navy sounds refreshing compared to my sentence. If I don't marry, I must go live with my Aunt Maude, never to be seen or heard from again."

He looked at me frankly. "Is the reason you have to get married because you took your clothes off? To dilute the scandal, so to speak?"

"There are other reasons. My father feels the steadying influence of a husband would be good for me. But if he thinks I'm going to quit drawing and painting just because I'm married, then he's sorely mistaken. I plan to be a great artist, no matter what he says."

I must have looked irritated, because Edmund placed his hand over mine and laughed. "Never fear, Miss Darling. We will be our own masters, I shall see to that. We'll do anything we like." He shifted a bit closer to me, squeezing my fingers for a moment before dropping his hands onto the veranda wall. He nudged my shoulder with his. "It's a cliché, old thing, but I think we're two peas in a pod."

"Seems so."

"Few marriages have begun with so much in common." He laughed.

"My parents were barely acquainted with each other. I'm not sure if my mother knew whether she was marrying my father or his best man."

"I hope that will not be the case with me, although my best man, Kenneth, is much better looking, so you might want to hedge your bets."

"Aren't you terrified of marrying a scandalous woman?" Although Edmund had besmirched his own name, it was easier for a single man to recover from scandal than a woman. But because a married man was thought to be responsible for his wife's behavior, a husband was often painted with his wife's tarry brush.

But truly, Edmund didn't seem to care a whit. "None of my friends give a toss about society whispers. The king doesn't let scandal mark his life, so why should the rest of us?"

"That's a refreshing view."

"A modern one. Time to sweep away the past and embrace the new, that's what I say."

We looked out into the darkened garden for a bit. India was under the pergola; her dress glowed a ghostly blue in the moonlight. It felt strange to be standing next to a boy I barely knew but who would be the person I would have breakfast with every morning and share a bed with for the rest of my life. How would we go from being acquaintances to intimates? Perhaps it could start now. Edmund had been so humiliated by his father. Maybe if I showed him that I understood . . .

I turned to Edmund and put my hand over his. "I'm so sorry about what your father said to you earlier," I said. "I know that must have hurt you."

He looked at me and shook his head. "Hurt me? Don't know what you mean."

"Oh, I'm sorry if I misspoke . . . only—"

And then, without any warning, Edmund took me in his arms and kissed me. Startled, I took a step back, but instead of letting go, he followed and gripped me with even more determination.

I had never been kissed by a boy before, and my mind flickered through several emotions at once: shock, embarrassment, and then a tiny bit of excitement. My arms hung at my sides, and I wasn't sure what I was meant to do with them, so I just left them there.

The kiss went on and on and on, and Edmund's arms began to feel too tight around me, his cologne too cloying.

My corset pressed hard against my ribs. I forgot the warning from Bailey to breathe from the top of my lungs. The brandy rose up inside me.

I broke from Edmund's embrace, leaned over, and was sick all over his brilliantly shined shoes.

Twelve

T HE STENCH OF the manure in the streets and the smog from coal fires and motorcars made my pounding headache worse. My eyes were sore and hot from crying. It was the morning after the dinner. I was on my way to my charity, Friends of London Churches, at St. Martin-in-the-Fields in Trafalgar Square, accompanied by Emma, our parlormaid. And I was, once again, in utter disgrace.

My father was angrier than I had ever seen him. It wasn't my vomiting over Edmund that made him angry; he'd never discovered I'd been drinking brandy. Edmund had stepped forward and defended me, saying I'd probably gotten a bad oyster at dinner.

No, Papa was angry because I had spoken my mind. After the Carrick-Humphreys left, my father accused me of purposely trying to sabotage the engagement and humiliate him in front of Sir Henry. He paced round the sitting room calling me a wicked, wicked girl, over and over.

"Sallying forth with that ridiculous speech about women's suffrage and arguing with Sir Henry is inexcusable."

"What did I say that was so wrong? Am I not allowed an opinion?" I said.

"No, you are not! You, like many women, are overly emotional and have no ability to judge a matter well enough to form an opinion. If you behave in this fashion again, Victoria," my father went on, "you will be on the next train to Norfolk."

And then, true to his word, he had the servants remove every pencil, every paintbrush, every pastel and piece of paper that he could find in my room, even my childhood drawings. And worst of all, they took away my sketchbook, which I had left sitting on my dressing table.

Because I knew Mamma had been on my side once, I sought her out in her bedroom while Bailey was readying her for bed, and begged her for my art things, but she would not budge.

"But you convinced him before, he told me," I said.

"And I see now that I was wrong," she said. "Your father is quite right. He feels that this obsession you have with art has turned your head and is the source of your willful behavior." She flapped her hand. "So no more drawing. You shall concentrate on your social obligations and your trousseau."

"What about my sketchbook, Mamma? What has Papa done with it?"

"I have it."

"*You* have it?"

"And you should thank me. If your father saw what was in it, he would chuck it into the fire," she said.

I swallowed. "You looked inside?" Mamma had never seen any serious work I'd done. I couldn't bear it if she cast aspersions. I held my breath, but she looked away for a moment, saying nothing. Then she spoke again.

"I won't give your art things back to you now. But I will give them to Mr. Carrick-Humphrey once you are married, and it will be up to him as to whether you can have them back."

"Mr. Carrick-Humphrey?"

"Of course!" My mother looked exasperated. "He will be head of your household, so he will make your decisions for you. The everyday running of the household will be in your hands—dinners, parties, decoration and the like—but my dear, what did you think?"

"My husband will not be my jailer, Mamma. Times are changing, for heaven's sake."

"Not that much," she said, "despite your little speech on women's suffrage. I would advise you to be kind to Mr. Carrick-Humphrey so that he gives you what you want. If you harangue him and are willful in your behavior, then he may not grant you what you wish."

"Edmund Carrick-Humphrey is a new man, Mamma, not some buttoned-up, dusty old Victorian. I don't think he wants a simpering wife hanging on his every word so he'll be inclined to hand out wishes like sweeties from Father Christmas. My brother doesn't treat Rose that way."

My mother sighed. "Frederick has no need to. Rose is not a willful girl. She understands what it means to be a good wife. She follows his lead, and that is the way it should be. I fear you will come down to earth with a bump, my dear."

I had no chance of going to the RCA now. How could I create enough work for my application in such a short space of time, with no implements or supplies? And finding models to sit for me would be a near impossibility. Lily and the models at Monsieur's studio were the best models I'd ever had. In the past, whenever I'd asked people to model, they'd fidgeted with embarrassment under my steady gaze or chattered to hide their discomfort, shifting away from the light and rendering pointless the whole exercise. If I tried to draw people in public on the sly, they'd see me staring and leave or rebuke me for being rude. And of course no one, *no one* would be willing to pose for me undraped.

It was a problem that had hounded me all night, and I was still fretting over it as the carriage turned toward Trafalgar Square, and I saw the four bronze lions surrounding Nelson's Column. Usually this sight cheered me, but nothing could make me smile today. The carriage paused behind a queue of traffic. We sat there for the longest time, not moving. Finally, I let the window down and poked my head out. The reason for the traffic queue seemed to be the crush of people milling around.

I saw a line of women joining up by the fountain in the square. They were wearing sashes and carrying banners that said **Women's Social and Political Union**. Some of the women stood arm in arm, singing, while others handed out leaflets to passersby. In the back, several younger women dressed in matching green livery marched in step, playing recorders and beating drums.

A thought struck me. Lucy had said Christabel's sister Sylvia Pankhurst had graduated from the RCA and was looking for artists to help paint a mural. If I helped with artwork for the WSPU and showed Sylvia what I could do, she might write a reference letter. Of course I would still need new art supplies and models, but at least securing a letter of reference would be a start.

If only I could remember where the WSPU head-quarters were. I'd left the leaflet in my sketchbook, but I vaguely remembered Lucy saying it was in an inn off the Strand. She must have meant one of the Inns of Chancery, where solicitors used to live and work. There were a group of such buildings that had been turned into apartments and offices. But which one held the WSPU?

I opened the door to the carriage and stepped out, Emma trailing behind me. John, my father's coachman, looked down at me with surprise on his face.

"We can make our way from here, John. Don't worry about me." I pointed to the women. "There are so many other women about. It's as though I'm being chaperoned already," I joked. "By the time you get the carriage through, I'll be quite late. The church is just there anyway."

John looked at the women and then at the traffic near the church. Thankfully he was sensible and not prone to fits of drama like our housekeeper was. Mrs. Fitzhughes would have abandoned the carriage in the street rather than risk the chance I might run astray in the hundred yards between the carriage and the church. "Righty ho, then," he said. "I'll return home and be back for you in two hours." John had turned the carriage around and headed back toward Pall Mall.

I glanced at Emma, who was looking at a man selling sugared almonds by the pavement. I dug into my reticule and pulled out a tuppence. "Go on, Emma. Buy us a packet each."

"Oh, thank you, miss!" She took the coin eagerly and headed over to the seller.

I picked up my skirt and darted over the road. As the line began to move down Whitehall, the musicians drew near and I caught up with a girl who had a snare drum slung across her shoulder, her knees lifting high as she marched along. I touched her sleeve.

She glanced up, startled, her drumsticks in midair. And then a smile spread over her face. "Oh, hello!"

"I was wondering if you could assist me. I'm interested in helping with Sylvia Pankhurst's mural for the Women's Exhibition."

"Oh! Are you?" she said, her drum thumping against her leg as we walked. "The exhibition is going to be ripping! They'll be selling hats and cakes and all sorts. The band is going to play, and Mrs. Pankhurst is speaking. Should be heaps of fun."

"I was told to go to the headquarters, but I don't know where it is."

"Four Clement's Inn, just west of the law courts and north of the Strand before it turns into Fleet Street. Just follow the chalk arrows on the pavement. If you go Monday at one o'clock, Sylvia Pankhurst is sure to be there."

Suddenly, Mamma's charity scheme was a godsend. I could tell Mamma my charity was meeting at the Temple Church off of Fleet Street. John would take me there easily enough.

"Thank you. Where is everyone off to?"

"Marching to Parliament to protest the imprisonment of suffragettes. Then the fife-and-drum band are going to Holloway Prison to play music outside to keep the girls' spirits up. They can hear us, even the ones in solitary confinement."

We turned the corner and were onto Whitehall. I could see the spires of Parliament poking up through the foggy gloom of the city. But then I saw police constables milling around the side of the road.

The women in the queue, unhappy with the police presence, muttered their dismay.

"Are they always around the suffragettes, the police?" I asked the girl.

"An awful lot, as of late," she said. "Wherever we turn up, they're there. In some ways it's good because the police protect us from men who want to do us harm. You wouldn't believe what some men will do. Last week, one of the girls was chalking meeting times on the pavement, and a man shoved her into the railings. She knocked her head badly and had to go to hospital. The story made the newspapers and some wrote that she deserved it. The *Daily Bugle* said if she'd stayed at home where she belonged, it wouldn't have happened, and that's supposed to be a women's newspaper." The girl banged the head of her drum angrily with one stick. "And now, for safety, the WSPU will only allow us to chalk in groups."

Suddenly I saw something else that made my blood run cold: PC Catchpole eyeing the line of women marching past, a look of disdain on his face. The moment I saw him, his gaze met mine. And held it.

He recognized me. Fear coursed through my body. I was marching with the suffragettes. I had claimed I wasn't with them before. If Catchpole decided to arrest me, I wouldn't be able to talk my way out of it again.

I looked behind me. A crowd had gathered in the street; there was no chance of attempting to walk back through such a mob. I stepped up on the pavement, trying to find an easy exit. There, between a pub and a bookshop, was a small alleyway. Perhaps I could make my way through there and then double back behind the buildings.

I saw Catchpole take a step forward. I saw him point at me. I heard him shout.

I broke through a group of people and dashed down the alley.

The cobblestones clattered under my high-heeled boots, and soon the skin of my heels was rubbed raw. I rushed on, but the alley curved around instead of turning back toward Trafalgar Square, and soon I was hopelessly lost.

I stopped to get my bearings. The smoke from countless coal fires made the fog thicker. It was stifling and spooky. I gathered my wits about me and chose the closest turning.

And then I heard footsteps running behind me. *Catchpole!*

A whimper caught in my throat and I began to run; my boots pressed painfully against my blisters. The steps behind me picked up in pace.

I was approaching the back of a public house; workmen were rolling barrels of beer from a brewer's dray down a long ramp and into a cellar. I darted a look over my shoulder. I heard the voice behind me shout again.

A barrel spun into me, kicking my legs away. I slammed onto the ground, my arms shooting out in front of me. The impact was so great that my felt beret flew off, and my hairpins fell in a shower around me. I skidded along the brick ground on the palms of my hands.

Someone knelt down beside me.

I turned my head and looked into the eyes of the person chasing me. It wasn't Catchpole.

It was PC William Fletcher.

Thirteen

Behind the pub,
PC William Fletcher's beat

I SAT ON A stack of crates, trying not to cry, while PC Fletcher picked the gravel out of my palms. He had shown no signs of wanting to arrest me. After I fell, he helped me to my feet, had a quiet word with the publican, sat me on a crate, and began to doctor my hands. As friendly as he had been yesterday, I did not fully trust him. I was well aware of the handcuffs hanging from his belt and his prior threats to haul me back to the police station.

"I need to be on my way. My hands are fine." I tried to pull them back, but he tightened his grip.

"I don't think so. Those cobbles are filthy with muck of all sorts. You don't want these scrapes to go septic."

"So who are you? Florence Nightingale?"

Instead of getting angry, he grinned. "No, but I've been in enough pubs to know what lands on the floor after several pints."

"Don't be vulgar! I'll clean them as soon as I return home. I'm meant to be going to a charity meeting at the church and I'm horribly late now."

"I'll finish, and then you can be on your way to your meeting."

"I—"

"For once in your life just shut your gob and do as you are told."

"How rude!"

"Just shush and let me work."

"I'd better had, because you'll only chase me down again if I try to get away."

"I wasn't chasing you just now." He leaned over me so as to see my hands better. He had taken his helmet off and set it on the ground, so I was staring straight into his hair. "I was worried you'd become lost, because these streets are like a maze. The lads and I sometimes get turned about; that's why I followed you. Were you with the demonstration?"

"If I say yes, then you'll only haul me in front of the magistrate again."

He scowled. "What makes you think that?"

"Oh, let's see . . . could it be because you arrested me once before?"

"I never arrested you." He looked different without his helmet on. His wavy brown hair was cut short on the sides but left long on top, but his hair made a mockery of this style; as he spoke, the top flopped down over his face. He pushed it back in a casual manner, as if this happened all the time.

"Well, you didn't let me go, either."

He fixed me with a pointed frown.

"Yes, all right," I said. "That was for the judge to decide. At least you weren't horrible. Not like that other man."

He frowned. "Catchpole? I hate how he treats the suffragettes." He dropped another pebble to the ground. "Well, that is the last of the stones."

The publican's wife came out and left a cloth and a bowl of water on a nearby barrel. PC Fletcher busied himself rinsing my hands with the cloth. My fingers began to tingle under his gentle touch and my headache began to fade. I found myself no longer wanting to run away from him. I felt as though I could stay there in the dirty back alley behind that pub all day with him.

He drew a handkerchief from his pocket. "It's quite clean," he said, grinning up at me. He bound it round one the worst of the abrasions, tying a neat bow. "I had better see you back." He took my hand and helped me down from the crates. The pain from my blisters made my knees buckle, and he caught me by the elbow.

"Careful," he said.

His touch compelled me to step a little closer to him. I hadn't noticed before how his mouth lifted up at one corner, as if he found life too humorous to stop smiling completely. Such a smile should be preserved forever in a drawing. If only the feeling of his hand on my arm could somehow be captured and kept. My stomach fluttered strangely and my mind recalled that moment when I fell on top of him. I found that it wasn't an unpleasant memory anymore.

"Your hair seems to have come undone," he said.

My hands flew to the back of my head. "My hairpins came out when I fell."

We searched around on the ground and found several by the barrel that had tripped me. My beret lay on the other side.

With the pins found, I bunched my hair up and tried to put them back in, but my sore hands wouldn't allow me to.

"Here, let me help." I turned around, and PC Fletcher gathered my hair up in his hands. "Um, I'm not sure what to do; I've never dressed a lady's hair before."

"Wind it all up and ram the pins in as best you can. Try not to skewer me in the process."

He laughed. "I'll give it my best attempt."

I felt his fingers gently comb through one of the tangles in my hair, and little tingles flashed through me. I closed my eyes, wanting to lean into his hands, but I forced myself not to. Thankfully he finished quickly.

"I don't think it looks too clever. Rather like a Chelsea cinnamon bun."

I turned around, feeling suddenly shy. "Thank you for helping me. I don't think I would have found my way out if you hadn't come along."

"I was only doing my job," he said, reaching for his police helmet. "You shouldn't walk about on your own. Not in London. There are a lot of villains knocking about who wouldn't hesitate to take a swipe at a woman, especially lately. A lot of blokes hate suffragettes."

"I thank you all the same, PC Fletcher."

"Call me Will."

Somehow the name Will suited him very well indeed. "And you must call me Vicky."

"Vicky Darling. Not Smith," he said in a matter-of-fact tone, as if he'd known it all along. "Your real name was in your sketchbook."

Feeling embarrassed for the lie, I said nothing. I simply shrugged.

"Well, then. Allow me to escort you back, Vicky."

We set off. With Will next to me, the fog no longer seemed ominous; instead, it felt peaceful. The fog blotted out the surroundings and any passersby, making it feel as though we were the only people about.

"So you believe in votes for women?" I asked as we walked.

"I don't see the point in denying half the population the right to vote. I think the politicians are frightened women will take over if they have it." He shook his head. "My mum and sister are more capable than my dad and me put together, so I see no reason to worry about that. It's daft. So yes, the suffragettes have my sympathies. I can't work out which side you're on, though."

"With the women, of course."

"But you don't fight with them?" He looked at me, his eyes questioning.

"I'm going to help them with the artwork. I'm not the fighting type." I twirled my beret around my hand.

He grinned. "And an artist can't fight?"

"Not this one."

"I don't know about that."

The sun was beginning to cut through the fog, and a shaft of light fell upon William Fletcher's face, illuminating the angles of his cheekbones and the length of his jaw. I thought once again that he had the perfect face to draw. And then the vision of him on a battlefield struck me once more, and I thought of how I would like to draw him: as the knight Lancelot in the Arthurian legend. I wondered if *he* would pose for me. Perhaps he might be willing to if I took him up on his offer of illustrating his stories. Doing so was certainly worth the risk for me now that my parents had taken away my sketchbook.

"Your offer from yesterday. Does it still stand?" My fingers gripped an imaginary pencil.

"Too right! Have you changed your mind?"

"Maybe. If you'll do something for me in turn."

"Name it." He waved his hand. "Anything."

"I need a model."

He looked confused. "A model?"

"Yes. I'm submitting work for my RCA application and I need an artist's model. Someone to pose for me."

He swallowed. "You mean, like the drawing in your book? Of that man?"

I smiled. "Yes."

"You mean you want me to model for you with . . . without my kit on?" Even in the fog I could see his cheeks flushing bright red.

"Would you?" I held my breath, hoping I hadn't crossed a line, but Will seemed like the only person I had met in London who understood art and its process. And because of his political views, he didn't seem a slave to convention either. I did need a model, desperately. But also the thought of seeing him without his clothes brought the flutter back to my stomach. An unclothed man wasn't the most awful thing to gaze upon—the broad shoulders with the lines of muscles down the arms and back, a strong chest, a long thigh. No, drawing Will without his garments wouldn't be the most arduous task a girl could embark upon.

"I . . . well . . . I . . ." He laughed a little. "Blimey. I never thought you'd ask me that. You already have pictures like that. Can't you show the school those?"

"I would, but I don't have my sketchbook any longer. My parents took it. They don't approve."

"Of you drawing?"

"Yes. They've forbidden it, but obviously I'm not letting that stop me."

He digested this. "That's why you lied about your name." His face fell. "And then there's me, behaving like a rotter. I'm sorry. I'm so sorry. I should've given you a chance to explain."

"You couldn't have known. But yes, that's the reason why I lied about my name. I didn't want my father to know I'd snuck out of the house to draw. That and the fact I was around the suffragettes."

"It's a shame you lost your book. It was really good."

"I hope I'll be able to replace the work in time, but what really worries me is the lack of life studies. They would really impress the examiners, but now I don't have any to show."

He frowned, taking things in a bit more deeply. "Life studies?"

"The undraped form. The nude? No clothes on and all that."

"Why is it important to know how to draw people in the buff?"

"It's not so much about drawing people in the buff. There's a difference between naked and nude."

Will looked unsure. "How do you mean?"

"The nude figure is inspiring, sensual. Naked is simply the result of the everyday act of removing one's clothes. Someone who is naked is often embarrassed to be looked at, and that's certainly not what an artist is after. Depicting the nude is the most difficult thing for an artist to master," I said, remembering Monsieur Tondreau's lecture on the subject. "Get one thing wrong and the person will look skewed. And when you draw the undraped form, you learn about anatomy and how the clothing should fall upon a person. And there is an emotional component that is challenging as well; the muscles show tension, relaxation, fear. That kind of thing is clearer with no clothing on."

"I see." Will looked thoughtful.

"A life-drawing session is always professional, mind, never risqué," I added.

"Hmm," Will said. "What will I have to do?"

"Stand as I tell you, keep very still, and don't speak; it's dead easy."

He stopped walking and leaned against the brick wall of a building. "Without my clothes on."

"You don't have to worry about it. I've seen men undraped before." I watched him mull it over in his head. He kept tapping his fingers nervously against the brick and shooting little glances at me. I hoped he would say yes, but I knew it was a lot to ask of a person.

"I don't know," he finally said. "Can I think about it a bit?"

As Bertram had pointed out to me that day in France, it wasn't the done thing for an artist to press a model to take his clothes off. Although I was disappointed, I nodded. "I can draw you as you are, if you're more comfortable with that."

"That sounds like a better starting place. Where?"

I bit my lip, realizing I had no place to draw him undraped anyway. I hadn't quite thought it all the way through. "Can you meet me at the Royal Academy? By the Burlington Arcade; do you know it? There's a place there where we can work undisturbed. Lots of artists work there, and people tend to leave them be."

He nodded. "I have Thursday afternoons off. We can meet then. Say two o'clock?"

The Royal Academy was close to my house. I could get away with a church-charity excuse and meet Will for an hour or two. I would have to find art supplies in the meantime. Somehow.

We started walking again, and after a little while Will turned down a small lane that opened out to Northumberland Avenue. All too soon, Nelson's Column came into view. I felt a pang of guilt. Emma stood exactly where I had left her, two paper cones of nuts clutched in her hands, scanning the crowd, a look of panic on her face, which changed to relief when she saw me.

"Here I am!" I said. "I got dragged along in the crowd and I couldn't get back. I fell, and then P.C. Fletcher helped me."

"I was that worried about you, miss," she said. "I didn't know what to do. I went to buy the nuts and just like that you was gone! I'm sorry. I shouldn't have left your side." She pointed at my bandaged hand. "You've hurt yourself!"

"It's nothing, Emma." I said. "Only a little scratch."

Will walked with us all the way up the steps of the church.

"I will leave you then, miss," Will said, his face crinkling into a smile. He bowed slightly and then trotted down the steps. I watched him walk across the street toward Whitehall. I couldn't help but notice other women glancing at him as he went.

Perhaps my artistic sensibilities weren't so misguided after all.

Fourteen

Darling Residence

AFTER WE SPENT a crushingly boring morning replacing old hymnals with new ones, John met Emma and me at the church door and escorted me back to the carriage, and we headed home. My new prison warden and lady's maid was due to arrive at any moment, but I wasn't looking forward to meeting her. Despite the maid's reported ability to transform Joan Hollingberry from an ugly duckling into a swan, she would have to be someone of whom my mother approved: someone old, someone dull, and someone who shared the same fashion sense. She would probably keep a hand on me at all times and report back to my mother every time I sneezed. At least I could slip away from her with an excuse to work at the charity. I would have no need of a chaperone within the saintly walls of a church and under the watchful eye of the vicar.

Mrs. Fitzhughes, our housekeeper, was waiting in the hall when I walked in the door. "Your mother wishes to see you in her drawing room," she said. "The new lady's maid has arrived." Mrs. Fitzhughes drew herself up tall. "She has red hair. It's very bright. Not befitting a servant at all."

It took everything I had not to laugh. "Oh," I said. "That's . . . that's a shame."

"A letter arrived for you earlier, delivered by Mr. Carrick-Humphrey's footman. I had Emma put it in your room."

A personal letter from Edmund boded well. If my behavior had made Edmund's father change his mind, Sir Henry would have written my father and I would have heard nothing from Edmund himself. I left the house-keeper and went upstairs to the drawing room. I heard a murmur of voices coming down the hall.

"Have you seen the latest *La Mode Illustrée*?" asked a voice tinged with a northern accent. "There's a ball toilette illustrated there that I think would suit. It has a higher waist with ruching round the hips. The skirt is narrow with a slight train, and the bodice is sleeveless with a rounded décolletage."

"Yes! I know the gown," my mother said, excited. "What do you have in mind for garniture around the décolletage?"

"Plain, I think."

"Oh?" Mamma sounded disappointed.

"Yes, I think that's more suited to a young lady. You don't want too much frippery or else she'll look overdone. I can do a sash round the waist, folded at the hip and held on with a silver buckle."

Definitely a creature of my mother's.

I peeked around the door. My mother was sitting in her chair, and the lady's maid was standing in front of her, but they leaned toward each other, eyes sparkling with unbridled fashion frenzy. They were clearly ecstatic in the realization that they were able to communicate in the style devotee's native tongue.

Miss Sophie Cumberbunch was younger than any lady's maid I had ever met, maybe only eighteen or so. She was dressed in the usual simple black gown appropriate for her station, but it was fashionably cut and fit her perfectly, as if made for her. She had red hair, as advertised by Mrs. Fitzhughes. But it wasn't flowing down her back in a flaming fall of siren's curls. It was gathered in a loose roll at the nape of her neck. She wore a pair of steel spectacles, which would look dowdy on most women, but the juxtaposition of the workmanlike accessory with her elegance made her look intriguing.

"Hello," I said, stepping into the room, and taking care to hide my bandaged hand in the folds of my skirt.

"Cumberbunch, this is my daughter, Miss Darling," Mamma said.

The lady's maid turned toward me and curtsied. "Pleased to meet you." Those eyes behind the spectacles were as green as emeralds, and she had a dusting of freckles across her nose.

I felt childish and plain compared to her. "And I you," was all I could think to say. I had never been tongue-tied in front of a maid before.

"We've been discussing the gown for your coming-out party, Victoria." Mamma said. "I'm going to set the date of the ball for the evening after your presentation at court. Cumberbunch says she can make the dress herself."

"I can select the cloth and notions from Liberty on

Monday after luncheon," Cumberbunch said, "and begin immediately."

"Take Victoria with you. You can choose shirtwaists and chemises for her. Have a look at the hats and whatever else you think she'll need."

I couldn't help but notice that Cumberbunch looked dismayed when Mamma said this. *The feeling is mutual.*

"I would go along," Mamma continued, "but I have a luncheon party to attend."

"Actually, my charity is meeting at Temple Church on Monday after luncheon, and I don't want to miss it." I watched Cumberbunch out of the corner of my eye as I said this. She looked relieved.

"I'm happy to walk to Liberty, madam," Cumberbunch said. "It's not far. Perhaps we can all go together another day. I think it would be better if you were there to help choose."

Definitely not better.

This settled, Mamma waded in with the second phase of Victoria Darling's reformation. "Now, Victoria, since you're missing the final classes of finishing school—the preparations for coming out—I've enrolled you in a school in Kensington called Miss Winthrop's Social Graces Academy. Cumberbunch will escort you there once a week, and you'll be taught the popular dances of the coming social season, important etiquette for the debutante, and, most importantly, the court curtsy."

Cumberbunch didn't look dismayed at that chaperone duty, oddly. She looked as friendly as she had when I first came into the room.

A few more pleasantries were exchanged, and then I was excused. But Cumberbunch remained. As I went along the corridor to my room, I heard her telling my mother about the new machine-made lace she had spotted during the grand opening of Selfridge's earlier that week, and Mamma's exclamation of delight.

In my room, I removed Will's handkerchief and soaked it in a basin of water. It was a simple cotton handkerchief, frayed at the edges and torn in one corner. My heart tugged a little to think of him carrying such a shoddy thing about.

I tossed my beret onto my bed and was starting to pull the pins out of my hair when I caught sight of myself in the mirror. I held up a hand mirror to look at the back of my head. Actually, Will had done a stellar performance. He had wound my hair into a coil and laced the pins through to hold it all together. I lifted my hands to undo it but changed my mind and left the bun in place.

Edmund's letter was lying on my writing desk. I picked it up and flopped onto my bed on my back. The envelope was expensive-looking cream-colored paper with a wax seal. I broke the seal and drew out the note.

Dear Miss Darling,

I do hope you've gotten over your bout of dyspepsia and that you're feeling much better today. I apologize for not coming by to see you and express my wishes myself, but I had to return to Oxford for rowing practice.

I will be in touch regarding the Boat Race. It would be my honor to have you there.

Sincerely,
Edmund Carrick-Humphrey

I dropped the letter onto the bed. *Dyspepsia.* How gentlemanly of him to continue the indigestion charade. My mind jumped to that cringe-worthy kiss. Our first, and I had been sick all over him! How humiliating. It would be a long while before I touched brandy again.

I stared up at my canopy and tried to picture what married life would be like with Edmund. Despite the outcome of the evening, I had enjoyed my time with him. But when I tried to picture Edmund doing homey things like sitting by the fire reading a book, *or lying next to me in a bed*, William Fletcher's face appeared instead of Edmund's.

Alarmed, I turned over onto my stomach and buried my head under my pillows. *Goodness gracious!* What took my imagination in that direction? Possibly because Will was my inspiration for art. But why didn't I long to paint Edmund? He was handsome, with romantic good looks, yet I had not the first urge to draw him at all.

But that was the peculiar way with artists. You never knew who was going to inspire you. Étienne's muse was Bernadette. He had told me that a muse usually wasn't conveniently available. Often the person was out of one's reach. Before Bernadette, he himself had pined over a mayor's daughter for years, drawing her from afar, until her father threatened him and he had to leave his own home village. Dante Gabriel Rossetti poached Lizzie Siddal from his friend and fellow artist Walter Deverell, creating a rift in their relationship.

Don't be so naive and stupid and girlish as to believe that Will is anything but your muse, I told myself firmly. I reminded myself that attraction for an art model was acceptable—as long as it fed the creative process and not the physical passion. However, the image of Will lying next to me in my bed wouldn't depart from my mind's eye as quickly as I would have liked.

Later, after Mamma went out to tea with friends, I sat down to write Edmund a letter. There was no writing paper in my desk, so I went into my mother's drawing room to look for some. There was a box sitting on her desk with the lid off to one side. Thinking it was stationery, I took the first page out. But it wasn't stationery.

Inside the box were sketches. Not sketches for needle-point patterns, but amazing sketches. I took them out, one by one, and looked at them in the light streaming in through the window.

My mother must have drawn these years ago, because the sketches were of my brother and me when we were children. There was a young Freddy, holding his cricket bat, looking off in the distance at something, a sad expression on his face, as though hoping for something that would never come. There was me as a toddler reaching toward a flower where a butterfly sat feeding, an expression of joy on my little face. Each drawing was better than the last, showing mastery and skill that must have taken years to perfect.

And then I took out the final one. It was of me, about seven, squatting down to throw corn to a bird in the garden. But I was half drawn; only one side of my face was finished. It was as though she had been called away in the middle and never returned.

Why was Mamma dead set against my art ambitions when she was so talented herself? Why had she put her art away so long ago? And why was she looking at her drawings now? Was it because she, like me, had a voice inside her that told her she wasn't any good? That she was *preposterous* for trying?

Whatever her reasoning was, it had been enough for Mamma to put it all away and to dissuade me from trying to be an artist. I put the sketches back where I found them. I didn't want to ask my mother what had happened to her art, because I wasn't sure I wanted to know the answer.

IN LIGHT OF the discovery I had made about Mamma, I had hoped that she might be more on my side than she let on. So on Sunday after church, I decided to ask her if I might have my pocket money returned to me. At school my parents had sent me money each week, but I had had nothing since I returned. I had spent the last on hansom cabs the day I went to the RCA.

But she laughed when I asked for money.

"I do not understand why I cannot have pocket money," I said. "Surely if I am old enough to be married, I can have the responsibility of money."

My mother stood arranging flowers in a large crystal

vase that sat upon the table in the hall. "I hardly think one follows the other, Victoria. I can well imagine what trouble you would get up to if you had the means. I'm sure you're after art materials."

"No! I want to shop for my trousseau," I said.

"If you want something for your trousseau, put it on your father's account, just as I do." She snipped a little off the bottom of a stem and placed it carefully into her arrangement. "I'm not sure Harold can grow roses. These look as though beetles have been at them."

"Mamma, can you just consider what I'm asking?"

She frowned and pulled the roses out of the arrangement, discarding them on the table. "It won't do. No, these are dreadful."

I stared at the red roses lying there. A petal was damaged on one bloom. She had dismissed the entire bunch based on one flaw. For a moment I wondered if the sketches I had discovered had truly come from her, because there didn't seem to be any sign of an artist left in my mother. I nearly opened my mouth to ask her about them, but she was staring at the roses angrily, so I gave up.

I went to my room and sat on my bed. There were so many things of value in my room. Maybe I could sell something. But what? I scanned the top of my dressing table. No, my mother knew everything that sat there, and she'd ask questions. I thought of my grandmother's jewelry that I had inherited. There was a silver-and-jet ring that Mamma deemed unfashionable, so I had never worn it. She'd never notice it gone, I was sure of it.

I took the ring out of my jewelry box and turned it over

in my hands. It was solid silver, and the jet was fine, so it must be worth a fair bit. But how would I sell it?

The only person who was able to come and go without question was John, my father's coachman. John wasn't that much older than I, and as he'd shown the previous day, he didn't appear to be as old-fashioned as servants who'd been entrenched in their occupation forever like Mrs. Fitzhughes or the cook. If Mamma asked, they'd tattle on me without pause.

I found John at his usual spot, in the mews behind the house, where our two Cleveland Bay carriage horses, Chance and Ruby, were stabled. My mother was ever after Papa to replace them with a Daimler motorcar, but my old-fashioned father refused. He said motorcars were only a trend and would never replace horses. I was glad he said no, because I loved the horses.

I explained to John that I'd purchased the ring in an antique shop in France, meaning to give it to my mother as a gift, but only just discovered that she had one already. Did he know of a shop that might be interested in buying it?

He did. And, promising me he'd get a fair price, off he went. An hour later he sent Emma up to my room with an envelope. There were several notes tucked inside: enough money for art supplies and a little left over.

Fifteen

N MONDAY, I left in the carriage after lunch to go on my first clandestine outing. I felt daring and wicked and filled with giddy freedom, just as I used to feel when Lily helped me slip away from finishing school to attend Monsieur's atelier. An ache of longing filled me, thinking about Lily. She would have loved this caper. She always delighted in finding new excuses and ruses for sneaking me out of the school. I wished she were here now. I wished I could write to her, but I knew Madame Froufrou would have seized any letter from me, even opened it and read it.

John escorted me to Temple Church, and I hid in the vestibule for a few moments while he walked back to the carriage. I pinned the DEEDS NOT WORDS badge that Lucy had given me on my lapel and left the church. I walked along the Strand and past the Royal Courts of Justice, and as the girl in the band had said, I saw the notices for the WSPU headquarters chalked upon the pavement. Many people walked around them, as though the markings would somehow contaminate their shoes.

I followed the arrows pointing the way, and fell in

behind a group of women—two older women and a teen-age girl—headed in the same direction. Even though I was going to the headquarters to meet Sylvia Pankhurst and sign up to work on the mural, I was curious about the WSPU. I found that I was eager to see what they were about, how it all worked.

Clement's Inn turned out to be an old chancery inn that had been turned into flats and offices. The headquarters were in the basement and resembled a busy office space, not unlike my brother's publishing company. The first room I stepped into was a visitors' entrance. Boxes of leaf-lets and pamphlets were laid out on a table, and a woman sat at a desk, talking on a candlestick telephone. The group I came in with made a beeline to a table filled with goods and began selecting postcards, badges, and banners for purchase. Another woman sat behind the goods table, waiting to take their money.

A dapper gentleman with thinning hair, perhaps in his late thirties, came forward from the back of the room. "Can I help you?" he asked me.

"Yes, um, I'm interested in signing up to help Sylvia Pankhurst with her mural. I'm told this is the place to come."

"Yes, indeed. Well, that's lovely! Come through. She should be along any moment. I'm Frederick Pethick-Lawrence. I manage the headquarters here and keep things running smoothly, as it were."

A woman poked her head out from a hallway and asked for his help with a jammed typewriter.

"Is Jane not available?" asked Mr. Pethick-Lawrence. "She's better with mechanical things than I am."

The woman shrugged. "Haven't seen her yet."

"Feel free to look around while you wait," he said to me, and then hurried off to help.

I stood in the foyer, feeling slightly awkward and out of place. Everyone else seemed to have a job to do. The telephone rang often, and the clicking sound of typewriter keys accompanied by laughter drifted in from the back. Women floated in and out of the room, carrying boxes filled with leaflets. More women came in the front door, filling the place up. I went to the back of the room and waited in a dark hallway between two rooms. One on the left looked to be a newspaper office. A huge stack of newspapers titled *Votes for Women* teetered precariously near the door. Men and women leaned over broadsheets spread out on tables. Other people sat at tables cutting things out with scissors or typing. I saw Mr. Pethick-Lawrence patiently helping the frustrated woman unstick her typewriter.

The room on the right was much calmer. Here a group of young women sat stitching letters to banners and talking. I felt a prick of jealousy and loneliness. Their camaraderie reminded me of the relationship I used to have with Lily and a few of the other girls at school.

A girl by the window looked over and smiled at me. I was about to step inside and introduce myself when one of the women stood up and stretched, and I saw the signature red hair and steel spectacles of Sophie Cumberbunch, my lady's maid.

Gone was the somber dress she had worn at home. Now she was dressed in a tailor-made suit, but instead of the jaunty pinstripe seersucker or somber face cloth of most tailor-mades, hers was bottle green. Knotted around her neck was a man's tie printed with peacock feathers. On one lapel was a green-and-purple enameled badge. Her bright-red hair was gathered in a braided knot at the nape of her neck, and a small straw boater trimmed in yellow ribbons sat at a jaunty angle on her head. She was as colorful as a stained-glass window.

I backed out of the room so fast that I collided with Mr. Pethick-Lawrence coming out of the newspaper room.

"My word!" he exclaimed.

"Sorry!" I stumbled away from him and dodged through the scrum of people in the visitors' entrance, ignoring the cries of *I say! Watch out!* and shot outside. I didn't look back to see if anyone was following me. I walked away from Clement's Inn as fast as I could without actually breaking into a run.

Thoughts clashed around my mind. What was Cumberbunch doing there? She had told my mother she would be at Liberty right now. What if she saw me? I was filled me with so much anxiety that I felt I might start tearing at my hair. I could almost feel Aunt Maude's terriers nipping at my ankles.

"Queenie!" I heard a voice call out in front of me. Lucy Hawkins was coming down the pavement. She was wearing the same tailor-made suit she had worn the day I met her, although she had swapped the hideous hat for an equally ugly cloche. Today she was wearing a full-length apron, upon which were written mottoes and meeting times.

"Well, this is a turnup," she said when she reached me. "The way you acted at the police station, I didn't expect to see you anywhere around here."

"Must you insist on calling me *Queenie*?"

"I don't mean anything by it," she said cheerfully, swinging her arms as she walked. "It's cute. It suits you."

I'd heard Americans were brash and forward. That was certainly true of Lucy Hawkins.

"I can't stop," I said. "I have to go."

"I can see that. Where's the fire?"

I glanced at her. "Pardon?"

"Where are you running to? Or running from?"

"I'm just late for something." I sped up. There wasn't enough distance between me and Clement's Inn for comfort yet. "What are you doing here? I thought you were in prison."

"Early release. I think they needed the space for some shadier characters. But forget about me. What happened to you?"

"They let me go straightaway."

"Well, that's good. But why are you here? Did you give that donation you were talking about?"

"I want to sign up to help with the mural, but I can't wait for Sylvia Pankhurst. I have to be somewhere."

"Really? You're going to help?" Lucy lifted her hands, placing them on her cheeks as she said this, eyes widening in mock surprise.

"Yes, so you see I'm willing to do the *heavy lifting* after all," I said.

Lucy could dish the sarcasm, but she didn't rise when it was directed at her. "Don't worry about catching Sylvia. I'll tell her you're coming. Just go to Avenue Studios at seventy-six Fulham Road whenever you can. She's there every day from sunup to late in the night. She's only at Clement's Inn for a little while on Mondays."

I could barely focus on Lucy's words; my mind was still racing with the fear that Cumberbunch had seen me. "Are you acquainted with a woman in the sewing room? She has red hair and wears spectacles."

Lucy looked at me, puzzled. "Sophie? I know her, sure; why?"

"Does she help with the mural?"

"No, she mainly sews banners and helps sell papers and whatever else we need. Why do you ask?"

"Never mind." I was relieved, but then I realized Sophie Cumberbunch might prove to be an ally. Mamma would never knowingly employ a suffragette, so Cumberbunch had to be sneaking. If she wouldn't help me, I'd threaten to tell on her.

"Well then, just pop in and help when you can. Maybe I'll see you there."

Lucy had turned to go when I called out, "Wait! Just one more thing. Are there any churches near the studio?"

Lucy scrunched up her nose as though I had asked her if there were any dead mice lying about. "Churches?" She shrugged. "I suppose. It is England, after all. Land of churches on every corner. Why?"

"Do you know the name of one?"

"I've seen one called All Saints, if that helps you." She looked at me oddly.

"It does."

"All right, then. Far be it from me to cast aspersions on the devout. Hope to see you there."

I left Lucy and headed back toward Temple Church, passing the time in Lincoln's Inn Gardens until John would collect me. I sat on a park bench and thought again about Cumberbunch. She had to be a secret suffragette. Perhaps Cumberbunch wasn't as much of a creature of my mother's as I had thought.

MY MOTHER WASTED no time tasking Cumberbunch to make an assessment of my wardrobe and a list of things I would need. As my mother had pointed out, I would be making my debut in June, so my youthful ankle-length skirts were no longer appropriate. Nor could I keep wearing my mother's gowns. So the next morning I had to go through my clothing with Cumberbunch.

"I don't really care much for fashion," I said to Cumberbunch. "I'm not one of those girls who feels the need to swan about all done up like a maypole."

"Hmm, is that so?" Cumberbunch said. She was pulling skirts and blouses out of my wardrobe and arranging them in piles on the bed. She was all business now—such a contrast to her carefree demeanor and dress at the WSPU headquarters.

"I don't want a dress that requires one of those long

corsets," I said. "I wore one of my mother's on Friday, and I don't wish to repeat that experience."

"S-bend corsets are going out of fashion," she said. "I can make a ribbon corset for you, Miss Darling. You'll wear it around your middle, and it'll be more comfortable. I'll get some boning tape and ribbons at Liberty."

Liberty, my Aunt Fanny, I thought. More like a quick side trip there and then off to the WSPU headquarters.

"You go to Liberty a lot, it seems," I said, watching her carefully. She was folding one of my shirtwaists and paused. "You know you can place an order. Mrs. Fitzhughes can telephone it in for you."

"That's very kind," Cumberbunch said quickly. "But I prefer to look at the goods before I make my selection." She surveyed the things on my bed. "You have a lot here that I can recut to make new garments. Do you like tailor-mades? The jacket and skirt with a shirtwaist? That will give you the practicality you're looking for. And they aren't cumbersome to wear."

"I liked the green one I saw you—" I snapped my mouth shut. "I mean, I liked one I saw on a girl once."

Cumberbunch blinked. "I . . . all right." She looked taken aback but then she shook her head. "Here, wait a moment. I have something in my room that might do for you." She went away and came back a few moments later with a tie in her hand. "I make these ties from offcut fabrics I find. This one would suit you well, I think." She held out a tie patterned with a repeating design of navy and green plants, red strawberries, and blue and golden birds.

I took it from her and went over to my mirror and

held it up under my chin. I had never seen anything like it. The birds and the flowers mixed with the red berries created an artistic pattern that was reminiscent of the Pre-Raphaelites. The blue of the birds' wings and the flowers brought out the blue in my eyes.

I wanted it. I wanted to wear it more than anything. And I wanted to wear it on Thursday when I met Will.

"What would I wear it with? I don't have a tailor-made."

"You have an older brother don't you?"

"Yes, why?"

"Any chance his boyhood clothes are still about?"

"If they are, they would be in the attic."

"Let's go have a look," Cumberbunch said.

We trooped up the two flights of stairs to the attic. I searched around and found Freddy's trunk under the window next to his old rocking horse and my dollhouse, which was the worse for wear after I had decided to decorate the walls with inky scribbles when I was eight. My mother had not been amused.

Cumberbunch opened the trunk lid, rummaged around, and pulled out a shirt and a collar, setting them to the side. She handed a blue flannel jacket to me. "Try those on, Miss Darling. There are several jackets, summer and winter fabric, in here, all sorts of colors. I can do a lot with those."

I removed my blouse and put the shirt and jacket on. I went over to a hall mirror, which my mother had pronounced old-fashioned, relegating it to the attic forever. I looked ridiculous. I laughed. "This will never do. It's miles too big." I spun around to show her, holding my arms out to my sides. The jacket fell to the middle of my thighs, and the sleeves hung over my hands. "My brother is tall. Even when he was at school he was tall."

"Never mind. That's what I'm here for." She came over and looked at the jacket carefully. Then she pinched in the sides and secured them with pins from a cushion tied around her wrist. "Nip this in a bit here." She folded up the hem so the jacket hit just above my hips. "We'll shorten it to here. See, it will fit you a treat. This is how I get a lot of my clothes. From reach-me-downs on Petticoat Lane in the East End. Can't afford new."

I looked in the mirror again, and suddenly I could see the possibilities. Many tailor-made jackets had puffy sleeves, which I had always thought fussy. This one, being a boy's, did not, but the way Cumberbunch altered it made it look very feminine. It was almost cheeky, as if I were saying, *I could fit right in with the blokes, but I prefer not to.*

"You're very good at this," I said.

"Thank you, miss." She attached the collar and then slid the tie around my neck, wrapping a long end twice around a short end, and then looping it through to create a knot. "There." She stepped back. "I can let the hem down on that silk russet skirt you have. A tailor-made skirt is only meant to be just below the ankle, so there's heaps of room in the hem."

I untied the tie and then tried it myself.

She knelt on the floor and began pinning the bottom of the jacket.

"Do you think you could have this done by Thursday?"

"I don't see why not." She looked like she wanted to ask

me why, but it wasn't her place to ask, and I certainly didn't volunteer any information.

Cumberbunch stood up, fished around in the trunk, and pulled out my brother's straw boater. She reached up and placed the hat on my head and smiled at me in the mirror. "How do you feel about fashion now?"

I adjusted the hat, cocking it forward. I couldn't wait for Will to see me in this new outfit. What would he think of it? What would he think of *me* in it? "I changed my mind," I said. "I like it."

Sixteen

Darling Residence, Tuesday, twenty-third of March
Later in the day, Miss Winthrop's Social Graces Academy, Kensington

THE NEXT DAY, Cumberbunch helped me get
dressed for Miss Winthrop's Crushingly Boring
Social Graces Academy. I sat at the dressing table
while Cumberbunch did my hair, and I thought
about the final piece of the puzzle—art materials. I had a
model, an idea for a reference, and some money. But the
acquisition of art supplies was proving the hardest of all
because the only art shop I knew was in Kensington. There
were no churches nearby, as it was on a busy high street.
Furthermore, I could only fake a charity visit once or twice
a week or Mamma would get suspicious, and I needed
those precious days for drawing Will and for working on
the mural. As it was, I'd have to go to a real meeting once
a week in case Mamma should ask the charity organizers.

What really rankled was the proximity of the art shop
to Miss Winthrop's academy. It was so close—a minute's
walk down Kensington High Street, if even that. If only I
could escape for just a few minutes, I could—

Goose bumps rose on my arms, and I sat very still. I
knew how I could do it. I knew how! But it would take a bit
of planning and some acting.

"Miss?" Cumberbunch was holding my hair in a knot at the top of my head. "Would you like your hair swept up here or rolled at the nape of your neck?"

"Uh, I don't mind. Whatever you prefer." And then I put my hand to my forehead. "Actually, I'm feeling a bit poorly."

"Shall I tell your mother you're unwell?"

"No . . . it's important I should attend. Maybe I'll feel better soon," I said.

"I'll get you some headache powder," Cumberbunch said. She looked at me sideways, hesitated for a moment, and then went to fetch the medicine.

WHEN WE ALIGHTED from the carriage, I waded in with the first part of my scheme.

"Cumberbunch, actually, would you mind at all going to Harrods to purchase some Turkish delight for my aunt's birthday? She loves the pistachio and rose flavors." I held my breath, waiting for her reply.

"Your mother said you were dancing today. Don't you need help changing into your skirt and dancing slippers?" Cumberbunch looked at me strangely when I said no, but it was not a maid's job to question, so she accepted the money I held out and went off toward Knightsbridge.

Thankfully I knew none of the eleven other girls in the class, so there would be no reports to my mother through other girls' mothers. Girls my age were the biggest tattle-tales going. Not a one of them could keep her mouth shut.

Without Cumberbunch's help, it took me longer to

change into my dance things, which was to my benefit. I was able to hold back for a moment as the other girls and their maids went into the ballroom. I tiptoed into the hall and bundled my dance bag behind a potted fern next to the door. Then I joined the class.

Owing to the fact that it was a girls-only class, we were to dance with one another, taking turns to lead. My dancing was terrible because I couldn't concentrate. I was so nervous about my scheme that I kept stepping on my partner's feet and turning right when I was meant to go left.

"Ouch! I say, do pay attention!" my partner said after I had mashed her toes for the third time.

I didn't have a moment to waste, so ten minutes into the class, I told Miss Winthrop that I was unwell. She took me to the dressing room and bade me rest a moment. As soon as she returned to the other dancers, I jumped up from the chaise and crept down the hall, grabbed my dance bag from behind the pot, and stole outside. It was all I could do not to break into a run, so I walked as quickly as I could, dodging around the other pedestrians on the crowded pavement.

And then I was there. My favorite place in all the world: Baldwin Art Purveyors. I had purchased my art materials there practically ever since I could grasp a pencil. I always felt as if nothing horrid could ever happen to me in such a wonderful place.

The tiny shop was at the end of a small arcade of shops. It sat underneath its sign: a drawing of a paint palette. I always loved to see what the owner, Mr. Baldwin, chose for his window display. This time he had arranged a life-size art mannequin dressed in a painter's smock in front of an easel, while another mannequin posed in front of him, arms held aloft.

A bell tinkled as I stepped inside. Although it appeared tiny from the outside, the shop was an Aladdin's cave on the inside. The long room stretched far back and was filled with every imaginable kind of art material. Drawers were crammed with tubes of paint with names like burnt umber, copper beech, cadmium blue, and vermilion. Shelves bristled with jars of paintbrushes, and boxes upon boxes of pencils and pastels of all sorts were stacked from floor to ceiling against one wall. A coal fire flickered merrily in the small fireplace near the till, creating a cozy atmosphere. And there was that deliciously earthy scent of pencil shavings, oil paint, and mineral spirits that I loved so well.

A clerk I had never met before came to the front of the shop. "Good afternoon, miss," he said. "Do you require assistance?"

I looked around me. I hardly knew where to begin. "I am in need of just about everything."

"You are in luck. We have just about everything," he said, smiling.

I drew my list out of my bag, and the two of us went round the shop selecting everything I needed: a Reeves & Sons charcoal set in a pretty beech-wood box with a sliding lid; a silver dip pen; a bottle of golden iron-gall ink and a pot of ebony bister ink; a small tin of conté crayons in portrait colors; a wooden box set filled with both Derwent graphite and colored pencils; two erasers, gum arabic and kneadable; several blending stumps; a glass-paper sanding block; and finally a beautiful new sketch pad with an Italian leather cover filled with cream-colored cartridge paper. I hesitated over a wind-up easel, but it was ridiculous to think I could sneak something that large into my house.

As the clerk toted up my purchases at the till, I wandered over to look at the watercolor caddies, considering whether I needed one or not. Should I show the examiners I had a grasp of something other than drawing? Watercolors weren't my favorite medium—I preferred colored pencils—but I did like the effect of gouache on tinted paper. Maybe next time. My dance bag would be full as it was.

"Miss Darling," a soft voice said.

I turned, and there stood Mr. Baldwin, the shop's owner. He had a solemn look on his face.

"Mr. Baldwin!" I said. "It's been ages since I've seen you. How do you do? The shop looks beautiful, as usual. I've been admiring these caddies. Are they new?" I held one up.

"Miss Darling, I . . . I'm terribly sorry, but I'm going to have to ask you to leave." His homely face crinkled into a frown.

I set the caddy down. "Pardon?"

"It's your father, you see. He sent me a letter saying we weren't to sell you anything, and he closed his account here."

"My father?" I said stupidly, barely able to take in what Mr. Baldwin was saying.

"I do beg your pardon. Mr. Ashby is a new clerk here, otherwise—"

"I have money of my own; I don't need my purchases to go on my father's account, Mr. Baldwin."

He shook his head.

I had known Mr. Baldwin since my childhood. I considered him a friend. He always welcomed me in the shop, even putting to one side new things I might like. The shop was like a second home, and now it was barred to me because of my father. Anger flickered inside me. "But Mr. Baldwin, I'm begging you. All my art materials are gone. I haven't a single stump of pencil to my name."

Mr. Baldwin looked dismayed. "I simply cannot go against your father's request, Miss Darling. I'm sure he has your best interests at heart."

"Who is to know, Mr. Baldwin?" I said pleadingly.

"I feel very badly about what went on in France, Miss Darling. Perhaps if I hadn't encouraged you as much, this wouldn't have happened. And indeed your father made the same assumption in his letter to me."

My face burned, and I was filled with an equal measure of shame and outrage.

No matter how much I begged, he would not budge, and in the end I left the shop empty-handed.

I didn't have time to go to another art shop, even if I knew where one was. Trying desperately not to cry, I walked back to the school. I felt like a marionette where my father was concerned: helpless to do anything on my own, and with one twitch of a cord he could spin me in any direction he wished. Soon, soon I would be away from his control.

I would have married Edmund the next day, if I could have.

I turned the corner to Miss Winthrop's, and there was Cumberbunch standing by a lamppost, arms folded, green eyes regarding me from behind her steel spectacles.

I stopped short. My mouth went dry.

"Lovely afternoon for a walk, don't you think?" Cumberbunch said.

"Uh, well . . . I—"

"Went shopping, did you?" she asked matter-of-factly.

I started, and then looked at her, incredulous. "How did you know? Were you spying on me?" I spluttered.

She regarded me. "No. Your mother told me you weren't to go near an art shop. I wondered if you'd try to find a way."

"So what if I did?" I asked. "What do you intend to do about it?"

"I'm assuming they wouldn't sell to you?"

I quickened my step and strode ahead of her; my dance skirt swished about my ankles.

"I know you don't wish me to pry into your affairs," Cumberbunch called.

"So don't!" I threw the words over my shoulder. "I know you're planning on telling my mother."

"I won't tell her."

I stopped abruptly and turned around. "Whyever not?" I said, watching her draw near. "My mother employs you, and your loyalties must lie with her, after all. But know that if you tattle on me, then I'll tattle on you. I saw you at the WSPU headquarters, and my parents would not be glad to know they have a suffragette in their employ."

Her eyes widened and her mouth dropped open. "You were there?" she said quietly.

"I was."

We were blocking the pavement, and people were moving around us, grumbling, so we started walking back to the academy.

"If you feel you need to tell your mother that I belong to the WSPU, then do," Cumberbunch said. "But I won't tattle on you."

I was still wary. "Why not?"

"Your mother hired me to sort your clothes and chaperone you about, not to spy on you and stomp on your dreams. You saw me at the WSPU so you know we're all about helping women, and I've pledged to do that, no matter my occupation. I had someone help me when I was just an orphan. She taught me all about sewing and fashion and helped me get my first job with the Hollingberrys. I know I'm only your lady's maid, granted, but I can't see as that's a barrier between us. May I ask why *you* were there?"

I hesitated, unsure of how much to trust her. "I wanted to see what it was about. I was meant to go to my church charity, but I went there instead."

She nodded. "Now, do you want those art things or not?"

"What do you mean?"

She held out her hand. "I can't buy them without money."

I stared at her for a long moment. Then I handed her my purse.

"Do you have a list?"

I handed that over and my bag as well.

"So get back in there, dance your feet off, and I'll go to that art store and get them for you."

"I won't tell I saw you at the headquarters. I wouldn't. I was just saying that, Cumberbunch." I felt ashamed.

"I know you wouldn't."

And good as her word, she met me after the class, my dance bag filled with everything I wanted.

Seventeen

TRUE TO HER word, Cumberbunch completed the alterations on my brother's garments in time. The tailor-made fit perfectly. She had removed the fussy flounce from my skirt and dropped the hem. I didn't feel as though I looked like anybody else, even though tailor-mades were very popular. Cumberbunch had made this one my own. She had even trimmed my brother's boater with a navy-blue satin ribbon, tying it into a large bow on one side, which gave the otherwise masculine hat a very feminine touch. She braided my hair into one long plait and then twisted that into an intricate bun at the base of my neck.

With the patterned tie knotted under my collar, and the altered jacket, I felt so much surer of myself. I stood a little taller, held my head a little higher in it. I felt more grown-up in it, too. Gone was the teenage girl with her hair dangling down her back and ankle-length skirts with babyish flounces.

I hugged Cumberbunch hard. "Thank you. I can't wait for Will to see me in this."

"Who's Will?" she asked, readjusting my tie. "I thought

your fiancé was called Edmund. Or did I get that wrong?"

I felt the smile fade from my face. In my excitement over the new frock, I'd let Will's name slip out.

"Am I wrong?" Cumberbunch asked again, confusion on her face.

I sat down on the edge of my bed. "Can I tell you something? A secret?"

She nodded, watching me carefully.

I took a breath. "Will is my art model. I'm drawing him so that I can work on my application to art school. By the time school begins, I'll be married, so it's really nothing to do with my parents. But if they knew, they'd forbid me. You might as well know the rest, because you might hear about it anyway. I'm going to help Sylvia Pankhurst with the mural, the one for the Women's Exhibition."

Cumberbunch's eyes brightened. "But that's wonderful! I'm helping trim hats and make scarves for the exhibition, myself. And the art-model thing sounds innocent enough. Your secret's safe with me."

I stood up and hugged her again. "Thank you, Cumberbunch!"

She blushed deeply and looked pleased. "Can you call me Sophie? I know it's not the done thing to call a lady's maid by her Christian name, but I can't stick my surname."

"Sophie it is, but I'd better call you Cumberbunch in front of my mother or she'll have both our heads."

I couldn't imagine ever confiding in any of the servants like that, and I suppose Sophie made me think about them in a different light. My mother always forbade me to engage them in conversation apart from discussing the business at hand. I knew my mother was close to her lady's maid, Bailey, but that closeness was one-sided. My mother controlled that relationship completely. If she grew tired of Bailey, or if Bailey overstepped the line, my mother could dismiss her. I had to remember that Mamma could do the same with Sophie.

I WAS ON my way out to my adventures, heading down the stairs of my house, when I saw Papa standing in the hall, a look of bewilderment on his face. He was staring at the new telephone, a copper upright desk stand with ornamental finishing, on the hall table. I was surprised to see him home in the middle of the day.

I paused, my hand on the newel post. "Good afternoon, Papa," I said.

He looked up. "Victoria. My, you look so grown-up. Very fetching, my dear." He stared at the telephone again.

"I'm going to my church charity. Do you wish to make a telephone call?"

He rubbed his hand over his jaw. "I would prefer not to, but Frederick says I must embrace this new machinery or else be left behind." He clasped his hands behind his back. "I must say I feel the fool. How does one speak into such an apparatus? I feel as though I'm talking to a doorstop."

"It is intimidating the first time you make a call."

"Have you made one?" Papa looked surprised.

I nodded. "Lily's family has a telephone. When I was visiting their home in France, she showed me how to work it. It's ever so much fun, once you get the way of it." I held out my hand. "Would you like me to show you?"

"Hmm, yes. I would."

I sat and demonstrated. "You sit on this little bench here and rest your elbow on the table, like so. You want to hold the receiver to your ear with that hand. And speak into the mouthpiece here."

"How do you contact the person you want to speak to?"

"Press down this little lever and wait for the operator to answer. You give her your party's details and she'll connect you. If you want to answer when it rings, simply lift the receiver and speak."

"Well, I never! Aren't you clever? Does one have to shout to be heard?" Papa asked, warming to the subject.

"Not at all. Only your normal voice is required." I stood up. "Would you like to have a go?"

Papa sat down and I directed him through the steps. He flinched and pulled the receiver away from his ear when the operator answered, but he soldiered on and placed his call. I waited to make sure he was comfortable before I went on my way. When I left, he smiled at me.

JOHN TOOK ME to All Saints Church in the carriage mid-morning. I'd told Mamma I'd be coming home in a friend's carriage. Of course, in reality I'd make my own way back.

I walked up and down the Fulham Road but I didn't see the address or anything that resembled an art studio. I was growing frustrated but then finally I found it behind the main buildings, down a quiet tree-filled mews. The studio was a large brick building with arched windows and a large black door bordered by a white colonnade. AVENUE STUDIOS was printed on the window. Someone had planted pansies and daffodils in tubs on either side of the door.

I went inside and immediately the scent of art hit me: an earthy aroma of clay and the woodsy perfume of oil of turpentine. I walked down a long hallway bordered by doors leading to art studios. Avenue Studios was a much larger space than Monsieur Tondreau's, which had consisted of one small room. Some of the doors were open, and I saw sculptors at work in one and a painter working on a large canvas in another. Behind a closed door, someone was playing classical music on a gramophone. There was a lot of activity coming from a studio at the end of the corridor. I could hear a murmur of voices, a bang as someone dropped something, and the swooshing sound of someone dragging heavy material across the floor. Then I saw *Studio 1a: Sylvia Pankhurst* written on a sign outside a door. I stepped inside.

When Lucy first mentioned the mural, I assumed it would be a simple affair, a large picture with a motto to hang against one wall, but what I saw took my breath away. The cavernous space of the studio was hung floor to ceiling with several canvases. Some were still blank and some were traced with patterns of angels, flowers, trees, doves, and wildlife. One of the canvases was already finished; it featured a figure of a woman sowing grain. It was ten feet high, maybe even more. There were several artists at work—half were women and half were men. Some stood on ladders or knelt on mats filling in color with paintbrushes; others were moving huge canvases around.

"Excuse me," said an artist carrying a panel. "Can I get by, please?"

"I beg your pardon." I stepped out of the way, and he hoisted the panel over his head and continued on. I took a couple of steps after him. "Excuse me, I wonder . . ." But he didn't stop.

I looked around. Everyone was busy doing something. I felt completely insignificant. Engrossed in their work, as artists were wont to be, no one took any notice of me. I eyed the door, thinking maybe the best action would be to leave and come back another day.

No. I was here now; I'd just have to wait.

Over by the window, I spotted a taboret laden with an untidy jumble of oil-paint tubes, mahl sticks, rags, and jars with brush handles poking out. From time to time, I had cleaned the brushes for the more experienced students at Monsieur's, so I knew how to do it. I headed for the table and got to work. I wiped each brush clean with a rag dampened with turpentine and rinsed it in a bottle filled with mineral spirits. Under a pile of rags I unearthed a paintbrush comb and ran it through each brush to get the dried paint out. I was organizing all the oil tubes according to color—mostly white, purple, and emerald green—when someone spoke.

"You look like you know what you're doing there." A woman dressed in a plain cotton blouse and wool skirt stood by the table. Her dark-blonde hair was piled up onto her head in a messy bun that was held together with two pencils. She had a kindly look about her, but dark circles smudged her eyes, as if she'd had no sleep for some time.

"It's good of you to do that. Someone's always meaning to do it, but we're so busy around here that brush cleaning gets put off." She pulled a face. "Shame to treat good brushes that way." She held out her hand. "I'm Sylvia Pankhurst."

What luck! I shook Sylvia's hand. "Pleased to make your acquaintance. I'm Vicky Darling. I was told by Lucy Hawkins that you required artists to help with the mural."

"I do. I've undertaken a vast project, I'm afraid to admit," Sylvia said. "I began in February and already I'm exhausted. Several of my friends from art school have helped me, but it's still a huge undertaking." Then she broke off; her gaze fell on the tie Sophie had given me. "William Morris's *Strawberry Thief*, isn't it?"

I looked down at my tie. "Is it?"

"I'd know that pattern anywhere. We studied Morris when I attended the RCA. He was the leader of the Arts and Crafts movement, and a student of the Pre-Raphaelites. How clever of you to wear it as a tie." Sylvia smiled. "Very artistic."

How had Sophie understood how to reflect my personality so quickly? To suggest an accessory that harkened to the Pre-Raphaelites? I had assumed she was in league with my mother then, but she had dressed me exactly the way I wanted to dress without my knowing it myself.

"Your mural reminds me of the Pre-Raphaelite Brotherhood," I said.

"They were my inspiration for the mural! Their use of symbolism is extraordinary." Sylvia's face held the slightly maniacal expression all artists seem to have when discussing painters they love. "The woman planting grain symbolizes hope. I'm going to add another woman har-vesting the wheat. So she's reaping what the other woman has sown. I need to draw some ideas first."

Needing to make an impression on Sylvia right away, I waded in. "I . . . I could sketch it for you," I said, feeling suddenly shy. "If you like, I mean. I attended an atelier in France. I have nearly a year's training in life studies. You don't have to say yes. I'm happy with doing basic work, too."

I was happy to see that Sylvia looked relieved when I suggested this. Sometimes artists didn't like others to inter-fere with their designs. So far I'd impressed Sylvia with my brush cleaning and my sense of fashion. If she liked my sketch and I showed commitment to the mural, maybe she'd write the reference letter for me. I had to put in the time, however. I knew I couldn't just come once or twice. I had to show Sylvia exactly what I could do. I needed a true reference that reflected my work, not just some generic letter.

Sylvia set me up at a makeshift table and I got to work, and for the next hour I was so engrossed that I barely noticed when someone came up. I felt a tap on my shoul-der, looked up, and saw Lucy standing there, but for a moment I didn't recognize her. Gone were the serviceable clothes. Today she was wearing a loose scoop-neck dress with wide sleeves and an elaborately embroidered bodice. Her dark, curly hair, freed from the clutches of her felt hat, tumbled down her back.

"I was wondering when you were going to show up," she said. "How was church?"

"Church?"

"Didn't you go to church first?" Lucy said, raising her eyebrows.

"Oh, that!" I shrugged. "I don't actually *go* to church. I tell my mother I'm going to a church charity. It's how I get out of the house."

Lucy hooked her foot around the leg of a stool, dragged it over, and sat down. "What's the matter? She won't let you keep company with suffragettes?"

"Let's just say the word *suffrage* is not to be uttered in our home. Among many other things."

"Welcome to the club." She waved her hand at a girl around our age, standing on a ladder painting. "Clara isn't supposed to be here either."

I touched the embroidery on Lucy's sleeve. "You look like a medieval maid. Beautiful."

"I only wear that other hideous outfit at the rubber factory and when I'm working for the WSPU. As you saw, sometimes the coppers get a bit handsy. Often people throw rotten veg at us, too."

"Why do you work in a rubber factory?"

"Some of us have to work," she said, looking at me askance.

"Oh," I said, feeling like a toff. "Of course. I didn't think."

"It's not like I get my fun there or anything. I need the money. I came over to study jewelry making at Goldsmiths College, but my dad won't send my tuition," Lucy said, resting her chin in her hand. "He wants me to come home. So I do piecework at a factory in Lambeth. It pays for my tuition and I rent a flat in Clement's Inn, above the headquarters. Mr. Pethick-Lawrence owns a bunch and lets them out cheap to WSPU members. That doesn't leave much else, but I make jewelry in suffragette colors and sell it at department stores. Suffragette jewelry is very chic, and Selfridge's, that new department store on Oxford Street, buys all I can make."

At that moment, the door opened and a disheveled teenage boy burst into the room. He was very delicate, almost elf-like, with blond hair and blue eyes. Tall and whippet thin, he looked as though the slightest breeze could bowl him right over.

"That's Sylvia and Christabel Pankhurst's little brother, Harry," Lucy whispered. "He showed up on Sylvia's doorstep awhile back. Did a bunk from his job as a builder up north in Clydesdale. Best thing he did, really. Can you imagine him carrying bricks and climbing scaffolding? Some say he's the only girl in the family."

"He looks very young," I admitted.

"He's nineteen. He's been helping Sylvia with the murals, carrying things and filling in color."

Seeing Lucy and me, Harry came over. Lucy introduced us.

"Hello." He waved his hand.

"I'd better go help," Lucy said, standing up. "I'm not much of a painter, but I do the grunt work."

"Are you an artist, Harry?" I asked after Lucy had gone off.

"I dabble. I'm nothing like my sister. I'm really just putting in the colors."

"Oi, Harry. Who's your girl?" one of the artists, a slender

blond man in his twenties, dressed in a purple waistcoat and striped trousers, called down from a ladder.

I could see a slow flush crawl up Harry's neck. He shot a quick look at me. "She's . . . she's not my girl, Austin." To me, Harry added, "That's one of Sylvia's friends from the art college. Austin Osman Spare."

Austin waved his paintbrush at me. "How d'ya do?"

"I'm quite finished with my sketch," I said, looking up at him. I had a little time to spare before I had to leave to meet Will at the Royal Academy. "Would you like some help?"

He gestured at an empty ladder near him. "Come on up!"

Harry set me up with paints and brushes, and I got to work between Austin and Harry filling in the colors—violet, green, and white—on the garland of ivy and flowers that arched over the canvas.

ur we all broke for tea. I met some other owning, who was another friend of Sylvia's nd Clara Watson, the other girl whose par- t her at the mural.

vas laughing and eating sandwiches and ut of chipped mugs. The scene reminded Le déjeuner des canotiers, which depicted a luncheon at the Maison Fournaise restaurant held after he and his artist friends had been boating on the Seine. The mural artists had the same carefree and exuberant expressions as Renoir's friends in the painting. Automatically, I reached for my sketchbook and began to draw.

No one chastised me or looked embarrassed to see me drawing them. Artists knew what it was to have an idea and itch to get it down on paper as soon as possible. I drew

Austin sitting on a stool, his elbow braced on his knee. I drew Harry sprawled in his chair, nibbling a digestive biscuit, head ducking shyly; Amy, Clara, and Lucy leaning forward, laughing at what Austin was saying to Harry. And then Sylvia sitting with her hands resting in her lap, eyes closed, stealing a moment's calm. I didn't know Will all that well, but I could see him sitting there, too. He'd fit right into the picture.

A familiar feeling washed over me as I drew. It was the one I'd had with Bertram and the other artists in the café that day in France after I had posed. I felt accepted for who I was. I didn't have to sort the words in my head first, making sure they were socially acceptable before I said them. I groped around for a word that fit.

Peace. I felt peaceful. I had come looking for a reference, but I had found so much more. I knew I would come back.

Eighteen

I CHECKED MY PENDANT watch for the third time as the driver pulled the cab up at the Burlington Arcade. Because of traffic, I was a quarter of an hour late. I hoped Will was still there. *What if he left, thinking I'd changed my mind?* I paid the cab driver and hurried through the crush of pedestrians to the stately Burlington House, home of the Royal Academy.

Will hadn't left. He was waiting underneath one of the arches, leaning against the stone, hands in his pockets, watching the people walk by on the pavement. He was not in his police uniform; instead he was wearing a flat cheese-cutter cap, dark-green trousers, and a herringbone tweed jacket that looked a little big for him.

I hurried up to him. "I beg your pardon, I'm ever so late."

But Will simply glanced at me and then went back to scanning the crowd.

"Will!"

He glanced at me again. "Vicky? I didn't recognize you." Close up, Will's ill-fitting jacket was frayed at the cuffs. But it was clean, and his trousers were neatly pressed, which gave him an endearing shabbiness.

"I'm not surprised. Almost every time you've seen me, I've been in some sort of horrid state, either falling on you or dripping with rain or running away from you."

"You forgot tripping over barrels."

"That too."

He looked at me for a moment. "You look so different. You look . . . smashing, actually."

"Thank you." I was pleased that Will noticed. More than pleased, actually. Far too pleased.

"Talking of those barrels. How are your hands?"

"Much better." I held out my palms.

"I thought my clumsy nursing might have made them worse instead of better." He ran his fingers over the fading scrapes, and I shivered at his touch. He had beautiful hands: large, callused, and strong, the sort of hands an artist dreams of sketching. I thought about drawing them in a study, his hand lying on the curve of Guinevere's breast; male strength against female vulnerability. I wondered what the RCA examiners would think of that?

"I hope you haven't been waiting long," I said, taking my hand away from his before I had any more wicked ideas of ways to draw him.

"Not long." He looked through the archway toward the entrance of the academy. "I've never been in here. I've gone by it lots of times on my beat."

"My favorite painting hangs here. I come by to see it whenever I can."

We went through the archway and to a place in the courtyard where I liked to sit and sketch while my mother went shopping in the arcade next door. It was bright and peaceful in the courtyard. Will and I sat down on a bench, and I got my pencils and sketchbook out. I took a graphite pencil out of the box and sharpened it with a fruit knife I had taken from the kitchen pantry. I planned to sketch Will's face. Faces were difficult to draw. They caught and reflected the light in so many different ways. Expressions were ever changing and were complicated things to capture on paper.

"I wish to make sketches first. I have an idea to do a study portraying you as Lancelot, just after he sees Guinevere for the last time." I had decided I would include the studies in my sketchbook for my application and then show a pastel sketch for the further work that was required for the examination. "Do you know the story?" I asked.

"Of course. Lancelot and Guinevere fall in love, and King Author sentences her to burn at the stake for it. Lancelot rescues her, but they can't be together. She goes to a nunnery, and he goes to war."

"Dante Gabriel Rossetti portrayed their last meeting. I'd like to show only Lancelot as he watches Guinevere walk away."

"What should I do?" Will asked. "I know you told me to keep still and keep my gob shut, but I suspect there's more."

"Do you mind taking your cap off so I can see your face?"

He did so and ran his fingers through his hair.

"If you can think about what Lancelot thought and felt when he saw her, that will appear in your expression," I said. "I won't tell you what to think because that would ring false."

"Like this?" He opened his eyes wide.

"Uh, less like you're longing for presents from Father Christmas."

He laughed. "How about this?" He stared at me with a startled look.

"Now you look as though you've backed into a cactus."

He put his chin in his hand and gazed at me. "Well then, how do you mean?"

"Don't try so hard. Think about something you really want but that's denied to you . . . your stories. Think about what it would feel like if they were never published."

"That makes me feel sick. Father Christmas and the cactus might be preferable."

"Don't worry about it; we'll work on expression later." I began to sketch an oval outline that tapered down at the bottom. I divided that with vertical and horizontal lines, which would help me block the basic details in the right proportions. I looked up to get the measure of his eyes.

"Um, do you mind turning your shoulders a bit that way?" I gestured with my pencil. I was suddenly feeling shy in front of him. Drawing someone, especially someone sitting so close, was an enormously intimate endeavor. The artist had to really look at the person's features closely. And it felt awkward to look at Will so. I'd only ever drawn people in a studio setting with other artists, and strangers from a distance. I'd never had a personal model before. I was frustrated. With such a large body of work to complete in such a short while, I didn't have much time for this nonsense. I was sure the Pre-Raphaelites never felt nervous around their models. Then again, the Pre-Raphaelites and their models were often lovers. *Will and I, lovers?* That thought flitted across my mind for a brief second before I pushed it away. Such a traitorous thought for a woman engaged.

"This way?" He shifted the wrong way, and the light fell upon his lap instead.

"No, actually . . ." I stuck my pencil in my mouth and placed my hands on his shoulders, turning them so that a flash of sunlight fell upon his face. Then, realizing what I was doing, I dropped my hands away from him quickly. I took my pencil out of my mouth and bunched my hands in my lap, my fingers squeezing the pencil. "I'm sorry; forgive me." I felt like a stupid girl, dressed in her brother's clothes, pretending to be an artist.

"It's all right, Vicky, I'm not bothered," Will said gently.

I returned to my sketch, but every time I looked at his face, his eyes met mine and I got flustered. This was pointless. If I didn't get over my nerves, then what was the idea of the whole exercise?

"I'm putting you off," Will said. "But I understand. We didn't start out on the best foot, as it goes. Why don't we just talk a little more?" He reached over and took my pencil from my hand. "Forget the drawing for a bit."

I shrugged, casting about for something to ask him. I'd never had a conversation with a boy like him before. Most of the boys I knew wanted to talk about shooting grouse or yachting at Cowes or how their racehorse did at Newmarket. They were crushingly boring, actually. "How long have you been a police constable?" I finally asked.

"A little under a year. I joined at seventeen. Coming to

London was a shocker for me. I still haven't gotten used to the noise and the crowds of the city. I'd never been out of East Sussex before, see."

"Really? Never ever? East Sussex is only a couple of hours away from London by train, is it not?"

"It's not far, which is good because I get home every once in a while. My mum and dad and sister and nephew still live in East Sussex. My dad is the constable in a little village there called Rye, as was his father before him."

"What's it like there?" Will was right. Talking helped ease some of the nerves I had around him. I could feel my shoulders relaxing. I loved the way he spoke. Will didn't have the drawn-out gentrified drawl that the boys I knew affected, learned at some boarding school. He spoke in a quick, almost cheeky, manner.

"It used to be a smugglers' den, if you want to know the truth of it. There's an old inn there where they used to do their evil deeds. They say it's haunted as anything. You'd like it. Lots of artists do because of the beauty and solitude. The American writer Henry James lives near my parents' house, and my mum does his laundry. He's quite friendly, always happy to give me advice. One time I went over to deliver his laundry, and H. G. Wells and Rudyard Kipling were there." There was wistfulness in Will's voice.

"It sounds as though you miss it."

"I do. Very much." He looked down at my charcoal pencil, turning it over in his fingers.

"So why did you leave?"

"To make my fortune, I suppose, although a London bobby will never make a fortune, but it's a sight better than what a small-town copper would make. My story is set in London, so I wanted to stick myself in that setting. Helps me understand my characters better."

"It's such an artist thing to do," I said.

"It is?" Will looked surprised. "That's good to know. I'll have to tell my parents that. They still aren't thrilled I left. My dad was hoping I'd join the police in Rye."

"My friend Bertram moved to France because the light is better there for painting."

I studied the cover of my sketchbook, traced my fingers over the leather. I felt less anxious now, but I didn't want to stop talking to Will. "Will you tell me about your story?" I asked.

Now it was Will's turn to look anxious. He had an expression on his face that I recognized: unsure, as though he might not describe the work well enough; worried that the person might misunderstand and he would appear foolish.

"It's a modern-day retelling of Robin Hood," he started out slowly, fixing his gaze on one of the paving stones in the courtyard. "Only my character's name is Robert Hoode and he's a politician." He darted a look at me, seemingly gauging my reaction. I nodded, *Go on*. "He steals from the upper class and gives to the poor in the East End. Because he couldn't right the wrongs done to the poor through the law, he finds ways to swindle the rich and give the prizes to the poor."

"But that's a brilliant story, Will! I can think of illustrations already." I wasn't just saying that; the story was intriguing, and ideas were popping into my mind.

"Really?" Will asked, his eyes hopeful. "I've never told anyone about it before. Only you."

"It's exactly the kind of thing my brother does in his publishing company." I took my pencil back from Will, opened my book, and did a quick scribble of Hoode. Will leaned over, watching closely. "Something like this?"

"Yes! That's it. You've got the way of him."

"I'll see what I can do."

He grinned. "So enough about me. What about you? What are you going to do?"

I shook my head. "I'm going to the art college, like I told you before." *And I will be married then, and I won't know you anymore,* I thought. I doubted Edmund would welcome my having a personal model, especially a male one—especially one as handsome as Will. Despite how modern Edmund was, for his wife to keep company with another man would border on scandalous. I didn't wish to have my marriage end up like Louis Trevelyan and Emily Rowley's in Anthony Trollope's novel *He Knew He Was Right.* At Madame Édith's Finishing School for Girls, the literature tutor wielded the book as a cautionary tale to us hapless girls. *Never be alone with a man, ladies, lest you be accused of something unsavory,* she had said. I don't think my tutor understood the irony of the book, and that Trollope was sympathetic to the wife, but that was Madame Édith's Finishing School for Girls.

"Yes, but then what?" Will asked. "Do you want to live somewhere else? I hear there are many artists in Cornwall, in Newlyn. Or do you want to go back to France?" His face softened. "You look upset. I'm sorry; I shouldn't have mentioned France."

I looked away, praying that I wouldn't start blubbing. Thinking about France still hurt. Will, thankfully, stopped asking questions. Instead he glanced around the courtyard. Then he finally broke the silence.

"Say, why don't you put your sketchbook away, and you can show me that painting you mentioned before?" he said.

Grateful for the suggestion, I put my things in my satchel and we went into the Academy. As we approached *A Mermaid*, I could feel that eager tug I always had when I came to see her. It was as if she were an old friend I couldn't wait to greet.

Will and I turned the corner and there she was, sitting on her tail on the shoreline, combing her long red hair with her mother-of-pearl comb, her mouth open in song. I could almost hear the waves of the sea as they purled toward the shore, and smell the brackish scent of the foamy water in the bay and the seaweed on the shingle. The towering cliffs stood sentinel, protecting her from prying eyes. Her gaze looked out at the viewer as if to say, *Where have you been? I've been waiting for you for ages.*

The carefree independence of the mermaid constantly touched something inside me. I supposed that was why I liked the Pre-Raphaelites and their successors so much. They chose to paint things that human beings would never see on earth, only in imagination. Fanciful things, like this mermaid. Subjects like these made you imagine that life could be far, far different than you ever thought.

"'Who would be a mermaid fair, singing alone, combing her hair,'" Will quoted as we stopped in front of her and stood side by side.

"You know Tennyson's poem?" I said, surprised.

"Yes, 'The Mermaid.'"

"They say the artist of this painting, J. W. Waterhouse, drew his inspiration from that."

"I believe it. She's Tennyson's poem in perfect illustration." He clasped his hands behind his back and leaned forward for a closer look, giving her his full attention. Would Edmund look at her in that fashion? I wondered. And if he didn't, would it matter to me?

"Waterhouse is such a successful artist," I said. "People love him. When he donated this painting as his diploma work, everyone raved about it. See how her tail shimmers? And the rocks and seaweed around her have such texture and color. Each one is different. And the iridescence in the abalone shell where she keeps her pearls? No one can match Waterhouse for that technique."

"Maybe you will someday. You'll go to the art college, learn lots, and be a big success, like this chap."

"I should like to be a mermaid fair. Like her."

"Why do you say that?" he asked, pulling his gaze away from the painting and squinting at me.

"She knows where she belongs, where she fits in. No one tells her what to do or how to spend her days. She's completely and utterly free."

"And you are not?"

I shrugged. "Who is? No one really. Well, no woman at least."

"That's a very melancholy thing to say," Will said, a note of surprise in his voice.

"It might be to you. You're a man; you can do as you wish, Will. Women cannot."

"Rubbish. That doesn't have to be so."

"It's very difficult." I shot him a look of irritation.

"So why should that stop you from doing what you want?" He sounded agitated, almost cross with me. "What would you rather be? Free, or trapped in a place where it isn't difficult?"

"Who says I'm trapped?" I could feel the tension returning between us, taking us back to the place where we both started. I was almost sorry I had brought him to see *A Mermaid.* Here he was judging me once again, when he truly knew nothing about me.

"Don't let's quarrel in front of her." I backed away from him and started to walk down the hall, leaving Will standing by himself.

"Wait." Will came up behind me and said quickly, "Vicky, I wasn't trying to argue with you. Will you slow down?"

I stopped and glared at him.

"I've known you for only a little while, yet I've seen that temper of yours come out lots." People were beginning to stare, so Will lowered his voice. "You're happy to cause a ruck over some things, but it seems to me not when it counts most."

"Cause a ruck? How dare you!"

"I don't mean that in a bad way. You told me yourself, your parents won't let you draw. That isn't fair. Do you think you're the only woman who is prevented from living her life as she sees fit? Instead of accepting all of this as 'oh, well, that's just the way it is,' you should be doing something about that."

I snorted. "And how could I do that, Will? Barge in to Parliament and demand justice? You've been reading too many penny novelettes."

"The suffragettes are doing that very thing."

"What is my life to do with you? We have a business arrangement between us, William Fletcher, and don't you forget it." I knew from the look on his face that my words had stung him, but I didn't give a fig.

He nodded, his face suddenly serious. "Please yourself."

We walked out of the building, but we really weren't walking together. It was as though we were both simply heading in the same direction.

"Here." Will pulled a bundle of papers folded in half and tied round with rough twine from his jacket pocket. "It's my first chapter. See what you can come up with for illustrations and we'll talk it over next Thursday."

I took the papers. Our fingers touched briefly, and without another word Will left.

Nineteen

*Darling Residence, Liberty, Miss Winthrop's Social Graces Academy,
Avenue Studios, Piccadilly Circus, twenty-sixth to twenty-eighth of March,
Friday, Saturday, and Sunday*

"ELL, HOW DID it go with your art model?" Sophie asked me that night as she helped me get ready for bed.

"He's pigheaded," I said. Even hours later I was still in a foul mood from my row with Will.

"What man isn't." She smiled at me in the mirror.

"He has an extra measure of pigheadedness, then." I picked up my jar of face cream and then plonked it back down again, too irritated to care about my complexion.

"All right then, what about the mural?"

"I loved that! I had no idea how much art the WSPU used and how they used it. Truly the mural is amazing. I think I want to be part of what they are doing."

"I'm glad. I'm happiest when I see young women fighting for the right to vote."

"Have you been going there long?"

"I started in Huddersfield up north, where I'm from. Dora, the woman who taught me to sew, told me about the WSPU. I went to a meeting with her there and I bought a pin. But when I came down to London to seek a position as a lady's maid, I was daft and wore it to an interview. As soon as I sat down, the lady of the house saw the pin and asked me to leave."

"That's so unfair!"

"That's the way it is." Sophie shook her head. She picked up my silver hairbrush and began to brush my hair. "So many women of the older generation are the same. They think life is never going to change and they either like it the way it is or they think they'll just put up with the struggle."

She set the brush down and unbuttoned the top buttons of her blouse, and I saw the enameled badge she was wearing the other day pinned on her chemise. Up close I saw it had an angel blowing a trumpet, with a scroll at her feet that read **Votes for Women**. "Even if no one else can see it, I know it's here." She folded the skirt back and patted it. "Dora and the WSPU made me believe I could be more than just an orphan, and that's helped me change my life. I'm happy you're of the same mind."

In the next few days I was the dutiful daughter. I did my mother's bidding, attending Miss Winthrop's, going to the church charity on Saturday, and arranging my trousseau with Sophie every afternoon.

But the mornings were mine. I worked as soon as the sun rose in the sky. During the hours before breakfast, I could work on my college submissions and Will's illustrations uninterrupted and without anyone knowing about it, as long as I had sufficient sunlight and didn't have to turn on the lamp. I worked on Will's story illustrations, and, from memory, finished the sketch I had started of his face. I even started a study of my own hand to demonstrate my grasp of anatomy.

I would draw until Emma knocked on the door with my cup of chocolate. Then I hid my art materials, taking care that not a pencil shaving or a stub of charcoal was left out. Everything went back into a hatbox, which I shoved deep into my wardrobe where no one but Sophie would ever look. I also had to make sure that not a spot of ink or smudge of charcoal remained on my hands. Ink was ever so hard to get out, and I had to scrub my fingers with carbolic soap and a pumice stone till they were nearly red raw.

I had been right: Will's story was brilliant. My brother Freddy and all the tuppenny novelette publishers in London would be lining up to publish it. In the first installment, Will introduced Robert Hoode as a politician working to change the labor laws but to no avail. I drew Hoode standing in the House of Commons giving a passionate speech while his peers ignored him. I drew some politicians yawning, some laughing, and some sleeping with their heads lolling to one side. I drew a group of men playing whist and another group tucking into a large meal of roast goose. I used diluted ink to wash the room in basic tonal elements, but then I used my dip pen with a fine nib to pick out the decorative architecture of the House of Commons and the angry expression on Hoode's face.

I liked the work so much that I wanted to include it in my submission to the RCA. So I did several preliminary sketches in my book first, and then a final illustration on its own to give to Will when we met again on Thursday.

On Sunday after church, my parents and I went to Freddy's for tea. Rose had not come to church, as she had begun her confinement. She had grown huge as a draft horse in the ten days since I had seen her last; it was impossible to imagine her having a child that large. My father looked appalled and avoided her completely, choosing instead to drink his tea quickly and insist that he and Freddy leave for the Reform Club earlier than they usually did. Rose did not appear to notice the snub, but I was angry with my father. As much as I disliked Rose, she was not at fault for getting so fat. Surely having a child grow within you was bound to wreak havoc with your figure. Then I started thinking about how that might be me in not such a long space of time. I wasn't stupid. I only hoped that I could put a baby off until I had finished college. But how could I do that? Nature would certainly take its course.

And so I was feeling quite gloomy all round. When my mother and Rose went up to inspect the nursery, I declined to go. Instead I sat with Charlotte in the window seat, reading *The Tale of Peter Rabbit* to Charlotte. A policeman walked past the window then, swinging his stick, and my mind leapt to Will.

I felt badly about what had happened between us in front of *A Mermaid*. A boy had never spoken to me so frankly before, and it quite took me off guard. Telling me that I wasn't willing to fight for what was important? He had no idea how hard I had to work to put pen to paper without my parents knowing it. Why Will bothered to say such things to me I couldn't fathom.

But why I cared at all was even more of a mystery to me. As I'd said, we had a business arrangement. That was all.

IT WAS RAINY and gray and foggy on Monday, and there was little light to work by, so I stuffed a petticoat into the crack under my bedroom door and turned on a lamp. But I was too tense to really concentrate; I was worried one of the servants would see the door stopped up and make a comment. So I gave it up as a bad job and climbed back into bed, feeling very cross.

I swear the sky brightened the very minute Emma knocked on the door with my morning cocoa. But then there was no time to spare for drawing. Sophie, Mamma, and I went off to Liberty on Regent Street straight after breakfast to choose material and sundries for my trousseau. To add even further insult to injury, I would have to endure Miss Winthrop's after we left Liberty.

"Victoria will need an automobile coat, an excursion suit, and several lingerie gowns for her at-homes," Mamma said. We were standing in the dry-goods department at Liberty, surrounded by bolts of cloth, froufrou lace trim, and whim-whams of all sorts. The sharp scent of starch, sizing, and cotton made my nose clog. "What color do you suggest for her engagement ball gown? Something in pink, perhaps?"

Pink was my mother's favorite color and my least. I must have looked dismayed, because Sophie waded in with a suggestion. "I think Miss Darling would look smashing in a sunny yellow mousseline de soie."

"Yellow?" My mother looked doubtful. "Yellow is not very chic, Cumberbunch."

Sophie pulled out a wooden spindle that was hung with a daffodil-yellow material. She held a swatch of the fabric to my face. "You see, saturated colors—deep yellow, blue, orange, green—suit Miss Darling well. Pastels wash her out a little, I find. As far as fashion goes, you want your daughter to set the trends, not follow them. She'll be beautiful in yellow; no one else will be wearing it, but soon everyone will want to wear the color because of her."

My mother regarded me, head to the side. "Hmm, I do take your meaning, Cumberbunch."

I stood against the wall, chewing at my nails, frustrated and bored beyond endurance. A morning going through my wardrobe with Sophie was one thing, but this fashion bacchanal was taking up precious time.

"Victoria, stop biting your nails, and do pay attention!" Mamma frowned. "She has no head for fashion," she remarked to Sophie.

"It's not that I don't have a head for it, Mamma, it's that I'd rather be doing other things."

"Like what?" she snapped.

Sophie shot me a warning look.

"Uh, Miss Winthrop's. Yes, I'm having such a lot of fun there." A little note of sarcasm crept out despite my attempts to quell it.

"Honestly, you have plenty of time. Now, Cumberbunch, Victoria will be wearing my coming-out gown for her debut, and my wedding dress as well, so I suppose you can work on altering those at home on Bailey's sewing machine. But she'll also have to have waists and skirts for everyday wear." Mother sighed. "I know this is such a lot of work, so do say if you are feeling pressed."

"Not at all, madam. We can purchase made-up shirt-waists and even lingerie gowns here."

It seemed Mamma purchased the whole of Liberty. Finally, after another hour, we left the shop. But the interminable day drew on at Miss Winthrop's; she had decided to add a new dance, the mazurka, to our repertoire. This time I trod on my own foot during the crossover step. My partner's face went pink with the effort of trying not to laugh. Honestly, all these dances were the most impossible waste of time. And the step patterns were mind-boggling and quite gave me a headache.

Our teacher divided us into groups and had one dance while the other watched. I was in the second group. The dance Miss Winthrop chose was the one I dreaded most of all: the quadrille. The quadrille struck fear into my heart more than any other because I could not blag my way through the steps by skipping and hopping as I could in the waltz and the polka. The quadrille was done by a group of four couples that made patterns within a set space upon the floor. If one went wrong, then the whole pattern collapsed. Worst of all, a dancer going wrong would be stranded in the middle of the figure, looking daft as her fellows cavorted around her and her forsaken partner continued on alone, arms in hold as if escorting a ghost dancer around the floor, for one never stopped in the middle of a dance if one could help it.

I felt quite sick watching the girls dance. They all knew

the steps perfectly and were able to make the intricate patterns the dance demanded. They glided through the little hops in place and the slides and twirls from one partner to the next when the music changed. They looked so delicate and feminine, taking tiny little measured steps across the floor, shoes poking out whimsically from underneath their skirts.

I just knew I would make a fool of myself at the ball. I knew I'd be the one to go right when I was meant to go left, bumping into the other dancers. And then poor Edmund would be lumbered with me, dragging me around the dance floor as if I were a sack of coal someone had handed him to dance with as a jest.

As predicted, I was perfectly awful when it was my group's turn. It seemed as though the girls had decided in advance that they would just ignore me, and they danced the entire figure around me. I must have looked like a stray dog trying to get someone's attention. I saw Sophie sitting along the wall with the other maids, a dismayed look upon her face.

Miss Winthrop took me to one side after the dance and told me I'd have to have private tutoring if I did not improve soon. I think she took it as a personal affront that one of her students would have such a poor showing at the season's balls.

"You're making very heavy weather of that dancing, if you don't mind me saying so, Miss Darling," Sophie said when we walked out of the dance studio. The sun was beginning to come out and a wind was freshening. I felt as though I had been released from prison.

"I don't think I'm cut out for dancing, Sophie. I'll be the most terrible flop."

"You don't know how lucky you are to get an invitation to such things."

"You go in my place, then," I said.

"Me, go to a ball? Chance would be a fine thing. I'd love to go." She had a dreamy look on her face. "All the beautiful gowns and lovely people. Dancing the night away with handsome men . . ."

"You wouldn't like it if you danced like a cart horse, like I do."

"You'd be all right if you paid attention to your instructress. Half the time you're away with the fairies. I've seen you. Looking out the window when you're meant to be looking at the teacher. And what was that you were saying to your mother? About you loving dancing? You nearly gave it away."

"I'll never get it," I said gloomily. "And then I'll have to come to extra classes, which means less time spent on my artwork."

Sophie heaved a sigh of exasperation, grabbed my hand, and pulled me off the street and into a little public square behind a wrought-iron fence bordered by beds of daffodils. "Oh for goodness' sakes, your whinging is driving me barmy. It's not difficult."

"How do you know?" I said, following behind her.

"I've been watching." The park had a square of grass, which Sophie made a beeline for, stopping in the middle. She took my hands. "I'm the bloke. Come on now. We walk about side by side, arms crossed; marching around the little square, see? And now we go back to the spot where we started. Now you weave in and out with the other ladies." She pushed me forward, and I made the little pattern.

"Sophie, this is silly. People are looking!"

"Let 'em look. You want to learn, don't you? Now come back, and we march about arm in arm once and then you do the little pattern with the ladies again. Ba, bum, bum, bum, ba, ba," Sophie sang out as I wove the pattern in the middle. "See, you're doing it. You're dancing. Now come back here, and we turn to each other and do that little jig step. Step, one two, hop, one two. Now go out and make a star with all four ladies."

I felt quite foolish holding my hand out to imaginary ladies and marching around, but I began to get the idea of the pattern, and as Sophie said, it really wasn't that hard.

"Bum, ba, bum! Now back to me, and we hold each other and skip around the circle." Sophie and I dashed around the circle, facing each other in a waltz hold, giggling our heads off. Several nannies with perambulators and some children sitting on nearby benches laughed and clapped out a beat for us. Two little children, a girl and a boy, ran forward and skipped around with us. "Now the blokes make a star." Sophie trotted into the middle and held out her arm to the little boy, the other tucked neatly behind her back. "And then we go around the circle again!" All four of us skipped about the circle. The little girl and boy danced together.

"Now we turn to each other and bow." Sophie stuck out her leg toward me and bowed low; I curtsied deeply. The children watched us and then did the same.

"Again!" the little boy called. So we did the whole thing again. And then again, and then once more. Finally, exhausted, we called the impomptu ball a success.

"See?" Sophie said, after we said good-bye to the children and made our way back to the street. "It's not so hard." Her eyes glittered with merriment. "Tomorrow we'll give the polonaise a whirl, shall we?"

"Thank you, Sophie. As ever, you're my lifesaver." For a moment, I thought about confiding in Sophie about Will and the way I felt about him. I missed confiding in someone, and whenever I was with Sophie I was reminded of my friendship with Lily.

But as lonely as I felt, and as much as I liked her, Sophie was my lady's maid. Even though I called her by her Christian name, she wasn't my friend.

THAT THURSDAY AT Avenue Studios, I kept a close watch on the time, determined not to have a repeat of last week. I cleaned my brushes, tidied my work space, and said good-bye to the mural artists in plenty of time. Out on the Fulham Road, there was no cab stand about, so I stood on the pavement with my arm up for ages, but all of the cabs, motorized and horse-drawn, were full, and the ones that weren't didn't seem inclined to stop.

Finally, with no choice, I took a horse-drawn omnibus. The only vacant seat was at the top in the open air, and I had to sit next to a man who kept sneezing into his handkerchief. A child behind me insisted on tugging at my hat, and it took several pointed glares from me before his mother reined him in. And the entire carriage, or whatever it was called, reeked of musty old curtains stirred in with mildewed library books. What was more, the streets were so crammed with traffic that I could have dismounted the conveyance and walked to Piccadilly faster.

The row with Will was in the front of my mind, and I worried that if I didn't arrive on time, he would leave, thinking I'd snubbed him. And so I was in near hysterics when the horses trundled past the winged figure of Anteros on the Piccadilly Circus fountain and came to a lumbering stop. I was twenty minutes late. I rushed down the bus's steps, picked up my skirts, and ran to the RA.

Will was still there at the Royal Academy, in the same tweed jacket, waiting under the archway. "What time do you call this, then?" he said, not sounding perturbed in the slightest.

"I'm so sorry!" I said, breathless. "The traffic's a nightmare. I was at the end of Fulham Road. It took ever such a long time to get here in the horse bus."

"A horse bus?" Will looked incredulous. "Those old things? They are so slow with the horses plodding along. Why don't you take the Underground? It's much faster," he said. "You'd be here in a heartbeat."

I shivered. "Can't bear the thought of it."

"Why not?"

"I can't stand being in close places. It's a fear I have, you see. I expect you find that silly."

"Not at all. My sister, Jane, has the same fear. I have a horror of spiders." He shuddered comically. "Can't stick them."

"You won't ever find me near the Underground," I said emphatically. "The name alone gives me the collywobbles."

"I don't think there is any shame in being afraid. But I think it's important to conquer your fears." He grinned.

"How do you mean?"

He held out his hand. "Come on, I'll take you."

"No, Will! I don't . . ."

Will reached down, took my hand, and strode toward Piccadilly Circus.

I tripped along behind him. "Will! I don't have time for this. The drawing!"

"We won't go far. Just a quick nip down the line to the next station and back. Won't take a moment, and then you'll see it's a doddle. No sense spending the whole of your life behind a horse's arse."

"William Fletcher!"

He laughed.

It was only a short walk to Piccadilly Circus Underground station, yet in that brief space of time my knees had begun to shake and I found I was having trouble breathing properly. But Will didn't give me time to pause. He towed me through the crowd and trotted down the steps, into the station, and up to the booking office. "One ticket, please," he said to the ticket seller behind the gated window, and handed over the coins. "I have a season ticket," he said to me. "It's much cheaper and it will get you on any train you like as many times as you like."

I made a face. "I don't think I'll be purchasing one of those anytime soon, William. I won't be repeating this exercise."

He took my hand again. "Oh, come on, don't be such a noodle. It's fun."

One more flight of stairs, and we were on the platform. It wasn't as bad underground as I had thought. The area was well lit, and there were even newsagents selling their wares along the tiled walls. Women, men, and children stood patiently along the platform.

"All right?" he asked me.

I shrugged. The longer we stood there waiting, the worse I felt. What would it be like inside that tunnel? I thought my heart would burst out of my chest, it was beating so loudly. My palm was damp inside Will's hand, but he didn't seem to care; he grasped my hand tighter.

"It's easier to stand something difficult when you picture happy things. A *Mermaid*, how about that? Pretend you're in front of her. Close your eyes."

I closed my eyes, imagining myself standing in front of the painting. The feelings I usually had when I saw her began to fill me, and I felt calmer. I took a deep breath. Will stepped a little closer.

"Don't worry, Vicky. We'll just go to Oxford Circus. If you're too scared, we'll walk back. I promise."

The conductor shouted into a bullhorn that the train was approaching and we should step back. A moment later a loud squealing noise came from deep inside the tunnel, a rush of air filled the arched room of the platform, and then the train arrived. It was not at all what I had expected. It was a narrow iron engine with several linked cars behind it. The train was quite elegant.

"I thought it would look like a goods train, like a steam locomotive."

Will laughed. "Those went out ages ago. These are electric. Smooth as anything."

Will opened the door on one of the cars, and we entered. It was spacious, with a wooden floor; upholstered benches lined both walls. We sat down on one by the door. Will took my hand again. "Ready?"

I nodded.

"If you feel afraid, just squeeze my hand."

"I've decided that I'm going to collect as many spiders in a jar as I can and then pour them all over you, William Fletcher. Seeing as how it's good to face your fears."

"Fair enough."

The conductor blew his whistle, and the train moved forward with a jerk. I expected the lights to turn off and pitch us into darkness, but they didn't. There was nothing visible out the window; it was not unlike riding an overland train at night. And before I knew it, we arrived at Oxford Circus. It would have taken me nearly half an hour to walk that distance.

"Well?" Will said. "You want to ride back or walk?"

"Ride!"

Will and I stepped onto the platform at Oxford Circus station and walked over the footbridge over the rails and onto the other side. We waited only a minute for the next train to come along, boarded it, and rode it back to Piccadilly.

"Now then, miss. What do you think to that?" Will

asked as we stood safely back on the platform. The conductor looked at us oddly.

"You're quite right; it's very efficient and not scary at all," I said. "But how do I know what train to get on?"

"Right over here on the map." Will led the way to a large poster that said

LONDON UNDERGROUND
RAILWAYS

on the top. The map below was traced with colored lines. "Here we are." Will pointed to Piccadilly Circus. "The Bakerloo Railway and the Piccadilly Railway leave from this station. Each route has its own color. Piccadilly is yellow; Bakerloo is brown. Where is the studio?"

I put my finger on the map. "Here. It's not far from South Kensington."

"Well then, you're in luck. It's a straight shot down the Piccadilly Railway; only seven stations and you're there." Will traced his finger along the route.

"Yes, I see! That's quite simple."

Feeling brave, I bought a weekly season ticket from the ticket seller. The seller also gave me a pocket map.

We returned to the street and headed back to the Royal Academy. As we walked, I realized that Will and I were still holding hands. My hand seemed to fit perfectly inside his.

I found I didn't want to let go of his hand, but I did so reluctantly.

"Thank you, Will," I said. "And I . . . I wanted to talk to you about last week."

"Actually, I was going to fall on my sword and apologize directly I saw you. It was my fault. My mum always says I'm too hard on the people I care about. So let's say no more about it, hey? We have a lot of work to do to get you ready for your submission. How long do we have, actually?"

"I need as much time to draw as I can get, so I'm handing everything in on the last possible day, April thirtieth. My eighteenth birthday, as it happens." I was relieved he had changed the subject. I wasn't quite sure what I was going to say to him.

"We'd better concentrate, then. No more messing about."

We went back to the courtyard, and I handed Will the illustration I had worked on during the week, which I had encased between two pieces of card to protect it.

He leaned over me to study the picture more closely That's when I started feeling anxious again. It was one thing for people to look upon my work without me there, but it was quite another to watch them look upon it. It always made me feel slightly sick. I always wondered what they were thinking. Were they trying to work out what to say to be polite? Could they see all the flaws?

He was so quiet for such a long time that I started to get nervous. Maybe he didn't like my rendition of Hoode. Maybe the politicians were too ridiculous. "I can do another if . . . if . . . you don't like that one."

He jerked his head up. "Another one? No! This is perfect. Hoode's better than I imagined him. And the lords! They are so funny in the way you have them ignoring him. This is better than I've seen in any penny dreadful. You are going to be famous someday; you know that, right? I don't just mean with my story, but on your own, too. I can see people emptying their wallets for a picture of yours."

"Will, stop. I'm not that good."

"Don't say that. Don't *ever* say that! You're talented. You're not changing a thing." Will carefully put the illustration back between the cards and slid the picture inside his jacket pocket. "Now enough of that. Let's get to work on your project."

I found that it was easier to draw Will this time. I felt more comfortable around him. I supposed the ride on the Underground helped. And his expression was perfect. When he looked at me, he had a measure of longing in his gaze. Just like Lancelot's when he looked at Guinevere. I did several studies of his face and even of his hands.

I spent the day doing exactly what I wanted to do. This was the life I wanted. No crushingly boring social-etiquette classes to take or deadly dull tea parties or idiotic social functions to attend. At the end of the afternoon, I walked down the pavement to join Sophie, and then I remembered what Will had said earlier. *I'm too hard on the people I care about.* I stopped and looked back to watch him weave through the foot traffic.

Will cared about me. The realization filled me with such happiness that it was all I could do to stop myself from picking up my skirts and skipping down the pavement.

ATURDAY WAS THE day of the Boat Race, and I was looking forward to seeing Edmund again. It was a fine day and a light wind was blowing, which was a good thing; it wouldn't be too choppy out on the Thames for the fragile boats. Sophie and I traveled to the Westminster School Boat Club, near where the race would begin, in a chauffeur-driven motorcar Edmund had sent to the house. We were to meet India and her French lady's maid there, cheer Edmund on at the start at Putney Bridge, and then be driven in the motor to Hammersmith Bridge—midway point of the race—and finally to the end at Chiswick Bridge.

Edmund, in his dark-blue uniform, looked as handsome as ever. When we arrived, he was with several of his team-mates, standing in a cluster round their boat. But seeing us, he broke away from the group and came over.

India kissed Edmund on the cheek. "I wish you the best of luck," she said. "But I'm absolutely gasping for a lemonade. Come along, ladies, let's leave Miss Darling and Edmund alone." India gave Edmund a pointed look, and she and the two lady's maids went off and joined the queue in front of a refreshment stand.

"Are you nervous at all?" I said, casting about for something to say. Even though I was glad to see Edmund, I still felt somewhat tongue-tied in front of him after that disastrous dinner a fortnight ago.

He leaned back against the low wall that bordered the river, drumming his fingers against the stone. "Not at all. We have a superb team this year. Cambridge hasn't a chance. Don't tell my father, but I have a little wager riding on the outcome." He grinned sheepishly. "Can't make a leopard change his spots, as it goes."

I laughed. "Your secret's safe with me."

"Say, this probably isn't the right time, but I have something for you. If I don't give it to you now, I'm afraid I'll lose it. I'm daft that way." Edmund reached into his pocket and drew out a small velvet box. He opened it and removed an enormous sapphire-and-diamond ring. He lifted my left hand and slid it onto the third finger. "Your engagement ring." The sapphire was oval and set with a trio of square diamonds on either side.

"Oh!" I didn't know why I was so surprised that Edmund would give me a ring, but all of a sudden the engagement seemed so very real.

"Is it all right?" Edmund pulled my hand toward him and peered at the ring, as if seeing it for the first time. He looked at me quizzically. I couldn't help but think how the sapphires matched his eyes. They were both a perfect ultramarine blue. "Mother said girls love sapphires and diamonds."

"Oh. No. I mean, yes, of course. It's lovely."

"It's official, then."

"Yes," I said faintly. "I suppose it is."

"Jolly good. I suppose I can stop calling you Miss Darling now. And you should call me Edmund."

"I suppose you're right."

"I'd better get back to my mates or they'll think I've lost my nerve and jumped ship." Edmund kissed my cheek and then ran down the towpath to his teammates, who welcomed him with hearty slaps on the back.

I should have been happy, but I wasn't. I held my hand out in front of me. The jewels sparkled in the sunshine. The ring was pretty—beautiful even—but it wasn't me. It looked wrong. It felt wrong.

What was I doing, marrying someone I didn't love, like some old-fashioned Victorian girl? I felt claustrophobic, just as I had when I'd worn my mother's gown. I looked around. There were too many people here. *I just wish I could go home.*

The ladies came back, and India handed me a glass of lemonade. I reached to take it, and she saw the ring. She squealed. "He gave it to you? Oh, it's beautiful, Miss Darling."

I smiled and nodded. I took a sip of the lemonade, hiding my face in the glass.

A girl in a striped tailor-made and boater hat came over and started talking to India. Grateful for the distraction, I turned away from the two. Sophie caught my eye.

"What's the matter?" she asked.

I shook my head. "Nothing."

"Something's the matter. You're pale as death, Miss Darling," she said.

"It's nothing, Sophie. I'm quite well, really."

Sophie looked at me doubtfully.

India came back, hooked her arm through mine, and began to chatter away about the race, but I was barely able to take in what she was saying.

We returned to the motorcar, and the chauffeur drove us through the crowded streets to Putney Bridge. We found an empty space near the embankment wall to watch. The ring felt heavy and cold on my finger. I could not stop twisting it around and around, trying to find a better fit. I caught Sophie looking at me, so I stopped and tried to concentrate on the race.

Since Oxford had won the toss of the sovereign coin, the team picked the north station on the Middlesex side of the river, which had the advantage on the first and last bends, leaving the south station on the Surrey side for Cambridge. The two teams rowed downstream for a bit, warming up. Then the boats' coxes raised their arms while the teams got into position, lining up with the University Stone on the south bank. The umpire waved a red flag, starting the race. Edmund's boat got off the mark quickly, rowing to the center of the river, where the fastest water was.

When the boats disappeared round the bend, we got back into the motorcar to follow the race farther. Oxford was ahead at Hammersmith Bridge, which boded well, the driver told us; most boats ahead there went on to win the race.

As we reached Chiswick Bridge we saw, turning the bend at Watney's Brewery, the dark-blue uniforms of the

Oxford crew, at least a boat's length ahead. Cambridge caught them up as the two teams pressed for the finish, just before the bridge. I saw Edmund, pulling at his oar, perfectly in synch with his teammates, his brow damp, his jaw tight. The coxswain, sitting in the bow, shouted at the team through his bullhorn. The tip of the boat surged past Cambridge's, and they won in nineteen minutes and five seconds, breaking Cambridge's three-year winning streak.

When the crew stepped ashore, a crush of spectators surrounded them. India grabbed my hand, and I tripped along behind her as she rushed up to greet her brother. Edmund saw us and pressed through the crowd.

"Congratulations," I said. "You were brilliant. I'm so glad I was here to watch you. Well done, you!"

But my words sounded false. It was as if someone else were speaking them, as if I had become some other version of myself.

I could not sleep that night. My mind kept going over and over my reaction to the ring like a stuck disc record on a gramophone.

Somewhere close to midnight I finally put it down to nerves. I was nervous. How could I not be? After all, I hadn't wanted to become engaged in the first place, and it would take some getting used to. I did not love Edmund, but I hadn't known him that long. Affection would take time to build as we came to know each other better. I just needed to concentrate on my work and let the rest sort itself out.

Y MOTHER WAS so thrilled with the ring, you'd have thought she'd been given one herself. To me it felt uncomfortable and foreign, so I kept it in my pocket or art satchel whenever I wasn't around my parents or Edmund.

My mother began to employ her next scheme for stitching back together my tattered reputation. Or at least patching it up a bit. This meant making endless rounds of deadly dull calls, and driving the length and breadth of London in the carriage to the houses of people Mamma knew would accept me, such as the aristocratic Dowager Viscountess Somersby and the immensely powerful Mrs. Georgina Plimpton. These were my mother's very close friends who had decided to rally round her and pretend my terrible behavior had not actually happened.

Once word got round that these ladies had returned my mother's card with one of their own or with a call during one of my mother's at-homes, then all the underlings in their social circle would follow suit, like sheep following their bellwether. Calling cards for my mother and me would fill our silver salver in the hall. And so it would go.

In time the horrid behavior of Victoria Darling would be a faint, distant memory. Or so my mother hoped.

The Monday after the Boat Race we went round to five houses. While we waited in the carriage, John took my mother's engraved calling card, with the corner folded down to indicate she'd been there personally, with my name penned in just underneath hers, to the front door to give it to the butler. At three of the houses, the women had daughters my age, so my mother included a card for each of them as well.

As my mother predicted, all five cards were returned with cards. So we spent the next few days in the carriage paying calls during the women's at-homes. I wore my engagement ring silently, letting the women notice it and remark upon it themselves. In time, word would get round that the newly engaged Miss Darling was not as unfit for society as once thought.

Mamma was very shrewd, paying strict attention to etiquette by arriving at each house early, between three and four o'clock, and staying no longer than a quarter of an hour so as not to presume anything.

But when the Dowager Viscountess Somersby and Mrs. Georgina Plimpton and her crushingly boring daughter Georgette came to my mother's at-home on Thursday, she rolled out the tea table in all its glory, piled high with French fancies, Battenberg cake, and Victoria sponge. One by one, as predicted, the other women and their daughters came to call. Much chatting about the weather and fashions for the upcoming social season ensued. I sat on the edge of my chair and made charming conversation with the other girls. When I asked after the health of Georgette's little spaniel, Bridie, my mother smiled at me and nodded.

But all the while I was thinking of the cartoon I would draw of this day when I found the chance.

When the teapot had gone dry and the last crumb had been eaten, the visitors left, and my mother sat back in her lingerie gown and declared my reentrance into society a success.

"Providing you do nothing more to damage your reputation, my dear," Mamma said, with a pointed look.

I smiled and assured her I wouldn't. But I was tired and fed up. I had not had a single moment to spend on my artwork in three days.

A moment later Emma came into the sitting room, curtsied, and handed my mother a crystal tray with a gentleman's calling card upon it. "Mr. Edmund Carrick-Humphrey wishes to know if Miss Darling is available."

My mother took the card, looked at it, and nodded. "Show him up, Emma." She turned to me. "Pinch some roses into your cheeks, Victoria. You look quite pale."

I was just rousing myself to do this when Edmund entered the room. He was dressed in a motoring duster; he held his bowler hat.

"I wonder if Miss Darling might be amenable to joining me for a ride in my motorcar?" he asked my mother, and then flashed a smile in my direction.

My mother looked as though she had been kissed under the mistletoe. "I see no problem with that, Mr. Carrick-Humphrey, as long as Cumberbunch chaperones."

Emma was sent to fetch Sophie, and I went to put on

a light paletot and collect my gloves from my bedroom. When I took the jacket from my wardrobe, I saw the edge of the hatbox filled with my art supplies peeping out. I nudged it farther back with the toe of my boot. *What I wouldn't give to be able to spend one whole day just working on my art. Soon, soon*, I reminded myself. Only a couple of months until I was married and I could work whenever I pleased and however long I pleased.

I pinned on my new hat—a straw chapeau trimmed with a wide velvet ribbon and black feathers—and since we were motoring, I secured it with a long chiffon scarf tied under my chin.

"Pretty as a picture," Edmund said as I came down the stairs to the hall. Edmund's open-topped motorcar sat outside at the curb. It was expensive looking—long and sleek with a leather settee in both the front and back. It was painted a cream color, and the fenders and bonnet were highlighted in black striping. The front of the car shone with bright chrome.

"Edmund, it's beautiful," I said. "I didn't know you had a motorcar!"

"It came in from the coach builder's yesterday. A present from my father for winning the Boat Race."

"Is it a Daimler?" I asked.

Edmund scoffed. "Better than that. It's a Rolls-Royce Forty/Fifty HP—the Silver Ghost! Best motorcar in the world. I don't really like the color; my father's choice. I wanted blue, but my father said it was too flash. Still, I suppose it will grow on me."

He opened the back door for Sophie and then the passenger door for me. I stepped up onto the running board and climbed in. I arranged my skirts around me and pulled my chiffon scarf over my face. The inside of the motorcar was luxurious, leather and polished wood everywhere. It smelled faintly of Edmund's cologne, that spicy scent I had come to associate with him.

Edmund put a pair of driving goggles on. He did something complicated to the many levers and dials in the car, and then drove it out into the London traffic.

"You're clever to drive," I said. "It looks ever so difficult."

"It's dead easy," he said. "I'll teach you."

"I don't know. I'm not very coordinated."

He looked over and smiled at me. "Not to worry. I had a very good teacher myself and I'm quite sure I can pass on the skills to you."

The traffic cleared a little, so Edmund coaxed the motor even faster. It was smooth and easy, and we went along at a good clip. The speed was exhilarating and frightening at the same time. I sat forward and gripped the dash. The wind tugged at my hat.

"Where are we going?" I shouted over the engine. "It's a fine day; perhaps through Hyde Park?"

"Oh, I think we can do better than that," he said.

"Better than Hyde Park?"

He overtook a hansom cab and blew the hooter. The horse shied, and the driver shook his whip at Edmund. Edmund simply laughed and accelerated the car in a burst of speed.

"How would you like to see our new house?'

"*Our* house?"

He grinned. "Our very own. I went to see my father at his club this afternoon, and he gave me the keys."

"Edmund! A house of our own. The idea of it!"

"I thought you'd like that. It's in Chelsea. Not such a fashionable address, but on the rise. It's a large townhouse on Paulton's Square, so it has a garden."

We turned onto a tree-lined road, which was a quiet oasis after the bustle of the main streets. Edmund pulled the car up to the pavement and we alighted. We stood on the walk and looked at the house. It was a three-story brick townhouse with a green door. Ivy crawled up one side and window boxes filled with pansies framed the windows on the ground floor.

Edmund let out a little laugh. "Can you believe it? In August we will be married and snuggled up like two pigeons in a roost in this delicious house."

I slid my hand through Edmund's arm and we walked up the brick path to the front door; Sophie followed behind. Edmund fished for a key in his pocket, slid it into the lock, and swung open the door.

A small hall led to two rooms on either side: a sitting room and a study. Then straight ahead was the stairway.

"The dining room is farther back. Bedrooms are upstairs," Edmund said.

"Oh, Miss Darling," Sophie said. "Isn't it lovely?"

"Servants' rooms are in the attic. Go on up, Cumberbunch, and choose your bedroom. My father says they've all been done up recently. Two of them have basins with running water."

Sophie went upstairs eagerly, and Edmund and I went

into the sitting room. It was a spacious room with a coal fireplace and a mantel. Huge Palladian windows let in light that fell upon the oaken floors. Flowered Victorian wallpaper covered the walls. "Don't think much of the wallpaper," Edmund said, picking at it with his finger. "Those flowers would give a bee a headache. Still, we can get rid of it. Father said we could change anything we want."

"I can't get my head round it, Edmund. It's so beautiful."

The caretaker came inside just then, so Edmund started talking with him about the changes he wanted. I pushed open the French doors off the sitting room and went out to look into the garden. It was a mass of spring flowers: fragrant sweet peas climbed up trellises, daffodils nodded their heads in the breeze, and camellias opened their faces to the sun. A stone wall divided the garden, and there was a wooden door in the middle. I walked across the lawn and went through this, and it was like stepping into another world.

I stopped, staring, unable to believe my eyes, for there in a little clearing sat a small summerhouse, a tiny little cottage no bigger than my bedroom in Mayfair. It had a rounded wooden door with wrought-iron hinges, three large windows framed in flower boxes, and a sweet little porch. Clematis vine blooming with purple flowers as wide as my palm crawled over the roof. I could imagine Little Red Riding Hood popping out at any moment, with her basket over her arm.

I stepped up onto the porch and turned the door's iron handle. I expected it to be locked, but it swung open easily. Inside, the summerhouse was empty save for a couple of wooden chairs and a desk, but the walls and floor were lined with polished wood. Best of all, the room was flooded with north light.

I could not believe it. It would make the perfect atelier. Mentally, I began to fill it: a model's dais could go there, just under that north-facing window, my easel just in front of it, in the middle of the room. And by the door, a table where I could place my brushes and paints and such.

And then I realized that I didn't have to wait. The house was ours and there was nothing to stop me from drawing Will here. All I needed was a key.

I heard the door creak open, and I felt a hand on my shoulder. I turned and Edmund was there. He pulled me to him and kissed me. And any lingering feelings of doubt I had about the engagement were gone.

Twenty-Two

The summerhouse, Chelsea,
Thursday, fifteenth of April

ON THE FIFTEENTH of April, the Thursday after Easter, I met Will, as usual, at the Royal Academy on time, as I was now a veteran Underground traveler. I held up my key ring. "I have a place for us to work in private in Chelsea," I said.

"Blimey," he said. "How did you manage that?"

"It's um . . . a friend's," I said. "He's away right now, so we'll have it all to ourselves for a fortnight."

Will held out his arm. "Well, then, let's go." We headed off to the Underground and made our way to Chelsea. It was a short walk from the station to the house. Once inside the summerhouse, I pulled the door shut quickly. I didn't think the caretaker was about, as I'd had a quick look in the windows when we went past the house, but I wasn't taking the chance.

"It's so peaceful," Will said. "Lucky whatsit. What luck to have such a place. This is bigger than my entire flat."

Will helped me pull the desk and chairs into the middle of the room. "Let's get to work on your project first, and then we'll do mine," I said. *My first project in my own atelier,* I thought with pleasure, looking around the room.

Will worked on writing his next episode, while I finished my latest illustration. "Dash it. Will, I drew a mustache on Hoode and he doesn't have one." I looked for my kneaded eraser in my pencil box to fix a mistake, but it wasn't there. "My satchel is by you. Can you see if my eraser is in it? Not the square one; the one I squish up." I studied the picture as Will rummaged through my art satchel.

"I was thinking when you draw him at Spitalfields to hand round the money to the silk weavers, he should definitely . . ." Will's voice trailed off.

"Definitely what?" I added a touch more shading to the church steeple. "Definitely what, Will?"

I looked up and saw Will holding my satchel in one hand, a bit of paper in the other, and it was this he stared at, his mouth open, a look of shock on his face. Shock and something else.

It was Bertram's drawing of me he held. I could feel a hot flush spread up my throat as Will studied the drawing of my naked body.

"Is this you, Vicky?" he whispered.

"You know it is! Stop staring at it like that!" My chair screeched on the wooden floor as I stood up. I snatched the drawing from his hand and held it tight against my side in the folds of my skirt.

"It's beautiful . . . the drawing, I mean. He's . . . talented." Will cleared his throat. He seemed to be nervous, which made no sense. After all, it was *my* naked self he'd stared at. "Is this why you had to leave France? Because you let them draw you without your clothes on?"

I couldn't bring myself to speak. I was nearly breathless

with fear. If Will judged me like other people had, I would run mad.

But the expression on Will's face was not one of judgment; instead he looked as though he was trying to understand, so I began to tell him what had happened, haltingly at first, but then I let the story come out. "At first I was just taking lessons at the art school; I didn't pose. But the other artists posed nude from time to time if there was no model, and so one day I did too. But a girl from finishing school tattled, and I was expelled. I would do it again, even though people judge me for having done it. I see no reason why I should ask anyone else to do something I'm not prepared to do."

Will was quiet then. He seemed lost in thought. "That's fair enough," he said at last. "If other people are brave enough to get their kit off for art, then you should be too."

And then he reached a hand over his shoulder and pulled his jersey over his head.

I took a step back. "What are you doing?"

"If you are brave enough, then I should be too." His voice was muffled from inside his shirt. His head emerged, his hair mussed up.

"Are you certain you want to do this?"

He tossed his jersey onto the floor.

I watched him unlace his boots, kick them off. Then he pulled his undershirt off. It was nothing like watching the other artists disrobe. They tended to make it funny so that the humor dispelled any tension. It felt different with Will. I had studied the other models with an artist's scrutiny. But with Will, I longed to see him without his clothes. If I was honest, I'd admit I'd even imagined him without his clothes on before. Would he look like the other nude men I'd seen?

He was down to his drawers now. Without even pausing, he hitched his thumbs in the waistband. I squeezed my eyes shut for a moment, and then I slowly opened them.

My hand unclenched, and Bertram's drawing fluttered to the floor.

Will was Michelangelo's *David*, as I had imagined him from the first moment I saw him. Like *David*, Will was finely made, long and lean, with well-sculpted warrior's muscles. I kept my eyes to his chest, not wanting him to catch me looking elsewhere. I tried to calm my nerves, but it was to no avail. *A life-drawing session is always professional, never risqué*, I reminded myself. But my emotions took no notice.

Will watched me warily.

I took a deep breath; let it out. "Do you mind if I touch you?" I asked.

"Eh?" he said, confusion in his eyes.

I gestured with my hands. "To pose you." I hoped he didn't hear the quaver in my voice.

He made a slight shake of his head as if he didn't quite trust himself to move.

I laid my hand on his left shoulder; his skin felt warm, his muscles firm under my hand. "Put your weight in your right leg and relax the left. It's called contrapposto, a classic standing heroic pose." I bent his arm and held it to his shoulder, shaping his fingers into a cup as if they were holding a sling. I turned his chin with the tips of my fingers so that his gaze was just over his shoulder. "You're Michelangelo's *David*, looking defiantly toward his enemy."

I chose a conté crayon, turned my sketchbook to a fresh page, and sat down and began to sketch.

Will did not budge. It was as though he didn't dare. I could barely see his chest moving as he breathed. The pastel I had chosen was a rustic bronze color, and it lit his figure with a burnished glow that seemed from another time. He was no longer Will. He'd become my muse once more. The desire to touch him turned into the desire to draw him. We were artist and model again. I was so inspired it was as though Michelangelo himself guided my fingers, and I fell into the dreamlike state that happened when art took me in this way. And nothing mattered anymore.

THE LIGHT WAS starting to fade when I realized that nearly an hour had gone by. I sat back and put my pastel down.

"Is that it, then?"

I nodded. Once the model's job was over, an artist shouldn't continue to stare, so I busied myself with my sketchbook to give some privacy while he dressed.

"That wasn't as strange as I thought it would be. I mean, no one's ever seen me in the buff like that before," Will said. "Actually, that's not true. One time I was out with a bunch of my mates. It was a scorching-hot day and we just stripped off and jumped into the river. Problem was a bunch of girls from the village came down the path just as we were getting out!"

"So what did you do?"

"Jumped back in." He laughed. "Quick as we could. Well, apart from Charlie. He stood there staring at the girls with his mouth dangling open."

"I can't tell you how much it means to me that you posed like that. Honestly." I looked away. I felt bashful all of a sudden.

He waved his hands. "Aw, that's just standing still. I didn't do anything."

"Being a model is more than just standing still. It's a collaboration with the artist. The Pre-Raphaelites always said they were nothing without their models. They fought over them."

"Do you like to draw people in the buff?"

"I do. I love it."

"Why?"

"There's something about it that makes me feel like a real artist, like I'm not pretending. I don't know if you feel this when you write, but so many times my head is filled with voices telling me that I'm only playing at being an artist. But those all leave me when I draw from the nude figure. I don't know why."

I felt shy for saying that and a little embarrassed. But the look on Will's face told me that he understood completely.

We were only able to go to the summerhouse once more because the builders were due to start the renovations. In one way I was relieved, because I began to have stronger feelings about Will. I didn't feel at all like I had when I'd drawn Bertram or any of the other artists.

Truly, the Pre-Raphaelites had had similar feelings.

Rossetti married his model, Lizzie Siddal, after all, although that ended disastrously. Hunt considered marrying Annie Miller for a time, and Millais ran off with John Ruskin's wife, Effie Gray, after he painted her portrait. And the more I thought about it, the longer the list of famous artists marrying or having affairs with their models grew. One didn't have to act on that impulse. I certainly wouldn't marry or have an affair with mine.

I thought I would feel better at that realization, but somehow I didn't.

I NEEDED ONE MORE day at the mural to impress Sylvia, and so the last Thursday before the deadline, I decided to work the entire afternoon at the mural. There was nothing for it; I had to sacrifice my session with Will. Harry scurried down his ladder to greet me as soon as I walked in the door of the mural studio. Sylvia set me to work on filling in the mottoes that would hang from the ceiling. Harry tailed behind me.

"Siddhartha Gautama, do you know of him?" Harry asked after we had been working for several minutes. He shoved his hands into his pockets and leaned against the brick wall of the studio.

"Not personally, no," I replied.

Harry crouched down beside me, his long, skinny legs jutting up on either side of him like grasshopper's limbs. He picked up a piece of chalk and began to sketch a picture on the floor of a man sitting cross-legged. "Siddhartha Gautama is the Buddha. Buddhism is the very foundation of life. Buddha was here long before Jesus, yet most contemporary religions are based on Jesus' teachings."

"Mmm," I said absent-mindedly, trying to close my ears to his patter.

"Buddha believed that suffering was an essential part of life," Harry went on, adding two arms to the man in his picture, one with the hand in his lap and the other held up, palm out. I glanced over. It was a good effort for a boy who said he only dabbled. Art talent ran strongly in the Pankhurst family. He regarded the drawing with his head cocked to one side, and then smudged a bit of the pastel with his thumb, creating a pleasing shadow. "This gesture is the *Abhaya mudra*, which represents protection and peace."

"Is that so," I murmured, moving on to another section of the banner. Harry stood up and trailed behind me like a loyal puppy, jabbering on.

"Eastern religions . . ."

"Right." Harry didn't seem to realize I wasn't taking any notice of him.

". . . hobby of mine . . ."

"Mm, you don't say?"

Finally I had finished my task and began to walk back across the room to the supply table where the paints were kept. Harry moved up to walk beside me and seemed to be wrestling with himself about something. He'd slant his eyes in my direction then shake his head, clench his fists, and open his mouth to speak and then close it again. I didn't mind this new quirk of his much because at least he had stopped his infernal rabbiting. He rubbed his palms on his trousers, and all of a sudden he reached down and grabbed my hand. He stared at it with a startled expression, as if he had caught a fish with his bare hands on the first try.

"Harry!" I snatched my hand away. "Steady on."

Harry's face went red as a beetroot. "Sorry," he muttered. He slumped his shoulders and shoved his hands back into his pockets, as if he didn't quite trust them to be out on their own and roaming freely.

I touched Harry's arm. "It's all right, Harry. But I'm engaged. I should have said. Friends though, right?"

He looked horrified. "I'm awfully sorry, Vicky."

"You're really sweet, Harry; please don't feel bad."

Harry looked like he was going to cry. He turned away and hurried back to his place at the mural, his shoulders up around his ears.

I felt guilty then for not wearing my ring. If I had, Harry would have known right off. I sighed and went back to work myself.

I stayed at the studio as long as I could, until everyone had gone. Finally, at four o'clock, just Sylvia and I were left. I only had an hour before I had to go home, and I was growing more anxious with every passing minute.

I was working on transferring Sylvia's master drawing of the vine-leaf border pattern onto a blank canvas with tracing paper when Sylvia climbed down from her ladder and stretched, her hand on the small of her back. "I think we ought to break for tea, Vicky."

I laid down my materials with a sigh of relief and went to join her. Finally, a chance to talk to Sylvia about the letter.

"Do you think it will be ready for the exhibition in

time?" I asked as I watched her make the tea. "Only a fortnight to go."

"It will have to be. We've done such a lot already. I think we're close."

We sipped our tea in silence for a moment, and then I waded in. "You're such a thoughtful artist, Sylvia. I admire you so. The mural is magnificent." It was true. I wasn't just buttering Sylvia up. I really did mean it. You couldn't help but look around the studio and know what she was trying to say with her design.

"That's kind of you. But I agonize over my art all the time." Sylvia looked at the murals. "Sometimes I wonder whether it is a waste of time to devote my life to painting when so many people are suffering and women are not free. My friends from the art college feel that art is all there is to life, but I can't in good conscience agree with them. What do you feel about that, Vicky?"

"Art does inspire people, does it not? The world would be a far bleaker place without it. You only need to look at your work here to know that."

"You're so right. The way I can reconcile myself is to use my painting skills for social reform. I saw so many women in the north working in sweated labor who have nothing and earn nothing. Art moves people to see things in a way they may not have thought of before."

Sylvia was voicing the same thought that I'd had that day in the French café. It heartened me to hear such an opinion from another woman, especially someone as talented as Sylvia.

"You know, there's a suffrage atelier that's started up

in a member's garden in South Hampstead. It's going great guns at the moment," Sylvia said. "It's more of a craft atelier at the moment, but the organizers are thinking of bringing in artists and offering some fine-art classes, if there's demand. The atelier makes all sorts of things to sell at the WSPU headquarters and some of the shops throughout England. After we've completed the mural, I think you should consider helping out. The woman who runs it, Clemence Housman, is looking for people to do illustrations for our newspaper *Votes for Women*. Could you help?"

I couldn't say no to Sylvia. But what was more, I didn't *want* to say no. I didn't want my only art outlet to be working all alone in my bedroom before the sun rose. The thought of joining another atelier and working in the company of other artists appealed to me greatly.

Sylvia leaned forward over the table and squeezed my hand. "I'm so glad you've come to us. Your talent is a blessing to the WSPU."

Now was my chance. "But my skills are limited, Sylvia." My heart started to beat a little harder. "I wish to go to art college, as you have done. It's been my dream to study at the RCA, but I don't have the reference letter the college requires."

Sylvia was quiet, which worried me.

"If you're happy with my work here, would you be willing to write a letter of reference for me?"

She shook her head sadly. "I wish I could."

My heart sank. That was it then. It was over. I knew it. It was preposterous of me to ask her. *Who do I think I am?* But still, I had to ask, as much as I didn't want to hear Sylvia's opinion out loud. "Am I . . . am I not good enough?"

"Oh no! Quite the contrary. I just don't think a letter from me would help. It would probably make things worse for you. I butted up against the establishment one too many times. I can't say I enjoyed my time much at the school but I did learn, and that is what is important." She thought for a moment. "Austin could, however. A letter from him would hold a lot of weight. He was very well respected."

Austin! Brilliant, even better. I hadn't thought of asking Austin. And then I felt a prick of guilt that I would prefer a letter from Austin, a man, over one from Sylvia. "Oh, would he, Sylvia? I'd be ever so grateful."

"Of course he would." She picked up a scrap of paper. "I'll make a note to ask him."

I had it all now. I had everything. Now what I needed to do was to get through the exam and marry Edmund.

THE EVENING BEFORE my eighteenth birthday, Rose gave birth to a boy, whom she and Freddy named George. My parents, Sophie, and I went to Freddy's the next morning to see the baby and Rose. My mother was over the moon to finally have a grandson, proclaiming him to resemble Freddy exactly. She cuddled the baby for a moment. Papa stood back, admiring the baby from a safe distance, and then the two left the nursery to congratulate Rose.

"You and my son born nearly the same day," Freddy said, and handed little George to me. "I'll take that as a good sign."

The baby woke up then and yawned, his little mouth shaped into a circle. He blinked at me, his blue eyes unfocused.

"I'm your Auntie Vicky," I told him, and shook his little starfish hand. "How do you do?" He regarded me solemnly.

Charlotte came up and leaned against my leg. "He doesn't know how to talk yet, Auntie Vicky," she said.

"I can't tell who he looks like." Freddy peered over my shoulder.

"Mamma's right. He looks exactly like you," I said. "His face is the picture of a sponge pudding, round and podgy, just like yours."

"Brat." Fred nudged me with his shoulder.

"I don't want a brother," Charlotte said. "Can we give him back, Papa?"

Freddy laughed.

I pushed her hair away from her face. "I don't think so, dearest. Besides, brothers aren't so bad. Why, your papa and I are the best of friends."

It was nearing ten o'clock. I had to get going to the RCA, but I had to wait for my parents. Thankfully Papa wanted to leave quickly, and so I put George down and left Charlotte peering into her little brother's basket, looking doubtful.

Sophie had smuggled my sketchbook out under her coat. And with the excuse that Sophie and I wanted to stroll around Kensington Gardens, which was a short walk from the Royal Academy, I had John drive us there.

While Sophie waited in the anteroom, I looked through my drawing book once more. I had several studies of Will, a collection of the illustrations for his story, and sketches of the mural angel and of the artists at work. Austin's reference letter was tucked inside. I had done the best I could, and I could do no more. It was in the lap of the gods.

At the RCA there were several other artists submitting work. Only one other woman was there, dressed in a navy-blue tailor-made, a hopeful look on her face. We nodded to each other in passing, but she looked as wary as I did. The men did not look at one another this way; in fact, several were standing in a group going through one another's books, making admiring comments.

I handed in my work at the clerk's office, and Sophie and I walked out of the RCA and into the bright sunshine. I saw a police constable watching the door. My eyes adjusted to the sun and I realized the PC was Will.

"Wait here a moment, will you, Sophie?" I ran down the steps.

"Happy birthday!" Will said when I reached him. He handed me a small parcel wrapped in brown paper and tied with a green ribbon.

"Will! You didn't have to do this."

"I wanted to. It's just a little thing."

He watched carefully as I undid the package. Inside was a slim volume of the poems of Tennyson.

"Turn to page twelve," Will said.

I found the page, and there was the mermaid poem. Above the poem was an illustration, a woodcut of Waterhouse's *A Mermaid*. The illustration was signed *JW Waterhouse*.

Without any warning, tears filled my eyes. No one had ever given me such a kind and thoughtful gift before. I pictured Will going into the shop, looking over the books, and then discovering the very one he knew I would love. I even pictured him watching as the clerk wrapped the volume in brown paper. I wondered if the clerk had tied the green bow on it or if Will had gone into a notion shop and chosen it himself. These were all small things, but kindness was built of small things.

"It's the closest I could come to the actual picture," Will said. "I found it in a bookshop in Charing Cross."

I brushed at my eyes. "Thank you." My voice cracked.

He hesitated. "I need to get back to my beat, but . . . I'm given a whole rest day off once a month, which is Saturday week, and I had planned on going to Rye to see my family. Would you like to go with me? We could work, of course. There is a hill there that overlooks the marshes. If the weather is fine, you could draw."

A whole day out of the city to spend drawing Will appealed to me greatly. I'd have to fix an excuse with Sophie first.

"I'd like that," I said.

"In the meantime I'll write my mum and tell her to expect us. You'll love my mum. And I can't wait for you to meet my nephew, Jamie."

We parted, and Sophie and I went off to meet John.

I could tell Sophie was dying to know who Will was. Of course, as a lady's maid, it wasn't her place to ask, but when we were in the carriage, I told her anyway.

"That's your art model?" Sophie looked at me, her eyes wide. "That's Will? He's a bit of all right, isn't he?"

I smiled. "I suppose you could say that. He gave me this for my birthday." I handed Sophie the book of poems. She turned the pages carefully. There was an illustration above each poem. Each one by a different artist.

I took the book from Sophie and looked at the cover again. "I've heard of these books, Sophie. They're hard to find and very dear."

"How much does a police constable earn?" Sophie asked.

I shook my head. "I don't know."

Sophie and I looked at each other. Neither of us said anything, but we both knew that the book had cost more than a constable should spend.

My parents had a birthday party that evening, and Edmund came, bearing champagne, roses, and a diamond bracelet. They were beautiful. But they didn't compare with Will's gift. If I was honest, nothing about Edmund did.

THAT SATURDAY, A week after my birthday, the Charing Cross train station was a hive of activity with people bustling all around. When Sophie and I arrived, I spotted Will waiting by the newsagents, leaning against the wall and reading a newspaper.

Sophie blew out her breath. "Gosh. Lucky girl, getting to stare at him whenever you want."

"I suppose," I said, in an attempt to sound as though I didn't care a whit one way or another.

Sophie and I had cooked up a scheme to tell my mother that a friend from Miss Winthrop's had invited me to her country home in Royal Tunbridge Wells for the day. Tunbridge Wells was in Kent, far enough away to account for the length of time I would be away. Mamma at first said no because she didn't know the girl's mother, but then, having anticipated Mamma would ask, I handed her the invitation from her mother—the one that I had created myself in my bedroom. While I watched Mamma read, my heart was thudding so hard I was surprised she didn't hear it. Mamma looked up from the note and, finally satisfied, gave her permission. She told Sophie to go with me, and I argued a little, just to keep her from becoming suspicious. But this gave Sophie the day off too, which she planned to spend at Clement's Inn making scarves and helping trim hats to sell at the Women's Exhibition.

Will saw us, waved his hand, and came over to greet us. I introduced him to Sophie.

As she shook his hand, I thought about what a good match they might make. Maybe I should try to get them together. But then I imagined Will kissing Sophie, pulling her close against his body while her arms wrapped around his neck. I pictured Will combing his fingers through Sophie's red hair, as he did to mine that day in the alley when my hair came loose. The thought made me want to scratch Sophie's eyes out, although I knew I had no claim on Will.

When Will went off to buy tickets, Sophie turned to me. "You fancy this bloke. I can tell. Your face is glowing. Your face doesn't glow like that when you're looking at Mr. Carrick-Humphrey."

"That's not true. I'm just a bit warm." I fanned my hand at my face. "It's close in here with all the people about."

"Does he know you're engaged?"

I shook my head. I didn't like the accusatory look on her face.

"Why?"

"It's none of his business." *And it's none of yours either!*

She pointed at my hand. "Why don't you wear your engagement ring?"

"I don't like to wear rings when I draw. They get in the way."

"You're not drawing now."

"I forgot it," I said sharply. "Sophie, leave it alone."

She looked doubtful. "Well, he fancies you, I can tell."

"He doesn't! We're only friends."

She snorted. "Friends?"

"Sophie, you overstep yourself!" I hissed. "You're my lady's maid, not my confessor!"

I regretted the words as soon as they left my mouth. I sounded like some of the girls I knew who bossed their servants about and treated them like they were less than human. "I'm sorry. I didn't mean that." The hurt look on Sophie's face made me feel horrible. "Please forgive me."

"No, I'm sorry. I had no right to devil you."

"Let's say no more about it," I said, squeezing her hand. It was my fault Sophie had said those things. I'd made her believe we were friends, so she behaved as though we were. Perhaps I shouldn't be so familiar with her. It wasn't fair to her.

After Will came back with the tickets, Sophie went off to the Underground. I tried to forget my conversation with her, but I couldn't quite do so. Her question about why I hadn't told Will about my engagement bothered me. Saying *I'm engaged* should be as easy as saying when and where we would meet next. I should have told him when he held my hand on the Underground. I had told Harry straightaway when he tried to hold my hand. I had had no compunction there. I should have told Will that the summerhouse belonged to me and to Edmund, my fiancé. That would have been a better time to tell him. But Will was so honorable. If I'd told him, he wouldn't have been my friend and creative partner like this. Certainly he wouldn't have ever posed nude for me.

And then I wondered if Sophie was right. *Did* Will fancy me? He had given me that book of poetry for my birthday, and now he was taking me to meet his parents. Perhaps he was just being kind, being a friend. On the other hand, maybe his actions meant something more. Either way, I could never return such affections.

Despite this truth, a little feeling of joy started to flicker inside me.

Our train was announced, and Will and I headed out onto the platform. I stopped at the first-class carriage and waited for him to open the door. I hadn't meant to—it was force of habit—but I cursed myself for it all the same. Of course Will wouldn't be able to afford the cost of such a ticket. In fact, I should have offered to pay my own fare, but it was all too late now.

Will had continued on up ahead and I couldn't catch up with him quickly enough. He'd noticed what I had done. The gap between Will's life and mine yawned wider than a chasm. I felt horrid to have put him in such a position.

"You don't mind second-class, do you?" He looked down at the tickets in his hands. "I didn't think. It's a long journey, two and a half hours. Perhaps you won't be comfortable. I should change these for first. Perhaps there's time. . . ." His voice trailed off.

"Not at all, Will! I'm happy with second-class."

Will looked unsure.

"Please, Will. I'm not such a delicate flower. Let's not spoil the day."

This settled, we carried on down the platform and stepped into a second-class carriage. I had never been in such a carriage before. In first class, one traveled in a private wood-paneled compartment with comfortable upholstered seats and a little table. A waiter would come by and serve a five-course luncheon or tea and cakes.

The second-class carriage was worlds away from that. It rather reminded me of a music hall, with benches grouped in two lines, facing forward. But instead of a stage, the passengers gazed at a wall papered with a map of the railway line. And instead of a porter hanging one's things up, people simply shoved their belongings onto racks above the seats or carried them in their laps. The carriage was full of people talking and leaning over one another to be heard. One man was eating a sandwich over his knees in broad view of everyone. A crying child sat next to his exasperated mother, who was staring out the window, a grim look on her face.

We made our way down the noisy aisle and found a place. There was no armrest dividing the seat, so Will and I had to sit very near to each other. I edged as close to the window as I could and pressed my knees together so I wouldn't brush against him. I looked out the window, pretending to be immensely interested in the scenery. It was a beautiful day with the sky blue and the sun shining down. Soon, the city scene began to turn into a country setting. Cows and horses cropped grass in the fields; houses with thatched roofs dotted the rolling hills, and in the distance a castle loomed.

"You look like you're trying to become part of the wall, flattened against it like that," Will said, breaking the silence. He laughed. "Do I pong or something? Shall I go find another seat?"

I turned away from the window and smiled. "Don't be silly. You smell fine."

"You've been so quiet. Did I say something?"

"I'm sorry, Will." I shook my head. "I don't mean to be distant. I just have a lot on my mind. It's nothing, really. Tell me about your sister. She's older than you?"

"Yes. She was married, but her husband was a soldier and he died in the Second Boer War seven years ago."

"How sad."

"She was only seventeen, and Jamie was just a baby. So she moved back in with my parents. She's lived there ever since."

"Are you very close to her?"

"I am. She likes to boss me about, and I like to pretend to let her." He grinned.

I laughed. "My brother, Freddy, whom you met, is much the same."

"I got the feeling that was true. He seemed very exasperated when you pitched up that day. I've seen that look on Jane."

Will went on about some of the things Jane did when they were young. While I listened to Will talk, the train's rocking began to make me feel sleepy. In anticipation of being invited to sit the exam, I was continuing my early-morning drawing sessions in order to work on my final presentation, and they were beginning to take their toll. I tried to concentrate as Will told me about his father. I yawned and leaned my head back against the seat. I would just close my eyes and listen.

"... village constable ... for ..."

"Uh-huh ..."

"He said I should ... London ..."

I nodded. It was so warm, sitting there in a shaft of sunshine next to Will. So warm and comfortable that I fell asleep. And I began to dream. I dreamt I was walking with Will, hand in hand, in a meadow filled with wildflowers so beautiful I could almost smell their sweet scent. Bees buzzed and butterflies floated all around us. And then Will turned to me and pulled me so close against him that I could feel his heart beating. He felt so lovely, so solid and strong. He felt like a place I had never been to before, a place I never wanted to leave.

"Vicky," he whispered in my ear; his breath fluttered across my face.

I cuddled closer, pressing my cheek against his coat.

"Wake up, Vicky," he said louder.

My eyes popped open. Will's face was only an inch away from mine, an amused look in his eyes. I had fallen asleep on his chest, my hand in his. I sat back. "Oh."

"We're here." He smiled. "I don't think they'll let us stay for much longer."

The conductor stood in the aisle. "Final stop, lad. Or are you heading straight back to London?"

I stood up and followed Will off the train, embarrassed beyond measure and blasting my traitorous heart.

WILL AND I walked along the harbor past people hawking their wares and toward a cobblestone street that led up a hill. I felt even more awkward around him now. Thankfully he didn't tease me about falling asleep on him. Instead he pointed out sights as we walked.

"I've been mad to show you this street for ages," Will said. "It's called Mermaid Street. Not sure why, but there's an old hostel here named the Mermaid Inn, too. Just up the way there."

Mermaid Street was lined with medieval, Tudor, and Georgian houses all crowded together higgledy-piggledy along the cobbled street. They had peculiar names like The House Opposite and The House with the Seat. It was like walking into a Turner landscape painting, it was that picturesque. Its old-fashioned charm reminded me of the French village of Trouville, where I'd attended finishing school. I wondered if Bertram had ever visited Rye. I could see why many artists wanted to live and work here. The light was beautiful, and there was a harmonious feeling to the place that beckoned to an artist's spirit.

After a bit, we turned down a narrow alley and through a shaded garden. We heard a shout, and then a young boy came blazing through a small vegetable patch, dirt flying, and threw himself at Will. The breath left Will with an "oof," and he staggered.

"What the devil, Jamie? You nearly knocked the stuffing out of me!"

The boy untangled himself from Will and grinned up at him. "I've been watching for you all morning!" The boy was very young, maybe seven or so, and he had a mischievous look about him, with freckles spattered across his upturned nose and a rooster tail of hair poking up on the back of his head.

"Jamie, this is my friend Vicky. Vicky, this is my nephew, Jamie."

Jamie stared at me. "She's prettier than Eliza."

"Jamie!" Will warned. "Hush now."

Jamie slid his hand into mine. "You're prettier than Eliza," he repeated. "She had a pig's face with a nose like this!" He pushed the tip of his nose upward with his thumb. "She even had pinky-red hair. And she snorted when she laughed, just like a pig." He demonstrated loudly. I was beginning to like Will's nephew.

"Jamie, that's not nice," Will said, trying not to laugh.

Jamie eyed him. "It's true," he said, his voice rising indignantly.

"Who is Eliza, Will?" I asked.

Will shrugged.

"Well, this must be the artist we've heard so much about," I heard a feminine voice say.

A young woman stood in the garden gate, arms folded, watching us.

"She's my friend first, Mumma!" Jamie clutched my hand with both of his so hard I winced.

"I can well see that from the state of my runner beans."

She smiled wryly. "Trampled to bits, nearly. Well, give us a kiss, then, Will."

Will stepped forward and kissed his sister's cheek. He pulled me over and introduced me. She shook my hand briefly and then folded her arms again. Jane's brown hair was caught into a bun, and she wore a long apron over a navy-blue serge skirt and brown linen blouse. It was a no-nonsense outfit, and I had a feeling Jane was not the kind of woman who would tolerate silliness.

"Mum and Dad are waiting inside. Dad's just got home from his beat, and Mum is getting lunch ready."

We followed Jane around the house and through a small yard where chickens pecked at corn strewn on the ground. I hung back, eyeing the cockerel warily.

Jane looked bemused. "You're not frightened, are you? Have you never seen chickens before?"

"Um . . . not like this, no." I sheltered behind Will as one of the chickens came over to investigate, pecking at the silver buckle of my boot. Jamie thought that was hilarious and bent in half with laughter.

"Vicky lives in the city, Jane," Will said. "No chickens in London houses."

Several other hens ran over with wings flapping to see what had interested their sister. Just as I was playing with the idea of bolting out of the yard, a short, round woman came out of the house and shooed the chickens away. She smiled broadly.

"Now, Jane, you should have brought Will and his sweetheart to the front door, not round the back. She'll think we're not civilized with all these biddies about."

Will glanced at me quickly, his face reddened. "Vicky's not my sweetheart, Mum, I told you. We're working together, remember?"

"So you said," she replied, patting Will's cheek and grinning. Jane, who didn't seem to find her mother's comment to her liking, scowled at the chickens. Will's mother then put her hands on her hips and eyed Will. "Now, let me take a look at you." She tutted. "I've seen more meat on a butcher's pencil!"

"I'm fine, Mum!" Will said. "I eat plenty."

We followed Mrs. Fletcher into the cottage. It was dark inside, and it took a moment for my eyes to adjust. But there wasn't much to see; it was the tiniest house I had ever been in. The entire first floor was no bigger that my mother's sitting room. The room was divided in half by a staircase. One side held a table set with china for lunch. The other side served as a makeshift sitting room. A settee and two battered upholstered chairs were grouped in front of a blazing coal fire. A man slept in one of the chairs with a newspaper on his lap, his stocking feet on a little stool close to the fire.

"Up you get, sleepyhead!" Mrs. Fletcher said in the direction of the man. He stirred and blinked at us. "Will and his friend are here."

"Well, now. PC Fletcher come home to visit! That's grand!" He got to his feet and we went over so that he could greet his son. He shook Will by the hand, at the same time patting him on the shoulder affectionately. Will was taller than his father, but the resemblance was uncanny. They shared the same kind eyes and floppy hair that refused to be tamed.

I was overcome by shyness, but I made myself shake Mr. Fletcher's hand. Will and I sat on the settee together. Jane sat on one of the chairs, pulling Jamie onto her lap. Mr. Fletcher settled back down, and his wife perched on the stool at his feet. It was a very close fit, but it looked as though all of them were quite used to being this near to one another.

"What's in there?" Jamie asked, and pointed at my art satchel, which I had placed at my feet.

"Jamie, don't be rude!" Jane said, folding his small finger back down. Jamie glared at her.

"I keep my art materials in there, but I've also brought some things from London." I had splurged and bought presents for Will's family from my grandmother's ring money. I had enjoyed buying the gifts, browsing through the shops in Mayfair, looking for the perfect choices with Sophie's help.

Jamie immediately slid off his protesting mother's lap and came over to lean on my knee.

"Did you bring something for me?" Jamie asked. Will and his parents laughed, and Jane spluttered.

"I did, indeed!" I took up the satchel and drew out a bag of sweets, which held a mixture of bull's-eyes, humbugs, and licorice allsorts, as well as a small box of painted wooden policemen I found at Hamley's Toy Shop on Regent Street.

Jamie's eyes grew round with amazement. He stared at

the packages I held out as if he didn't know what to look at first. Finally he took the bag, opened it, and stuffed his mouth with a peppermint humbug. Then he tore the lid off the box of policemen and drew one out.

"See, Mumma!" Jamie hopped over to his mum to show her one of the policemen. "It's Uncle Will!"

We all laughed. It was fun to make Jamie happy. I smiled and watched him go through the box and show his mum every figurine. I glanced at Will and found he was not looking at Jamie, as everyone else was, but at me.

"I have something for you too, Jane." I pulled out the foil-wrapped box of rose and violet creams I had chosen at the confectioner's in the Royal Arcade. "I hope you like Charbonnel et Walker. I hear the king adores them." I realized I sounded like a snob just then. As if Jane was used to eating luxury chocolates. My face burned hot. I'd even said *Charbonnel et Walker* in a French accent.

Jane took the box. "I've never et them," she said with a short smile. "But I suppose the king's favorites must trump good old Cadbury Dairy Milk any day of the week."

I thought I heard a note of sarkiness in her voice, but I acted as if I hadn't noticed and finished handing out the other presents, which I had purchased at Liberty: a decanter of port for Mr. Fletcher and a little casket of bath items for Mrs. Fletcher. But my pleasure in the gift giving had faded.

Mrs. Fletcher was as thrilled as Jamie with her gift. She undid the lid and drew out the bottle of rose bath oil and then the cake of lavender soap done up in sprigged paper. She held the soap to her nose and breathed deeply.

"That's lovely, that is. I can't thank you enough, Vicky." She replaced the soap in the box. "I'll keep that in my bottom drawer for best. Now, I'd better see to the lunch."

For best. It was only toiletries. I pictured Mrs. Fletcher eking their use out for months, maybe years.

Mrs. Fletcher disappeared down a narrow corridor toward what I assumed to be the kitchen, judging by the smells coming from that direction. Without a word, Jane set Jamie on his feet and went off to join her mother, the box of chocolates discarded on a side table.

I felt like a massive toff, throwing my expensive gifts about, showing off. Like my pause at the first-class-carriage door, my gifts had only highlighted the differences between myself and the Fletcher family. And Jane had felt it too.

AFTER LUNCH, WILL and I went outside so I could draw. Will took my hand as we walked, as though it was perfectly natural for him to do so. And I let him; we walked, hand in hand, up Mermaid Street, and then across to a long, sloping lawn behind a copse of trees overlooking the Romney Marsh.

"This is blissful," I said, looking around me. The oak and horse chestnut trees made a verdant background, and the long grass and wildflowers were the perfect stage. "We should work in a natural setting more often. There is a place near the boathouse in Hyde Park. Let's meet there next time."

Will took up his pose near the horse chestnut. "When do

you expect to hear if you've been accepted for the exam?"

"They're posting the list at the RCA on Thursday."

"Are you nervous at all?"

"Nervous?" I laughed. "I've been having nightmares over it."

"Well, don't. You're sure to get it. I know it."

I felt embarrassed. He started to say something more, but I interrupted. "Now be quiet. I can't draw you if you're talking."

Will rolled his eyes.

"You're getting much better at standing still," I said when I was finished and Will had come over to sprawl beside me. "Not so much fidgeting."

"I never fidget."

"Maybe not." I turned a page over and began a quick sketch of him lying on the grass as he was with his head in his hand.

"I love watching your face as you draw," he said. "It's all aglow, like someone has lit a lamp inside you." He ran his fingers over my cheek. His touch made me quiver, made my skin tingle. I wanted him to do it again. I wanted him to cup my face in his hands. I wondered what that would feel like.

"You make me sound as if I have a fever," I said, attempting to jest with him like I did with Freddy. *Yes, he's just like your brother. Keep believing that, Victoria!* I glanced at him quickly. He wasn't smiling at my stupid jape anyway.

"I'm completely serious. Your face changes."

"I love to draw; I suppose that shows in my face," I said.

"Why do you love it so much? I'm just curious."

I shrugged. "If I'm not drawing every day, then I don't feel alive; do you know what I mean? And I'm not very good in social settings—I don't quite say the right things or act the right way—but with my art I can express myself through what I see and feel. It helps me understand how I fit into the world, which is something that has quite escaped me since I was a little girl."

"How do you mean?"

"I never liked the same things as other girls—dolls and frocks and such. My parents sent me to finishing school in France so that I might learn how to behave as they thought I should. It was unbearable until I met my friend Lily. She let me draw her. She understood me. And then I met an artist named Bertram in the town, and he told me about the art studio. I felt as though I had come home. When I lost all that, I thought I would never feel whole again. But of course, then I met you, and the artists at the WSPU. I know one thing is certain, Will. I would die if I could not draw."

He looked at me frankly. I wondered if I had said too much. I stared down at my hands, covered with charcoal dust and pastel smudges.

"I feel the same way about my writing. All those hours spent walking my beat, I'm really thinking of new stories." He laughed. "Some of the other blokes tell me I stare off into space quite a lot, that I look gormless." He demonstrated: his eyes shifted upward; his mouth hung open slightly.

I giggled. "I expect that's what I look like too."

"Not at all. You look as though magic has taken hold of you. It must be magic because I don't know how you can draw like that. I can barely manage a stick figure." He nudged closer to me and picked up one of my conté crayons, turning it around in his fingers. "And all these bits and pieces you have. They fascinate me."

I set my drawing book in Will's lap and turned it to a fresh page. I handed him a graphite pencil. "Here, have a go." He grasped the pencil; his fingers tightened around the tip as though he were writing. "Relax your fingers. If they are all bunched around the tip, your drawing will be cramped." I pulled his fingers away from the tip and loosened them so they gently cradled the pencil. "This will give you more movement." With my hand over his, I guided the pencil, making a series of quick, loose lines across the page to create a tree. "You see, all these little marks make up the subject. Some will be lighter or darker; some will look like scribbles. It all depends on how you see your subject. Every artist interprets things differently."

I let go of Will's hand with reluctance and watched him as he drew. On the right hand, his third finger had a callused lump on it created from endless hours of writing. I couldn't keep my eyes on his hands only. My gaze wandered to his face and fixed on his mouth. I found I wanted to lie down on the grass with him, our faces side by side, our hands touching. And perhaps our lips.

He looked at the page, head tilted sideways. "I think I'll stick to writing."

"Well, that is an art form, too," I said, closing the drawing book and closing my mind on all those wicked thoughts I kept having. Will might not know I was engaged, but I knew that I should act like I was instead of daydreaming about kissing him. I never daydreamed about kissing

Edmund. I should make myself try. "When are you going to start sending out your story to publishers? We have, what? Four episodes finished?"

He shrugged and dug at the hillside with his heel. "When they're ready, I guess."

"You need to get them out there, Will. They're really wonderful. I'll give them to Freddy."

"Not yet."

"When?"

"Soon."

I nudged him with my shoulder. "I will hold you to that."

He glanced at me shortly and grinned a little. "Surrounded by bossy women."

We sat quietly side by side for a little while, looking out at the view. A song thrush sang from high atop his perch in a pine tree nearby. I wrapped my arms about my knees and pressed my chin into my arms.

"So," I said, glancing at Will sideways. "It's funny your mother thought we were sweethearts. Didn't you find it funny?"

Will said nothing, but I thought I saw his shoulders tighten. "I suppose."

"I'm dying to know. Who is this Eliza?"

Will gazed thoughtfully out at the river, chewing on a piece of grass. "She was my best mate's sister. I'd known her for a long while—since childhood. I suppose it was just natural that we should walk out together. Everyone assumed we'd be married, but—" Will hesitated.

"But what?" I asked, holding my breath. *But I didn't love her*, I hoped he'd say.

He shrugged. "I dunno. She went into service, became a parlormaid, and I joined the police." He pulled the grass out of his mouth and tossed it down. "Why do you wish to know about her?"

"It just . . . well, Jamie mentioned her. I think it's lovely you have a sweetheart. Do you ever see her?" For some torturous reason I wanted to know more about this parlormaid who'd claimed Will as hers, who'd run her hands over his body, the body I'd drawn; pressed her mouth to his, the mouth I'd sketched. I clenched my jaw at the thought. I'd had no idea I was such a jealous person. In the space of one day I'd wanted to do battle with two different women because of Will. I pulled up a piece of grass and tickled Will's ear with it. "Come on, out with it!" I laughed. Giggled really. I sounded like a flibbertigibbet. *Tra, la, la! Do tell or I shall sulk!* Ugh!

Will batted my hand away and looked annoyed. "She's not my sweetheart. Like I said. We went our separate ways. I haven't seen her in months, if you really want to know." He looked at me for a long moment and then looked away. He kicked at the grass on the hill again.

This tidbit of information did little to assuage my jealousy. Mindful of how stupid my thoughts and actions were, I realized that maybe the antidote lay in telling Will I was engaged. But how to begin? I would just say it: *Will, I'm engaged.* No, that was too blunt. How about: *Actually, I forgot to tell you something. It's so funny that I haven't said anything before. I'm getting married in three months' time.* No, that was worse.

If I was truly honest, I didn't want to tell Will. He saw me as an artist, and I liked that. I didn't want him to see me as belonging to a man.

These days with Will would be gone soon enough. I knew this even as we sat next to each other in the sunshine. I couldn't let them go quite yet.

Twenty-Six

ON WEDNESDAY MORNING I was sitting with Papa at breakfast—Mamma, as usual, was still abed with her breakfast tray—when Mrs. Fitzhughes brought in the letters and left them at the silver salver at Papa's elbow. He put his newspaper down and sorted through the neat stack of envelopes. A moment later, he drew in his breath so sharply that I looked up from my boiled egg. He was holding a cream-colored envelope heavy with inky black calligraphy and embossed with a wax seal and ribbon.

"That's lush," I said. "Who sent you that?"

"It's not for me. It's for you!" His eyes were wide. "You've done it, my dear!"

"Done what?" For a dimwitted moment, I thought Papa meant I'd been accepted to sit the RCA exam. I must admit my heart beat a little faster, but of course that couldn't be. Then I saw the wax was embossed with the king's arms of dominion.

He handed the envelope over. "I'm sure you've been invited to Court."

I put down my toast and sliced the envelope open with my fruit knife. Papa watched eagerly as I tugged out a cream-colored engraved invitation.

Miss Victoria Darling
To Be Presented by
Mrs. Elizabeth Darling, Mother,
To King Edward VII at Court
Friday, Fourth of June 1909
Ten o'clock in the Evening

I sat back in my chair. Everything was truly going according to plan. The reinvention of Victoria Darling was complete. I had done everything they asked of me. Now all I had left to do was to meet the king, not make a fool of myself in front of him, and marry Edmund. I could feel the chains loosening. Soon I would be on my way.

"Well?" Papa asked.

I nodded, handing him the invitation. "It's as you say."

Papa read the invitation and stood up. "Well done, my dear. You must go and tell your mother right away."

I stood up to do as he asked, and as I passed him, he reached out and took my hand. "I'm so proud of you, my dear," he said, squeezing my fingers. "So proud." His dark-brown eyes looked at me earnestly, and for a moment I pretended he was saying he was proud of me because I had gotten into the RCA. For a little moment I afforded myself that tiny luxury.

I kissed his cheek. "Thank you, Papa," I said, and then went off to find Mamma.

THE NEXT DAY, Thursday, I went to back to the RCA to see if I had been accepted to sit the examination. With Will's words of confidence boosting me, I marched up to the list and found that I was accepted, and that I was to present myself to the panel on the first of July. I swear I had to stop myself from running to Hyde Park. I couldn't wait to tell Will.

When I reached the boathouse where we were to meet, he wasn't there, so I sat down on the steps and waited. After a bit I could see him approaching. His head was down as he walked with long purposeful strides, looking at the path, lost in thought. As he drew near, I stood up and ran down the steps to greet him. I couldn't help it. I threw my arms around his neck.

"I did it, Will! I got accepted!"

He stood still for a moment, but then he put his arms around my waist and hugged me hard.

"What happens now?" he asked as we walked to a little clearing underneath a tree by the Serpentine, the lake that flowed through Hyde Park.

"I need to show further work," I said as I unpacked my sketchbook and pencils. "It has to be even better than what I've shown already. I thought I'd do the pastel study of Lancelot, to show the examiners what I'd like to accomplish at the school."

We got to work, but gray clouds had been rolling in, and after a few minutes the first raindrops began to fall.

Will and I jumped up and dashed for cover. Just before we reached the boathouse, the skies opened up, and it bucketed down, drenching us. Will reached back and took my hand, pulling me the final distance underneath the eaves of the boathouse. He shook the raindrops out of his hair, laughing. "Well, so much for that."

We watched the rain come down in stair rods, filling the paths with puddles of water. The wind had whipped up tiny waves on the Serpentine. Several people were stranded underneath nearby trees. Two little boys ran by us, stomping through the puddles and laughing.

"Blast this weather," I said. "We have so little time until the exam. I wish we had someplace to work indoors." If only I could take Will back to the summerhouse in Chelsea, but, with so many builders about, I couldn't chance it. "It's pointless to go back to the Royal Academy. The Summer Exhibition is open now, and it will be ever so crowded if we tried to work in the galleries." The Summer Exhibition heralded the start of the social season, and so the chances of being seen by someone who knew my mother or me would be much greater.

Will looked thoughtful. "Actually, my flat isn't far from here, near Praed Street Station in Paddington. We could work there. What do you think?"

"Your flat?" I hesitated. I wasn't sure I trusted myself enough to be alone with Will in his flat, but I had been alone with him before in my summerhouse. Surely I could resist temptation. "Of course," I said. "Why not?"

WILL LIVED IN a groom's quarters over a stable. His entire flat consisted of one long, narrow room. Shelves crammed with books hung over a table made from a plank of wood atop two trestles. A single bed lay under the eaves; an apple crate served as a nightstand. His clothes hung from a peg on the wall. His kitchen consisted of a pitcher and bowl, two tea mugs, a stack of plates on a shelf, and a tiny paraffin stove. Two mismatched wooden chairs faced a coal fireplace. It was damp as well, and I could feel a draft whistling round my ankles. The large skylights let in a good amount of light. But that was about the only thing in the room's favor.

I caught Will looking at me, uncertainty on his face. "It's not much," he said. "I expect you're used to something . . . well, different."

I went over to the window, grasping for something nice to say about the flat. The rooftops of London stretched in an endless forest of chimneys, and there was not a single human being in sight. "Oh, look at the view."

Will moved to stand behind me. "You can see clear across the rooftops. It's like another world up here."

I glanced around. "Where is your lavatory?"

"Outside. I share the privy with the other tenants. I bathe at the public baths."

I sat down in one of the wooden chairs by the fire; one of its legs seemed shorter than the others. Will bathed with other people. I couldn't imagine it. I had my own lavatory at home, with piped-in hot water, a huge claw-foot bathtub, and all the warm towels and French-milled soap I wanted.

"How long have you lived here?" I asked.

"Not long. I used to live in the Section House near Cannon Row Police Station, but I can't write with so many blokes about, so I choose to live here. It's not much, I know. To be honest, I was a little embarrassed to bring you here."

I couldn't help but compare Will to Edmund with his new motorcar and our house in Chelsea full of rooms we didn't even need. I'd be willing to wager that Will wouldn't care about the flowered wallpaper in the sitting room. The flat touched something inside me and made me like Will even more.

"Don't feel that way, Will," I said. "I think it's grand you have a place of your own."

He looked relieved. "I suppose we'd better get to work. That's what we've come here to do, after all."

The flat may have been poky, but despite the noise from the street, the room was peaceful. I watched Will over the top of my sketchbook. He was leaning over the make-shift table, his pencil flying across his notebook. When he reached the end of the page, he lifted the pencil and bit the end of it as he scanned what he had written. As attractive as Edmund was in his expensive clothes, he would be eclipsed by Will in his simple muslin shirt with his sleeves rolled to his elbow. I made a quick sketch of Will at work in the corner of my sketchbook and then returned to Lancelot.

"Will you show me what you've drawn?" Will said after a few moments. He set his pencil down and came around to peer over my shoulder.

I held my hand over the paper. "It's not ready yet."

"Come on, Vicky." He held his hand out. "You've read all my work, so there's no secrets between us. Give it over.

You're going to have to show the examiners, so why not just start with me?"

"Fine." I handed him the sketchbook. "Bossyboots."

He took the book over to the window.

"Blimey," he said. "It's really good."

I stood up and took it back. "I don't know. I think the perspective is a bit skewed."

Will made a little noise of exasperation. He set the book down and took me by the shoulders. "Will you stop finding fault? Listen, you dafty. When are you going to realize how talented you are? You made my carcass look halfway decent, and that's saying a lot." He gave me a little shake. His eyes were warm, his expression kind. His hands felt so good on my shoulders. I thought about when he hugged me earlier in the park and when I fell asleep in his arms on the train.

And then the image of him nude flashed in front of my eyes, leaving me feeling slightly dizzy, weak, and hungry for something I didn't quite understand. I had seen Will undressed in person. He had seen me undressed in a drawing. Amazing that two people could know each other's bodies so intimately and yet . . .

This thought was barely taking shape in my mind when Will leaned forward and kissed me.

I SHOULD'VE WRENCHED myself away and left. But my hands flew up and found their way to the back of his head, and I leaned into the kiss, lacing my fingers through his hair. A little sound left him, and his lips opened with mine.

I didn't care how scandalous it was to be kissing a boy in his own flat. I didn't care that I was engaged to another. The way he felt against me, the hardness of his chest, the strength in his arms that pressed me to him, and how he smelled overcame any sense I had. The city noises of horseshoes ringing on cobbles, workmen shouting, and motorcar horns blowing faded into the background. All I knew was Will.

The next moment we were on his bed, kissing each other as though we would die if we stopped.

I could not get enough of him, and it felt as though he could not get enough of me. His kiss grew more urgent. His fingers tightened around my waist and pushed me back until I was lying beneath him. Will's mouth left mine and fell against the hollow of my throat, and his lips trailed down from my neck to the top of my bodice. I could feel his breath flutter under the lace of my chemise, like gentle shivers on my skin. He'd seen me undressed in Bertram's drawing, but I wished him to see me, my body, and not a charcoal rendering of it.

My hands ached to touch what I had drawn for so long, so I pulled his shirt free of his trousers and ran my hands over the muscles of his back, tracing each curve and dip as if my fingers were a paintbrush and his body my canvas. "Vicky," Will murmured, and the way he said it, so desperate and adoring, made something clench inside me. Edmund never made me feel this way.

Edmund.

Edmund!

His name clanged around inside my head, and I reached

for the last shred of sense I possessed. I braced my hands against Will's shoulders and shoved him away from me.

Will let me go, startled. His face was flushed, his hair mussed. "I'm so sorry. I didn't mean to—"

I jumped up from the bed. "I have to go." I grabbed the Lancelot drawing and went back to the table to collect my things. I shoved the sketchbook into my art satchel, throwing pencils on top and cramming loose papers in. I swung my satchel over my shoulder and spun around, nearly bashing my face on Will's chest, he was standing so close. I backed away.

"Vicky . . ."

I should have told him that the kiss was a mistake and why, but heaven help me, I could not. I gripped the strap of my satchel. "I have to be somewhere."

"I shouldn't have done that. I'm sorry, Vicky. Honestly, I didn't bring you up here to do that. Let me walk you to the Underground."

We walked in silence back to the station at Praed Street. I felt stripped naked, my emotions raw. My lips still tingled from his kisses; my skin yearned for his touch. Once Will's hand brushed the back of mine as we walked, and I drew it away quickly.

We stopped in front of the Underground entrance. People bustled all around us, but I felt we were the only two standing in the street.

"I'll meet you Thursday week, then?" He sounded unsure. "By the boathouse in Hyde Park again?"

"I can't. It's the Women's Exhibition in Knightsbridge. I promised I'd draw portraits in the art stall." I had been disappointed to give up a day with Will, but now I was relieved. I stared at his mouth, thinking of how I had just kissed it, how I had felt his body against mine. It felt wrong to be standing in the street feeling this way. Did the people walking around us sense it?

"Oh," he said. "The Thursday after, then?"

I just ducked my head and walked down the steps to the platform. I did not turn around to see if he was watching me.

On the Underground train back to Piccadilly, the clicking of the tracks and the noise from the engine seemed louder than usual. A man sitting near me must have tipped half a bottle of bay rum cologne over himself, and the scent made my stomach churn. What had I done? No matter how much I tried to rearrange in my mind what had happened, the simple fact was that even though Will had kissed me first, I had been only too happy to kiss him back. And I had let it go on for so long, let it go so far. If I hadn't stopped, how far would it have gone?

What kind of person was I to do such a thing when I was engaged to another? Was my father right? Was I, like other females, overly emotional? Was I wanton and tawdry like everyone thought I was? Out to have a mindless fling with my muse, like some male artists did with their models? This was why female models were held in such disrepute, after all. Why so many artists were considered louche. People assumed an affair was the next logical step.

I pulled out my sketchbook and looked at the drawing I had done of Will working. And in that moment, I didn't see him through an artist's eyes, mentally placing a border around him, thinking of how the light would reflect best off his features, and how I could portray him. I saw him for real, as the person he was: stubborn, kind, full of a sense of fairness and integrity.

Then I knew: this wasn't just a passion I felt for my model. My feelings about him had nothing to do with how his looks inspired me; he was far more than a muse. With every stroke of pencil and crayon, I had drawn Will into my heart.

I was in love with him.

My fingers clenched on the edges of the sketchbook. Will and I could never be friends. I could never see him again. I had to end it. Another kiss like that, and I would give my body to him with no hesitation. He already had my heart. I had to take it back. I had to.

But the thought of never seeing Will again, of never talking of writing and drawing and laughing with him, or kissing him again, filled me with grief. I couldn't help it; I burst into tears, right there on the Underground. I tried to stop crying, but it was like trying to push back the tides.

CONCENTRATE ON MY art. That was the solution to the problem of Will and Vicky. I knew it was. And I was grateful to have somewhere to direct my mind to when Sophie, Lucy, and I headed to the Women's Exhibition the day after it opened to volunteer. Sylvia's grand mural was finally completed and hung in place at the Prince's skating rink in Knightsbridge. The rink was huge: a vast and cavernous space that had hosted the figure skating events of the Olympics last year. The ice had been removed in February, and now events and bazaars were held in it.

Sophie turned in a slow circle, taking in the vast iron-and-glass ceiling festooned with banners in the WSPU's colors. The spring sun cast rays of light through the rink. The Aeolian Women's Orchestra sat on a platform in the middle of the rink, tuning their instruments.

The twenty-foot-long murals covered the walls of the rink, looking for all the world as if they had been painted in situ and had always been there, just as Sylvia hoped. The winged angels looked down at the crowd, giving the space a mystical air. The woman sowing seeds with doves over her head and thistles at her feet took pride of place at the middle of the hall, and the design I'd helped with, of the woman reaping the rewards, was directly across.

"Sylvia must be over the moon," Sophie said.

"She must be exhausted," Lucy added. "I don't think she slept much in the last few days."

"This is what you've been working on, Miss Darling?" Sophie said.

I pointed. "That's my design."

She looked at me in wonder. "It's so beautiful."

"Thank you, Sophie, but I didn't complete her. Another artist did."

The fact that I hadn't been there at the end rankled. I had gone back to the mural at the beginning of May to help one more time and to collect my reference letter from Austin, but I could find no time to help finish. I pictured all the artists filling in the final colors, stepping back from the work to admire it, and celebrating with a bottle of wine. I imagined them at the exhibition supervising the installation, sitting together on the skating rink's floor, and absorbing the beauty of the work, exhausted but happy. Meanwhile, I had probably been practicing my court curtsy at Miss Winthrop's or choosing the right color drapes for the sitting room or inquiring about the health of Georgette Plimpton's spaniel again, as I'd never worked out anything else to say to her.

Never again. I would never let that happen again.

Fifty stalls had been set up, and in them women were setting out farm produce, confectionary, books, and post-cards. The millinery stall was filled with wide-brimmed hats, cloches, and straw boaters, all trimmed in WSPU colors. Others were in the adjoining stall readying the posters, badges, and jewelry for sale. There were several stalls from regional WSPU branches throughout the country selling local fare such as Yorkshire parkin and Kentish cherry pudding.

Close to the entrance, where no one could miss it, was an exact replica of a Holloway second-division prison cell, where the suffragettes were commonly held. Next to it was a replica of a first-division cell where the suffragettes, as political offenders, should have been held. A suffragette stood in prison garb, an ill-fitting green wool gown with a long apron tied at the waist, and a white cap on her head. The whole outfit was marked with arrows to denote prisoner status. Three times a day, a former prisoner would offer guided tours showing the public the difference between the way female and male political prisoners were treated. Although their protests grew from the same types of political unfairness, the male prisoners were allowed to keep their dignity; the female prisoners were not.

Lucy laughed. "That's Vera. Talk about game for anything. She's been in the clink lots. This must seem like home to her."

"Costs a sixpence to get in," Sophie said, digging into her purse. "Come on, Miss Darling. Let's have a look."

"I've seen it in real life," Lucy said. "I'm off to help at the jewelry stall."

Sophie and I paid our admission to the suffragette, and she opened the iron door to the first-division cell. It was a

small bedroom with a rug on the floor, blankets and pillows on the bed, and books on shelves.

And then we crossed through to the second-division
cell. It was tiny, about four paces across. There was a small
wooden stool to sit on, and a shelf in one corner was only
large enough to hold an earthenware dinner plate and mug.
The bed stood about four inches off the ground and was
maybe two feet wide. The mattress looked full of lumps.
The cell was dark and foreboding.

"I admire the women who volunteer for this," Sophie
said. "I don't think I have the courage."

"Neither do I, Sophie," I said.

I READIED THE art stall, setting out easels and preparing
the space for customers who could commission painted or
sketched portraits from us. While I waited for customers, I
sketched the prison cell.

At that moment a man approached the art stall, holding
the hand of a little girl, and requested a sketch of her. I put
my pad down and crossed to the easel.

"Sit here." I pointed to the chair we had set up. "You must
sit very still and not fidget. Do you think you can do that?"

The little girl put her thumb in her mouth and stared up
at me, big brown eyes wide as saucers.

Her father laughed. "She's a shy one, miss. You won't
get much out of her."

I smiled at her father, but I felt sad. I could not picture
my father bringing me to such a place when I was a child.
I couldn't even remember ever holding his hand. My father

had certainly never looked upon me with pride like this man did his daughter.

I stood behind the easel and began to sketch. The drawing was nearly completed when I happened to look up across the hall to the entrance, and my fingers squeezed so hard that I snapped the pastel in half.

"Something the matter, miss?" the father said, frowning.

"I . . . no. I need to be somewhere." I took the picture off the easel and handed it to him. "No charge for the portrait. I'm sorry I couldn't complete it. Perhaps you'll come back." I was babbling like a fool. I had to get out of there before I was seen.

Because coming down the aisle were two men. And one of them was Sir Henry Carrick-Humphrey. Edmund's father.

"Come on, old chap," the other man said to Sir Henry. "We need to be getting on."

"Look at this nonsense," Sir Henry replied. "Do they think selling hats and cakes will get them the vote?"

They were coming toward the stall, and so I didn't wait about any longer. I left, moving as quickly away from them as I could. I went outside and walked to Hyde Park. I sat on a bench near Rotten Row, where the gentlemen and ladies rode their horses along the path.

Sir Henry could have seen me so easily. He would have told my father, and I would have been sent to Aunt Maude's house to wait for my wedding day—or not have had a wedding day at all. I could almost smell the scent of boiled cabbage and beef tongue, the eau de cologne that permeated Aunt Maude's house.

Still, I was ashamed of myself for running away from Sir Henry and leaving the exhibition. I was a rabbit-hearted girl down to my toes.

SUFFRAGE ACTIVITY SETTLED as soon as the exhibition drew to a close so as to let the peaceful efforts of the event sink into the minds of the people and the government. The Pankhurst family scattered. Sylvia, exhausted, went to Kent to paint and recover. Christabel left for Germany for the summer to restore her own health. Their mother, Emmeline Pankhurst, sent Harry to Fels Farm in Essex to work the land while she toured the north to gain support.

As for me, I never went back to see Will again. I wrote him a letter explaining that I couldn't meet him any longer, that it had become too difficult to sneak out of the house. I sent the letter to his flat along with the story illustrations I had finished. Ending things with Will was a worthwhile sacrifice, because for all Will meant to me, he could not send me to art school. I hadn't set out to find love; I'd set out to become an artist, and that was exactly what I needed to do.

It was over. William Fletcher had gone from my life as abruptly as he had entered it. He would be nothing more to me now than images on paper made with pencil and pastel, just as he should have been all along.

Edmund came home from Oxford for good at the beginning of June. I walked in the park with him nearly every day, went to parties with him, smiled and laughed in all the right places. I went with Mamma to choose linens and china for the new house; I worked with Sophie on my trousseau. I had tea with India and her friends and tried to join in their conversation.

But Will was entwined with my emotions and my artwork so much that I could not unpick him from them. Thursdays were a misery. I kept up the scheme of my church charity so as to get out of the house and be on my own. I tried to resume drawing in the Royal Academy courtyard, but the first time I went there I nearly burst into tears, remembering Will's face, his smile, the lips that had kissed me, the hands that had touched me. Even *A Mermaid* held memories of him. When I went to visit her, I found her gaze, which once seemed so welcoming, to be almost accusatory.

I worked on the pastel drawing of Lancelot each morning. I had only less than a month left before I would present it to the examiners on the first of July, but without Will, the work was uninspired. The more I tried to get inspiration back, the muddier and more muted the colors looked. Worse, the expression on Will's face in the drawing tore at me. More than once I longed to hide the portrait far away in the back of my closet because I could not bear to look at it. If I hadn't needed to finish it for the exam, I might have given up on it altogether. I once took out the undraped drawing of Will, hoping to find inspiration again, but memories of the day he kissed me came flooding back, so I did not look at it again.

I saw Will once on Oxford Street while I was with Sophie and my mother, choosing flowers for my wedding. My mother had stopped with Sophie to look at a hat display in Selfridge's window, and that was when I spotted Will. He was walking his beat but he was on the other side of the road and did not see me. He was speaking to a gentleman, pointing out directions. After the gentleman had gone, I thought I saw Will looking toward me. I turned around quickly and pretended to be interested in a wide-brimmed hat trimmed with daisies. It took everything I had not to dash across the street after him.

It seemed I could not keep Will squashed into the back of my mind, no matter how hard I tried.

Twenty-Eight

"REMEMBER TO HOLD your train over your left arm," Mamma said. "Say nothing to the king unless he addresses you. Curtsy to him and the queen and then to any of the royalty around him, then back away, curtsying as you go. For heaven's sake, Victoria, do not turn your back on the king. Remember that most of all." My mother looked dismayed, as if she were picturing me greeting the king by waving my entire arm back and forth like a semaphore flag, shouting, "Cheerio!" and then lifting my skirts to my knees and skipping from the room like the Dame in a Christmas pantomime.

"Yes, of course, Mamma."

We were on the way to Buckingham Palace in the motorcar Father had hired, finally bowing to my mother's insistence that we embrace the new style of transportation, at least for one night.

I looked out the window. The traffic to the ball queued all the way down the Mall from Buckingham Palace. There were several police constables about, directing traffic. For a fleeting moment I thought I saw Will, but when the man turned around, I saw it was someone else.

"And do try to look happy." Mamma tapped her closed fan on my knee. "This is the most important day of a well-bred young woman's life, outside of her wedding day."

Yes, the most important day, because now we were marriage material. Now we were truly alive. Of course, if a girl did not find a husband after two seasons, she was considered a failure and doomed to remain on the shelf, forever a spinster.

I shifted in my seat. "Yes, Mamma." I pulled at my bodice. I was dressed in her white full-court coming-out dress that Sophie had refashioned to bring it up to date. A long train was attached to my shoulders with lace loops. The dress had cap sleeves; my shoulders and neck were bare as was custom. Despite the summer heat, I wore white opera gloves that fitted well past my elbows. Sophie had fixed two white ostrich-tail feathers in my hair, which marked me as an unmarried woman.

My mother was also dressed in white, but her dress had a high collar and was trimmed with colored flowers. And as a married woman, my mother wore a trio of feathers, arranged in the symbol of the Prince of Wales's plume and styled to the left side of her head. We both wore long veils and carried bouquets of roses.

Sophie had had to lace me into the dreaded S-bend corset in order to fit into the wretched gown. I could feel the boning press into my ribs. The evening was sweltering hot, and it didn't help that we were at a standstill.

"Don't fidget."

"I'm not fidgeting!"

"Victoria, do try to look interested in what the other girls have to say."

"And speak to them of what? Hatpins and the weather? As if those are of any interest."

"Well, this is what society is like. This is how you will spend your evenings."

"Not if I can help it." I tugged at the dress once more. I felt Mamma's gaze on me.

"Just how do you think your life will be?"

"Doing what I want." I turned from the window and looked at her. "I'll be married and free to pursue what I want at my leisure."

"In the hour or two each day you have to yourself." She held up her hand and began to tick down an activity on each finger. "You'll have your at-homes and your visits to other ladies' at-homes; you will have to host dinners for Edmund, and there will be many of those, seeing as he's a new businessman. Luncheons out each day with the wives of Edmund's friends and others in your social circle. Meetings with your cook and housekeeper to arrange the day's menu."

I watched, horrified, as she moved on to her other hand. "But . . ." In the past several weeks it had taken all my will to submit the work I needed to the RCA. My time would be taken up all the more with these new social obligations.

But why was I surprised? Had I not seen my own mother immersed in these activities from sunup to sundown?

Was this the reason why she had abandoned her own artwork when I was a little girl? I imagined her drawing me as I tossed corn to the little bird. What was the final distraction that called her away from her drawing book that day? What had she felt when she laid her pencil down for the last time? Frustration? Anger? Or was it relief?

I studied Mamma carefully to see if there were any signs of the artist left. She never once looked out of the motorcar's window searching for a subject that caught her attention or inspired her, fingers curling around an imaginary pencil. Instead she sat still, posture perfect, head held high—a book could sit neatly on top with no danger of falling. Eyes were straight ahead toward Buckingham Palace, hands folded in her lap.

My mother no longer saw the things only artists noticed, things other people would walk straight past, like the light dappling the trunk of a tree; a cat turning its whiskers to the sun, eyes closed in contentment; or the quiet contemplation of a person's face as he sat reading. Instead she saw flaws. Things that were wrong with the house, with her embroidery or flower arranging. Things that were wrong with me.

And then I understood. These were the things a frustrated artist would see.

Suddenly my hands felt strange—restrained as if I wore a pair of manacles instead of silk opera gloves.

THE MOTORCAR ARRIVED at the palace and drove into the Quadrangle. Footmen resplendent in scarlet velvet livery handed us from the car and escorted us to the Grand Entrance. Another footman led us up into the Green Drawing Room, where a buffet of canapés and drinks had been laid out on gold plate. An orchestra from one of the Guards regiments was playing music. Servants milled about offering crystal glasses of punch from trays. My mother went off to deliver our presentation cards to the Lord Steward.

There was even more art than I'd realized. The green tabinet-covered walls of the Green Drawing Room were hung with huge paintings from the Renaissance era. Through the door I saw the work of Rembrandt, Vermeer, and Rubens hanging in the Picture Gallery.

A crush of girls my age waited along with me, standing in groups, giggling and chatting. Like me they were adorned in white gowns and shoulder trains, tall plumes in their hair. I recognized many from my dance class and several from my French finishing school, but none paid me any mind, apart from a few whispers and pointed looks in my direction. I bit back the urge to poke my tongue out at them. Mercifully, Mildred Halfpenny was not there as she was a year behind me and would have her presentation next year.

Excitement crackled in the air. This was the event that the girls had imagined all their lives. To meet the king and announce they were ready for marriage and society! What could be better?

I stood by myself, dressed in my finery, holding a cup of punch, a false smile on my face, and wondered if this life was truly what these girls wanted. And if so, what satisfaction did they glean from it? I wondered what the tall girl with blonde ringlets and a haughty expression really desired. Did she long to be a ballerina or maybe a writer?

What about that short, round girl with the rose-pink cheeks eyeing the French fancies? Did she desire to be a cook or a baker? Or the girl with her back to me, looking out the window. What did she wish to be?

And then I realized that the long neck and the set of those shoulders were familiar; I had drawn that figure many times before. At that moment of recognition, the girl turned and saw me looking.

There she was! Just as I had hoped. My dearest friend, Lily Northbrook.

Her eyes widened.

I set my punch cup down on a nearby table, and, picking up my skirts, threaded my way through the crowd of girls and footmen to her side. We grabbed each other's hands, laughing, giddy with happiness.

"Vicky Darling, how do you do?" Lily laced her fingers through mine.

"Much better now I see your familiar face here." I glanced around. "Everyone here acts as though I have a catching disease."

She smiled wryly. "How have you been? I have worried about you so. I saw Bertram before I left France, and he said he'd had a letter from you. I'm so sorry I haven't written. My father made such a fuss."

"Yes, I know." I was quiet. I didn't know what else to say.

The sound of heels approaching quickly on the marble floor interrupted our conversation. Those heels belonged to the very angry Lady Northbrook, Lily's mother and my mother's erstwhile friend. Her red face stood out against the backdrop of her white dress and veil. She did not share the sweet English rose features that Lily had. Instead I rather thought she resembled the rose's thorny stems: her nose was sharp and angular, her face pinched with disapproval.

My mother came up just then; her face blanched at the sight of Lady Northbrook. She drew in her breath.

"Mrs. Darling, we had an agreement regarding our daughters, did we not?" Lady Northbrook's smile was polite, but there was an undercurrent of tension to the words. "And I will thank you to remember that. I know your social circle has turned the tide with some people but not with me."

"I understand, Lady Northbrook," my mother murmured, looking mortified.

"Things have changed greatly since Queen Victoria's day." Lady Northbrook addressed my mother, but her gaze flicked to me. "*She* only received young ladies who wore the white flower of a blameless life. King Edward does not possess such high standards." Lady Northbrook held out her hand, fingers flickering at Lily. "Come away then, Lily."

Before her mother had a chance to pull her away, Lily leaned in and kissed me on the cheek.

It was clear that my mother was upset and humiliated by Lady Northbrook's tirade. She looked as though she might burst into tears. Several people nearby had heard the exchange, and there was much whispering from behind fans.

I pictured telling Lady Northbrook exactly what I thought about her. How dare she speak to my mother so? But I knew that would have only embarrassed my mother further. So instead I fetched her a cup of punch and stood in front of her, shielding her from the pointing fingers while she drank it.

Thankfully, Mrs. Plimpton came in with her daughter Georgette. I don't think I was ever so grateful to see two people in my life. My mother's tension dispersed as soon as she was back in the safety of her own social circle.

A footman came in and announced that the king was ready. We all followed him to the Throne Room, a huge room decorated in scarlet with an ornate gold-and-white rococo ceiling. I saw the king awaiting us, dressed in a red jacket with gold epaulets, standing underneath the Cloth of State; Queen Alexandra sat next to him; his lords-in-waiting stood to the side.

I couldn't help but think the king looked rather bored. I couldn't blame him. Greeting girl after girl for hours on end was surely enough to drive even the most stoic monarch round the bend.

I watched several debutantes go in front of me. When their names were called, their sponsors moved to stand at the back of the room. When it was my turn, Mamma let go of my arm and stood as far away from Lady Northbrook as she could.

One of the lords-in-waiting let down my train, spreading it behind me. I stood alone for a moment, underneath the massive crystal chandelier, as the Lord Chamberlain announced my name. I took a deep breath and approached the king.

Miss Winthrop had taught us to curtsy deeply so that we were nearly sitting upon the floor. I smiled demurely at the king, as I had been told to do, brought my left foot around behind my right, bent my knees, and sank to the floor while holding my bouquet over my right knee.

But when Miss Winthrop had taught us, we had all been wearing dance skirts, not long, narrow gowns with a train, a veil, and a tight corset and holding a bouquet of flowers. So when I tried to rise, I found I could not. I had trodden on the back of my dress with the heel of my foot when I brought it round my other leg. I had effectively pinned myself to the ground. The skirt was far too narrow to move my feet; if I did so, I'd teeter to the ground. So I just stayed there.

I heard feminine titters and giggles all around me. I could imagine the silent scream of horror that echoed through my mother's head.

I stared at the king's ankles, unable to work out what to do next.

"You may rise," the king said.

"I cannot, Your Majesty," I whispered. "I'm stuck."

And then the king laughed, rose from his velvet chair, and reached for my hand.

"Might I assist you, Miss Darling?"

I untangled my legs, and with as much dignity as I could muster, rose to my feet with the king's help. His whiskered face creased into a smile.

"I . . . thank you, Your Majesty." I went to curtsy again, but the king lifted his hand.

"I think we should desist with the curtsy, don't you? Otherwise you might find yourself wound round like a ball of twine again!" The king's attendants broke into laughter.

"Please forgive me, Your Majesty," I said, feeling my face blush red with shame.

"I shan't forgive you," he said in a gruff voice, "for you've done nothing wrong. You've quite made my evening. Makes a change from the usual parade of utterly proper debutantes that parade in front of me year after year. They all look the same, but you—you I shall remember! Who is your family?"

"My father is the proprietor of Darling and Son Sanitary Company, maker of the dreadnought flushing toilet, Your Majesty." I winced when the word *toilet* left my lips. I was about to apologize when he laughed and then spoke again:

"Well. Mr. Darling of Darling and Son Sanitary Company, maker of the dreadnought privy, is fortunate to have such a charming daughter." And then he took my hand and kissed it.

Gasps rose from all around me. The kissing of the hand had been done away with in the court presentation when Queen Victoria had died. She had only bestowed her kiss upon those girls deemed worthy of it. For King Edward to do so was tantamount to him stamping *acceptable* on my forehead in indelible ink.

I didn't have to worry about backing away from the king because he held out his arm and escorted me to the door. My mother had an expression of astonishment on her face. Lady Northbrook looked as though she had swallowed a cactus. Lily's face was bright red from the effort of trying not to laugh. And she had that familiar expression in her eyes that I knew so well: exasperation mixed with affection.

In the motorcar on the way home, my mother was beset with a case of the giggles. I had never seen her laugh so much in my life. She'd shake her head, look at me, and then titter. She had a musical laugh, three little trills: *ha, ha, ha!*

"I tell you, Victoria. I've never seen Lady Northbrook so tongue-tied in my life. She's always been such a stuck-up thing, thinking herself better than most people. I must confess that I nearly caught my shoe in the hem of my gown when I was presented. I don't think I would have handled it as well as you did." She beamed at me and then giggled again. "Papa will be very pleased that you mentioned his name, very pleased."

Mamma gazed out the window for a bit, smiling. She looked so young and happy just then. I could almost imagine her sitting next to me in a life-drawing class, leaning over to compare our sketches.

"Mamma, why did you stop drawing?"

She turned away from the window; her smile faded. "Whatever do you mean?"

"I found a box in March after I came home from school. I was looking for stationery to write Edmund. You weren't home, and I went into your room. There was a box on your desk filled with your sketches." Mamma's hand had gone up to her throat. She started pulling at the rope of pearls there. "One was unfinished. The one of me."

I saw her swallow.

"Mamma?"

She pressed her mouth into a tight line and looked out the window again. I should have just shut my mouth then, just left it there, but no, I could not leave it, as usual.

"You're so talented. I want to be as good as you some-day, do you know that?" I said.

She said nothing for a long moment. She just sat there staring out the window. And then she finally said, "Cumberbunch tells me your gown will be finished tomorrow morning, which is all well and good, but I think she should have had it finished sooner, given that tomorrow is your ball. Still, I think it will be worth the wait."

The door that had cracked open a little between us slammed shut. "Yes, you're right, Mamma. It will be beautiful. I can't wait to wear it."

My heart ached for my mother. And now, more than ever, I vowed not to follow in her footsteps. When I saw Edmund at my ball tomorrow, I would tell him about art school. I would tell him that I would not be a society wife.

THE NEXT EVENING was my coming-out ball at the Savoy Hotel on the Strand. The ballroom was lit by glittery electric lights and filled to bursting with friends, family, and business acquaintances. I finally met Jonty, Edmund's older brother, who would inherit the Carrick-Humphrey estates. He couldn't be more different from Edmund. He was tall, like Edmund, but with a more slender build. His eyes were a lighter color blue, and he held himself slightly aloof, as if he really couldn't be bothered with a debutante ball. Unlike Edmund, he hadn't a whiff of charm about him.

His wife, Millicent, a tall woman with dark hair, clung to his arm.

Several of Edmund's friends from Oxford were there, including a boy called Kenneth, who was to be Edmund's best man. I recognized him as one of the teammates from the rowing crew. Edmund seemed to hang on his every word and defer to him much of the time. Like Edmund, Kenneth was dressed in the latest style and wore his clothes as if they were a second skin.

I had arrived with my parents, and Edmund came to greet me. He was dressed in tails, a waistcoat, and a high collar, a white bow tie knotted around it. His hair was carefully combed and oiled back as usual. He resembled the hero I saw once at a bioscope at a Chelsea music hall with Freddy. The clothes looked natural on Edmund, as though he had been born to such riches, and his personality shone a bit brighter in them.

"You look very beautiful, Victoria," he said, and held out his arm for me to take. I slid my arm through his, and we walked into the Wedgwood-blue Lancaster Ballroom for the first dance of the evening. I was wearing the ball gown that Sophie had made for me. I couldn't help but notice Georgette Plimpton and a few of India's friends looking my way with envious expressions. No one else was wearing anything like it. Although it had been featured in *La Mode Illustrée*, Sophie had made it my own, adding a Pre-Raphaelite flair. I had drawn the gown from Waterhouse's *Lady of Shalott* for Sophie, and she'd replicated the sleeves' checkered decoration with silver embroidery thread on my bodice.

"So . . . how was the king last night?"

"Going a bit doolally. I think it was from the hoards of women coming at him from all angles. At least that's what he told me."

Edmund looked shocked. "He spoke to you?"

"I nearly fell over when I curtsied. He had to help me up."

Edmund burst out laughing. "Well, I never. It had to be you. I hope India has as much luck when she has her presentation with the king next year."

The orchestra struck up the music for the quadrille. Sophie's dance lessons held me in good stead and I did not disgrace myself. Edmund and I danced the quadrille and then the mazurka and the polonaise successfully. And not once did I tread on his feet or mine. I had several balls to get through in the next few months, and at least I wouldn't disgrace myself.

After an hour's dancing, Edmund persuaded me to go off with him and a few of his friends to visit the American Bar in the hotel for a cocktail.

I pretended to enjoy my drink, but really I was just gathering my courage to talk to him about art school. Finally, when we had finished our cocktails and headed back to the ballroom, I paused in the foyer and tugged Edmund's hand, letting the others go on ahead.

"Edmund, just before we go back, I wanted to talk to you. I wondered. Do you have a desire . . . a dream to be something or do something?"

Edmund looked confused. "How so?"

"I mean . . . do you wish to pursue your rowing? You did ever so well in the Boat Race, so perhaps you'd like to keep on with it . . . perhaps the Olympics. Shouldn't you like to row for England?"

He hunched his shoulders a bit and then leaned against the wall. "What extraordinary ideas you have, Victoria. Why would I want to do such a thing?"

I was slightly taken aback. I thought Edmund would have agreed with me immediately. "I don't know. . . . I expect for the glory. For personal satisfaction. Everyone has a dream they want to come true, don't they?"

Edmund lifted his hands and then let them drop. "Maybe. I've never given it any thought. Rowing was fun for the Boat Race but jolly hard work just for that one day. Not sure I'd like to spend the next three years getting shouted at by a coxswain. Say, let's go back to the ballroom. They'll be turning out the brandy soon. Cakes as well." He pushed himself away from the wall and took my arm. But I held back. Edmund crinkled his brow. "What's all this about, old thing? All this talk about Olympics and such. You do take on about the oddest."

This wasn't going at all to plan. I would just have to wade in and have done with it. "I . . . I have to tell you something. Well, you see, I've been preparing to go to art college. I didn't tell you because I didn't want our fathers to get wind of it. You know what they are like. I wish art to be my life and so I shan't have much time for parties and such, you know?" Edmund looked at me blankly. I went on. "An artist has to focus. If I'm to be any good, I'll be spending quite a lot of time on my work. Freddy told you I was going to college. Don't you remember?"

He shrugged. "I don't know. . . . Maybe. But your

father said you were done with all that art stuff," he said.

"I . . . no. He may have thought I was, but I assure you I am not."

"Well, if you're set on it, then you're set on it. So you'll go to art college—if you get accepted, mind. Maybe you won't. But if you want to spend your time shut away in a dreary classroom listening to some fusty old boy blather on about art, then that's your funeral."

"You don't mind if I miss parties and luncheons and such?"

"Go to parties; don't go to parties. I don't mind a whit." Edmund pulled the sleeves of his jacket down and brushed a bit of lint away.

"I . . . all right." I wondered if I should mention the tuition. "There's just one more thing."

An irritated sound left Edmund. "What now?"

"I'll need you to pay for it."

"Oh, let's talk about money now, do!" Edmund shifted from foot to foot. He was truly irked. "Oh, jolly good! Sometimes, Victoria, you are so middle-class! You'll have the money, and let's say no more about it. Now, let's go back or else we'll miss the refreshments." Edmund held out his arm. I hesitated and then slid my hand through the crook of his elbow.

I should have been glad that Edmund didn't care what I did. After all, this was what I had wanted when I agreed to marry him. But I thought he might have shown more happiness for me. Instead he just seemed resigned, as though agreeing reluctantly with the design of our new wallpaper or furniture.

Why couldn't Edmund be more like Will, who supported me in my endeavors fully and wholeheartedly? Sometimes I felt like Will believed in me more than I believed in myself. Without Will's support, Edmund's indifference to my dream was even more painful.

But truly, I'd spent more time with Will than with Edmund. Will and I had always been alone; Edmund and I were always chaperoned. We'd only been alone for a few minutes here and there, surely never enough time to let understanding—or passion—grow between us.

I pulled Edmund behind one of the pillars, out of sight of anyone who might be walking past. A scowl twisted his face. "Victoria, honestly—"

"Will you kiss me?" I asked.

"Of course," he said in a distracted manner. He leaned down and fixed a quick kiss on my lips.

Who could tell anything from such a chaste kiss? I tightened my fingers on his elbow to prevent him from leaving. "No, Edmund, really kiss me!"

I could tell that my request took him off guard. He hesitated for a moment, and then darted a look over his shoulder. Finally he made up his mind, and forgetting the cursed brandy, he backed me against the pillar, tilted my chin up with his fingertips, and kissed me with more passion. His mouth was soft; the kiss was tidy and efficient; his hands, now clasping my waist, were sure and strong.

Nothing. I felt nothing. I didn't even feel the urge to close my eyes.

There was too much space between us. Maybe I needed

to be closer to him, like Will and I had been that day in his flat. I slid one palm up Edmund's back and rested it against the bare nape of his neck, just above the starched cotton of his collar. I took a step forward and pressed against him.

Immediately Edmund twisted sideways, breaking the kiss. "Victoria," he said, laughing. He held me away from him, his arms braced, as though fending me off. His fingers were cold on the bare skin of my shoulders. "Steady on. Someone might come by. What's gotten into you?"

"Can't a girl kiss her fiancé at her own ball?" I said faintly. I was embarrassed, humiliated even. Even though I was fully dressed in layers of silk, cotton, and mousseline, I felt naked—more exposed than when I'd posed nude in front of a group of male artists. I crossed my arms over my bodice.

"There's a time and a place for everything Victoria, and this is neither the time nor the place." He tapped my nose with his forefinger and then held out his hand toward the ballroom. "Shall we make a move? At long last? Everyone will think we've eloped."

So we returned to the ballroom.

Earlier in the evening, my father had marked my dance card for a waltz, and he came to claim me from Edmund after the buffet. I had never danced with Papa before, and to say that I felt awkward would be an understatement. I didn't know where to look, so I fixed my gaze on his tie. His valet had shaped the piqué fabric into an even batwing shape and aligned it directly under his chin. His pearl dress studs marched in an unbroken line down his shirt, and his tailcoat had been brushed until the nap stood up.

Everything was perfect; nothing could be faulted. Unlike Edmund, my father wore no cologne, as he believed such fripperies unseemly.

"My dear, you were a smashing success with the king," Papa said, staring over my shoulder as he carefully maneuvered me across the dance floor. He moved through the stationary box step carefully and methodically. But he didn't dance along with the music like Edmund did. If the musicians suddenly stopped playing, Papa would most likely continue marching around the floor until the allotted time was up. "Most remarkable. You're to be commended."

"Thank you, Papa," I said, counting the steps in my head. *One, two, three; two, two, three.* I was terrified I was going to tread on his feet. I checked to make sure I wasn't clutching his hand or clinging too hard to his shoulder. What had Miss Winthrop said? *Light as a butterfly, girls! Don't clutch your partner like grim death!*

"You've done everything your mother and I have asked of you, and you've done it perfectly. Your mother has told me that you've even volunteered for extra duties with your church charity."

My slipper grazed the patent leather toe of Papa's shoe, narrowly missing treading on it fully. "Yes," I said. "I enjoy my time there."

"Sir Henry is pleased with you as well. You'll make a lovely wife and mother. I must say I was most astounded with your performance with the telephone. I had no idea you possessed such skills. You'll be a credit to Edmund, which is a great asset to a businessman, as your mother will attest. Since all is going as planned, I see no reason to keep it from you any longer."

Over Papa's shoulder I saw Edmund dancing with his mother. She was talking and nodding; the feathers in her hair bobbed emphatically. He caught me watching and grinned at me, rolling his eyes. Apparently we were both being subjected to parental conversations. I smiled at him, as though nothing was amiss, but another wave of embarrassment crashed over me as I thought about how he'd held me away from him with stick-straight arms, like some odious thing in need of discarding.

"Victoria, are you listening?"

I jerked my attention back to my father's bow tie. "I'm sorry, Papa. Keep what from me?"

"Now, the marriage contract has been drawn up, and there is a jointure included for your care if you should become widowed, but I have not settled a sum upon you. However, in light of your recent behavior, I have decided to give you a yearly allowance of seven hundred pounds."

Mercifully the music stopped, because if it hadn't, I'm sure I would have stepped completely upon Papa's foot, I was so startled. "Seven hundred pounds?" My voice rose. "A year?" Seven hundred pounds was a small fortune. And it would give me a measure of independence in my marriage. I wouldn't have to go to Edmund for every little thing I wanted. I wouldn't have to charge my purchases to his account. I could pay my own college tuition. The money more than made up for Edmund's indifference.

I kissed Papa's cheek. "Thank you!"

Papa squeezed my hand. "You're quite welcome, my dear."

I danced every dance the rest of the night perfectly, not putting a foot out of place, propelled by the giddy promise of seven hundred pounds a year. I'd made the right decision when I severed ties with Will. Of course I had.

Twenty-Nine

EARY OF BALLS, fidgeting with boredom, and lonely for the company of other artists, I decided to investigate the Suffrage Atelier. Sophie made inquiries at the WSPU headquarters and got the address for me. It was located in a garden studio at the home of Laurence and Clemence Housman, a brother and sister who resided at Broadhurst Gardens in South Hampstead. I worked out how to get there on the Underground and went there on the Thursday after our ball.

The Housman siblings lived in a quiet neighborhood on a tree-lined street. A wooden sign on the gate pointed the way to a little building behind the house in the garden. There were a few women inside who were sketching, painting pottery, and the like. I saw Lucy sitting at a small table underneath a window, working with wire and small, colorful stones.

She set her pliers down. "Hi, Queenie. I was hoping you were going to come."

I sat down in the chair next to her. "I've been busy. What are you working on?"

"Oh, some things to sell. I'm glad you're here because I've been thinking of asking if you'd like to design something. Figural work is very popular, and I'm not much of an artist when it comes to that. Why don't you draw something, and I'll make the wax mold and cast it at school this week. If the Selfridge's buyer likes it, I can cast more. We just have to make it in suffragette colors."

I thought about when Sylvia mentioned studying William Morris's textiles at school. Maybe I could impress the examiners with some decorative work. I turned my sketchbook to a new page. "What are the suffragette colors again?"

"Purple for dignity, white for purity, and green for hope, just like on the mural."

I sat sketching ideas. I tried a sailing ship, a horse, and a chalice, but none of them held the symbolism I wanted to capture, as Sylvia had with the mural. Finally I thought about *A Mermaid*. She had always been my inspiration, so maybe other women would feel the same. I thought maybe she would make a beautiful brooch. But instead of showing her combing her hair, as in the painting, I made her holding an umbrella of seaweed and sea lavender over her head. I showed the sketch to Lucy.

"I like that."

"I think a mermaid would make a wonderful suffragette, don't you? Mermaids sing and distract sailors at sea; so as a suffragette, she could sing and distract all the politicians in Parliament into giving women the vote!"

Lucy laughed. "And then lead the daft men straight to the bottom of the Thames. We need to find a school of mermaids right away. What's the umbrella for?"

I thought for a moment. "I suppose she's made her own shelter from the storm."

"Even better."

Lucy started to flip through my book. I was just about to take it back when her finger landed on a page. "That's PC Fletcher. What's he doing in your book?"

I tried to pull the sketchbook away, but she took hold of it and slid it closer to her. I watched as she leaned over the pages and studied the sketches of Will. I squeezed my fingers into fists, wanting desperately to snatch the book from her hands. "It's nothing—"

She shook her head. "This is not *nothing*. These sketches are really good." And then she turned the page, and there was my nude drawing of Will.

There was a sharp intake of breath from Lucy. She stared at the sketch, unmoving, and then she slowly looked at me, her dark eyes shining. "Oh, did I ever have you pegged in the wrong hole!" Her voice was marked with laughter. "Not only did you draw a copper, but in the buff as well! You're really something!" She burst into giggles. "I have to say," she said, after collecting herself, "I always thought that copper was a pretty nice guy, stepping in to help us any way he could. I never thought he was *that* nice." She lifted the sketchbook and turned it sideways, leaning in to take a closer look. "Hmmm." She raised an eyebrow. "*Very* nice."

Just then, the atelier's co-organizer, Clemence Housman, came over. She was middle-aged, with her hair bundled into a net at the base of her neck. Although she was dressed in black, she was anything but dowdy. She'd accessorized her bodice with a striking ornate circular brooch encrusted with fresh-water pearls and mother-of-pearl. After Lucy introduced us, she said, "You're the Vicky who does the illustrations! Sylvia said you might be willing to do some for us. Would you be able to draw the deputation to Parliament on the twenty-ninth of June? Our usual illustrator can't make it."

"A deputation?" I asked. "What's that?"

"Emmeline Pankhurst and a bunch of us are going to Parliament to see the prime minister," Lucy chimed in.

"That doesn't sound very interesting," I said, wondering what on earth I would draw.

"Oh, it might be," Lucy replied. "The prime minister hasn't allowed the WSPU to speak with him for ages, so a crowd of us are going to march right up to the door of the Commons and demand to see him. We won't take no for an answer, so it's likely we'll get arrested. The papers will carry the story and put suffrage back in people's minds again."

An artist came over and asked Miss Housman for help. "Let me know as soon as you can, Vicky," Miss Housman said, and then went off with the artist.

"Are you going to do it?" Lucy asked me.

"I don't know. I can't risk getting arrested."

"Why would you get arrested? You're just drawing. If you stand in the gutter, you won't be done for blocking the pavement. You'll be safe as houses. The only reason you got arrested before is because you wouldn't scarper when I told you to scarper." She grinned. "Just don't let anyone shove you onto any police constables. Not that there's anything wrong with that."

I didn't respond. I didn't want to talk about Will.

"All right. What's going on? There's something more to this story." Her eyes widened. "You kissed him, didn't you?"

"Shhh!" I glanced around. "Keep your voice down."

"That's romantic as all get-out. An artist falling in love with her muse." She gestured with a wide, theatrical sweep of her arm. "Did he have his clothes on when you kissed him?"

"Lucy!"

"So what's the problem? He doesn't feel the same way about you?"

"No. I believe he feels the same. At least the way he kissed me felt like it. It was really passionate."

Lucy leaned forward, rapt, listening to my every word. "Sounds good to me. What's the problem?"

"The problem is I'm engaged already!"

"What? I didn't know that! Well, if you love PC Fletcher, then you'd better break the engagement before it goes any further. You can't marry someone when you're in love with someone else. How's that going to work?"

I gaped at her. "Have you lost your mind, Lucy? I have to get married."

"Why?" She went back to work, sliding a silver bail into a pendant and pinching it closed with her little pliers.

"Because if I don't, my father will cut me off and send me to live with my great-aunt in Norfolk. No art school. And art school is what I'm about. Not love. Not some fancy I have for a working-class boy."

I put my head in my hands. *Working-class boy.* Just saying those words out loud made me feel like a toffee-nosed idiot. But that was what he was, and the way my parents would always treat him. There was a reason why Will had come to the servants' entrance that day to bring my sketchbook back. Will knew that was the door he had to use. Of course he did. What was more, I didn't think I'd ever walked through that door once in my life.

Lucy reached for her cigarette case. "You English are so strange about class. Listen to you." She drew out a cigarette, lit it, and exhaled, regarding me through a plume of smoke. "'Working-class boy'! Heavens to Betsy, Queenie."

"It's not I who care, Lucy. It's my father. And my mother. They would never accept Will. It's not the done thing to marry outside one's class," I said.

"If you ask me, the heart knows the way, and if you deny it, then it's hell to pay for you." She pointed her cigarette at me. "If money is what you're looking for, then you'll have a life of misery. Remember what happened to Midas, when he wanted the gold? Sure, it was all lollipops and rainbows at first, but then it all ended in tears."

"So you're telling me that I should break my engagement?" I was so frustrated I was close to crying. "And then do what after my father gets over his fit of apoplexy? Live how and where? He cut my brother, Freddy, off because he didn't want to go into the family business. When he came crawling back begging for forgiveness, my father gave him an allowance. My brother can't even manage without Papa's money."

Lucy shrugged. "So when you come crawling back, he'll probably forgive you, too."

I shook my head. "Oh, no. Stepping out with a boy

below my class would be the ultimate betrayal. My father would never, ever forgive me. My fiancé is joining the family business, too. There's no way around it, Lucy. Anyway, it's over with. I don't see Will anymore."

Lucy watched me thoughtfully, turning the cigarette around in her fingers. "I'm not one to say it's easy to break away from your family. Lord knows my pa didn't want me to come here, but I was willing to take the chance. The way I see it, you've figured out how to draw PC Fletcher, be a suffragette, and get yourself into art school on your own. You're a smart cookie. You'll figure it out."

I was more confused than ever now. I was sorry I had told her.

IN THE END, I told Miss Housman I would help illustrate the deputation. Using my church charity as an excuse, I told Mamma I'd be helping at St. Martin-in-the-Fields in Trafalgar Square.

The day of the deputation was scorching hot, and the sun blazed down. The black tarmacadam roads reflected the heat in shimmering waves. It was the kind of day that turned the gloomy, misty days of spring into a fond memory.

The deputation had made the papers, and a crowd had come to gape. There was a big police presence, on foot as well as on horses, lining the street. I scanned the constables for Will, but they all looked the same in their domed helmets and tunics.

I had taken up a position near the Members' Entrance,

but I stood in the gutter, as Lucy had suggested, so I would not be arrested for obstruction of the pathway. I had already made sketches of the entrance. I would sketch in Emmeline Pankhurst as she arrived. I shifted from foot to foot. The sun was hot on my head; my little straw summer cloche was no defense against its rays.

Several police constables passing by looked at me askance but didn't say anything to me. All the same, I didn't like them taking notice of me. When would Mrs. Pankhurst get here?

And then finally I heard some people shouting. I stood on tiptoes and looked toward Whitehall to see Mrs. Pankhurst coming down the pavement. A group of women, Lucy among them, trailed her like a wake behind a sailing vessel.

As they drew near, I began to draw, making basic figure sketches that I could finish with more detail later. I focused only on the women's essential features and actions. Mrs. Pankhurst didn't look anything like Christabel or Sylvia. Where her daughters were possessed of delicate beauty, their mother was what Mamma would call a "handsome" woman, with sturdy yet feminine features. She was dressed in a high-necked shirtwaist and a striped poplin skirt. And she walked with purposeful, quick strides, her gaze locked on Parliament.

I drew Clara tripping along behind, her hand clasped on top of her straw boater, her expression earnest. And Lucy, next to her, ignoring the jeers from the crowd and walking steadily, face calm, attention focused on Mrs. Pankhurst, like a bridesmaid behind her bride. I drew the angry faces of the crowd and the staid faces of the constables. My fingers began to cramp because I was drawing so quickly, trying hard to get down every detail that I could. The scene was too important to rely on my memory alone.

As the women drew nearer, some men shouted and shook their fists. I couldn't make out what they were saying, but Mrs. Pankhurst's contingent didn't like it. Some of the women yelled back at them. The men could do little in response, but they pushed against the police line all the same. The constables shoved back, holding the line. There was a sizzle in the air and a feeling of tension and sheer fury held in check.

One of the men cocked his arm back and threw an egg, which struck a woman in the side of her face. She staggered sideways and put her hand up to her cheek. She paused for a moment and then turned to stare down the crowd, wiping her face with the back of her arm. Lucy said something to her, and she shook her head and walked on.

Mrs. Pankhurst marched up to the Members' Entrance, the door that admitted the members of Parliament, and spoke to a red-faced constable guarding the door. He handed her an envelope and watched while she read it. Then she threw the letter to the ground.

"I will not accept the prime minister's refusal," Mrs. Pankhurst said, her voice stately. "I stand upon my right as a subject of the king to petition the prime minister. I am firmly resolved to stand here until I am received."

But the constable just shook his head.

"What's happening?" someone near me shouted. "I

can't see!" Like water rising to the boil, the people were growing restless.

"Asquith denied the Pankhurst woman leave to see him," a man with a broad Yorkshire accent answered. "I don't think that will find favor with her."

Several politicians came out to watch the proceedings. They hung on the railing like little boys on a climbing frame, laughing as though the scene was the funniest thing they had ever witnessed in their lives. Not a one of them seemed inclined to understand why Mrs. Pankhurst was there. It made me angry that none of them gave her the dignity that she deserved as a citizen.

I knew then how I would portray them. I would draw a cartoon of them as little boys dressed in suits and bowler hats. If they acted like children, then I would draw them as children.

There was a brief, heated exchange between Mrs. Pankhurst and the constable. Several constables came out to escort her away, but when one put his hand on her arm and tried to march her from the door, she dug her toes in. So he wrapped his arm around her waist and pulled her along with him toward the gate. They drew closer to me, so I could see clearly when she spun out of his grip and tapped him lightly on the face with her fingertips.

"I know what you're about," the constable said in an even tone. "You're striking me so I will arrest you, but I will not be perturbed."

So Mrs. Pankhurst slapped him again, twice, and another woman pushed the man's hat off.

"She's slapped a constable in the face! She's being arrested!" someone shouted.

The crowd exploded, shouting and pushing against the police line. The women who had been following Mrs. Pankhurst glanced around, fear marked on their faces, and shuffled up against the iron railings. An arrest was one thing, but reprisals from an aggressive crowd were not part of the plan.

The crowd shoved the line once more, and I didn't know if they did it with malicious intent, but several constables stepped away, allowing a space to open up. The constables on the other side tried vainly to stop the gap, but it was too late. Several men ran forward and rushed the women huddled near the gate, grabbing at them and throwing things at them. It was a rugby scrum of hostile spectators, suffragettes, and police constables.

Afraid of being caught in the riot, I stepped out of the gutter and struggled through the press to find a place farther back away from the crowd.

In the middle of this melee, I saw Lucy fall to the ground. The men surrounded her, and I didn't see her get up. I shoved my book into my satchel and pushed through the people toward her. A man in a flat cap grabbed hold of my arm, pulling me against him. I stamped on his foot hard with the heel of my boot and he let go, cursing. I finally reached Lucy. She sat on the ground, her arms over her head; people were churning and falling all around her.

"Lucy!"

She looked up. Her hat was gone, her dark hair in disarray. There was a long, bloody scratch on her cheek.

When she saw me, the fear on her face turned to relief. She grabbed my hand and I helped her up, and we ran.

WE ESCAPED TO Victoria Tower Gardens and collapsed onto a park bench. I clutched my satchel against me as if I could contain the horrors I had documented inside it. But it was like trying to slam the lid on Pandora's box. I couldn't get the images of what I had seen out of my mind: the hatred of the people who had attacked the suffragettes, and the utter disregard from some of the police for the safety of the women. The fear in the women's faces as the crowd surrounded them. My eyes burned and my blouse felt clammy with dampness.

"Did you know it would be like that?"

Lucy shook her head, wordless.

"You were nearly crushed! I was so afraid for you."

"I was afraid for me too, Queenie." Lucy's voice shook.

"Promise me you won't do anything like that again."

She let out a short laugh. "I can't promise that. Like I told you before, I'm always up for a fight."

"A fight like that? How can you? I saw how afraid you were."

"So what? I was afraid. If I let fear stop me, I'd still be back in America, washing another man's underpants. And you shouldn't let it stop you, either."

My throat was sore from the effort of holding back tears. "I wish I could be like you, but I'm not."

"How can you have what you want when you're denied the same rights as male citizens?"

I shook my head.

"Here are some home truths, Queenie. That art school you're hankering after? It gets money from the government, yet they are stingy with scholarships for women. Even though Sylvia Pankhurst won a scholarship, she didn't think it was fair other women weren't considered, so she challenged the school and they labeled her a trouble-maker. Did you know that?"

"She told me she butted up against the establishment, but she didn't tell me that." I couldn't imagine anyone disliking Sylvia Pankhurst, who was possibly the kindest person I knew. I could only imagine the doors that were shut against her in the art world. She couldn't even give me a simple reference letter.

"The dean hated her for it, and he's not someone you want against you if you want to be an artist. And Christabel. She got her law degree from Manchester University. She graduated with honors. Finished higher than most of the male students."

"But that's good, isn't it?"

"It might be if she were allowed to practice law. The Bar Council won't let women use their degrees. Christabel is forbidden to practice law because she is a woman. Is that fair?"

I bit my lip. "I didn't . . . I didn't know that. My neighbor is going to medical school. She might not be able to become a doctor?"

"If she dared to work alongside men, they'd treat her like a nurse, if even that. This is why we all fight so hard.

Not just for the vote, but for an equal opportunity in the world. A vote is a voice. I think you underestimate yourself, Queenie. This is your fight, same as it is mine." Lucy stood up, shoved her hands into the pockets of that ugly gray skirt, and leaned against a London plane tree. "If I could snap my fingers and give you the life you wanted, what would you say? What would your life look like?"

"I know where you're going. I don't want to play this game—"

"Yes, you do. Come on, what would it be? Dare to dream a bit, Queenie."

I shrugged. "I'd want to earn my own money with an occupation that means something to me."

"Go on."

"To be able to say what I want, to say what I believe without being disapproved of." I thought back to how Papa had berated me for expressing my opinion to Sir Henry.

"Sounds reasonable. How about loving who you want instead of settling for someone your parents have chosen for you? Wouldn't it be a real lollapalooza to bring him home and say, 'Ma and Pa, this is my guy and if you don't like him . . . well, then, too bad. I don't need your money or anyone's money, I don't even need *him* to have money, 'cause I got my own.'" She nudged me with her elbow and watched me carefully. "Like PC Fletcher?"

At the mention of Will, a stab of pain rent my heart. "Please don't say his name." I started to cry then. I couldn't help it. I tried to hold it back, but everything came crashing down around me. Will, my parents, Edmund, art school, the suffragettes, the riot . . . it all tumbled down like a landslide.

Lucy put her arm around me. "Hey, I'm sorry. I didn't mean to upset you." She mumbled something under her breath. "I'm such a disaster. I know it. Everyone tells me not to be so pushy, but I just get on my soapbox and I can't get off it. I forget this is all new to you. Sometimes things can get really intense, and we can't take it anymore. It happened to me before I left America. Even the Pankhursts get overwhelmed. Sylvia is in Kent painting, and Christabel is at that German spa. Why don't you concentrate on getting into art school and then see where you are."

Lucy pulled a cloth-wrapped package out of her pocket and handed it to me. "Here. I finished it this morning. I was going to give it to you after the deputation. I knew you wanted it to show for your exam. But I think you should wear her. Maybe she'll give you some courage. Remember why you made her in the first place? What you wanted her to mean? She makes her own shelter."

I undid the wrapping. Inside was the mermaid brooch I had designed. She held her sea-lavender umbrella aloft, a gentle smile upon her face as she sat on her tail. An unseen wind seemed to blow her long hair back from her shoulders.

Lucy nudged my shoulder with hers. "Come and find me at Clement's Inn when you decide what you want to do. You can even stay with me for a bit if you want."

A lump rose in my throat just then. "Thank you, Lucy."

She laid a hand on my shoulder. "Do you remember what Christabel said—'women who are unwilling to fight for the vote are unworthy of it'? That applies to life, too, Vicky."

A moment later I realized that she had not called me Queenie. For the first time since I had known her, she called me Vicky.

Thirty

IT WAS THE day of the exam. I waited in the hallway of the RCA with my drawing of Lancelot and another life study of Will safely between two large pieces of card, and the mermaid pin nestled in a box.

After the deputation I had pulled myself together and finished Lancelot. It wasn't my best, but I thought it was good enough. I also finished the sketches of the deputation and posted them to Clemence Housman. And then I stepped back from the WSPU. I couldn't think about it now. It was just too much.

The day after the riot, newspapers reported that Lucy and thirteen other women had protested the prime minister's refusal to see Mrs. Pankhurst, and had thrown rocks at the Treasury Building, breaking nearly every pane of glass. They had waited until nightfall when no one would be in the building. They had even gone so far as to tie strings to the stones so they wouldn't fly far into the rooms, just in case someone was there. The goal was just to attract police attention, not to injure anyone. As planned, they had been arrested and then released to stand trial later in the month.

Now I studied the RCA candidates, who sat on a long

row of benches in the hall while we were called in one by one to show our work. There were maybe fifty men there and only ten or so women besides myself.

I couldn't help but think about what Lucy had said about the RCA. It wasn't fair that so few women were given a scholarship. I supposed that was why the men had reason to look so confident while the women who needed financial help were apprehensive and worried.

When my name was called, I rose and went into the room. Five men sat at a long table against the window. Only one looked up when I came in. He was the youngest of them, maybe in his forties with hair that was long enough to touch his collar. The cut of his coat was a little more modern, and he wore a colorful waistcoat, whereas the others looked as though they had been dragged from a Victorian tableau. One man actually wore a monocle, of all things.

I placed my work on the table and watched, hands folded in front of me, as each examiner looked at the drawings and the mermaid brooch and passed them to the next man in line. One of the men looked at the nude drawing of Will and then at me with an expression of surprise on his face, but he said nothing.

"It appears you have a fascination with the Pre-Raphaelites, Miss Darling," the man with the monocle said as he studied the pastel drawing.

"I do, sir," I said with as much confidence as I could muster. I tried to keep the nervousness out of my voice, but I could hear it quaver just a little bit.

"The subject is Lancelot?" the younger man in the colorful

waistcoat said when it was his turn to look at my work. I saw him studying my William Morris tie.

"Yes. When Rossetti portrayed him, the subject was really Guinevere and her emotions. I feel that the subject of men in myth has never been fully explored. We've seen gods and knights and the like, but few show how they've felt as they've suffered loss, only triumph."

I hoped he would agree, but "hmmm" was all he said as handed my work to the next man.

Moments later the clerk collected my work and handed it back to me. I was confused. I looked at the clerk. "Is that it? Do they not want to ask me anything else?"

He inclined his head toward the door. "That's all."

I looked once more at the panel. I had been in the room two minutes. Three months of hard work, and they had given my art little regard. One of the men yawned. I pushed the door open and walked out.

"What was it like?" a woman sitting in the hallway whispered.

I shook my head. A lump was in my throat and I couldn't speak, but the look on my face must have been enough for her. She stared down at her sketchbook.

The exam was held in one of the classrooms. The adjudicator explained how much time we had and what the rules were as he handed out the booklets. We all picked up our pencils and began.

I sailed through the art history questions and the practical exam, and my confidence began to build. At least the panel would see that I knew my basics well. But when I turned the final page, I saw the paper was full of arithmetic problems; a good many of them were geometry.

Dumbly, I turned the test over as if I would find the answers on the back or something. I glanced around the room. Everyone else was studiously writing away, head bent over the exam.

I bit the end of my pencil and looked at the test again. Isosceles triangle? Pythagorean theorem? What did those words even mean? I had no idea. I was never taught such things in finishing school, nor was I taught them at the day school I had attended in London when I was younger. Instead I, like most girls, was taught comportment, music, religion, French, and only the very basics of geography, arithmetic, and science. I could add and subtract and work simple sums, but that was about it.

How stupid I was to think I could make the panel change their minds about women. I couldn't even get through the test. This realization, and the looks on the men's faces when I presented my work, had made that horrible whisper inside me start afresh. But this time my father's words joined it: *Why educate a girl as a boy? Advanced study makes girls discontent and unfit for the lives of wives and mothers.* And here it was in black and white, the proof that I was not qualified to be anything other than a wife and mother.

A prickle of a headache began to grow behind my eyes. I put my head in my hands and stared blankly at the test, the numbers seeming to run together in a blur. I felt as though I had rolled a huge boulder to the very top of a mountain, only to have it pushed right back in my face.

Then I thought of my little niece, Charlotte. If she wanted to become something other than a wife and mother, would she encounter the same obstacles as I had in twelve years' time, when she was my age? I hoped with all my heart that it would not be so; I wouldn't wish this humiliation on her or any other young girl.

I closed the exam book, gathered my things, and handed my test in to the clerk.

Maybe, just maybe, my artwork would be enough. It had to be enough.

I LEFT THE school in utter despair. As I trudged down the steps, I planned to go home, hide in my room, and lick my wounds. Then I caught sight of a familiar figure standing by the railing. It was Will. He was dressed in the same tattered herringbone jacket and cheesecutter cap. A rush of relief filled me. Will was exactly the person who would understand. I started to run to him and tell him what had happened with the exam, but then I caught myself. Instead I looked away, pretending not to see him, and headed off in the opposite direction, even though it wasn't where I wanted to go.

"Vicky!" I heard him call out.

I hunched my shoulders and kept walking.

He caught up, grabbed my arm. "Will you stop? I know you saw me."

I stopped but I did not turn around. "Let me go."

"What are you doing? What is all this about? Acting like you don't know me? I know you saw me that day when I was on my beat."

I turned around, but I couldn't look at him. I stared at his boots.

"How did the exam go?" His voice was guarded.

"Well enough." We stood there in uncomfortable silence for a moment. "What are you doing here?" I finally said.

"It was the only place where I knew you'd be. I've been waiting for ages, watching the door."

"I sent a letter. Did you not receive it?"

"I received it. You said you couldn't get away from your parents. I don't see anyone holding you back now, so why won't you talk to me?" Will looked upset.

"I thought I explained in my letter."

"You didn't, actually. You're trying to act as if nothing ever happened between us. That kiss didn't matter to you?"

"It was a mistake."

Will stared at me. "A mistake?"

"Sometimes artists feel things for their muses, and that's what I felt for you. It was a . . ." My breath jerked. "A passing fancy. That's all it was."

"A passing fancy?"

And then I launched in with the one word I knew would sever any remaining connection we had. "I'm engaged. I'm getting married. Next month."

Will flinched as though I had thrown cold water in his face. "Engaged?" It seemed as though an eternity passed before he spoke again. "To who?"

"It doesn't matter who. You don't know him."

"You love him?"

"No!" His question had caught me off guard. "I mean, yes. I don't know."

"So then why are you marrying him?"

"Because . . . because . . ." I couldn't explain to Will that the reason I was marrying Edmund was for money. He couldn't understand.

"Let me help you then." Anger flashed in his eyes. "It's because your family wants you to and his family wants him to." Will took a step closer to me. "Just like all upper-class families." He shook his head. "I thought you were different. I guess I was wrong."

"Why are you being so beastly?"

"Why didn't your fiancé pose for you? What did you need with me?"

"He hasn't the time. He was at university during the week; besides, he's a gentleman and—" I broke off. I had said the wrong thing.

"And a gentleman doesn't pose for artists, right?" He nodded. "Well, good thing I'm just a copper then."

"That's not what I meant. . . ." I felt sick inside, my feelings jumbled into a snarl. Tears filled my throat, hot and thick. I was desperate for Will to understand. "You know I don't believe that. You're more than a copper, Will. You're talented and wonderful."

Will's face was white. He stared over my head, his hands clasped behind him.

"You want to know the real reason why I don't draw my fiancé," I said. "The truth is that he doesn't inspire me."

"So I inspire you?"

"Yes."

He made a little noise, shook his head.

"You think me spoiled and snobbish, Will, but the one thing I want most in the world, my art, I can't have in my own home. As long as we're being honest, that's the truth of why I've agreed to this marriage: to get out from under my father's thumb and into a life of my own where I am free, where I can draw and paint as I like. And I'll do anything I can to have that. I should have told you about the engagement, but I didn't think it mattered."

"You're quite right," he said then. "It doesn't matter. You don't owe me an explanation."

"I'm sorry."

"No. I'm the one who is sorry. I should never have presumed we had more than an artistic partnership. It's my fault. I let myself . . ." His voice trailed off.

"You let yourself what?"

Something seemed to change in Will then. I could see him transforming in front of me: his happy-go-lucky expression hardening, the look in his eye turning aloof. "It's nothing. Let's forget this ever happened."

I didn't like the way his voice sounded, formal, not at all like the Will I knew. I would rather he shouted at me. This reversal, his change in attitude, back to the William Fletcher I had known months ago, hurt me more. I'd forced myself not to think of that day, that kiss, those desires he awakened in me. Now I knew he did the same, and right in front of me. I saw a door slamming shut in his eyes, and that day on his bed was locked behind it. He'd never open that door again.

I closed my hand around Will's, but he gently pulled it free of my grasp. I made to take it again, but he backed away and bowed a little. "I wish you the best of luck, Miss Darling." And then he turned around and left without another word.

Thirty-One

The Royal College of Art,
Friday, thirtieth of July

THE DAY AFTER the exam, the verdict came in on Lucy and the thirteen other women who had been arrested for throwing stones the evening of the June deputation. They were convicted and sent to Holloway Prison in the second division, in with the prison population, instead of in first division with the other political prisoners, who were allowed to wear their own clothes, write letters, and live in less stringent conditions.

A week later, Sophie had bought a *Votes for Women*, and the two of us hovered over it, reading about their ordeal. The women, including Lucy, had protested by refusing to eat. They hunger-struck for six days until they were too unwell to continue their sentences. The prison officials released them because they were concerned they would die, and the government did not want the deaths of the women on its hands.

In the same edition, Emmeline Pankhurst wrote an article on hunger-striking. She said that the government had closed the door on peaceful protest and she believed the WSPU had now found a weapon with which to defeat the government. Retaining control of one's own body had become a political statement. Hunger-striking was a way to passively resist the injustices women endured because they were not treated as equals to men. It was now WSPU policy, and if any woman or man wanted to go to prison, they were to hunger-strike or not go at all.

To endure six whole days without food in that noisome prison: I shuddered to think of it. Lucy was the bravest woman I knew.

WHILE I WAITED for the exam results, I tried to take my mind off of things. I attended several balls with Edmund and helped with the rest of the wedding details. The work in the Chelsea house was completed, the new furniture in place. Wedding gifts had begun to arrive. The Wedgwood china, the Elkington silverware, and the Waterford crystal took pride of place on the dining room table, where they would be displayed to visitors during my first at-home. Edmund and I organized our honeymoon, a week in Scotland, and met with the vicar at St. George's Hanover Square in Mayfair, where we would be married.

I went to Clement's Inn with Sophie to see Lucy in her flat after she'd been released from prison. I brought her some grapes and a book on jewelry I found in a shop on Charing Cross Road. Lucy was in good spirits and seemed even more determined to fight after her ordeal.

Finally, at the end of July, the day of the exam results arrived. I very nearly didn't bother to go back to the RCA for the results, but I had to see it through to the end. If Lucy could endure hunger for so long in a horrid prison, I could face my disastrous exam results.

Again, with the excuse of a stroll, John took Sophie and me to Kensington Gardens. Sophie waited in the RCA's vestibule while I went in to join the other prospective students. I found a place in the back.

The woman who'd gone in to meet the panel after me was sitting on a bench. "How did you get on?" she asked as I sat down beside her.

"I don't know," I replied. "The arithmetic section quite eluded me. And I don't think the examiners were much impressed."

She winced. "I found the same to be true. I couldn't get my head round those figures. I left them blank. I hope they don't grade too harshly on that. I need a scholarship to go here; I can't go without it. If I'm accepted," she whispered this last bit, as if she daren't speak it out loud.

I realized then that if I hadn't agreed to marry Edmund, I'd be in the same place as the woman.

The clerk came out of his office and pinned a paper to the notice board. He was nearly swallowed up as the students bustled about it, crying out in happiness or dismay. I hung back, wanting to wait until they had all gone. The woman waited at the back of the queue. When her turn came, she stared at the list and then pushed her way out of the crowd, I saw that her eyes were red and she was blinking back tears. She said nothing to me. She hurried from the hall, her arms crossed over her chest, staring at the floor.

I stood up and then sat back down. My life began or ended now. If my name was on the list, I would take that as a sign that the path I had chosen for myself was the right one. And if it wasn't? I closed my eyes. *If it isn't? What will you do then?* the voices whispered. *That will prove that you aren't an artist after all. That you're preposterous for even trying.*

Finally the room emptied, and I approached the list for the RCA School of Painting. The names were written neatly on lines. First the scholarships. My name was not there.

The main class list followed. I found my name among the *D*s and slid my finger over.

Victoria Darling. Accepted.

I had to read it again.

Accepted.

I ran my finger back to my name just to make sure I had read the line correctly.

It was true. I was going to the RCA.

I had done it.

I stepped back from the list. My dream of attending the RCA would become a reality. All of the hard work had been worth it.

On the way home in the carriage, I held Sophie's hand tightly. I couldn't keep myself from smiling. I must have looked insane sitting there with a mad grin on my face. But I couldn't help it. I was in. I had made it into art school. I was an artist. A real artist. I wanted to shout it to the whole world. I wanted to tell Will, the one person I couldn't tell. And yet even this didn't drown out my happiness. Today, nothing could.

Thirty-Two

MY PARENTS WERE getting ready to spend a fortnight in August on the continent, as they did every year. This year, however, I would not be joining them. Instead, I would stay home with Sophie to finish preparing the house and my wardrobe, and see to wedding details with Lady Carrick-Humphrey. My mother wanted to stay but felt a spa in Germany would be good for my father.

Although I was busy with India and Lady Carrick-Humphrey over the course of that fortnight, I didn't see much of Edmund. He had gone to Cowes Week on the Isle of Wight in the beginning of August to crew on a friend's cutter. My parents were nearly due back when an invitation arrived for a Friday-to-Monday party at his family manor house in Gloucestershire.

Sophie and I took the train to Gloucestershire, and India and Edmund met us in his motorcar. The Carrick-Humphrey country home was near the village of Dyrham in an ancient deer park in a lovely old baroque-style mansion. Sir Henry had recently purchased it from a newly impoverished earl. The house was a jewel in a setting of acres of woodland and parkland. The inside was decorated in the Dutch style with Delft pottery and tile. But no feeling of warmth lingered in the hushed rooms and hallways. It felt like a museum: a place to visit and look at but never to touch.

Luncheon was ready when we arrived. Jonty's wife, Millicent, spent most of the time in her room, suffering from "delicate nerves," as Jonty put it. Jonty's friend, Alfred, a balding man in his thirties, seemed glued to his side. Edmund's mother had left to take the waters in Bath, but his father remained, hanging on Jonty's every word and virtually ignoring Edmund altogether.

I was bored beyond redemption. I had forgotten how oppressing these noble country houses could be. Snobbery was right under the surface, bleeding through the shiny politeness like speckles on an antique looking glass. We all sat through lunch as if enchanted, listening to Jonty and his father talk about shooting grouse as though they were great white hunters bagging a man-eating lion in the Congo instead of Englishmen dressed in Norfolk suits shooting at birds that were raised in a cage and then enticed to fly by men whacking at the undergrowth with sticks.

The ladies withdrew for drinks on the veranda after luncheon, leaving the men in the library to their brandies and cigars. The day was growing chilly, and, remembering I had left my wrap in the sitting room, I went to collect it. Sir Henry was coming out of the library just then and he saw me.

"Ah, Miss Darling. I was just coming to collect you. I'd

like a word," he said. He held out his hand. "Shall we go into my study?"

I was a little taken aback but I went with him. He gestured for me to sit in a large leather chair by the fire and sat opposite me. He crossed one leg over the other and settled back as if we were going to have a nice chat, future loving father-in-law to future dutiful daughter-in-law.

"Well, my dear, the wedding day is getting close, only a fortnight away. Most exciting for you, I should say. I'm sure you will look charming in your wedding dress, most charming."

"Thank you, Sir Henry."

"Now, no more of that 'Sir Henry,' my dear." He smiled broadly. I could not help but think again how his mustache made him look like a walrus. Really, his valet should tell him so. "You must call me Papa."

"Thank you, Papa." I felt ridiculous calling him Papa, but if it pleased him, who was I to argue?

"Now, Edmund told me this morning of your request to go to an art school in London."

"It's not a request, Sir Henry. I'm going. I've done the work and I've been accepted." I laughed a little. Nothing could keep me from art school now. It was absurd of Sir Henry to think he could put his paw over me like that, but I wondered why Edmund had even mentioned art school to him. I hadn't told him I'd been accepted yet. Really, what business was it of his father's?

Sir Henry waved his hand as if my statement were nothing but an annoying gnat flying around him, something that could be swatted down easily. "I don't think so.

It's not the done thing for women in our family to be so, well, shall we say, present."

The smile faded from my face. "Whatever do you mean?"

"I mean the answer is no. You won't be going to art school," Sir Henry said in a casual tone. He rose and crossed to a side table to pour sherry into two glasses. He handed one to me. I set it down on the table beside me. I did not want to drink it. "Do not think that word of your scandalous behavior in France passed me by. I am not stupid, nor am I willing to tolerate any similar behavior in the future. I will not have a daughter-in-law going to college, nor a bohemian one who keeps company with the great unwashed. I suggest you spend your days as India and my wife do, working with their charities and attending to their social obligations. That should please you."

I stood up. "I have made my decision, Sir Henry. I don't intend to flutter through life without leaving my mark. I'm sorry if you don't agree with my decision."

"No. I'm sorry for you." Sir Henry's words held the promise of a threat. "I have no intention of my daughter-in-law 'leaving her mark' upon the world."

"You can't stop me."

"Oh, but I can!" Sir Henry spread his tailcoat out and sat back down. "Who do you think holds the title to your house? Who will pay your servants, buy your food, your clothing? I loosen and tighten the purse strings, my dear."

I had to stay calm. It wouldn't do to get angry with him. He was simply trying to control me, as my father had on so many occasions. "I don't wish to be rude, Sir Henry." His brows rose. "Forgive me—Papa. But I don't need your money. My father has settled an allowance upon me in the wedding contract, as I'm sure you're aware."

"He has, but it's tied. He will release the funds after bills are submitted for his approval. Do you think he'll approve of art school?"

My breath caught. I should have known. I should've have known that Papa would tie up my money in such a way. Freddy himself trod lightly when it came to his allowance, as he had attested that day when he said he was as much of a lapdog as I was. But Papa had not counted on the fact that Edmund was on my side. "Edmund will be working with my father and earning his own money. Edmund can pay for my schooling, then."

"Not so." Sir Henry settled back and took another sip of his sherry. "My son will only receive a small stipend until he inherits the business fully when your father passes. Do you think I'd let Edmund loose with money to gamble away just as he has done in the past, causing this family further shame and scandal? You will thank me for it later, my dear. Money slips through that young man's hands. Your father and I are in complete agreement. What's more, we will go to this *art college* and tell them you don't have our permission to attend. So it's no good you trying to wheedle anything out of him. We will have no more talk of this nonsense."

I clenched my hands at my sides so hard that my nails cut into my palms. It was pointless to argue with such an irrational man.

As politely as I could, I left the study and I went in search of Edmund. After searching around the enormous house, I found him sitting in a leather chair, drinking brandy, in the library.

"Do you know what your father just said to me?" I said.

"Haven't a clue, but most likely he's pulled you up, judging from the look on your face." Edmund watched me carefully, almost warily.

"He said I'm not allowed to go to art college. As if he has a say in my life! Edmund, you have to tell him that I'm going. Make him see sense."

I assumed Edmund would stand up immediately and go confront his father, but instead he shrugged as if I had asked for something so inconsequential that he couldn't be bothered to even get up out of the chair.

"There's nothing for it, old thing. Our fathers hold all the aces. If he says you can't go to college, then you can't go to college."

At first I thought I hadn't heard him correctly. I was kneeling down in front of him and reaching out my arms to embrace him when his words seeped into my mind. And it was as if Edmund's words had formed a fist that lashed out and struck me in the stomach. I could actually feel the breath leave my body.

Edmund was not going to stand up to his father for me. He didn't even have the courage to look at me. He sat there, slumped in his chair, staring down into his blasted brandy, running his finger round and round the rim of the glass. I wanted to grab it out of his hand and dash it in his face. The coward! The absolute and utter coward.

I stood up and backed away from him, shaking my

head. I couldn't find any words to say. I turned and fled the room.

"Victoria!" I heard him call, but I did not pause. I heard his footsteps on the marble floor as he ran up behind me. He grasped my elbow. "Will you stop!"

I glared at him. "Did you know he wasn't going to let me go to school?"

He glanced around. "I don't want to talk about this here." He took my hand and led me up the stairs to his rooms.

Edmund's valet, Haskell, was stacking shirts in a bureau drawer. Edmund waved his hand, dismissing him. "I told him about your wishes and he said no, straightaway. I was going to tell you, but he beat me to it, as it goes."

"Why can't you stand up to him?" I sat on the upholstered bench at the foot of the bed.

"Don't be ridiculous, Victoria. You've seen what he's like. It would be like banging my head against a brick wall." He took the stopper off the brandy decanter on his dresser and peered inside. "Blast! I've told Haskell to keep this filled." He grabbed the bottle by the neck, strode to the door, and jerked it open. He called the valet back and handed the bottle out to him.

"We don't need him, Edmund. We can find another place to live that's less dear."

"Victoria, consider what you're saying. I won't live in a mean flat somewhere and have to scratch for every ha'penny. My father doesn't care if you paint, just as long as you keep it to the house. You have that little shed in the garden to draw your little pictures and whatnot. Why can't that content you?"

"Because I want to learn more. I'm not satisfied with doing 'little pictures,' as you put it. I need to know more, Edmund."

"Why? For what? It's not as though you will exhibit your work."

"That is my dream: to exhibit my work. Of course it is. But I will never be able to show anything without instruction."

Edmund looked appalled. "It's a bit thick, Victoria. I'm not happy with you putting your work about in public. It's not the done thing in our circle, you know. Why not just leave it alone?" He began to pace the room. "Where is that damned Haskell with the brandy?"

"I won't marry you, Edmund, if I can't go to school." There was no point to my marriage with Edmund if I couldn't go to school. Mercenary though it might seem, both Edmund and I had reasons of our own for this marriage.

He stopped his infernal pacing and turned to look at me. He had an expression on his face as though I had told him I had decided to become a lead miner.

"You'd give up a grand life with me just so you can put paint on a bit of card?" He was outraged.

"Is that what you think I do? How would you like it if I compared your rowing to punting on the Serpentine?"

Haskell came in with the brandy just then. Edmund took it. I could see his hands shaking as he filled the glass to the brim. He drank the brandy in one long gulp. "What about *your* seven hundred pounds, eh? Why don't you talk to your own father? Why must I?"

"He won't listen to me, Edmund," I said, frustrated with

the way the conversation was proceeding. "I'm just a girl!"

A cold rush came over me. *What had just happened?* Those dreaded words tumbled out of my own mouth so easily, as if I knew them to be true. Hearing myself speak that phrase was worse than hearing it from anyone else. Immediately, tears flooded my eyes.

Edmund came over to me. He took me in his arms, but I was frozen in place and stood rigid as a marble statue. "You're right, of course. It's my duty to speak for both of us." His face was tender as he looked at me. He brushed his lips across mine. "Don't cry. I'll talk to my father, I promise. I'll talk him round. You'll see."

I went back to my room and sank down onto the floor of my lavatory. I pressed my forehead against my knees and cried. My dreams shattered one by one as my future unfolded in my mind's eye. I would bite my tongue and keep my opinions to myself. I would go along with plans laid out for me. I would hide my work away. The little summerhouse meant as my refuge would be my prison. And one day I would grow tired of pushing and shoving to take the tiniest of steps forward, and just like my mother, I would shut my sketchbook in the middle of a drawing and hide it away. I would lock the door of the summerhouse that held all my artwork inside, and leave it forever.

Because that's what someone who was *just a girl* would do.

I LAY ON MY bed, feigning a headache for the rest of the day. I didn't want to face Edmund or his father. Sophie came in a few times to check on me, a worried look on her face. She asked me once what was wrong, but I couldn't say. I couldn't bring myself to admit that my life had turned into utter shambles.

In the evening, Sophie dressed me for dinner in one of my new gowns, a dark lavender crepe de chine. I opened my jewelry box to choose accessories and I saw the mermaid that Lucy and I had made. I could use a little of her courage to face Sir Henry at dinner, so I scooped her out and pinned her to my gown.

Several of Edmund and India's friends had come to join us for dinner that evening, including Edmund's best friend, Kenneth. Edmund unbent in Kenneth's presence. All tension left him, and he relaxed utterly, joking and messing about with him and two other boys from Oxford.

Dinner passed without event. The men talked about pheasant this time and what the weather would be like on the hills for shooting tomorrow. I smiled and nodded, chatting with India's friends and feeling like a clockwork automaton. Edmund barely met my gaze at the table, apart from once when I caught him eyeing me nervously.

After Jonty and Sir Henry retired, Kenneth proposed a game of baccarat for the gentlemen. India and several of her friends played ragtime tunes on the gramophone and danced the turkey trot, giggling. I sat on a settee and watched, playing wallflower.

The clock struck midnight when I felt a hand on my shoulder. "Victoria," Edmund said. "I wonder if I might have a word."

He took my hand and drew me to the back of the room. Edmund looked flushed and out of sorts; his bow tie was crooked and he reeked of whiskey. "I must ask a favor of you." He put his elbow up against the wall by my head and leaned in. His breath was warm on my cheek as he whispered, "My father will not give me my allowance until next week, and I have need of money. Kenneth has emptied my pockets, damn his eyes, but I have a chance to win it back. I just need surety to do so."

"You need money?"

"Only a loan, see? Until Monday week, and then I will pay you back."

I shrugged. "I'm sorry. I have no money with me. Besides, I thought it was *middle-class* to talk about money." I couldn't resist the poke, but Edmund didn't rise.

He brushed his fingers over the brooch. "This will do."

"Edmund, that's out of the question. I love this—"

"It's only a bit of jewelry. If I lose it, I'll buy you another one later."

"I designed this myself. It means a lot to me!"

"Then just make another one."

"That's not the point—"

Kenneth leaned back in his chair and glanced at us. "Edmund. What's it to be? You in or out?"

"A moment, gentlemen; I'm just speaking with my fiancée," Edmund said, and then turned back to me. "You're making a fuss over nothing."

I twisted my engagement ring off and held it out to him on my palm. "If you are so sure you can win it back, then have this."

Edmund glanced at my hand. "You're being ridiculous! My father bought that. If I lost it, then it would be hell's delight!" He snatched up my hand and shoved the ring back onto my finger. "Now stop making a scene and give me your brooch."

"No! I won't give it to you."

A look of irritation bled through the calm expression on his face. He reached for the brooch, and at the same time I twisted away from him. I felt a sharp tug and heard my bodice rip. Startled, I looked down to see a long rent in my gown where my brooch had been. I clamped my hand to my chest.

I stared at Edmund in disbelief. I could see the mermaid's tail poking out of Edmund's fisted hand.

"Sorry, old thing. As I said, I'll make it up to you."

I set my jaw and reached down to grab his hand. I tried

to pry his fingers away to get her back, but he was too strong. He laughed as though we were playing a fun game.

It was useless to fight him. My hand fell away from his. And I turned and left the room. I felt sick in the pit of my stomach. As I walked down the hall, I could picture Edmund returning to the table, tossing the mermaid down upon the pile of tokens. And then with one snap of a card onto the green baize, losing her in an instant.

IT WAS ONLY jewelry, only a brooch, I tried to tell myself. But really it wasn't just the pin that upset me so much; it was the utter indifference that Edmund had for something I loved so much, and the calculated way he ripped it right from me. As if I needed any further evidence that Edmund would never stand up for me. He had so little regard for my wishes or my possessions. He only thought of himself. He would never side with me against his father. I had piled all my hopes on Edmund, as if he were a knight in shining armor who would ride into battle for me. But I had given my favor to the one who refused to leave the castle.

But Edmund wasn't all at fault. I'd happily played the role of damsel in distress. And if I didn't want to remain the rest of my days *just a girl*, I would have to stand up for myself.

I rummaged through my art satchel to look for Bertram's drawing on the day I posed at Monsieur's atelier. I found it and took it over to the lamp. That girl portrayed in the drawing would have gladly chained herself to the railing, would have joined the suffragettes in prison. She would not have depended upon someone else for her livelihood. She never would have run away from a fight. Who was that girl?

I didn't know, but I wanted to be her.

I SAT IN MY room for several hours, listening for Edmund to return. It was not hard to stay awake because my emotions were galloping through me like a Thoroughbred racing over the turf at Ascot.

At three o'clock in the morning I heard footsteps. I opened the door and saw Edmund reeling down the corridor. He stopped short when he saw me, and put out a hand to brace himself against the wall.

He was sloppy, stinking drunk. He grinned and acknowledged me with a little bow. "Well met, old thing. Waiting up for me?"

"I wish to speak with you."

Edmund waved his hand and staggered past me to open his bedroom door. Haskell was sleeping in a chair in the corner of the room; his mouth was open and his head lolled to one side. Edmund flicked the lamp on, and the valet jumped to his feet, squinting at the light.

"Ha! Caught you sleeping, you bugger!"

"Begging your pardon, sir," Haskell stuttered, moving forward to help Edmund shrug out of his jacket. But then he caught sight of me, and his arms dropped to his side.

"Get out. I can undress myself. Go to bed, will you," Edmund said to him.

Haskell bowed and left the room, closing the door behind him.

"The man is useless," Edmund muttered. He fumbled at his buttons and shrugged off his coat, letting it drop to the floor. "Now, what is it that you want?"

"I have something to say to you, Edmund."

Edmund made a face. "Is this about that poxy brooch?" He picked up his coat and fumbled in one of the pockets. "Here." He shoved the mermaid at me. "Kenneth didn't want it anyhow."

I took the brooch from him. I was glad to have her back, but that didn't change anything. "You were reprehensible, Edmund. You tore this right off my dress!"

"A mistake! I didn't mean to do it. I'll buy you a new gown."

"It's not the gown!" I was growing ever more frustrated with him. "I told you no, but you took it anyway, even though it was important to me. Art is my life, yet you don't even care to understand that. I can't be with someone who refuses to understand me."

"Not that new-woman claptrap! Mother said you would never be happy. She knew that night when you opened your mouth and wouldn't shut your noise about women's rights. I told her you were only trying to get a rise out of Father, and that you didn't really mean it. I see now that I had the wrong end of the stick."

"None of that matters anymore. I'm ending our engagement."

Edmund pulled his case out of his trouser pocket and took a cigarette out. He lit it and then sat down on his bed, settling back against the pillows. He looked at me with a calm expression. "You won't end the engagement. You're just cross right now. I doubt you want to spend the whole of your life with your aunt Maude."

As I watched him smoke the cigarette, I noticed what a weak chin he had and how his eyes turned down at the corners and how his lips pouted, as though always in a sulk. I couldn't believe I'd ever thought he was handsome.

"Believe what you wish, but I'm quite serious."

He leaned over to tap the ash into the crystal ashtray that sat on the nightstand. "So does that bloke you knock about with *understand* you?"

I stood there, looking at him, hoping I hadn't heard him say that. I wanted to pretend to myself that he didn't mean Will, that he was asking about someone else, maybe someone I had been talking with at my coming-out party. But Edmund hadn't left my side once, and most of the boys I'd talked to were Edmund's friends.

It was all unfolding in front of me; the two worlds I had been straddling since France were beginning to collide, and there was nothing I could do to prevent it happening. "I . . . I don't know what you mean," I finally said, having no idea what else to say.

"Don't play that game. You were with a bloke awhile ago at the house in Chelsea. The caretaker had come to check because a neighbor told him some people were in the back garden the week before. He saw the two of you leaving. I didn't believe him at first, but then he described that tie you wear, the one with the birds on, and I knew it was you."

"Why didn't you say anything to me?"

He shrugged. "I assumed it was your brother; maybe you were showing him the house. I didn't think you capable of an affair until now. This sudden revelation that you don't want to be married anymore made me think maybe it's because of this bloke. Your face told me true. So who is he?"

"I'm not having an affair. He's my art model. I drew him in the summerhouse a few times. I told you I didn't stop drawing—"

Edmund interrupted, his blue eyes icy. "When you say you drew him, what exactly do you mean?"

I hesitated. "I . . . I drew him . . . undraped."

"I don't know the lingo, Victoria; you'll have to help me out."

"You know what it means," I said carefully.

Edmund jumped to his feet and grabbed my arm. I shrank back. I didn't think Edmund would hurt me, but he was drunk and he was angry. "Say it! You did it, so *say it!* Out loud!"

I shook my head.

"Go on!" he spat.

"It means without his clothes on! I drew him like that and I'm not sorry about it. I'd do it again."

"Is that all you did? Draw?" His voice rose. "Tell me the truth, Victoria, because somehow I don't believe you."

"At first that was all we did, but then . . . then something happened."

"What? What happened?"

I swallowed. Edmund had every right to be angry, had every right to know the truth. "We kissed. It was just the once."

Edmund dropped my arm.

"I didn't mean it to happen, Edmund. I didn't. I ended it. I haven't seen him in a long time. He has nothing to do with why I'm breaking our engagement."

Edmund stepped away from me and pulled the tail of his shirt down. "You've certainly hidden your true colors."

"You're right. I tried to act like someone I wasn't. That's not fair to you. You never made out to be anyone else."

"Quite right," he said. "I'm no phony. You are, though."

I twisted off the engagement ring and held it out to him. He grabbed it out of my hand and tossed it into his ashtray, where it landed among the mashed-up cigarette butts and ashes. "I don't want you, anyhow. You're debauched, as far as I'm concerned. I'm breaking our engagement, and I'll tell everyone the reason why."

I knew he was talking out of anger, and maybe he wouldn't say such things to me if he weren't drunk, but it hurt me all the same. "I thought you didn't care about that. Isn't that what you told me before? The king doesn't care about such social conventions, so why should we?"

"The king was never made a cuckold or a laughing-stock by Queen Alexandra's actions. Think of it. A lowly caretaker saw my fiancée at our home with another man.

And I won't be packed off to the navy because of you."

"I'm sorry, Edmund. I'm sorry for everything," I said, and I left the room.

As soon as the sun rose, I rang for Sophie and asked her to arrange for our departure home with one of the footmen. And we left before anyone else awoke.

Thirty-Five

I TOLD SOPHIE EVERYTHING as we rode the train home to London.

"What will you do now?" she asked.

"I'm going to implore Freddy to help me get our father on my side." After all, Freddy had convinced Father that publishing was the right path for him. Perhaps if I laid out my plans, explaining exactly what I would do, so as not to appear like an impetuous girl, he might understand. I couldn't help but think about the look of admiration Papa had had on his face when I explained the telephone to him. I would talk to him in the same way. And Mamma—I would appeal to her, artist to artist. She'd defended me to my father before; surely there was a chance she would again.

I needed to cobble a plan together before they returned home from the continent tomorrow morning, before Sir Henry was able to speak to him. Edmund would have told his father about Will, and Sir Henry would tell Papa. Freddy had said he would always be on my side. If he spoke to our parents with me, helped me convince them, then I might have a chance.

It was nearing two o'clock, so Freddy would be at the

Reform Club in Pall Mall. As soon as the train alighted at the station, I sent Sophie home with my luggage and art satchel, and I took a hansom cab to the club.

A quarter of an hour later I reached the palatial building. Although my father and brother frequented the club weekly, I had never been inside; women were not allowed membership. I walked in and stood on the mosaic pavement in the atrium. The Reform Club turned out to be an ode to masculine sensibility. The paneled walls were decorated with large, foreboding portraits of its founding members. The space was cavernous, with a lead crystal ceiling that let in the light. A grand staircase led up to a gallery that wrapped around the central atrium.

A tall and scrawny young footman dressed in a tailcoat approached me. "May I assist you, miss?"

"I'm looking for my brother, Freddy Darling," I said. "I wish to speak with him."

He drew himself up. "Our club is closed to women, miss. I will get a message to him, and he can attend you at your home."

I glanced past him and noticed a group of men climbing the stairs, so I lifted my skirts and went around the astonished footman toward the staircase.

"Miss!" I heard the voice of the now very angry footman behind me. But I ignored him.

As I climbed, I could hear the clink of billiard balls and the murmur of masculine voices coming from one of the rooms at the end of the gallery, so I headed there.

There were many gentlemen inside the room. Some stood with billiard cues in their hands; others sat in leather chairs by the fire reading newspapers. The acrid smell and smoke of pipe and cigar tobacco hung in the air like fog.

"Frederick Darling? Is Mr. Darling here?" I called out. The men turned to stare. The way they looked, you'd think someone had released a milk cow into their hallowed halls.

"I say!" I heard one of them exclaim. "Where did she come from?"

One of the newspapers lowered slowly, and the astonished face of my brother was revealed. "Vicky! What are you doing here?"

"This isn't done, old chap," one of the gentlemen near him said. "Meet your fillies elsewhere."

"She's my sister," Freddy snapped. He stood and came over, took me by my elbow, and marched me from the room.

The footman hovered outside. "I'm sorry, sir," he said. "She just pushed in."

"It's all right, Thomas. I'll see that she doesn't stay long." The servant left, and Freddy turned to me. "What do you mean by coming here, Vicky? Actually, why are you in London at all? You're meant to be in the country." Then he saw my face, and his expression softened. "Oh, no . . . what's happened now?"

"I broke my engagement."

My brother looked alarmed. "Broke your engagement? Whatever do you mean?"

"Marrying Edmund Carrick-Humphrey would be the biggest mistake of my life. That marriage contract is but a gold cage."

"Vicky, I love you dearly, but you do overdramatize—"

"I can't have a life where I'm not free!"

"Calm down, Vicky."

"I can't calm down!"

"Vicky, an engagement can't be undone so easily. The marriage contract is ironclad."

"How can that be? I'm not married yet!"

"You might as well be. The engagement was announced formally, so the contract is in full effect. Do you know what a broken engagement means? There will be stories in the newspapers and scandal rags. At the very least, it will ruin your chances to ever marry."

"Ruin my chances to marry someone who cares about all that." Certainly someone like Will would never care about such social rules.

"That's as may be. But this might hurt Father's business, Vicky."

"How can you say that? Papa's company is called Darling and *Son* Sanitary Company, not *Daughter*! Where was your sense of familial duty back when you wanted a life of your own?"

That got him. He looked away and wouldn't meet my eyes. And then finally he spoke. "So have you thought about what you will do?" he finally said.

"I want to go to art school."

"How will you do that? Surely they only accept established artists—"

"I've been accepted! The Royal College of Art accepted my application."

Fred gaped at me. "How? How did your mange that?"

"I managed it. And on my own."

"Good God." Freddy slumped against the wall and rubbed his forehead, his newspaper held slack against his side.

"Maybe Papa will still give me an allowance, like he's given you, so that I may keep my own home and pay my tuition. I don't need anything much: just a small flat and art supplies. I can't see what's wrong with that, Freddy; Papa won't even notice the money. When Papa sees how much work I did to get accepted, and how the examiners were impressed with my work, he'll see sense. Just like with the success of your business. I need you there to help me convince him."

Freddy said nothing, and I became frightened he would say no. "For just a moment, see yourself in my place, Freddy," I pleaded. "You left of your own accord. What if you were forced to work in Papa's business? Could you do that, knowing your heart was not in it? Knowing your whole life that your heart was elsewhere?"

"I couldn't."

"Then don't I deserve the same chance at happiness?"

Freddy regarded me for a moment, looking unsure. It was clear that Freddy was wrestling with himself, trying to find a way around my reasoning, and then he pushed himself away from the wall. "All right. I'll see what I can do. But breaking your engagement means more than a scandal, Victoria. It means the end to Darling and Son. Father has much to lose, including his pride. I wouldn't count on an easy time of it."

I T HAD BEGUN to rain, and the day had grown cold and dreary, so Freddy took me home in a hansom cab. He would come back in the morning when our parents arrived home.

By the time we arrived in Berkeley Square, fog had purled in, and the streetlamps were lit. More ominously, the lights inside my father's study were on.

"They're home," I said. My stomach flipped over.

"What the devil?" Freddy leaned past me to look. "I thought they weren't due home until morning."

Not many country houses had telephones, but the Carrick-Humphrey manor did. It would have been nothing for Edmund's father to pick up the blasted thing. In my imagination I could hear Sir Henry's voice, reduced to a tinny rattle through the earpiece, as he relayed the story of my broken engagement to my horrified father. "What if . . ." I swallowed, feeling sick with nerves. "What if Sir Henry telephoned Papa? You know what he's like when he's angry, Fred. There'll be no talking to him."

"There's nothing for it." Freddy stepped out of the cab.

"Well, let's gird our loins and face the lion in his den."

We went inside and, as suspected, found our parents in my father's study. We stood there in the doorway; Freddy held my hand tightly. Papa was sitting by the fire, a glass of port in his hand. He looked haggard. The wrinkles round his eyes seemed deeper. My mother sat on the settee; her eyes were red, as if she had been crying. Our parents did not greet us, and my heart sank. I knew then that they had already heard.

I saw Sophie standing near the window. I tried to catch her eye, but she wouldn't meet my gaze.

"Your mother and I arrived home to find an urgent message from Sir Henry waiting for us," Papa said, getting right to the point. Although his voice was calm, his words were tinged with anger. "I rang him, and he told me that you ended the engagement with his son because he would not let you go to art school. Is this true?"

I drew myself up tall. I needed all the bravery I possessed. "Yes."

My mother sucked in her breath.

"Please, Papa, listen to me," I pleaded. "There's more to the story than that."

He barked out a short laugh. "Sir Henry tells me that you've been accepted to this school already. I had forbidden you to draw, yet you defied me! Your willful behavior continued, and under my nose!"

Freddy stepped forward, put a hand on his shoulder. "Steady on, Father! Hear her out."

"We found a suffrage badge in your art satchel,

Victoria," Mamma said. "And drawings of women at that riot where the Pankhurst woman was arrested were in your sketchbook. You were there?"

"You went through my satchel?" I cried.

"I'm sorry, Miss Darling," Sophie said. "They stopped me as soon as I arrived home and went through your things."

"Be quiet, Cumberbunch," Mamma told her, taking on that imperial tone she always used with the servants.

Sophie pressed her mouth closed. She looked at me, her eyes desperate.

"Explain this." Father fumbled for something alongside his chair. He held up my art satchel and dumped it upside down. My sketchbook tumbled out, accompanied by a cascade of WSPU leaflets, charcoal pencils, conté crayons, and the DEEDS NOT WORDS pin. "Every secret you harbor is in this bag." He threw down my satchel and snatched up my sketchbook. He turned to a page and held it out. I stared at my nude drawing of Will. His face was half covered under my father's thumb. "This . . . filth . . . this muck. Sir Henry said you've been meeting a man at his home in Chelsea and saw him . . . unclothed. Had a sordid dalliance with him, too! Who is he?"

I could not breathe. I could not speak. My knees sagged and I sat down on the footstool.

"Cumberbunch!" my mother said. "You are her chaperone. Surely you knew about this?"

"I did," she said boldly, stepping forward. "It . . . it's not right for you to stop her from drawing and the like. She loves it. She helped the suffragettes with art for their mural, that's all. She did everything else you asked. She was even a success with the king! She wasn't doing anything wrong or hurting anybody—"

"That is none of your business," my mother snapped. "Our rules for our daughter were laid out for you when I hired you. It's not for you to say what she should or shouldn't do."

"Leave her be, Mamma. It's not her fault," I said.

"You are dismissed, Cumberbunch," Mamma said. "Pack your things and leave in the morning."

Sophie wrenched her spectacles off and rubbed her eyes with the back of her sleeve. Her face looked so different without them, vulnerable and naked.

"That's not fair, Mamma! Sophie didn't do anything!" I said.

"And that is exactly why *Sophie* must leave. She should have come to me directly this nonsense began. Utter betrayal. Now I see what the true reason was behind Joan Hollingberry's marriage to that unsuitable man. It was you, wasn't it? You encouraged it, and now you've ruined my daughter. And if you think you'll get a character reference from me, Cumberbunch, you are sorely mistaken."

"You can't do that to her!" I said. "If you punish her for my behavior, I'll never forgive you—"

"You wouldn't have been able to get up to this mischief without her help."

"Enough of this!" my father said. "That will be all, Cumberbunch."

Sophie bobbed her head. "I'm ever so sorry, Miss Darling," she whispered, and then dashed from the room.

"This isn't right!" I said, but my parents ignored me. "Freddy, please tell them."

But no one listened to me.

"I cannot believe this." Papa's voice rose. "I cannot! How did I lose control over my entire household?"

"Papa, please let me tell you," I said, hoping that he'd listen, hoping that I could reach through his anger and convince him. "I've been accepted into the RCA. Let me tell you what I plan to do—"

He rapped his fist against the mantelpiece. He shook the sketchbook at me. "This is over, do you hear me? You will forget these silly notions of yours!" And then, before I could blink, he cast my book into the fire.

"No!" I fell to my knees at the hearth and reached into the fireplace.

"Vicky, stop!" Freddy dropped beside me, grabbed my shoulders.

I reached in to drag the sketchbook out, my fingers blistering as the flames licked round them. But I was too late. The book caught fire, and I could only watch as the flames engulfed the pages and the undraped drawing of Will turned to cinders. Rage began to bubble up inside of me then. It was like a spring that had lain quiet for a very long time, just waiting for the right pressure to give way and turn into a geyser. I stood up.

"You don't care about me, do you, Papa? You don't know anything about me, who I am, or what I love!" I shouted at him. "I'm nothing to you. You only care about your business! You have never been a father to me and you're never going to be!"

My father covered the short distance to me in two long steps. He raised his hand and slapped me across the face so hard that my head snapped to one side.

"George!" Mamma cried out.

I pressed my hand to my cheek. My father had never raised a hand to me in the whole of my life. I didn't know what was worse, the pain or the humiliation.

Papa stared at his hand, stricken, as if he couldn't quite believe what he had done. Then he turned on his heel and left the room. A moment later I heard the front door slam.

Freddy came to me and pulled my hand away. I saw my reflection in the mirror over the fireplace, and there was a red hand-shaped mark on my face. I saw my mother in the mirror, too, her eyes wide with disbelief.

Freddy began to pace the room, shoving his hands through his hair so many times that it stood up in a tangle. "What a terrible, terrible mess this is. My God," he kept muttering over and over.

I couldn't say anything. I couldn't make any words come out.

"What shall we do, Frederick?" Mamma asked, once again turning to a man for help. My mother couldn't rely on herself, even in a crisis. In that moment, I think I hated Mamma for her weakness.

Freddy stopped pacing. "She'll come to my house. Let things settle for a bit." Freddy pulled the bell sash. Emma came in, looking scared. "Can you please pack a valise for Miss Darling? Go with her, Vicky."

The pain in my heart was astonishing in its intensity.

Just drawing breath took effort. My legs felt leaden, but somehow they carried me out of the room. I did not weep. The tears could not come. I wanted only to crawl into bed and sleep. And when we reached Freddy's house, that was exactly what I did.

Thirty-Seven

FOR THE FIRST time in my life I had no interest in art. I had no desire to draw; nothing inspired me; everything seemed wrong. *I* felt wrong. I didn't know where I belonged anymore. Or who I was.

When I was a little girl, I would draw and paint and dream. I would play all day in our garden and pretend I was a famous artist and my toy bears and dolls would come flocking to my studio to sit for their portraits. That creative spark had lived inside me all the time. But that spark blew out when Papa slapped me. I wasn't sure I could rekindle it. I felt ridiculous, as though everything I had ever tried to do was laughable. Mamma was right. Who did I think I was?

One day slipped into the next. Tension at Freddy's house hung in the air like coal smoke. I knew Rose did not want me there. Whenever I came into a room, she found a reason to leave it. Freddy was kind to me, but I could see uncertainty in his eyes. Charlotte, with her sweet childish ways, was over the moon that I was staying in the house, and many a morning I woke to find her in my room, escaped from the nursery. One morning, for good measure, she had pushed baby George's bassinet down the hall and parked him next to my bed. I took comfort in their presence.

That night after Freddy brought me home to Pimlico, I'd begged him to intervene for Sophie, to write a letter for her himself if he had to. Without a character reference, Sophie would be unable to find a job even as a charwoman. The thought of her ruined because of me made me cry so hard I thought I'd never stop. Freddy promised he would help. I loved my brother dearly, but that night my love for him deepened. I didn't know what I would have done without him.

Freddy went straight back to Mayfair and waited with Mamma for Papa to return. Freddy told me later that Papa was full of remorse and dismayed that I had left before he could speak to me. He had locked himself in his study and refused to come out. At least Mamma had acquiesced to Freddy's pleas and had given Sophie a character reference. Freddy saw Sophie before he came home. She told him that she'd stay with a WSPU friend until she'd found a new position.

I knew I needed to go to the RCA and resign my acceptance but I found I couldn't. I suppose I held on to some hope that Papa, in his remorse, would change his mind. He would yield, appear at Freddy's house apologizing, and hand me a pot of money.

But I was childish and fanciful in my hope, because I should have known that Papa could never forgive me. Despite his remorse for slapping me, in his eyes I had humiliated him, created a scandal that had far-reaching consequences. Sir Henry had wasted no time telling his side of the story at the Reform Club, and Freddy told me that Papa, ashamed, could no longer bring himself to attend. So I was not surprised when Papa didn't come to see me. But I was surprised that Mamma didn't either.

A week later, I went to join Freddy and Rose in the sitting room. As I reached the door, I heard Rose say my name. I hung back in the shadows outside the door.

"Why did you try to speak for Victoria, Frederick?" she was saying, irritation in her voice. "Whatever were you thinking? You should have known your father would react the way he did." I could picture Rose's face as she said this, eyes bright with righteousness. She always hated it when Freddy leapt to my defense.

"Sweetheart, I had no idea she had been carrying on as she had," Freddy replied. "All she told me was that she wanted to go to art college. Drawing that bloke was bad enough, but she was alone with him while he was unclothed!"

"What a disgusting man!" Rose said. "To sit there naked and let a girl look at him? It's not to be borne."

"It's a jolly good thing Father doesn't know his name, or he'd see to his ruin," Freddy said.

"She's come out now, so she's responsible for her own actions. Nothing your parents can do will save her." Rose pointed this last bit out helpfully. "Not a wicked girl like that."

"She's ruined. I know she is," Freddy said sharply. "You don't have to spell it."

Rose sighed. "What is she going to do with herself? She can't stay here, Frederick. I won't allow a black mark on our name to match the one she's painted on your father's. There is talk in my circle already. I went to June Arbuthnot's today to play bridge, and all discussion in the room stopped when I came in. I was so embarrassed I came straight home."

"London is no place for her now." I heard the shuffle of the fireguard and the sound of coals falling as Freddy poked the fire. "I don't see her ever finding a husband. I fear this will follow her until the day she dies."

Rose spoke, driving the knife in further. "Without a marriage, she'll never have a life of her own. She'll be as a child. A spinster's life is a dreadful one."

There was a long moment of silence, and I thought about going in and pretending I hadn't heard, but then Freddy spoke again.

"She has to be sent away," he said. "It's what's done in these circumstances. Father wants her gone permanently, but I've convinced him to keep her away for a year and then see where things lie. That will give a chance for the gossip to die down. And maybe she can come back and start anew. It grieves me to say it, but I think Great-Aunt Maude's is the only place for her. At least she'll be safe in Norfolk, and away from anything that will turn her head again."

Sent away. Like some unloved orphan in a Dickens novel. I was a problem that must be dealt with and then forgotten about. Would Papa ever think of me again? Would Mamma? Or would they excise every memory of me from the house and their minds?

I wished with all my heart that Will were there beside me. I could see his eyes, kind, as he heard the conversation unfolding behind the door. I could feel his arm, heavy and warm around my shoulders, as he held me to him to comfort me.

But then I remembered the hardness on his face as he backed away from me that day at the RCA.

I had never felt so unloved and unwanted in my life. I swallowed and swallowed; I thought I'd choke on the tears that threatened to overcome me.

"When will she go?" Rose sounded relieved. Of course she did.

"I'm to take her home tomorrow night, and she'll be in Norfolk by the weekend."

I pulled my shawl around my shoulders and leaned against the wall. All I could do was breathe in and out, in and out. This wasn't happening to me, surely. This was someone else's life. But then Freddy said something that saved me, that brought me out of the deep well of pain I had been lost in for the past seven days.

"It's extraordinary what she's done, really," he said. "She was accepted into the Royal College of Art! How did she do that? She had no money, no time on her own, no art supplies, nothing, yet she did it. When I bolted, I had money, your support, friends, and resources. She had, what? A lady's maid to help her?"

"She's always been a tenacious girl," Rose said.

"But the thing is, such tenacity would be admired in a man. Father came round to my choice because he saw how determined I was, and that reminded him of his own start. Vicky tried the same thing, and everyone saw it as bad behavior."

"The world doesn't work the same way for women."

"Well, maybe it ought to. I used to think it shouldn't, but now I'm not so sure."

"It's no good to wish the world were different, Frederick," Rose said. "The truth is, there's no place in the world for a girl like that."

I backed away from the door as quietly as I could and went back upstairs. I sat on my bed, closed my eyes. My hands were trembling and I gripped the edge of the mattress to calm them.

I waited. I waited for the usual whispers to tell me I was preposterous. But they didn't come. Instead, I heard new ones. There were Freddy's: *It's extraordinary what she's done. Such tenacity would be admired in a man.* Rose's: *The world doesn't work the same way for women.* Lucy's: *How can you have what you want when you're denied the same rights as male citizens?* And then Will's: *When are you going to realize how talented you are?* Most of all, I found the whisper of *preposterous* had been replaced with *tenacious.* And then I felt myself coming back, fighting through the sadness and pain and humiliation. That girl in Bertram's picture was sparking to life.

In the morning I woke up to find Charlotte lying next to me, escaped from the nursery once more. Her dark lashes lay against her cheeks; one hand was thrown up over her head.

What would life be like for Charlotte when she was my age? Would tenacity be admired in a woman then as it was in a man? I imagined her at age eighteen, going out into the world with courage, living her life as she pleased.

But how could she do so if there was no one to show her how? Charlotte needed someone to show her all the possibilities of life, someone who knew what bravery was.

I may have had only one option in my father's world, but there were plenty of options left in another.

After breakfast, I wrote Freddy a note telling him I was going back home, gathered up my things, and slipped out of the house.

I took the Underground to Dover Street Station and wandered about in Green Park until midmorning, when Papa would be at his place of business, and Mamma at her charity.

The house was quiet when I came in. No one was about. I went upstairs to my bedroom to find that everything had been packed away in trunks, most likely waiting to be shipped to Aunt Maude's.

I searched through the trunks until I found the one that held my grandmother's jewelry box. I could sell the jewelry, and that would keep me going for a bit. I had no reason to care now if Mamma noticed it missing. I unpacked one of the trunks to repack it with my tailor-mades and shirt-waists and a few hats. As I lifted out a stack of silk chemises on the bottom, I saw the leather cover of my sketchbook, the one I'd had in France. Packed neatly next to it were my Reeves & Sons charcoal set in its beech-wood box, the silver dip pen, the bottles of ink, the tin of conté crayons in portrait colors, the Derwent pencils, and the glass-paper sanding block. Everything my parents had taken from me, months ago.

I took out the sketch pad and flicked through the pages, expecting to find the drawings torn out, but they were all there: the sketches of Lily, the one of a nude Bertram standing contrapposto, the one of the Black Maria with Will's profile in the corner, marked by a scribble of pencil when Lucy had pushed me away. All the silly scraps of paper were in it too—the leaflets and notices and bits of paper that I had hoarded. And then I discovered, behind all this bumf, the drawing Mamma had done of me as a little girl. But it was no longer half drawn. Mamma had completed it.

I understood now why my mother had turned her back on her own talents. It was scary enough in my world; it was utterly impossible in hers. But her packing my sketchbook and giving me her finished drawing meant as much to me as being accepted to the RCA.

I tore a page out of my sketchbook and sat down to write.

Dear Mamma,

I'm not going to Norfolk to stay with Aunt Maude. I'm going to stay with a friend. I have to find my own way in the world. Don't worry about me. I will be in touch soon.

Thank you for packing my art things. I

*see that you finished the sketch of me. I
will cherish it.*

*Your loving daughter,
Vicky*

I left the page on my dressing table and finished packing.

I dragged my trunk down the staircase, thumping on each step. Mrs. Fitzhughes and Emma stood at the bottom of the stairs, watching me openmouthed.

"Miss Darling?" Mrs. Fitzhughes said. "May I ask—"

"Actually, if you can ask John to fetch a cab for me, I'd be most obliged," I said, as the trunk dropped off the last step. I stood up and blew the hair out of my eyes. "If he could do that, I'll be on my way."

Mrs. Fitzhughes blinked and blinked. "I . . ."

"I'll sort that for you, Miss Darling," Emma said, and then hurried off. I thought I heard her giggle as she rounded the corner.

"I'll be off then, Mrs. Fitzhughes." I dragged the trunk through the hall and outside.

"Where are you going? What shall I tell your parents?"

"Tell them . . ." I hesitated. "Tell them not to worry."

I directed the cab driver to the RCA in Kensington, and asked him to wait. I went inside, pausing in the anteroom to look at the art. *Someday, someday I'll be up there,* I vowed.

I went down the hall toward the clerk's office, but on the way I saw Mr. Earnshaw, the man who had given me advice on applying back in March, coming down the corridor. His face creased into a smile when he saw me.

"Miss Darling!" he said. "It is so good to see you. My heartfelt congratulations to you. I heard you were accepted."

"Thank you, Mr. Earnshaw. But unfortunately I must resign my place."

Mr. Earnshaw looked taken aback. "I'm sorry to hear that, Miss Darling. I saw your work and I was most impressed. Most impressed. True, you have a lack of technique, but that can be learned. The panel agreed there is a strong sense of emotion in all of your subjects, in particular the figure study of the young man posing as David. That is very rare in a young artist and almost impossible to teach, because one must see the emotion in one's subject and know how to portray it almost intuitively."

This was all astonishing for me to hear. It heartened me greatly but saddened me, too. Will would have been the first person to celebrate that with me. But I couldn't tell him, not after what happened the last time I saw him.

"May I ask why you've had such a sudden change of heart?"

"It's not my heart that has changed. It's my circumstances. I can no longer afford the tuition. But I wish to try again next year, if I may. Now, please tell me what I can do to gain a scholarship. I'm sure I lost it because of my poor showing on the arithmetic section."

Mr. Earnshaw smiled. "No, not at all. The women who won the scholarships were no better on that part of the test than you were. But they are all more established in the art world. One has won a prize in an art show, and she's had some work published. If you come back a mature artist with something like that in your portfolio next year, you'll have an excellent chance."

"Do you really think so?"

"I do. And whatever happens, I hope you will never stop creating art, Miss Darling, for you have immense talent." He reached out his hand and I shook it.

"I won't, sir. I promise you that."

IT WAS MIDAFTERNOON by the time I arrived at Lucy's flat in Clement's Inn. I knocked on the door, and after a moment the door opened and Lucy stood there.

I set the trunk down. "Your offer of a place to stay . . . does it still stand?"

Thirty-Eight

Lucy Hawkins's flat,
August to November

LUCY'S FLAT WAS bigger than Will's, with two rooms instead of one. But unlike Will's, hers were gloomy and dark inside, though she had done much to brighten them, gracing them with the beauty of an artist. Two overstuffed upholstered chairs faced a little coal fire, and a table filled with jars of paste stones, beads, metalwork, and tools sat under a window. A large iron bedstead covered with a colorful patchwork quilt filled one corner. One of Alphonse Mucha's advertisements hung on the wall over the bed. It was a drawing of a woman sitting on a bicycle, a laurel branch in her hand. Over her stretched the words WAVERLEY CYCLES.

Lucy had given me a section of her wardrobe for my things and cleared a little space on her dressing table in her tiny lavatory. She had a flush toilet and a wash-hand basin, but like Will, Lucy bathed at the public baths.

Things were difficult at first, and I fear I tried Lucy's patience. I didn't mean to, but unused to doing for myself, I simply left my clothing in a pile on the floor, expecting it to be laundered in the morning. By whom, I did not know.

"Enchanted mice?" Lucy suggested once. After meals I got up from the table and left the dishes behind. Of course, when Lucy pointed it out, I dealt with the mess, but she always had to ask.

Finally, fed up with me, Lucy took things into her own hands. One day I found my breakfast dishes stored in my bureau drawer. Egg yolk and marmalade had dripped onto my chemises. Lucy calmly explained what I would have to do to get the stains out. I had never considered what work a stain could create. It was an entire ordeal. I had to rub the soiled marks with butter and then let the garments sit in ammonia and washing soda. Once the stains had faded, I took them to the City of London Municipal Bath and Wash House and waited in line to use the boiler and mangle. I hung my damp wash on a clothesline strung across the rooftop garden and then pressed the garments with an iron heated up in the coal fireplace. I never forgot to wash my dishes again.

Once a week we bathed at the wash house. Despite the noise and bluster, it was tolerable enough. The building was clean and tidy, with wrought-iron columns and green-and-yellow tiles on the floors and walls. To save money, Lucy brought soap so we wouldn't have to purchase a tablet. Still, we each had to pay a tuppence for the bath and another penny to hire a small towel. Each little slipper tub was behind its own curtain, and one could change in a private cubicle beforehand. There was plenty of hot water, and the towel was clean.

But once again, I behaved like a toff. I sat on the little

stool by the tub and waited for someone to come and draw the bath. When no one appeared, after waiting a quarter of an hour, I poked my head around the curtain into Lucy's cubicle and asked when the maid would come in. I think at that moment Lucy wanted to drown me in her bath.

Through all of this, my thoughts flitted briefly to the comforts of home, but I turned them back firmly toward the present. After all, I needed to learn to do for myself if I wished to be independent.

Lucy was as patient as she could be. She helped me find a shop to sell my grandmother's jewelry. The trinkets weren't the crown jewels, only oddments of old-fashioned things that no one ever wore, but because she knew jewelry well, she made the clerk give me a decent sum. Lucy and I joined together to make jewelry to sell to the local department stores, and Mr. Pethick-Lawrence gave me a job working at WSPU headquarters. I illustrated articles for *Votes for Women*, answered telephones, and performed other assorted duties three days a week. In all, everything added up to enough money to help Lucy with the rent and food.

A week after I'd left home, Lucy and I saw Sophie at the headquarters sewing banners. She had found employment with a family in Park Lane. The mother was one of the WSPU's biggest supporters, so Sophie didn't have to hide her politics anymore. She was even given a paid day off each week to help at headquarters.

I told Sophie all about what had happened when I went into the RCA. "If I'm to get a scholarship next year, I need to do what the female winners did," I told her. "I need to be published and to enter some sort of contest."

"What about PC Fletcher?" Lucy asked. "Why not see if the two of you can get your novelette idea off the ground? *Votes for Women* is all well and good, but I don't know how much sway it will have with the old establishment at the RCA. Remember how they felt about Sylvia Pankhurst. No sense putting their backs up if you don't have to."

"PC Fletcher and I are not a partnership anymore. We haven't been for a long time; I told you that before."

"Yes, I know," Lucy said. "But that was when you were engaged. You aren't engaged now, so what's to stop you?"

"You love him; you know you do!" Sophie said. "Every time you were with him, you'd come home smiling. Whenever you were with your fiancé, you were so serious."

Before I left home, I would have lied about my feelings for Will. I had only ever admitted them to myself. But now, hearing Sophie say *you love him* made a little thrill of happiness shoot through me. "But Will doesn't feel the same way about me."

"I'm sure he does!" Sophie insisted.

"Well, if he did, he doesn't anymore," I said. "The last time we talked, he didn't want anything to do with me. After the RCA exam he came to see me, and I told him I was engaged. I tried to explain, but he didn't want to hear. You should have seen the look on his face, as if he loathed me."

"Are we talking about PC William Fletcher, the knight in shining armor, who helped us all the time, risking the wrath of a lot of police constables?" Lucy said. "Vicky, I never thought you were dumb, but sheesh."

"What are you going on about, Lucy?" I said. I was growing impatient with both her and Sophie. It was enough for me to be rejected once by Will. If I heard him talk to me in that formal voice again, I didn't think I could bear it.

"You told him you were engaged!" Lucy said, exasperated.

"As a servant living in an upper-class household, I can see why he acted like he did," Sophie put in. "He thought there was more between you, and then he realized he really had no right to love you. And as Lucy said, he's a gentleman through and through. He backed away."

"Oh," I said.

"You never thought of that, did you?" Lucy said.

"It's probably too late, anyhow," I said, feeling hopeful despite my words. "It's been ages since I've talked to him. Not since July."

"At least go to him to see if you can work together again. You need a publishing credit for your portfolio."

"I suppose I could write to him."

"No!" both Sophie and Lucy shouted.

"You know where he lives, so go there," Sophie urged.

"I know one thing." Lucy picked up a box of leaflets. "If I had a chance with a guy like PC Fletcher, I'd grab hold of him and cling on until he cried uncle. No foolin'."

I looked at Sophie. She shrugged. "I've seen him. I have to agree with Lucy."

It took me several days to get up the nerve to go, but finally I took the Underground to Praed Street and walked to

Will's flat. When I arrived, I knocked on the door, but no one answered. After a moment, the door across the hall opened, and an elderly man with a walking stick stepped out.

"Are you looking for the police constable?" he said.

"I am. Do you know when he'll be back?"

"He's gone. He's moved away."

I felt myself grow cold. "When?" I whispered.

The man leaned on his stick. "Now, let's see. A month ago, I suppose."

"Do you know where he went?"

He shook his head slowly. "No, I'm sorry, miss. I don't know."

Everywhere I went, I looked for Will, but I never saw him. I even went to Cannon Row Police Station, but they wouldn't give me any information about him and eyed me suspiciously when I asked. I sat down several times to write a letter to him care of his parents in Rye, but I didn't know what to say.

I wrote my parents and Freddy letters from time to time, letting them know I was well. My parents never replied, but I knew that was my father's doing. I knew he could never forgive me for what I had done. I was sure he'd renounced all attachments to me. I knew my mother had to do as my father commanded, because she wouldn't dare do otherwise, but I didn't blame her anymore. She didn't know how to be any other way. But still, for all of our arguing, I found I missed my mother. And if I was honest, I found I missed my father too.

Freddy wrote to me and told me that Papa had returned to the Reform Club, and that little by little his compatriots began to speak to him again. I received a letter from Freddy on my would-be wedding day, telling me that Edmund had become engaged to Georgette Plimpton, Mrs. Plimpton's crushingly boring daughter. But for all my opinions of Miss Plimpton, I hoped that Edmund would be happy with her, and she with him.

ONE DAY IN late September, Sophie, Lucy, and I were on our way home from a WSPU poster parade when we saw a crowd bustling around a newsagent. Several men in the crowd were laughing and saying something about how the women finally got what was coming to them.

We pushed through the crowd to see Clara, one of the mural artists. She was holding a copy of the *Daily Bugle*, her face grim.

"What's happening?" I asked.

Clara passed me the paper; her finger marked a story just above the fold on the front page. Lucy and Sophie leaned over my shoulder.

SUFFRAGETTES UNDERGO HOSPITAL TREATMENT IN WINSON GAOL

A Home Secretary spokesman, Mr. G. Masterman, confirms the prison in Birmingham has resorted to the "hospital treatment" of feeding hunger-striking suffragette prisoners Laura Ainsworth, Charlotte Marsh, and Mary Leigh by way of the stomach pump.

Keir Hardie was the solitary voice against such practice. Many MPs in the House of Commons found the situation amusing and laughed when Mr. Hardie touted the dangers of force-feeding, stating that the last person who had received such treatment had died the next day. "I could not have believed that a body of gentlemen could have found reason for mirth and applause in a scene which had no parallel in the recent history of our country," Mr. Hardie said.

One Mr. C. Mansell-Moullin, MD, said, "As a hospital surgeon of thirty years' standing, I indignantly repudiate the use of the term 'hospital treatment.' It is a foul libel. Violence and brutality have no place in hospitals, as Mr. Masterman ought to know."

Mr. Masterman declared the government was within its rights to force-feed the women because they were weak-minded.

"As if they were inmates in an insane asylum!" Sophie said. I could feel her behind me shifting from foot to foot, beside herself with rage.

"It's front-page news." Clara gestured to the newsagent's window. Nearly every paper there had the story blazoned across the front page. "But not all the papers are on our side. Most of them are on the government's side. Several doctors have come out saying it isn't at all what the suffragettes are making it out to be. Have a look." She unfolded another broadsheet and pointed to the article.

The story was illustrated with a photograph of a woman neatly dressed in prison garb, sitting calmly in a chair while a smiling doctor held a tube to her mouth. The woman gazed up at him, a grateful look on her face, as though she hadn't the sense in her addlepated brain to work out the right thing to do until the doctor pitched up with his hosepipe.

I looked up from the paper. "Is this what force-feeding is like?"

"That's staged," Lucy said. "That woman is no one Birmingham headquarters knows. But there're many people in this country who'll think that's real." She made a noise of frustration. "It's gruesome, that force-feeding. Mr. Pethick-Lawrence received a telephone call from the WSPU branch in Birmingham this morning. A sympathetic wardress called to report what had happened. Four prison wardresses hold the women down; a doctor wrenches their mouth open with some sort of metal gag and then shoves a tube down it. He pours raw eggs and Benger's Food down the tube with a funnel. The wardress said she was resigning because she couldn't bear to be part of it. Said it was torture."

I felt nauseated thinking of having a tube pushed into my stomach. I could almost feel the rubber brushing down my own throat. My stomach roiled, and I swallowed hard to keep from retching.

"I'm not sure I understand the hunger-striking, Lucy," I said. "Why do you do it?"

"When we did it after the deputation in June, it was because we were denied the rights of political prisoners. Hunger-striking is protest, pure and simple. But now, with this barbaric force-feeding, this is war. The women's suffering will boost determination and encourage many women who wouldn't otherwise do so to stand up and take part."

"Only if they know the truth!" I said. "This photo certainly won't encourage anyone."

Later, at WSPU headquarters, I drew an illustration for *Votes for Women* bringing the horror of force-feeding to life on the page. I sketched a woman captive in a chair, held there by four wardresses while a man forced her head back and another poured liquid through a gruesome tube trailing into her mouth, wrenched open with a gag. At the top of the page I wrote in block letters:

THE TRUTH AS WE KNOW IT.

I had once thought that I could only express myself through a sketch or a painting, but now I knew that was not true. I could express my beliefs in many ways, be it an illustration, a cartoon, or even a chalk drawing on the pavement, if I was so inclined. With every stroke of my pencil, I felt more and more inspired and triumphant. So instead of my real name, I signed the drawing: *Victorious.*

Mr. Pethick-Lawrence printed it the next day. It was on the front page of *Votes for Women*. It was an honor, but I couldn't help but feel we were preaching to the converted.

LUCY, HAVING BEEN among the first to hunger-strike, wasn't content to let other women sacrifice themselves while she stood idly by, and so I knew something was up when she rose early on the ninth of November and dressed in the plainest clothes she had.

I leaned on one elbow. "What are you doing, Lucy?"

"A little something I've been planning." She pulled on a pair of kitchen sleeves.

"Are you cleaning something?"

"You might say that. Going to help the Lord Mayor."

The importance of the date sifted through my tired mind then. The ninth of November was the Lord Mayor's Banquet at the Guildhall, and every politician of note would be there to celebrate the new mayor. "Are you going to the Guildhall?"

"Good guess!"

"Why?"

"Never been to a knees-up at the Guildhall," she said. "Might be a laugh."

"Wait!" I said, fully awake now. "Are you going there to get arrested?"

Lucy made a face. "Not going for the canapés, I can tell you that."

"But . . . but . . . if they arrest you, will you hunger-strike again? If you do, they'll force-feed you." I was terrified for

Lucy. People died from being force-fed, like that man in the paper said.

"Look, Vicky, the government doesn't seem to know the weapon they've handed to us now because of this force-feeding. We're in all the papers, and if we don't stop, the truth will come out eventually, and people will be on our side. We've all got to do our bit. And this is what we're all about."

If the end result hadn't been so grave, Lucy's escapade would have been hilarious. Lucy and two other suffragettes, a fellow American called Alice Paul and a Brit called Amelia Brown, slipped into the palatial Guildhall by dressing as charwomen. Each time they saw someone, they'd ask the way to the kitchen. One time when they saw a police constable, they hid in a cloakroom. The constable, not knowing they were there, actually threw his cloak over them. Eventually they worked their way to the gallery in the banqueting hall, and when everyone was seated, tucking into their feast, Lucy and her friends shouted and threw stones through a stained-glass window.

They were, of course, arrested. Mr. Pethick-Lawrence went to the court to sit in at their hearing. The judge sentenced them to thirty days' imprisonment in the dreaded second division at Holloway.

A week dragged by. I missed Lucy so much. The flat was empty without her. I even missed sharing the bed with her.

Lucy had been in prison for ten days when Mr. Pethick-Lawrence got word from a sympathetic wardress that Lucy had gone on hunger strike and they had begun force-feeding her. I worried about her well-being in prison, though I knew she was proud to be there. If only I could make everyone see my cartoon for *Votes for Women*, make everyone understand what Lucy was going through right now.

Then I remembered Étienne's posters of the cabaret girls. I would make posters of the force-feeding and hang them where everyone would see them! The WSPU didn't have to be at the mercy of the newspapers. Anyone with eyes would see the truth.

"I HAVE AN IDEA to get the truth of force-feeding out to the public," I said. "I want to make an illustration for a poster that we can stick up."

It was the next morning, and I had sought out Mr. Pethick-Lawrence in the newspaper room at Clement's Inn.

"What do you have in mind?" he asked.

I pulled out my sketchbook and set it on the table, turning it to the page with my sketch. "This is an illustration of the wardress's statement. We can paste the posters on hoardings, pub walls, buildings, signs."

His finger landed on the bottom of the illustration. "What's *Victorious*?"

"That's me. My secret signature; a play on my real name. I want that word to be on everyone's lips in connection with force-feeding. They'll all wonder who Victorious is. But no one will know."

Mr. Pethick-Lawrence looked at the illustration thoughtfully. "The idea has great merit, but won't people just tear them down? The police tear down anything we post almost before the glue's gone off."

"I thought of that." I told him about Étienne's posters, and how he had put them up high.

He rubbed his chin. "Fly-posting is illegal. We'll have to find someone willing to risk arrest. That might take a little while, as most of the women who do such things are already serving time in Holloway. I'm sorry, Vicky. Maybe there will be another opportunity, when we have the resources."

I hadn't thought that far ahead. I shut my book, feeling deflated.

"It's a wonderful idea," he said. "It's certainly worth considering in future." He smiled at me kindly and went back to work at the layout desk.

I went out front to the visitors' entrance. Sophie and Clara had been sorting through the day's post but stopped what they were doing when I came over.

"I had this idea for a poster, but Mr. Pethick-Lawrence says there's no one to hang them," I said, showing them my sketchbook.

"That's good," Sophie said. "Really good. I can't see how anyone could ignore it."

"Why can't *you* hang them?" Clara said.

"Me?" I supposed the idea wasn't so far-fetched. Étienne hung his own posters. He didn't make anyone else do it. "I guess I could. I'm not afraid of heights."

"You'll need a lookout and someone to help lug your clobber," Clara said. "You can't do everything burdened down with pastepots and brushes and the like."

"I'll go with you," Sophie said. "It'll make a nice change from stitching banners."

"You'll have to go in the dead of night or else you won't get a lick of paste on the wall, much less a poster," Clara warned. "The only women about in the night are"—she lowered her voice—"*harlots*. What if you're mistaken for one of those?"

"What about delivery boys?" Sophie said. "Delivery boys are about at that hour. We'll go dressed as boys and ride the bicycles they have here for the bicycling corps. I'll kit us out in boys' clothes. No one will be the wiser."

Clara drew in her breath, her eyes shining. "It's just like Mary Frith and Lady Catherine Ferrers. Those highway-women who dressed as men and relieved many a gentleman of his purse."

We started to laugh so hard that several of the women working in the back came out to see what was funny.

"Just remember that Lady Catherine died from a gun-shot wound," Clara said after she had collected herself. "Let's not pretend this isn't going to be a dangerous caper. If a constable catches you, you might not be able to blag your way out of it."

"He'll have to catch me first. I'm pretty swift on a bi-cycle," Sophie said.

"Me too," I said. Although truth be told, I hadn't been cycling in years.

"Start with Whitehall," Clara said. "Lots of politicians, lots of traffic in the daytime to see the posters."

And so the scheme was put into motion. Mr. Pethick-Lawrence had my illustration printed up in four colors—gold, gray, black, and green—by a sympathetic printer on Fleet Street who'd agreed to keep quiet. I had postcard-sized versions to paste onto the backs of signs and park benches and broadsheet-sized ones for buildings and hoardings.

Sophie found boys' reach-me-down clothing—knicker-bockers with braces, muslin shirts, wool jackets, and flat newsboy caps—on Petticoat Lane, and altered them to fit. I loved the way the garments felt, especially the knicker-bockers, which were very freeing.

As the night of the fly-posting drew closer, I grew giddy with anticipation. I felt like a horse released in a pasture after a lifetime of living in a stall. I may not have been brave enough to volunteer for prison and risk force-feed-ing like Lucy, but I had been brave enough to leave home for an unfamiliar world, one I had grown to love. I was ready to join the ranks of the doers, those mad women making demands instead of asking politely. I was itching to use my artwork, put forth my point of view, in the fight. As I'd told Mr. Earnshaw at the RCA on the day I climbed out my window, my artwork would hang in pride of place where everyone could see it. I had just never imagined my first exhibition would be so public.

Two days later, we were ready. Sophie and I dressed at Clement's Inn about midnight. Some of the suffragettes who rented rooms upstairs came down in their dressing gowns to see us off. We wore our own boots, but we rubbed dirt into them to make them look shabby. A little coal dust on our cheeks hid our femininity. My hair proved a chal-lenge, being so long and thick. Sophie struggled to fit all of it underneath the cap. She glared at me when I suggested cutting it—once a lady's maid, always a lady's maid. She settled on coiling it into a spiral and pinning the flat cap on top.

She looked doubtful. "I'm not sure this will stay on." She tugged at the cap. "If I put too many pins in, people will cotton on that you aren't a boy."

I shook my head a bit to test the pins. "It will have to do. Just make sure you hide all of your hair under your cap. Your ginger hair attracts enough attention as it is."

I prepared the wheat paste next, a messy business that required mixing equal parts flour and water and heating the mixture over a paraffin burner until it turned into a glop that would hold the posters in place and make it difficult to tear them down in one piece.

And so it was well after midnight when Sophie and I (after a few wobbly starts) set off on bicycles with posters in canvas satchels over our shoulders, and a pastepot and long-handled brush rattling in my basket. I was afraid, but I thought about what Lucy was going through in Holloway, and that gave me courage. I was glad that it was Sophie who cycled beside me. I remembered that day when Sophie taught me to dance. I had thought she and I could never be friends. We had more in common than I ever guessed.

Whitehall, the center of His Majesty's government and home to its departments and ministers' offices, was largely silent during the night. We skirted the edge of Trafalgar Square and turned our bicycles down Northumberland Avenue and up Great Scotland Yard. It was so quiet on Northumberland Avenue that the hiss of our bicycle tires and the jangling of the pedals echoing off the buildings was the only sound. Shadows cast from streetlamps created shifting figures, turning trees into looming monsters with eerie, clawlike hands, and ivy-covered gates into other-worldly creatures. A brisk wind shot between the buildings, and I could feel my cap fighting the hairpins, trying to take flight. I dared not let go of the handlebars to clamp it down because I didn't trust myself to steer one-handed. I used to cycle a lot in Hyde Park before I went to finishing school, but that had been a few years ago. My skills were coming back slowly, but crashing into a bollard was still a possibility if I didn't concentrate.

"Have you ever been out this late, Sophie?" I whispered.

She shook her head. "No."

"It's terrifying."

"It is. I won't say no."

"We'll have to work fast," I said. "Wheat paste on the back, then brush the bill into place with more paste—that will make it harder to tear down."

We pasted the smaller posters onto benches, road signs, and statue plinths. The larger ones went up on any build-ing we could get to without being seen. To put the posters up high, Sophie would boost me up or I would climb trees and shinny out on the limbs to reach the building. It was so much easier to climb in knickerbockers. I wished I could wear them all the time.

"I want to stick one right on Ten Downing, where the prime minister lives," I said after pasting a poster on the door of the Red Lion pub. "But I don't dare. Too guarded."

"We'd be nicked for sure," Sophie said, pedaling next to me. "Cannon Row Police Station is a stone's throw away from there."

"How about Horse Guards?" I said. "You know the little sentry boxes for the Household Cavalry regiment? Just under the roofs would be a smashing place to slap up posters. If we do a good job of it, they won't be able to scrape them off before the cavalry take up their post in the morning. Everyone will see them over the soldiers' heads. Wouldn't that be a coup?"

"Damaging Household Cavalry property?" Sophie shivered. "I'm up for anything, but if they catch us . . . well, a second-division cell will be a blessing. We'll most likely be tucked away with the murderers waiting to be hanged."

Sophie had a point, but faint heart never won fair maiden, and the smooth empty space just below the pitched roofline was calling out to be fly-posted. I wanted to do it, no matter what. The soldiers on their horses always drew crowds, and so my poster would be seen by hundreds of people.

And so, as Big Ben rang out two o'clock, we cycled back up Whitehall to Horse Guards. We left our bikes against a bollard and had a look at our targets. The roofs were maybe only twenty feet off the ground, but there was nothing close to either sentry box that I could climb on.

"We'll have to use those little ledges," Sophie whispered. "You can reach the roof from there." The ledges she was referring to were two decorative plinths, no wider than the length of my toes, one halfway up the wall, the other a few feet from the roof. "You can push off my shoulders to the next ledge. I'll stand right there so I can grab you if you slide down."

I eyed the ledges. They looked really narrow. I took a

shaking breath and blew it out. "I suppose there's nothing for it. I'll have to try."

Sophie held out her cupped hands and I stepped into them and grabbed hold of the first ledge with my fingers. She boosted me up farther, and I reached up for the next one. I dangled in midair for a heart-stopping moment, toes scraping against the wall while Sophie got her shoulders under my boots and pushed me up toward the roof. It was difficult to get hold of the roof's edge with the pastepot dangling from my elbow, but with a few wriggles and a few shoves from Sophie, I made it.

I wiped the sweat from my forehead with the back of my sleeve. I had scraped my hands, and I was sure my knees would be blue with bruises in the morning, but I wanted to stand up and dance a jig on top of the sentry box.

I set to my task, pasting the back of the poster, unfurling it over the edge, and then reaching down with the brush and smoothing the paper into place.

It fit perfectly in the little space, almost as though it were made to be there. Now, just the next sentry box to do, and we could go home.

I perched for a moment on the ridgeline, catching my breath. Sophie was standing right under me, scanning the pavement right and left, keeping a lookout. Suddenly, I saw her stiffen. She lifted her hand, and I looked where she was pointing. A figure was approaching, casting a long shadow over the pavement. The shadow wore a tall helmet.

Sophie said it before my stunned mind could form

the words: "It's a police constable!" she hissed. She spun around and looked up at me, her hand on top of her cap. Her face was full of fear. "Get down!"

"Run, Sophie," I whispered. It had been my idea to climb the sentry boxes. I'd just have to chance it alone.

"I can't leave you!" she said, fidgeting from one foot to the other.

"Go!"

"Damn and blast!" Sophie glanced at me one more time, then lit off toward the bicycles, her boot heels clattering on the pavement.

I crept toward the back of the sentry box, hoping the constable wouldn't notice me, but he would have had to be blind not to see me crouching on the roof like a gargoyle come to life. My skin felt as if it were on fire with anxiety, and my legs were shaking. I swung out over the edge, jabbing my toes around, fully expecting to find a little ledge like the one on the other side, but it wasn't there. There was only sheer wall. Without a ledge, I would have to drop straight down. I didn't have the strength to lift myself back up and I was too terrified to let go. My arms burned with the effort of holding on.

The sound of the constable's feet crunching in the gravel grew louder and louder, and then they paused for a moment in front of the sentry box. I squeezed my eyes shut. The footsteps began again; this time they were moving quicker. Moving toward the back of the box, where I dangled in midair.

I took a breath and let go.

I slid down the wall, scraping my chin against the stone, and I landed hard, my right leg buckling underneath me as I fell. I felt something in my ankle give, and searing white pain flew up my leg. I shoved my palm into my mouth, biting hard on it so I wouldn't scream out loud. I struggled to my feet, ignoring the pain, and stumbled toward Horse Guards Parade.

"Stop!"

I shot a look over my shoulder, and the police constable was speeding up behind me. The light from a nearby lamp-post illuminated my pursuer. Instead of the irritated police constable, the light shone on a friendly face. A face I knew and had drawn many times.

I stopped running.

"Will!"

His eyes went wide, and everything seemed to stand still in that instant. "Vicky?"

The relief was so great that I did the daftest thing. I threw myself into his arms and burst into tears. I pressed my forehead against his coat, hiccupping with sobs like a little girl. The wool of his jacket felt rough against my skin and it smelled like him, green grass and clean laundry.

"So you're the one fly-posting these illustrations up and down Whitehall?" His chest rumbled with laughter. "You're Victorious?"

"I suppose you have to arrest me," I mumbled. "I won't fight you. I'll go."

"I don't want to arrest you!" Will held me away from him. "I was going to tell whoever was doing the fly-posting not to go this way; there are constables on the other side of the parade ground. Let's get you out of here before someone sees you. Come on."

"I can't . . . I can't walk!" I held my foot off the ground, clinging on to Will's coat for balance. My ankle was beginning to throb, and my bootlaces were so tight they felt as though they were cutting into my skin. "I think I broke my ankle jumping off the sentry box."

Will was suddenly serious. "Here, put your arms around my neck."

I did, and Will hoisted me in his arms. "My bicycle is over there," I said, pointing over his shoulder. "I can't leave it. It belongs to the WSPU."

"We'll take care of the bicycle, and then I'll take you home to your . . . I suppose it will be to your husband."

"I haven't got a husband, William."

Will paused. "You what?" His arms tightened around me.

"I haven't got a husband. It's a long story. Take me to my friend's flat, and I'll tell you. There are so many things I want to tell you."

Will groaned and then shifted me in his arms. "How much do you weigh? I feel as if I'm carrying a log."

I thumped him on the shoulder. "I'll get my own back for that."

He sighed. "I don't doubt that you will. And Vicky?"
"Yes?"

"You look rather cute in those knickerbockers."

IN THE END, we hid the bicycle under a bush and took the Underground to Clement's Inn. I was hopping on one leg up the stairs to Lucy's rooms, clinging on to Will, making a hellish racket, when one of the other suffragettes poked her head out of her flat. "Vicky? Is that . . ." Her voice trailed off. Her eyes widened when she saw Will.

"It's all right, miss," Will said. "Just escorting Vicky home."

The woman ducked her head back into the flat. "Sophie, she's here! There's a PC with her."

There were quick shuffling noises from inside the flat, and a moment later Sophie appeared, still dressed as a boy. When she saw Will, a huge grin spread across her face. Then her eyes traveled from Will's arm around me to my foot. "What happened? We've been waiting for a call from the police."

"I hurt my ankle jumping off the sentry box," I said. The conversation must have disturbed other suffragettes because startled faces began to poke out of doors.

"Is it all right?" Sophie asked Will, her expression worried.

"I'll see to it for her."

Inside Lucy's flat it was cold; the fire hadn't been lit all day. Will helped me hobble to the edge of the bed, and I dragged the bedcovers over my lap.

"This is your flat?" He shrugged off his police tunic and laid it over my shoulders. Underneath it he wore a simple white cotton shirt with braces.

"It's Lucy Hawkins's flat. You know her. She was the one chained to the railing the day I got arrested."

He knelt down and unlaced my boot, drawing it off carefully. "Yes, I know her. She's the one in jail just now with the others being force-fed. That's why I was trying to help whoever was fly-posting. I was walking my beat and saw the posters. I thought, *Finally people will know the truth of it.* I have to say, it took a lot of bravery to do what you did tonight."

"I wasn't very good," I said glumly. "It's probably my last caper. Caught on the first night. It was too difficult to pull off."

"Now, don't give up so easily. Where's that stubborn spirit of yours that I know so well?"

I nudged his leg with my good foot. "You shouldn't say that, Will. You're a police constable. You should have arrested me. In actual fact, you're probably in the soup tomorrow. We fly-posted on your beat, and they're bound to question you about that. You abandoned your post too. They'll think you helped me."

"I was going off duty anyway." He hesitated. "Hey now, there's an idea."

"What do you mean?"

He let out a laugh. "I can tell you where we'll be patrolling, and you can fly-post somewhere else. Simple."

"You? A turncoat? William Fletcher!"

He shrugged. "Let's just call me an informant. The way I see it, you could use someone on the inside to tip you off. It's not like I haven't helped the suffragettes before. Victorious would be able to give them all the slip."

I could imagine the frustration of the government, waking up each morning to a city wallpapered with my illustrations. Everyone would wonder who Victorious was, and surely the papers would take notice.

"'Deeds not words.' Isn't that the suffragette motto?" He pulled off my stocking and whistled. It was not a pretty sight. My ankle was puffy and swollen and already turning an unlovely shade of yellow.

"Blimey," he said. "You did a good job of it, didn't you?" His fingers pressed around my ankle. "I'm not sure it's broken; maybe just wrenched. Still, I'll strap it up for you, and then in the morning we'll get you to a doctor."

Will went to Lucy's fireplace, shoveled in some coal, and coaxed a fire to light. My chin stung where I had scraped it. I brushed it with the back of my hand.

Will went into Lucy's little kitchen, and I heard cupboard doors opening and closing. He reappeared carrying a bowl of water and some cloths. He dipped one into the water, came over, and pressed it to my chin. "Hold it there and it will ease in a moment. It's just a little cut; I don't think you need stitches. You'll look as though you've gone a few rounds with a bare-knuckle fighter, I expect."

He knelt on the floor and began to wrap a cloth around my ankle. "So out with it. What's all this about? Last time we spoke, you were off to marry a rich bloke. Now you're dressed as a lad, fly-posting illustrations up and down Whitehall. Surely you must have known you would have been arrested if you were caught? I doubt there are any art classes offered in Holloway."

His flippant remark stung me. "I suppose I deserve that."

"I'm sorry, Vicky." He shook his head. His voice was marked with frustration. "I don't mean to be a swine to you. I'm just a little confused."

"I couldn't go through with the marriage. There was no freedom in that life after all. I left home, and now I'm a suffragette."

"I can't imagine what that cost you, Vicky." Will's fingers hesitated on the bandage. He looked up, his face grave. "What about art school?"

"I got accepted. But it turns out I could never have gone."

Will looked at me in sorrow. "I'm sorry."

"I'm going to try again next year, this time for the scholarship. I tried to find you to see if you wanted to work together again. I went to your flat, but you weren't there. I even went to the police station, but they wouldn't tell me anything about you."

"After that day I saw you at the RCA, I moved out of my flat and back into the police barracks." He finished rolling the bandage and sat next to me. "After what happened with you, I didn't want to stay in that flat. There were too many memories of you there."

"But why?" I said. "I thought you hated me. The way you sounded that day at the RCA—it was the way you sounded when you thought I was an anti-suffragist. Disgusted."

He shook his head. "I wasn't disgusted with you. I was disgusted with me. When you told me you were engaged, I felt so daft. It was stupid of me to think I had a chance with you. Especially when I realized you had to get married in order to go to art school. I couldn't give you that. And then I thought I had mucked things up between us, kissing you as I did."

"Didn't you notice that I kissed you back?"

"I did." He looked at me in that adorable way that I remembered well. I watched his mouth turn up at the sides as he smiled.

Without even hesitating, I put my hands around his neck, pressed my mouth on his, and kissed him soundly.

Will made a garbled noise. He pulled away. "Vicky, what the devil are you doing?"

"Kissing you." I suddenly felt uncertain. "Isn't it obvious?"

He looked at me for a long moment. "Well, do it again so I can be sure."

So I did. And the same feelings I had had before bloomed inside me, as if they had never gone away—the same desire, the same need to feel him against me. And my love for him bloomed into life, too.

"Is that all right?" I said, a moment later, feeling more than a little breathless.

"Better than all right; grand, if you want to know the truth of it." He squeezed my fingers. "I had given up on ever kissing you again. But I don't understand. What's this about? Before, you told me what you felt for me was a passing fancy."

"It was a lie. The truth is, I can't ever imagine my life without you."

He pulled me close to him, and I rested my head on his chest. For the first time in maybe my entire life, I felt as if I was exactly where I needed to be and exactly who I needed to be.

—

WILL'S DIAGNOSIS WAS correct. Painful as it was, my ankle had only been wrenched, and a month later Victorious was fly-posting again, with her inside informer telling her where to go. For weeks I posted my illustrations, evading and frustrating the police. And slowly, as I worked, public opinion began to change, and more and more people understood that force-feeding was barbaric and torturous. My mother's favorite newspaper, the *Daily Bugle*, was the first to take the suffragettes' side. It denounced the force-feeding, saying, "No matter whether one agrees with the suffragettes, the government's brutal torture of the women cannot be justified." Because of the public outcry, the Home Office began an inquiry, interviewing all the prison warders. While the WSPU waited to see what the government would do, it called a truce.

Lucy and the other two suffragettes arrested with her had been released at the beginning of December. There were over a hundred of us at Holloway to greet them as they walked through the small door in the gothic iron gate. We draped them with flower garlands and paraded them home in an open-topped horse-drawn carriage, the fife-and-drum band marching behind them.

I was now among the top artists at the WSPU, and I asked Miss Housman if I could teach drawing classes at the atelier. My classes were exactly the kind that women should frequent. In my classes we drew from the undraped figure—the nude. I started out with six students, all female, from teenage girls to married women. But when word got round that my model was PC William Fletcher, I had a waiting list.

"Draw what you see, ladies, not what you know," I said, walking around the room, checking each drawing and making comments and corrections. "Don't gape, Violet," I said in a lofty voice to a teenage girl who was staring at Will posing on the model's dais. "A life-drawing class is always professional, never risqué." Violet blushed and returned to her drawing. Will looked at me out of the corner of his eye, trying valiantly to keep his expression still, fighting the compulsion to laugh.

Forty

WINTER HAD BEGUN in earnest, and snow lay thickly on the ground and covered the rooftops like cotton blankets. Everything was so white that it nearly hurt my eyes.

It was so cold I could see my breath in the air, and I felt sorry for a little house sparrow that pecked around for seeds in my mother's desolate rose garden. I looked up at the windows of my old bedroom. The remains of the wisteria vine looked ragged and forlorn in the winter light. So long ago I had climbed out that window.

I held in my hand a newly minted tuppeny novelette that featured Will's story, which Freddy's company had published. On the cover was my illustration of Robert Hoode dressed in a black cloak, robbing a lord who staggered drunken from the Reform Club. On top of it was written: *Magnificent Picture Printed in Full Color! Robert Hoode Steals from the Rich and Gives to the Poor!* And on the bottom: *Written by W. Fletcher. Illustrated by V. Darling. Published by Darling and Whitehouse and sold by all newsagents everywhere.* I looked forward to including it in my RCA application in April. I hadn't given up on my dream of going to art school, and I never would, no matter how many times I had to apply.

Mamma was the first person I wanted to show it to. I wanted her to see that I had become an artist and that I was earning money. I wanted to show her because I knew she would be proud of me.

When I lifted my hand to pull the doorbell, I saw a curtain twitch at the window. And there was my father peering out. I caught his eye and he nodded.

And smiled.

I LEFT MY parents' house and I stepped out into a day that had turned bright with sunshine and promise. Mamma had loved the novelette, and I left it with her, along with the promise to join her at Sally's Tea Shop on Saturday to meet Will. As for Papa, the smile was a start.

I walked to the Royal Academy and into the courtyard, past the statue of Sir Joshua Reynolds, holding his palette in one hand, brush held aloft in the other, making his mark on an unseen canvas. But Sir Joshua did not hold my attention for more than a passing glance. I saw Will leaning against statue's plinth. I threaded my way through the scrum of people to his side.

Together we left the Royal Academy and walked down the streets of London, a place brimming with hidden opportunity. And I knew that I would find it. For opportunity is nothing if you don't grab it by both hands.

Author's Notes

EDWARDIAN LIFE

The Edwardian era (1901–1910) was one of great change for women. Queen Victoria (May 24, 1819–January 22, 1901) had been very straitlaced, and her subjects often copied her behavior. Her son and heir, King Edward VII, for whom the era was named, was her exact opposite and had many very public affairs; his mistresses included the famous actress Lillie Langtry and socialite Alice Keppel (who was the maternal great-grandmother of Camilla, Duchess of Cornwall and second wife of Prince Charles, the Prince of Wales and future king of England).

Edwardian women were making their voices heard through the suffrage movement, and young women were finding employment, becoming better educated, and even becoming doctors and lawyers, although many universities did not award degrees, and many associations, such as the Bar Council in England, denied females the right to practice. Middle-class girls were rebelling against their parents and demanding treatment equal to that of boys. Upper-middle-class and aristocratic girls clung to tradition more than middle-class girls, but they too wanted the freedom to be more independent. Working-class single women were the most vulnerable without suffrage. The government turned a blind eye to their lives, which, if they worked outside the home, usually included sweated labor (sweatshop labor, as we know it in the United States) or long hours and no private life as a live-in servant. A great many working-class women were not paid a living wage and were forced to live in squalid conditions.

Vicky's arranged betrothal was very common for the time. People rarely married purely for love; a good match equaled marrying someone within your own class or someone who could further the interests and contribute to the betterment of the family. Vicky, as an upper-middle-class girl, would have been forbidden to date someone like Will, who was working-class.

EDWARDIAN CLOTHING

The elaborate and beautiful clothing worn during the Edwardian era was the privilege of those who could afford it, in other words the upper classes (the upper-middle class and the aristocracy). The fashion was vastly different from that of any other class. Women's fashions were all about the curves and required a corset, to produce tiny "wasp" waists. Women often "tightlaced" their corsets: pulling them so taut that they could barely breathe. Dresses were tight-fitting around the waist and bottom, and often ended in a long swath of material at the hem. Later in the era, during Vicky's time, skirts became much narrower, with slight trains, and the silhouette was longer and slimmer, requiring a new kind of corset called the S-bend, which ended mid-thigh instead of at the hips. The S-bend was touted as a health corset because it put less strain on the stomach. However, because the corset pushed the torso forward, it caused a new health problem: backache. Women would use parasols or walking sticks to help take the strain off the back. Hats were huge—often twenty-four inches in diameter—trimmed with feathers and ribbons and secured through the hair with a long, decorative hatpin.

Vicky's tailor-made was very much in fashion around the turn of the twentieth century. It was essentially a man's suit combined with a long skirt. Very comfortable and informal, it represented the changing nature of the Edwardian woman.

TUPPENNY NOVELETTES

The penny dreadful and the tuppenny novelette were the graphic novels of the Victorian and Edwardian eras. These publications were made very cheaply so that the young working class would be able to afford them. The booklets contained serialized stories released over time. They were usually thrillers. Early stories included *Black Bess, or the Knight of the Road, Varney the Vampire,* and *The String of Pearls: A Romance* (introducing Sweeney Todd). A popular Edwardian serial about a fictional detective called Sexton Blake, which first appeared in 1893, was published up until the 1970s.

VOTES FOR WOMEN

The reason why women were not given the right to vote seems ridiculous viewed through our twenty-first-century eyes. Many men thought women too irrational to make important decisions. They feared women would become the majority voters and use emotional arguments to change policies, particularly on moral and sexual issues, imposing higher standards. It was also felt that women would lose their charm, and men their dominance over women. Women were allowed to vote in municipal elections, and it was thought that this was sufficient, because local government dealt with social issues, which were deemed women's concerns. The national government dealt with wider issues, such as defense of the realm, something that was not a woman's concern.

Many women also opposed suffrage. An anti-suffrage

group—largely formed of women—called The National League for Opposing Woman Suffrage was formed to put their case forward. These women believed firmly that a man was better equipped to make decisions, and that women had enough to do running the household. They believed women could influence their husbands to make the right voting decision. Queen Victoria was appalled at the idea of women's suffrage, and in 1870 she urged her subjects to check "this mad, wicked folly of 'Women's Rights.'"

In the United States, there were many women in the temperance movement, and it was feared that women would be able to bring about Prohibition. Ironically, Prohibition came in before women received the right to vote.

British suffragettes did indeed chain themselves to railings, heckle political meetings, throw rocks and tiles at cars, and smash windows. Later, their actions increased to arson and destroying works of art. It's unclear whether their militant tactics had any weight in the final decision to give women the vote. Instead, it is thought that women's part in winning World War I (1914–1918) actually turned the tables in their favor. Because they successfully took on roles that men had to abandon to become soldiers, they were no longer seen as "half angels, half idiots," as the famed pro-suffrage politician Keir Hardie put it.

British women began demanding the vote in 1865 and were finally granted it in 1918 for those over thirty years of age. In 1928, women were granted the same voting rights as men, which was over the age of twenty-one.

What's the difference between suffragettes and suffragists? In 1906, the journalist Charles E. Hands of the *Daily Mail*, a British newspaper known for its conservative views, called the WSPU *suffragettes*, meaning it to be a slur. The WSPU embraced the name and responded that they were actually suffra*gets*, because they were going to *get* the vote. Groups other than the WSPU were simply called suffragists. The definition of *suffragist* is someone, male or female, who advocates for extending voting rights (also known as suffrage). Today the word *suffragette* is widely used as a blanket term to reference any woman in the nineteenth or twentieth century who fought for the right to vote.

In the United States, the fight was just as strong, although suffragists weren't as militant as those in the Great Britain. Their demand for the vote began in 1848. Elizabeth Cady Stanton, Lucretia Mott, Lucy Stone, Susan B. Anthony, Lucy Burns, and Alice Paul were some of the stalwart warriors fighting for women's right to vote. Alice Paul and Lucy Burns attended school in England and joined the WSPU (Paul in 1908, Burns in 1909). Paul was force-fed in England in 1909 after hunger-striking. As noted in the story, Paul was arrested after gate-crashing the Lord Mayor's Banquet. The character of Lucy Hawkins is based on these two women.

Wyoming became the first state to grant women's suffrage, in 1869. In 1920 Woodrow Wilson signed the Nineteenth Amendment, which prohibits state and federal agencies from gender-based voting discrimination.

We modern women are fortunate to have had such

brave souls fighting to give us the vote. It's a gift to treasure, certainly never one to ignore. The spirits of the Pankhursts, Susan B. Anthony, Lucretia Mott, and hundreds of others who sacrificed their peaceful existence for women in the future must always follow us into the voting booth.

THE PANKHURSTS

In 1878, Emmeline Goulden (1858–1928) married Richard Pankhurst, a lawyer who was passionate about women's suffrage. They had five children: Christabel, Sylvia, Frank (who died in infancy), Harry, and Adela, who was also involved in the movement, but largely in the north of England. Adela was banished to Australia in 1914 by her mother and sister Christabel after they falsely accused her of being useless to the suffrage movement.

Emmeline cofounded the Women's Social and Political Union with Christabel. She was very stalwart about women's suffrage, and often sacrificed her children's happiness for the movement. During World War I, Emmeline put aside the suffrage demand temporarily to help with the war effort. She encouraged women to chastise men for not going to war by presenting them with a white feather, which was a symbol of cowardice. Two years after her death, a statue of her was erected in Victoria Tower Gardens, next to Parliament. It stands there today.

Christabel Harriette Pankhurst (1880–1958) was cofounder of the WSPU. She was very beautiful, feminine, and charismatic. She received a law degree from Manchester University but was unable to practice law because she was a woman. The Bar Council in England drew up its own regulations, which excluded women from practicing until 1919, when the Sex Disqualification (Removal) Act made it illegal to disqualify a person from a post, public function, civil or judicial office, vocation, or incorporated society on basis of sex or marriage. Christabel was a talented orator, and hundreds of women admired her and would do anything for her. She was, like her mother, very autocratic, and dismissive of anyone who took a view other than her own. She and her mother highly approved of militant action, but Christabel preferred to direct operations, and was jailed only three times, the last in 1909.

Christabel fled to Paris to escape prison in 1912, and directed WSPU actions from there. She returned to England in 1913 at the start of World War I. She was arrested, but served only thirty days of her three-year sentence. She moved to the United States in 1921 and died in Los Angeles at the age of seventy-seven.

Estelle Sylvia Pankhurst (1882–1960) was a talented artist, pacifist, and active member of the WSPU. Her civil disobedience caused her to endure multiple imprisonments that included sleep, thirst, and hunger strikes—the last of which resulted in many force-feedings. Her beautiful artwork was featured heavily in WSPU publicity. The panels she created for the Women's Exhibition in 1909 were later destroyed by police when they raided WSPU headquarters. In 1914 Sylvia began to disagree with the WSPU's tactics (such as arson and destroying priceless works of art) and political decisions. Wanting to help improve the lives of working-class and impoverished woman, Sylvia turned her attentions to the East End Federation of the WSPU and founded the East London Federation of Suffragettes (ELFS). Christabel and Emmeline, angered by Sylvia's association with this group, gave her an ultimatum. If she did not leave the ELFS, then they had no use for her, which seems horrible considering the sacrifices she had made for the WSPU. A staunch feminist, Sylvia refused to marry, and lived with her partner, Italian revolutionary Silvo Corio, for thirty years (they had a son, Richard, in 1927). Emmeline, scandalized about Sylvia's home life, never spoke to her again. From 1936 until her death, Sylvia fought against fascism in Italian-occupied Ethiopia. She died in 1960 and is buried in Addis Ababa, Ethiopia.

Henry Francis "Harry" Pankhurst (1889–1910) was the only son of Emmeline and Richard to reach adulthood. Harry was a fragile boy and often very sickly. His mother forced him into masculine jobs, such as bricklayer and farmhand, in order to toughen him up. Harry tried to join in with the WSPU. He chalked pavements and spoke at street corners. Harry contracted polio and died in January of 1910.

The ghastly practice of force-feeding continued until 1913, and was a widespread method of trying to prevent women from protesting through hunger strikes. Because the newspapers and public became outraged at this treatment of women, hunger strikes became an effective way of protesting for the suffragettes. Sylvia Pankhurst was arrested fifteen times in the years between 1913 and 1921 and went on hunger, sleep, and thirst strikes, resulting in her being force-fed more than any other British suffragette.

The poster that Vicky fly-posted is based on a real one that was drawn by Alfred Pearse (1865–1933) for the WSPU's propaganda drive in 1910. Pearse called himself "A Patriot," and his poster was indeed fly-posted and sold as a postcard in order to show the public what the current government was capable of. The illustration was labeled *The Modern Inquisition.*

The Prisoners (Temporary Discharge for Ill-health) Act of 1913 allowed prison officials to release hunger-striking prisoners until they were well enough to be rearrested to complete their sentences. This was enacted in order to sidestep force-feeding. The act was nicknamed the Cat and Mouse Act (so called to reflect a cat's habit of releasing its prey to recover slightly before attacking it again). It was ineffective because the women would simply disappear, hidden by suffrage sympathizers, and the police were not able to rearrest many of them.

In the United States, a group of suffragists, including

Alice Paul and Lucy Burns, were force-fed in 1917 at the Occoquan Workhouse in Virginia.

THE ARTISTS

The Pre-Raphaelite Brotherhood was formed in 1848 by Dante Gabriel Rossetti, William Holman Hunt, and John Everett Millais. They created their own art movement by rejecting the art of the day and putting forward their own ideals of embracing the vivid colors, subjects, and style of fifteenth-century Italian and Flemish artists. In addition, the Brotherhood studied nature and made sure their ideas stemmed from passionate and genuine thought. *Beata Beatrix* (1864–1870), one of Rossetti's most famous works, is an homage to his late wife and fellow artist, Lizzie Siddal, who died from a laudanum overdose.

John William Waterhouse (1849–1917) is one of the most esteemed Victorian painters. His sensitive and beautiful portrayal of women and femininity is famous all over the world. His subjects from myth and legend formed a common bond with his predecessors in the Pre-Raphaelite Brotherhood, although he is considered an inheritor of that legacy rather than one of the Brotherhood. *The Lady of Shalott* (1888), *A Mermaid* (1892–1900), and *Ophelia* (1894) are some of his most enduring works.

The suffrage movement relied heavily on its artists

to produce the huge amount of publicity needed to get the word out to the public and to potential members of women's unions. Illustration and cartooning were among the best ways to do this, and just as it can today, a funny cartoon could speak and show the truth where an article might miss the mark. The Suffrage Atelier (from a French word meaning artist's studio or workshop) Vicky belonged to is historically accurate. It encouraged women to express themselves through art and to create things to sell in the many suffragette shops throughout Great Britain. And yes, life-drawing classes were taught at the atelier!

Victoria's Favorite Pikelets

Pikelets are similar to English crumpets, but a little bit thinner, and were popular tea cakes during the Edwardian era. Stored in a plastic bag, they will keep for up to three days. Reheat and serve with butter, jam, or honey.

INGREDIENTS:
one cup of self-rising flour
one tablespoon of sugar
one egg
one tablespoon of butter, melted
$\frac{1}{2}$ cup of milk, or more if needed

Sift the flour into a medium bowl and stir in the sugar. Make a well in the center of the dry ingredients and crack in the egg. Stir while pouring in the milk slowly until the batter comes together. Add more milk if you want thinner pikelets. Stir in butter.

Heat a griddle or skillet over medium heat, and coat with a small amount of cooking oil or spray. Drop a large spoonful of the batter onto the hot skillet. Flip when bubbles appear, and cook until browned on both sides.

BIBLIOGRAPHY

Atkinson, Diane. *Funny Girls: Cartooning for Equality.* London: Penguin Books, 1997.

Atkinson, Diane. *The Suffragettes in Pictures.* Stroud, U.K.: The History Press, 1996.

Blackman, Cally. *Costume from 1500 to the Present Day.* Andover, U.K.: Pitkin Guide, 2003.

Brimacombe, Peter. *The Edwardians.* Andover, U.K.: Pitkin Guide, 2005.

Crawford, Elizabeth. *The Women's Suffrage Movement: A Reference Guide 1866–1928.* London: Routledge, 1999.

Dawes, Frank. *Not in Front of the Servants.* London: Hutchinson, 1984.

Gardiner, Juliet. *Manor House: Life in an Edwardian Country House.* San Francisco: Bay Books, 2002.

Gernsheim, Alison. *Victorian and Edwardian Fashion: A Photographic Survey.* Mineola, N.Y.: Dover, 1963.

Hardwick, Clara. *The World of Upstairs Downstairs*. New York: Holt, Reinhart, and Winston, 1976.

Harris, Kristina. *Victorian and Edwardian Fashions for Women 1840–1919*. Atglen, Penna.: Schiffer, 1995.

Harrison, Shirley. *Sylvia Pankhurst: A Maverick Life, 1882–1960*. London: Aurum Press Ltd, 2003.

Hattersley, Roy. *The Edwardians*. New York: St. Martin's Press, 2005.

Hayward, Edward. *Upstairs and Downstairs*. Andover, U.K.: Pitkin Guide, 1998.

Johnson, Eleanor. *Ladies' Dress Accessories*. Princes Risboorough, U.K.: Shire Publications Ltd, 2004.

Karlin, Zorn Elyse. *Jewelry and Metalwork in the Arts and Crafts Tradition*. Atglen, Penna.: Schiffer, 1993.

Laver, James. *Costume and Fashion: A Concise History*. London: Thames & Hudson Ltd, 1969.

Liddington, Jill. *Rebel Girls: Their Fight for the Vote*. London: Virago Press, 2006.

Marlow, Joyce, ed. *Votes for Women: The Virago Book of Suffragettes*. London: Virago Press, 2001.

Mendes, Valerie D., and Amy De La Haye. *Lucille Ltd, London, Paris, New York and Chicago: 1890s–1930s.* London: V & A Publishing, 2009.

Olian, JoAnne. *Victorian and Edwardian Fashions from "La Mode Illustrée."* Mineola, N.Y.: Dover, 1998.

Phillips, Melanie. *The Ascent of Woman: A History of the Suffragette Movement and the Ideas Behind It.* London: Little, Brown, 2003.

Steinback, Susie. *Women in England 1760 to 1914: A Social History.* London: Weidenfeld & Nicolson, 2004.

Trippi, Peter. *J. W. Waterhouse.* London: Phaidon Press Limited, 2002.

Worsley, Lucy. *If Walls Could Talk: An Intimate History of the Home.* New York: Walker & Company, 2011.

Acknowledgments

This novel would not have seen the light of day had it not been for the many people who lent me their talent and wisdom.

Thanks to John M. Cusick, my incredible agent, for making my dream of becoming a novelist come true, and for being so generous with your feedback and support. Having you on my side makes me a very lucky writer girl.

To Scott Treimel, for taking care of those little details that make a writer want to tear her hair out. I knew I was in good hands from the start.

To Martha Alderson, the Plot Whisperer, also known (by me, at least!) as a writer's "oracle." Thank you for helping me find Vicky's voice and for guiding me along the plot path.

To Gloria Kempton, instructor at Writer's Digest University, who lent her expertise in the early drafts of *Folly* when the paint was still wet on the canvas.

And to editorial consultant Sarah Cloots, who put her stellar red pencil to work, not once but twice, and helped me shape the final drafts.

To my editor, Leila Sales, for helping me find Vicky's story through her patient questions and thoughtful remarks. I'm a better writer for having worked with you and I'm forever grateful!

To all the incredible people at Viking Children's Books,

especially Regina Hayes, Ken Wright, Kendra Levin, Kathryn Hinds, Janet Pascal, Kate Renner, Kim Ryan, Janet Frick, and Lori Thorn.

To my father, Richard Biggs, a fine artist in his own right, who showed me the fundamentals of art and shared his own stories about art school. But especially for taking me to the Art Institute of Chicago when I was a little girl and holding my hand in front of Georges Seurat's *A Sunday on La Grande Jatte* (1884). You instilled in me a love of art.

To art professor Christine Boos, my friend and a brilliant artist, who explained mural making, painting technique, and art history. Any mistakes are definitely mine!

To my writer friends who gave me valuable and honest advice, but who also patched me up with kind words and sent me back into the fray when it was needed: Jennifer Salvato Doktorski, Katie Mitschelen, Tori Avey, and Tiffany Reisz. But especially to Melissa Azarian and Terri King, who were with me through every single draft.

To Elizabeth Crawford, author of *The Women's Suffrage Movement*, the bible of British suffrage. Thank you for writing such a compendium, and thank you for answering my questions about obscure things, such as what Clement's Inn looked like. And to Beverley Cook, curator of Social & Working History at the Museum of London, for helping me with the museum's suffrage collection and answering my many, many questions. And to Dr. Helen Pankhurst, granddaughter of Sylvia Pankhurst, who very kindly answered my queries about her venerable grandmother.

To Evangeline Holland of Edwardianpromenade.com;

Stephanie Pina of PreRaphaelitesisterhood.com and LizzieSiddal.com; and Jennifer Parrish of Parrishrelics.com for creating beautiful and inspiring websites of the Edwardian era, Pre-Raphaelite art, and jewelry inspired by the Pre-Raphaelites.

To my family, who understood that I wasn't being anti-social; I was simply writing. And to my niece, Ashley, who gave me some invaluable insight.

And to my husband, Mark, who always knew.

And finally, a humble thanks to the suffragettes who fought and sacrificed so much for women's rights.